Evidence

By

Ray Lawrence

Copyright © Ray Lawrence 2021

**The moral right of the author has been
asserted.**

CHAPTER ONE

"For Pete's sake, Bailey, if you can't take it why did you come into the force in the first place?" Detective Sergeant Mark Dolby snapped at the young Police Constable. Dolby felt particularly out of sorts this morning. It was not just the sickening sight and smell of violent death that greeted him as he walked into the kitchen of the house; he also resented the feeling that, like some green rookie policeman, he had to start proving himself to his superiors all over again. Still, he reflected with a prick of conscience, he should not take out his personal frustrations on his subordinates. "All right, Bailey," he grunted, relenting, "go outside and get some air! You can help Saunders put up the cordon."

With a word of apology for his squeamishness the younger officer, his face drained of colour, fled through the open door into the garden, gulping the fresh air into his lungs. For the briefest moment Dolby was tempted to follow him. Instead, he swallowed down the bile that was rising in his throat and taking his notebook from his pocket, flicked through the leaves to find the first blank page. He squatted down on his haunches at the edge of the pool of congealed blood that had gathered about the corpse. There were curious markings in the blood and as he looked more closely, he realised they were tracks left by an animal, probably those of a dog. A cat's paw marks, he figured, would have been smaller and possibly rounder. He had little experience of animals. The tracks, smudged and marked out in the dark, almost black blood, indicated that the animal - whatever it was - had run around the body two or three times before making a bee line for the garden door. Apart from these animal paw markings there were a number of short parallel score lines at the edges of the pooled blood, as if somebody had drawn something through it.

He placed his feet outside the darkened area, taking care not to further disturb the pooled, viscous liquid and examined the body carefully. It was a man - or, should he say *it had been* a man? - white, probably aged between 45 and 55, powerfully built, but running towards fat. He might have been ruggedly handsome in his youth, but heavy drinking had puffed out the flesh of his face and rimmed his eyes with red. They were bright blue and wide open, staring upwards in an expression of surprise, as if amazed at the turn of events that had left their owner lying here dead on the kitchen floor. The man's nose was large and broken, but the injury had been inflicted many years before and, now well healed, the protuberance lay in the centre of his face like a flattened strawberry. He was in his shirtsleeves.

His tie, once a sober blue to match his hand stitched suit, lay askew across his chest, firmly stuck to the expensive cotton shirt by a layer of congealed blood. It was probable he had died from a stab wound to the throat that, judging by the blood that had sprayed across the room, had severed his jugular vein; but there were other wounds lower down that had ripped open the flesh of his chest and stomach, leaving gaping slits in his shirt. There was no sign of the murder weapon.

Dolby was making careful notes in his book as Dr Peter Williams, acting Police Surgeon, pushed open the door from the hall and came through into the kitchen. "It's upstairs in the bedroom," he said, reading Dolby's thoughts, "with the woman. She's probably his wife." The policeman looked blank, not connecting his own thoughts with the doctor's words. "A kitchen knife," Williams explained, speaking slowly as if to a retarded child. "The weapon, Mark, it's up there on the bedroom floor covered in blood. Looks like she went upstairs carrying it, then dropped it on the floor when she laid down on the bed to take her overdose. If, of course, that's what she actually did - it certainly *seems* that way." He walked around the body towards the garden door. "There's an almost empty bottle of pills by the bedside. It looks as though she tipped the lot down her gullet and then topped them off with a bottle of brandy. It was good stuff too - *Remy Martin* - what a waste!"

Dolby stood up, straightening to his full six feet and flexing his limbs to drive out the early morning stiffness that lingered in his joints even after his drive from home. He worked out regularly in the station gym, but he had only to miss a session or two - as he had in the last week - for his body to remind him that he had nearly reached the end of his thirties.

"Thanks, Doc. At least we won't have to spend days on end searching for the weapon." He crossed to the sink, skirting around the blood that liberally stained the floor tiles. There were four knives in the wooden knife block that stood on the windowsill. They were sheathed to their hilts, but there was an empty slot for another. "It probably came from here. One like this could certainly have done the job." He noted a splash of blood on the cupboard door under the draining board, by the sink unit. There was no crockery out on the surfaces, but a plastic drum containing washing up liquid lay on its side on the edge of the draining board as if it had rolled there after being knocked over. "Looks like there was a struggle and she stabbed him." He shook his head with disgust. "Another case of domestic violence, I guess."

"It looks that way," agreed Williams. "But by the look of her she may have had good reason to do for him." The Doctor held a more pessimistic view of marriage than did the Detective Sergeant, for he had been married and divorced twice. Now he lived alone and, without the slightest inclination towards homosexuality, enjoyed the company of men friends who had either, like himself, tried marriage and failed, or had never taken connubial vows. He was cynical of Dolby who professed to have a good marriage and a devoted family. Williams returned his battered trilby to his head and, wrinkling his nose in mock disgust, picked his way gingerly across the room to the garden door. "And a particularly messy case this is if I may say so. You'd think they'd be more careful where they spilt their bodily fluids."

Dolby pursed his lips. He disliked the way this middle-aged medic made bad jokes about victims of violence, but he had known Williams for too long to expect him to change. It was probably the doctor's way of coping with the evidence of evil he had met so frequently during his long career. "Presumably you're able to certify them both officially dead? Is there anything else we should know?"

"Yeah, they're dead as doughnuts." Williams nodded in answer to the first question. "Have been for some hours I'd say. As for anything else - I think you'd better wait for the autopsy. After all, you're the detective." He grinned. "Speaking of which - I'm surprised your new boss isn't here yet, picking her pert little nose over the clues - if you'll excuse the expression."

Dolby ignored the doctor's attempt at humour. "For Pete's sake, the neighbour who found the bodies - or I should say body, he didn't hang around to look for any others when he walked in here and found *this* mess - he only rang through to the station half an hour ago - so DCI Caine is hardly late!" He surprised even himself at this vigorous defence of his new boss. "Well, I expect she'll be here at any minute," he went on gruffly. "She doesn't know the drill yet, does she!"

The doctor grinned wryly. "Still feeling sore about your newly appointed DCI then?"

"Well, Bill Walker and me, we made a good team," said Dolby. He was embarrassed. He had been sorry when they put Bill out to grass. They had worked well together. But it wasn't just that - he had worked more or less on his own during the months of "the interregnum" - as he called it - whilst the powers-that-be and the hotchpotch of bureaucrats were choosing Bill's successor and he had enjoyed being virtually his own boss. Now he was finding it hard to get used to the idea that he would have to work under supervision again. And, he had to admit, if he was frank with himself, that the fact that the new DCI was a woman - and an attractive woman at that - had thrown him slightly off balance.

Williams was still grinning mischievously, as if he understood the reason for the Detective Sergeant's pique. He opened the door leading out to the garden and walked through onto the side way. He glanced out to the street. "I see the world's up and about at last. See you..."

Dolby watched the doctor as he walked briskly past the window, up the path towards the street. Noises from outside came to him through the open door. A car starting up a couple of houses away, the distant rumble of rush hour traffic from the B road that ran past the housing estate, the metallic clang of a dustbin lid being replaced somewhere along the street. They were the normal sounds of a middle-class residential area waking up in the morning. There had been almost nobody about when

Dolby arrived fifteen minutes ago, but now he wondered how long it would be before the neighbours began to crowd inquisitively around the police barrier tape PCs Bailey and Saunders were now busily stringing up around the perimeters of the house and garden. Some of these people must have known the now dead occupants of the house. Perhaps they had been friends. More likely they had barely been on nodding terms with the dead couple. It was usually that way nowadays in these new housing estates. Generally, people kept themselves to themselves, although there were always the inevitable curtain twitchers who kept a watching brief on their neighbour's activities. One thing was certain - as soon as word got out there had been a tragedy in this otherwise ordinary house, morbid curiosity would bring the locals flocking here like bees to a honey pot. The Press, no doubt, would be hot on their heels.

Dolby could hear a television set playing upstairs. According to the officers first on the scene after the neighbour's call, the TV - which was in one of the bedrooms - had been on when they arrived at the house and had probably been playing all night. He looked up at the kitchen clock, noticing for the first time its particularly loud 'tick'. It was just on a quarter to eight. He crossed the kitchen again and made his way to the front door. It was closed, but the security chain was not in place indicating that the occupants of the house had not locked up properly the night before. He turned and made his way up the carpeted stairs, meeting Tony Ash, the police photographer, on the landing.

"Morning, Tony," Dolby acknowledged the other man, who nodded and made his way towards the stairs, turning to greet him and comment "G' Morning, Mark. All done up here, mate - and you'll be glad to know she's in nothing like the state of her old man. There's not much blood at all, in fact apart from her hands she's as clean as the proverbial whistle!"

Dolby followed the sound of the TV set and pushed open the door to the room from which the photographer had come. In the subdued light filtering through the closed curtains, he made out the shape of a woman's body slumped on her back across the double bed, on top of the bedclothes. They were practically undisturbed, indicating that she had not slept in the bed the night before. One of her arms was thrown over the edge of the mattress, the other was crossed over her stomach. Her legs were closed together, and she was scantily dressed in a filmy negligee, black and crisply clean, through which he could see clearly the outline of her upper body, her breasts sagging, the flesh no longer supported by the vital forces of life. A pair of skimpy pants barely covered her lower, private parts. He switched on the light and moved closer. The woman looked to be in her middle to late forties and he could see now, against the whiteness of her flesh, several bruises across her body and up her arms. Her medium length hair, dark, almost black, showing only the slightest traces of grey at the roots, partly obscured the upper part of her face, but he could see that here, too, there were badly bruised areas.

Curiously, since, probably, she had been dead for six or seven hours, her cheeks were tinged a ruddy pink.

Dolby moved forward, bending over the body to take a closer look. The dead woman's face was heavily made-up. Tiny particles of foundation powder still clung to her skin like a fine down and blusher had been applied to her cheeks. The outline of her eye sockets gleamed with mascara and the shimmer of lipstick clung to her lips. Dolby stroked his chin thoughtfully. Although she was nearly naked and looked ready for bed, for some reason of her own she had 'powdered her nose' just a short while before her death. The Detective Sergeant moved slowly away from the bed, his eyes tracing their way down her body once again, lingering over the mottled blue and purple of the bruises that stood out so starkly against the woman's otherwise clear and unblemished skin.

Dolby turned his attention to the rest of the room, ignoring the shrill voice of some sort of muppet-like creature on television, which was trying to persuade him to buy a particular brand of ice cream. Apart from the bed, which lay against the wall opposite the window, there was a large curved fronted burr walnut wardrobe and dressing table to match, which were too big and did not suit the characterless squareness of the room. A wooden chair stood a few feet away from the wardrobe. It was draped with discarded women's clothing carelessly dropped across its seat and a rolled-up pair of tights lay on the carpet a few inches away as if they had been thrown in the direction of the chair, but had fallen short. A black leather handbag hung by its strap from one of the struts of the chair back. The dressing table was laden with cosmetics. On the floor, a foot or so away from the discarded tights, was a greetings card which had been torn in half. Dolby picked it up and opened it, noting the birthday greeting "to Valerie" inscribed above the usual rhyming doggerel. He found the other portion of the card under the knee hole of the dressing table. Somebody had signed that part "all my love, Martha."

Dolby's foot knocked against something and he bent down to look more closely at an empty bottle of Remy Martin brandy which lay on the floor, eighteen inches or so from the bed valance. He left it where it was and moved across to the bedside cabinet. There was a glass on the top, next to it a small plastic pill bottle, turned on its side. The glass was almost empty but for a small amount of amber liquid settled in the bottom and its rim and outer surfaces were marked with bloodstains. He picked it up in his gloved hands, careful not to touch the bloody areas and swirled the contents about in the bottom, peering into it and sniffing. It was almost certainly brandy, but he would know for certain after the forensic team had carried out their analysis. He put the glass down and returned his attention to the floor. About six inches away from the bottle lay a long-bladed knife, clearly the missing quintuplet from the knife block down in the kitchen. The plain, beige coloured carpet was stained with congealed blood that had run off the edge of the blade. His eyes flickered back to the body, to the hand that hung over the side of the bed, finding as he had expected, the rusty bloom of congealed blood on the fingers, partially obscuring the dead woman's wedding ring.

"Good morning, Mark." The bedroom door creaked slightly as Jacqueline Caine entered the room. Dolby turned to greet the new Detective Chief Inspector. The navy-blue suit and white blouse suited perfectly her tall, slim figure, and her white gloved hands clutched a black leather handbag. She wore on her feet what Dolby's wife, Lorna, would have called sensible shoes, navy, matching her suit.

"Good morning, Ma'am."

DCI Caine moved her eyes from him to the figure on the bed. She smiled weakly, without humour. Dolby thought her face, set against her short brunette hair, looked slightly pallid and he reminded himself that she had just come up from the kitchen, away from a sight that would turn even the strongest of stomachs.

"What a bloody unpleasant way to start a new job, Mark," she said with a heavy sigh. "Statistically speaking Fen Molesey gets only six or seven suspicious deaths a year - and I get *two* on my second day!"

"As the poet said *'Love and murder will out'* " said Dolby, "although judging by the bruises on this poor woman's body there was precious little love to be had in this house!"

She went closer to the bed, grimacing. "By the look of her you may be right." She glanced at the TV screen, for a moment distracted into watching a few details of the weather forecast. "I don't think we need that on anymore." She found the on/off button and pressed it, watching the screen go blank before turning to face the Detective Sergeant once again. "What have you got for me so far, Mark?"

"Not much," said Dolby, lamely. What did she expect when he had been here for only ten minutes? And he resented the "me" which seemed to imply a "me and you" mentality rather than an "us" working as a team. She was waiting, frowning and he hurried on. "The man downstairs is - or rather was - a Mr Bruce Southam. He was some sort of businessman. We got that from the neighbour who found him." He indicated the body on the bed. "As for the woman - Doc Williams thinks she probably killed him and then OD'd. We don't know who she is yet. She's probably the wife, but nowadays who can say? We've not had time to make a positive identification. After finding that blood bath down there in the kitchen Mr Ford, the neighbour, didn't venture this far into the house and he didn't see her, so we don't know for sure who she is." He wanted to say more, but he thought he was rambling and abruptly stopped speaking.

Caine nodded thoughtfully and walked around the bed, carefully skirting the overturned brandy bottle and stopping in front of the bedside cabinet. She picked up the pill bottle that lay there on its side and peered closely at the label. "I think this may be your answer," she said. She squinted at the tiny label in the way people do when they should be wearing spectacles. "**Mrs Valerie Southam**," she read "we'll have to get that confirmed, of course."

"According to the next-door neighbour they have a son of about nineteen," said Dolby. "It won't be pleasant for him, but I suppose he'd be the best one to do that. When we can find him, that is - he wasn't anywhere in the house when the squad car arrived, and he hasn't come in since."

DCI Caine nodded. "Maybe he didn't sleep here last night. You know what kids of that age are like." She peered again at the bottle and read the description of the pills from the label. '**Ergotamine - one to be taken when needed'**. Mrs Southam had migraines, perhaps?" She shook the bottle, rattling the pills inside. "Only three left." She replaced it, putting it down beside the open packet of Black Silk cigarettes, her nose twitching with distaste as if seeing the packet had made the smell of tobacco in the room more apparent and unpleasant.

"Who did this neighbour, this Mr Ford, speak to?" she asked.

"PC Bailey. He was in the first squad car to arrive."

"But how come Ford found Southam's body? It's not the usual thing around here for neighbours to pop into next door's kitchen at the crack of dawn - or is it?"

Dolby shrugged. "I think it was something to do with their dog." Caine looked blank. "The Southam's dog. So far as I can gather it came to Ford whining and screeching and with a lot of blood on it. Ford thought it had injured itself, so he came next door to report it to the Southams..."

"...And walked in on the mess in the kitchen." DCI Caine nodded and crossed the room to stand beside Dolby in front of the dressing table, studying the cosmetics bottles of various colours, shapes and sizes, the profusion of which was multiplied by the reflection in the mirror. Body lotions, moisturising creams and fragrances fought for space with lipsticks, hair sprays, defoliants and hair colourants. More intimate items - an opened packet of Tampax, a small box of cotton Buds - were strewn about on the surface. The now dead Valerie Southam, presumably, had made up here every morning. Here, at this mirror, she had waged her own, personal, daily battle against age. Curiously, it seemed to Dolby, at the back of all this variety of beauty products, stood a carved wooden figure of two dolphins, their bodies entwined in play. He found himself reaching forward and running his fingers lightly over the wood. It was warm, highly polished, smooth, almost sensual to the touch and the initials of the sculptor "JP" were carved into its base. Pushed to the back of this haphazard arrangement of packets and bottles, almost hidden by them, was a photograph of a woman standing on a beach with her arm around a young boy, who was probably in his early teens when the picture was taken. They both wore swimming costumes - hers, a two piece, was so skimpy as to be almost non-existent. They were smiling at the camera. For a moment Dolby did not link the face in the photograph with that of the body lying on the bed. The woman's hair was the wrong colour. The face that smiled at the camera was that of a blonde. A closer look, however, at the heavy features, the wide mouth, the line of the jaw and cheekbones and the upper part of the not unattractive face, confirmed that this was Valerie Southam, albeit in happier times. He wondered who the young man was. Beside him Jacqueline Caine picked up the photograph and studied it for a moment, probably unaware that she was using one of her gloved fingers to wipe away a fine layer of dust from the frame.

"You carry on here, Mark," she said. "I'm going to have a quick look around downstairs and then organise a little chat with this Mr Ford. Join me when you're ready." She replaced the photograph and walked to the door.

Alone, Dolby resumed his examination of the room. An inch or so under the bed were two remote control devices, one for the TV set, the other for a video recorder. He looked across at the television set, realising for the first time that it was mounted over a DVD recorder. Valerie Southam had been watching TV before whatever it was had happened, maybe she had been watching a video? He shrugged, decided that whatever she had been watching was hardly relevant now and left the room to make his way slowly around the rest of the first floor.

Downstairs, Detective Chief Inspector Caine made her way into the lounge, wrinkling her nose as she breathed in air distinctly tainted by the cigarette smoke which had been absorbed into the furnishings and fabrics of the room. The house was part of a recently built estate and the accommodation was not large. The lounge curtains, at the front of the house, were drawn, but they were flimsy, allowing the bright light of the early morning sun to stream into the east facing room, throwing dappled shadows onto the shabby, smoke-stained wallpaper. The carpet on the floor was worn and the room was sparsely furnished with a low teak wood cabinet next to an old mahogany bureau running along one wall. There were two small armchairs in the centre of the room. All the furniture was old and battered and exhibited the marks of heavy wear. A large screen TV set stood in one of the corners. The dining room, which had a second door, leading to the left, into the kitchen, was empty but for an ancient dresser cabinet, a small table and four chairs. Caine thought the decor and furniture distinctly odd. In this relatively modern and expensive house, which would have been described by an estate agent as **an architect-built executive dwelling**, where one would expect reasonably modern and up to date accoutrements, everything seemed to be out of date and shabby.

Caine made her way towards the window, skirting around a brown leather briefcase leaning at a crazy angle against one of the chairs, suggesting it had been thrown down hurriedly onto the edge of the seat and had then slipped off onto the floor. A man's jacket lay where it had been dropped, on the back of the same chair.

The door connecting through to the kitchen was closed and it was quiet here in the back of the house. There was nothing in these rooms to suggest that, only hours before, there had been a deadly struggle between the two residents. Caine heard people moving about, probably the rest of the scene of crime team arriving, or forensics, but she put off the moment when she would have to go through to the other part of the house and introduce herself to them as the newly appointed Detective Chief Inspector.

She yawned, not yet fully awake. She had spent the weekend organising her possessions prior to moving them from her London home to the tiny flat she had rented, on a strictly temporary basis, in Fen Molesey town centre. Anxious to hit the ground running in her new job she had also set herself to reading the case files passed over to her by Superintendent Hansen. She had spent until the small hours of the morning poring over them. Consequently, the call summoning her to Marazion Road early this morning had not been welcome. She was in the shower when the telephone rang and she had not stopped for breakfast, which was probably just as well in view of the horrific sight that had greeted her when she entered the house via the kitchen just a few minutes afterwards.

Caine laid her handbag on the table and stood at the window for some moments, deep in thought, her eyes closed and her hands clasped together in the relaxing position she had learnt at meditation classes years before. She wasn't sure things had gone at all well with DS Mark Dolby just now. According to his file and the quite glowing report of the Superintendent, he was a good detective, so why on earth had he made such a hash of summarising his findings so far? All he had given her was the name of the dead man and the relatively unimportant fact that one of the neighbours had found his body. And he seemed to have gone along with the police surgeon's assumption that the woman, Valerie Southam, had killed her husband Bruce - possibly because he had been beating her - and then taken an overdose. It looked as though Dolby had entirely missed the point that if this was so there should have been blood on the woman's clothing. Lots of it. Judging by the state of her husband's body, if she had killed him she should have been drenched in the stuff, but the negligee and pants she was wearing were pristine clean. Had she bothered to change her clothes and take a shower before taking the overdose? It was not very likely. And what about the make-up? Had it not seemed strange to the Detective Sergeant that Valerie had made up like that, just before getting ready for bed? Had she really gone to all this trouble just for her husband? Was romance still so much alive out here in the suburbs of Fen Molesey? Not impossible, Caine mused, but not very likely either. No, for some reason DCI Caine had not hit it off with Dolby. He had obviously been uneasy in her presence and that would never do if they were to work successfully together in the future.

Caine brought her thoughts back to the matter in hand, striding back into the hall and opening the front door, careful where she put her hands although she was still wearing her gloves. Deployment of the cordon tape around the premises having been completed PC Bailey was now stationed at the front of the house and he turned towards her as the door opened behind him.

"Good morning again, Ma'am," he smiled the same, embarrassed lap dog smile he had rewarded her with earlier when she had introduced herself as the new DCI. "Er - there's something I think I should mention." He hesitated, waited for her smile of approval. "I don't know if it's important, ma'am, but this place was broken into a few weeks ago."

"Really? What was taken?"

PC Bailey shrugged. "Nothing - well, they said nothing was missing, but the place was turned upside down I can tell you."

Caine nodded thoughtfully. "That's a bit bizarre isn't it? Going to all the trouble of breaking in and not taking anything!"

Bailey smiled. "A bit weird if you ask me, but the same thing happened to one of the other houses up the road, at about the same time. We reckoned it was probably kids."

Caine made a mental note to call for the report on the burglaries as soon as she returned to her office. Behind PC Bailey, beyond the perimeter of the front garden and the blue and white incident tape which barred their further progress towards the house, a group of sightseers was gathering. Caine found her eyes drawn towards a blonde woman tottering on six-inch-high stiletto heels. The red leather mini skirt, which clung about her bottom, showing off legs that may once have been shapely but were now heavy and thick, did nothing to disguise the bulge of her stomach over a wide black leather belt bearing the word 'MOSCHINO' in large silver letters. Above the skirt she wore a flimsy, sleeveless orange blouse, the top three buttons of which were open to reveal her cleavage and the upper part of her brassiere which was stretched almost to its limits by her thrusting bosom. The woman was talking loudly to a WPC and gesticulating in the direction of the house. She looks, thought Caine, as if she has just knocked off from a stint at the local whore house, wherever that might be in a semi-rural area like Fen Molesey. Or, she was a reporter from one of the trendy tabloids, looking for a sensational scoop. Either way, she seemed distinctly out of place in this executive style housing estate.

Caine took her gaze off the woman. "The neighbour that found the man's body in the kitchen, Constable" she said to Bailey, "A Mr Ford, I think. Do you know where I can find him?"

"Yes, Ma'am - number 19. This is number 17 so he'll be next door." He indicated the house on their immediate right.

"Thank you, constable. The scene of crime team have arrived I take it?"

Bailey nodded. "Yes, ma'am and Sergeant Briggs, the fingerprint man, is here!"

She was about to tell Bailey she was going next door to see the neighbour, Mr Ford, when a bustling at the edge of the gathering crowd caught her eye. A young man riding a bicycle had turned off the roadway onto the run-in to the Southam's drive and had almost crashed into the sightseers. Amid shouts of anger he had swerved around them and was now pushing his way through to the police barrier. He was in his late teens, eighteen or nineteen, perhaps, stocky and fairly short for his generation, no more than five feet seven. His hair was hidden by his safety helmet, but his face, finely formed and well proportioned, was vaguely familiar. Caine thought she had seen him somewhere before. The WPC, breaking off her conversation with the woman, moved to intercept him, but he swung the handlebars of his cycle and, bending low, managed to sweep past her, under the incident tape and onto the drive leading to the house. He bumped over the uneven crazy paved surface towards Caine and PC Bailey, travelling fast and applying the brakes only a few feet away from them, pulling the bike in a wide sweep to come to a stop in front of the garage door. The tall policeman quickly closed the distance between them, striding over and grasping the young man by the arm.

"What's all this then? Who are you, me young lad?" The use of the word "lad" seemed ridiculous coming from Bailey, who was probably only in his early twenties and hardly more than a "lad" himself.

Caine could see the youth was alarmed and anxious. She remembered now where she had seen him before. He was the young man in the photograph which stood on the dressing table in the bedroom where they had found Valerie Southam's body. Her son perhaps? She went over to him. "Do you live here?"

"Yes - I'm Adam Southam."

"Then Bruce and Valerie Southam are your parents?"

"Yes. What about it? What's going on? What are all these police doing here?"

For a long time Caine had been used to the fact that there is no easy way to tell a person their loved ones have suffered a violent death. It is something that, once the telling has begun, is better told swiftly. She showed him her warrant card. "I'm Detective Chief Inspector Jacqueline Caine of Fen Molesey CID. I'm afraid we have bad news for you, Mr Southam. Your mother and father have been involved in an incident. I'm afraid they're both dead."

The young man drew back, momentarily stunned. There was a dumb acceptance in his eyes, as if for some time, he had been expecting something like this to happen. "It was that bastard wasn't it!" It was a statement, not a question, said coldly, without emotion, almost with the certainty of pre-knowledge. "I told mum she should leave him years ago." He paused and for the first time she saw the slightest flicker of sorrow and anger in his eyes. "How did he kill her?"

Caine laid her hand on his shoulder. "We don't know what happened yet, Adam, but it's not just your mother," she said with emphasis, " your father is also dead."

He almost laughed. "Good! I'm glad!" His face hardened and his eyes filled with hatred. "He had it coming!"

CHAPTER TWO

Jacqueline Caine was used to dealing with the reactions of people suddenly confronted with the death of their close relatives and those whom, by accepted standards, they should love, but she was taken aback at this young man's vehemence. Did he really hate his father that much? Now he had turned his head away, propped his bicycle against the wall of the house and started moving towards the front door.

"I don't think you should go into the house, Adam." Caine noticed, out of the corner of her eye, PC Bailey holding himself in readiness to pounce on the young man and she restrained him with a sharp look.

"Are you stopping me from going in? I do live here, you know."

Again, she was taken aback by Adam's aggressive attitude, by the way he had so easily shaken off the anxiety she had sensed when he first came on the scene. "I'm sorry, but I can't let you go in there for the time being, Adam. This is a crime scene and there are still things we have to do." She put her hand on his shoulder to guide him away from the door. "I shall have to take a statement from you, Adam, but not now. I don't think you're in a fit state. I think you need to calm down a little. Is there anyone you know close by who can be with you for a few minutes? Until you feel a little better?"

"Here, I've just heard the news -" The new voice was that of the gaudily dressed woman Caine had noticed earlier. In the temporary confusion caused by Adam Southam's arrival on the scene she had dodged under the security tape. Now she tottered down the drive on her high heels towards Caine, PC Bailey and the young man, pursued by the embarrassed policewoman. "Is it true Val and her old man are dead?" The words were directed at Caine. "It's terrible! Poor Adam!"

Caine stepped out in front of her. "And where do you think you're going, Madam?"

The woman stopped. "I'm only trying to help!" She turned towards Adam Southam. "You're all alone now, Adam, aren't you, you poor dear - it must be terrible for you. You can come and sit in my house for a bit if you like. You'd be very welcome."

"Breaking through a police cordon is anything but helpful, Madam," Caine told her. The woman looked flustered. Even through her heavy make-up Caine could see she was genuinely concerned at what was going on. Maybe she was not just a morbid sensation seeker after all. Caine relented, said less severely "I think you'd better tell me who you are and what you're doing here."

"I'm Susan Neale - from number 27." The woman could not disguise her cockney accent, which she was attempting to overlay with an imagined County brogue. "Me and Adam's mama are good mates. I mean..." She put her hand to her mouth as if realising she may have said the wrong thing, but was unsure whether or not to correct herself. The WPC, with an apologetic raising of the eyebrows to DCI Caine, laid a restraining hand on her arm. Susan Neale addressed herself directly to Adam once again. "You'd like to come and sit with me for a few minutes, wouldn't you Adam dear? It'll help you get over the shock."

A look of pure disgust creased the fine features of the young man's face. "You've got to be joking, you interfering old cow. You're just trying to get me into bed with you again, aren't you!" Caine would have wagered that this woman, who was dressed like a Soho tart, was incapable of blushing. She would have lost her bet, for Susan Neale blushed to the roots of her dyed blonde hair at Adam Southam's words and continued to blush and whimper with embarrassment as he rushed on with his accusations. "It's true you know, Inspector - she's a right old Mrs Robinson, seducing the students. Look at her, the old tart! As if I'd be interested in climbing into bed with *that* baggage!"

Mark Dolby had appeared in the doorway. He must have been in the hall watching and listening to the developing situation for now he moved up behind Adam Southam and took him gently by the elbow. "There's no need for that, Mr Southam. I'm sure Miss Neale was only trying to help." As he spoke he was guiding the young man away from the house and up the drive.

"It's Mrs actually," said the woman, "Mrs Susan Neale. With an "E". And an "A". And another "E". On the end." Adam Southam's verbal attack had thrown her off balance and she was simpering now, still trying to hide her embarrassment. She moved away, adopting an attitude of injured pride. "Well, I did my best for the boy, but he always was a bit of a handful. You know where to find me if you need me, Inspector. I'm at No 27." She marched away as best she could on her high heels, up the drive, holding her head high and thrusting out her bosom, trying to ignore Adam Southam as she passed him. He gestured rudely at her back with two of his fingers.

"Come along, Adam, there's no need for that." said Dolby. "Anyway, I think you should go next door and see how your dog is. He's with your neighbour, Mr Ford."

"Was Charlie hurt as well, then?" For the first time since he had been told of his parents' deaths Adam Southam's voice and manner showed concern. He moved quickly up the drive. "That's his name, my dog. Charlie."

"I don't think he's hurt," said Dolby. He watched the youth duck under the blue and white ribbon once again and push his way through the gathering crowd of onlookers, who had followed the proceedings with undisguised glee. "And you can tell Mr Ford that the Chief Inspector and I'll be round in a few minutes to take a statement."

Dolby walked back down the drive to join DCI Caine. "That boy's a cold fish and no mistake," he said.

"You handled him well, though, Mark," Caine told him. "I must admit his reaction threw me for a moment. Both parents dead and no tears, no emotion, almost nothing." She thought of the words Dolby had used as they had stood looking over the woman's body, up in the bedroom. There was, it seemed, precious little love in this family.

"Yes - well - maybe there's more to young Mr Southam than he's letting on," mused Dolby, "There's certainly more to his parents' deaths than meets the eye."

Obviously, thought Caine with some satisfaction, Sergeant Dolby *had* noticed there were some aspects of Valerie Southam's death that did not ring true. She was about to ask him to go into more detail when one of the other officers came out of the front door and walked purposefully towards them.

Dolby nodded a greeting. "Good morning, Eddie," he turned towards Caine. "This is Sergeant Edward Briggs, FM Fingerprint Division. Eddie, Detective Chief Inspector Jacqueline Caine. DCI Caine joined us yesterday."

Caine shook the hand that was offered to her by the tall policeman. He was about thirty years old, with quick intelligent eyes peering out at her from behind the thick lenses of his rimless spectacles.

"Nice to meet you, Sergeant," She said, "How are things progressing upstairs?"

"Very interestingly, as it happens." Behind his glasses Briggs's eyes twinkled with enthusiasm for his work, but he spoke slowly as if pondering every word. "Very interesting indeed." He repeated, smiling. It was a few seconds before he continued and Caine wondered if she and Dolby would ever learn what he had found so very interesting. "I've dusted the whole of the woman's bedroom - or what I assume is her bedroom, her and her husband seem to have slept in separate beds in separate rooms..."

"And...?"

"... And her prints are all over the place, as you would expect, except...there are none in the places you would expect to find them."

"How do you mean?"

"Well, for a start, Inspector, there are no prints on the door handles. They've been wiped. In fact, they've been polished and I doubt that the domestic did it. Even if she was in the habit of polishing door handles, she wouldn't have been at it late last night, after whatever it was happened happened." Briggs paused thoughtfully. "And even the brandy bottle on the floor and the glass Mrs Southam was drinking from are clean - apart from the bloodstains, of course - there are no prints on them." He smiled. "Curious isn't it, because she's certainly not wearing gloves!"

"But there's blood on her fingers," mused Dolby "which is why it's on the glass. But then, if she touched the glass to drink the brandy she would have left her prints on it."

"My tests show there are none. Maybe she was wearing gloves at the time and took them off?" Briggs immediately dismissed his own suggestion. "No, it's unlikely! But what I *can* assure you of is - there are no prints on the glass or bottle *now*."

"What about the knife?" asked Caine, "I suppose you're going to tell us there are no prints on that either."

"On the contrary! **There** the lady **has** been more than generous. The handle is copiously covered with her prints and there are one or two beauties on the blade as well." Briggs was enjoying himself. "There are no prints on the bottle or glass, but the weapon is covered with 'em. It gets curiouser and curiouser does it not?"

Caine nodded. "As you said earlier, Mark, there's more to these deaths than meets the eye." She turned to Briggs again. "Are there any other prints anywhere?"

"You mean any not made by Mrs Southam or her husband? I've not found any yet, but I'm looking."

"And don't forget there's a son," said Dolby. "You're bound to find his prints around the place."

"Right. I'll bear that in mind, Mark. Anyway, I thought you ought to know my findings so far. They are persuasive I think, leaning towards suspicious circumstances."

Caine sighed. "Yes, it certainly looks as though we have a double murder on our hands, Sergeant. But let's be sure of our facts. You'd better dust all the likely places. Get in reinforcements if you need them."

Briggs feigned shocked horror. "Reinforcements, Ma'am? Anyone could see you're new here. Everybody's economising here in the Fen Molesey Constabulary. I do hope you're not suggesting that the Council should put up the local rates just to help solve a few trivial little murders! Perish the thought! Now, if you'll excuse me, I'd better get on." He turned and retraced his steps into the house.

Caine followed him in through the front door and started up the stairs. "I think we'll just have another look around, Mark. Valerie Southam's room in particular."

Briggs was moving his equipment out as they entered the room. "I'll be in the bathroom if I'm wanted," he told them. "There are one or two nice surfaces in there where a careless killer may have left his mark."

Caine walked over to the bed and peered down at the body again. "The autopsy will tell us exactly how she died, of course, Mark, but I'm pretty sure, now, that it wasn't suicide, even if it's been made to look like it." She turned back towards him. "You were going to say something else before Sergeant Briggs arrived on the scene? Something about there being more to this than meets the eye?"

"Well, you've said it yourself, Ma'am - there's a lot here that doesn't add up. And I thought so a good bit before Eddie Briggs said anything about fingerprints, or more precisely the lack of them. If you want my opinion, I don't think the woman killed her husband and then took an overdose. But I do think that somebody out there wants it to look that way."

"And that somebody - whoever he or she is - killed both of them and tried to make it look like a domestic fight that went tragically wrong? Yes, Mark, you're almost certainly right. It's my guess that Valerie Southam was dead before she ever took the pills and brandy - or at least she was dead before the killer pushed the pills down her throat. And they used the brandy in an attempt to wash them down - to make it look even more like she'd overdosed."

"But they didn't think it through properly, did they? Apart from the lack of fingerprints on such places as the door handles they made one big mistake. There's no sign of her husband's blood on her clothes and there is no way she would have got away without getting blood all over her, not with the mess there is downstairs in the kitchen." Dolby warmed to the subject, moved across the room to look down at the dead woman's face. "And another thing - she's made up to the nines. Why? How many women make themselves up before going to bed at night? My wife doesn't - she usually spends half an hour taking off what she's put on during the day. And, of course, why make up if you're going to top yourself?"

Caine was pleased Dolby had put his finger on the points that had also been bothering her. "Yes, the make-up does seem strange, but then again it might not be. It depends when she put it on and what time she died - we don't know that yet. But it could be significant. We need to know more about the sort of woman she was before we can draw any firm conclusions. As for the blood - or should I say the absence thereof - maybe she washed it off in the shower? But then, if she had intended to commit suicide after killing her husband why bother to shower? No, it looks like murder to me."

"I've checked the showers," said Dolby, "there are two of them - one in the en-suite next to the main bedroom and the other one in the family bathroom. The one in the en-suite was completely dry - didn't look like it had been used for a day or so. The floor of the other one was wet and was almost certainly used late last night. Funnily enough, though, there were no towels in there. You'd expect to find towels wouldn't you!"

"Yes. And there aren't any in here either." Caine agreed, looking around the bedroom.

Dolby followed through his line of thought. "But even if she had killed him and then taken the trouble to wash off the blood before taking her own life - what did she do with her bloodstained clothes? There's no sign of them in the house so far as I can see."

"That's another reason to believe she didn't kill herself," said Caine. "Those who are about to take their own life do not bother to get rid of the evidence." She walked to the window and lifted the curtain aside to look out over the back garden. She could see over the wall to the meadow beyond and watched a young mother pushing her baby in a pram along the narrow path that cut across its diagonal, heading towards the distant, gaudily painted warehouses of the nearby retail and industrial estate. A little girl of about four ran alongside, skipping and dancing. "I don't think the Southams were a very happy family, Mark." She looked across the room again, at the body. "And the boy - Adam's - reaction - was he touched by the news that both his parents were dead? He didn't seem to be..." She shivered although the sun was well up by now and it was not cold here in the house. She thought of her daughter, Alison. How would she react to such news? She had been too young to know the meaning of death when her father - Jacqueline Caine's adored husband - had been killed so many years ago in the pursuit of his duty, but how would she react now to the news that her mother had died a violent death? Surely, she would show more grief than Adam Southam had shown, but then women did not keep their emotions bottled up like men; here, in the first two decades of the twenty first century, there had been talk of the patina covering men's passions wearing thinner, making room for a more emotional, more caring, more feminine caste, but Caine had seen very little evidence of this during her working life. No, young Adam Southam did not appear to be holding anything back. It seemed that he simply did not care.

"It looked like he hated them both," agreed Dolby. "And that Mrs Neale - he didn't like her much either. Do you think what he said about her was true?"

"What? That she tried to seduce him? If the way she dresses is anything to go by - yes, I do."

Dolby ran a hand through his hair and said thoughtfully. "With due respect, Ma'am," he blushed, "Don't get me wrong, but as a man I find what he said about her damned strange. O.K., she dresses like a Soho tart, but she is a good-looking woman and I can't see many inexperienced young man turning her down if the offer was there. Unless, of course, he's religious or puritanical - or maybe he's gay!"

"Don't let's jump to conclusions, Mark. He may dislike her for other reasons we don't know anything about. And let's be honest, at this stage of the game we don't know much about anything or anyone concerned with these two deaths."

"Yes. Yes, you're right." He squatted down on his haunches and looked closely at the drinking glass on the bedside cabinet. Its curved surfaces were squared off and congealed blood clung to two sides of the glass in long striations.

"These lines of blood on the glass," he said thoughtfully, tracing them with his finger a half inch or so from the surface. "Do you think they might have something to do with those peculiar markings in the pool of blood downstairs, around Bruce Southam's body? I mean, whoever did kill the Southams would have wanted it to look as if the wife had blood on her hands - literally and metaphorically - when she drank the brandy. Could it be that they rubbed the glass into the blood beside the body?...Ouch!"

He had caught his foot in the fold of the bed valance as he stood up, pulling it to one side and almost toppling over, crashing down onto his knees beside the bed. He rubbed his injured limbs.

"Hello, what's this?" He moved closer to the bed and peered underneath. DCI Caine joined him, squatting on her heels at his side, her skirt pulled modestly tight across her knees. She followed his gaze. There was a piece of cloth beneath the bed, tightly crumpled into a ball. It had been hidden from sight by the overhang of the valance. It was a large white handkerchief, a man's rather than a woman's and it was stained red.

"That's blood unless I'm very much mistaken." Caine leaned forward, reaching under the bed to extricate the crumpled cloth. In drying, the blood had darkened, become caked hard and small cracks spread across the stain as she opened the handkerchief. It was pure cotton, white with a simple blue border, expensive, but it could have been bought in a thousand different stores across the country. Embroidered into one of the corners was the large letter "P".

CHAPTER THREE

"Southam's name **was** Bruce, I suppose?" said Caine. "He wasn't one of these people who favour their middle name instead of their first?"

"You mean his real first name could have been something else, "Peter", for example?" said Dolby, "Peter Bruce Southam? But he called himself Bruce because he didn't like being called Peter? I suppose it's possible. We can easily check it out."

"It could be significant, Mark - especially if the blood is Southam's and the handkerchief isn't."

He stood and reached into his pocket, taking out a small plastic bag. "Forensics are still here. I'll take it through to them."

"OK. Now for Mr Ford, our friendly dog-loving neighbour."

Downstairs Dolby turned and walked back up the hall, carrying the handkerchief in its plastic bag and pushing through the door into the kitchen. Caine heard the murmur of voices as he disappeared into the other room and she turned to pull the front door open again, waiting deep in thought until he re-joined her. They went out onto the porch, passed PC Bailey and continued up the drive. She was pleased to see the number of people gathered on the other side of the incident tape had dwindled to no more than a dozen but groaned when she saw a small group of press people - identifiable as much from their demeanour as from their cameras and hand-held recorders - grouped in the shade of an old poplar tree that grew in the centre of the wide pavement. They pressed forward as she and Dolby ducked under the tape and onto the pavement, turning left to walk up to the house indicated earlier by PC Bailey. They evidently knew Dolby, looked curiously at Caine.

The Detective Sergeant held up his hand to ward them off. "No comments yet, ladies and gentlemen."

Representatives of the press - be they local, national or international - are not renowned for their reticence.

"How does it feel to have a double murder on your hands, Mark?" This from the oldest of the group.

"I said 'no comment', Tom." They pushed their way through the throng.

The man who answered the door of number 19 Marazion Road was short and thin, in his early thirties, dressed in a flimsy white "T" shirt with the words **Hewlett Packard** emblazoned across it in large red letters. His trousers were thick green corduroy. On his feet he wore open toed sandals, without socks. His face was round, bordered at the top by short, rapidly thinning mouse brown hair and at the bottom by a sprouting of wispy blonde whiskers that seemed more the result of neglecting to shave than of the active encouragement of beard growing. He looked ill, his face without colour, and his eyes - behind thick-lensed dark rimmed spectacles - tired and drawn, as if the after effects of discovering his neighbour's mutilated body were still with him. His head, which seemed too small for his body, bobbed nervously up and down on his long thin neck, like a bird's.

"G'Morning!" He looked at Dolby and ran a large, grubby handkerchief across his forehead, as if wiping sweat away from his brow. He blinked rapidly, nervously, said quickly, almost running the words into each other. "You'll be the police I suppose? About the - er - thingy next door?"

"Yes! Good morning," Caine stepped forward and showed him her warrant card. "I'm Detective Chief Inspector Caine and this is Detective Sergeant Dolby - Fen Molesey CID. We're sorry to trouble you, sir, but it is important that we have a few words. You are Mr Ford?"

"Yes - Barry, Barry Ford." He smiled nervously and held his hand out hesitantly, unsure of the etiquette required in greeting policemen and women who were visiting in the course of their duties. "Come in - I - er - apologise for the place being in such a mess, but I haven't been feeling too good since I - er ... found the - er - body."

His movements were tense, quick and jerky as he showed them through the hall and into the lounge. It was bigger than the Southam's and Caine realised that the wall originally separating it from the small dining room at the rear had been taken down, extending it backwards to the conservatory which had been tacked on to the back of the house. The curtains were closed, but due to the light-coloured wallpaper and white paint work the room was much brighter than the Southam's. It smelt fresher and there was not that acrid smell of stale nicotine smoke Caine had immediately noticed when she entered the house next door. The pictures on the wall were big and modern, but made no sense to Caine who was not one for contemporary art. They were just slabs of bright colour seemingly dabbed at random onto the canvases. Nevertheless, they gave a refreshing feel of movement and life to the room. But there was no feeling of homeliness here. The furniture was more suitable for an office than a home. The bookshelves lining the walls were full of paperbacks, magazines, DVDs and CDs, with not a leather-bound volume to be seen. The two low settees of white leather, set on opposing sides of a glass topped coffee table, reminded Caine of the reception area of a large office block rather than a domestic lounge. At the far end of the room, where she would have expected to see a dining table and chairs, were two computer consoles set on a larger desk.

Ford followed the Detective Chief Inspector's eyes and bobbed his head nervously. He was not a man used to having the privacy of his home - his workplace - invaded by the police, even in a non-accusatory mode. "Sorry for the mess, Chief Inspector," he said again, "I was working late last night - haven't had time to tidy up."

"You work from home then, Mr Ford?" asked Dolby, nodding towards the computer equipment.

"Yes. I haven't been into the office since the Corona Pandemic. I'm a Software Systems Designer and it's easier to work from home as well as safer."

DS Dolby had walked to the other end of the room and was peering curiously into one of the computer screens. "Looks bloody - er - *ruddy* complicated!" Caine noticed the quick glance in her direction and his subsequent slide away from the mild swear word. She sighed inwardly at this unwanted deference to her supposed feminine delicacy. It seemed that even Dolby was determined not to act and speak naturally in her presence.

"Oh, it's just a bit of code." Ford said, still nervous but eager to pick up on a comment that had relevance to a subject with which he felt at home. "Computers are not at all complicated, not really. Not when you get to know them."

Ford was warming to his subject, but whilst Caine did, in fact, find the whole concept of computers and cyberspace and the ever burgeoning universe of social media a fascinating one she was not ready to spend her whole morning listening to an explanation of the state of the industry and how it related to the consumer. She interrupted him, she hoped not too rudely. "I'm sure that's quite fascinating, Mr Ford and perhaps you could tell us about it some other time, but the Detective Sergeant and I don't want to keep you for too long. I'm sure you have lots of work to do, but we need to talk to you about what's happened next door."

Pulled back to the gruesome subject of the body he had found in his neighbour's kitchen, Ford removed his spectacles and started to polish the lenses furiously, blowing on them and rubbing the now far from clean handkerchief over their surfaces.

"I suppose you'd better sit down." He waved his hand vaguely in the direction of the settees. "Can I - er - get you anything?" His glasses were back on his nose again and he peered through the heavy smears he had just imprinted on the lenses. "A cup of tea - I - er - don't have coffee, I'm afraid. The kettle is on - actually it's just boiled. I'm having a camomile tea myself." He crossed to one of the computer consoles and retrieved his mug from the work top alongside It. "I got to drinking it when I was having the problem with my wife, Laura. It's good for the nerves, you know." He took a long sip from his mug.

"No thank you, Mr Ford," said Caine, remarking to herself that, judging from Ford's present nervous state, the tea could not be as efficacious as he thought. She smoothed her skirt and manoeuvred herself carefully down onto the seat of the extremely low settee wondering, as she did so, whether she would be able to stand up again with any degree of propriety.

"Oh. Right." Ford looked at Dolby and when he shook his head nodded quickly, put his mug down and moved, with his quick nervous stride, to one of the mobile office chairs that stood in front of the computer tables. He took the papers and books strewn over the seat, dropped them on the floor and then pulled the chair over to the coffee table. He retrieved his mug again and sat down, sipping at his camomile tea and waiting for his two visitors to begin.

"I understand" said Caine "that when you found your neighbour's body in the kitchen earlier this morning you were not aware that the dead body of his wife was lying in a room upstairs?"

Ford gulped down the last of his tea. "No!" He seemed genuinely shocked. "Valerie's dead too? How dreadful! I didn't realise. Adam, her son - he didn't say anything when he came in to see Charlie, his dog. Does he know?"

"Yes, he knows." Though whether he cared or not Caine was unsure. "It was good of you to take charge of the dog, Mr Ford. Adam is with him now?"

"Yes. They're in the kitchen." Ford's face had lost even more of its colour, if that was possible and he breathed heavily, leaning forward, bent over, with his hands grasping his shins rocking back and forth. "Sorry, this is a bit of a shock. I - er - knew her - Valerie - Mrs Southam - better than her husband. Not that I knew her very well. I didn't like her much, but he was a lot worse - a very unfriendly man. How did she die?"

Meaning - was she also the victim of a vicious knife attack?

"We're not sure yet, Mr Ford. We are proceeding with our inquiries."

"For which purpose, Mr Ford, perhaps you'd like to tell us exactly what happened this morning," Dolby, took out his notebook and flicked through it to the first blank page.

"There's not much to tell, really," Ford said. He rubbed his chin thoughtfully, put his mug down, took off his glasses and polished the lenses vigorously yet again with the dubious handkerchief. "I came down to have breakfast at about seven and Charlie - The Southam's dog - was whining outside my kitchen door. He was making a lot of noise and scratching on the door, which is not like him at all."

"He's usually quiet then?" asked Dolby "Not much good as a watchdog?"

"I wouldn't say that. He barks when a complete stranger comes into the house or garden, but he wouldn't actually attack anybody. He's not much of a deterrent dog, if you see what I mean."

"Go on."

"As I say, he was making a bit of noise, so I opened the kitchen door to see what was upsetting him. There was dried blood on his fur, mostly on his paws and muzzle. I assumed he'd hurt himself - so I thought I'd better take him next door, to the Southams, and suggest they take him to the vet or something. I rang their front doorbell. They didn't answer, so I went around the side way thinking I'd leave Charlie in their back garden..." He broke off, rubbed his chin again. "The kitchen door was slightly ajar, so I pushed it open. Bruce - Mr Southam - was lying there on the floor. I realised when I saw him that he was dead - well, he had to be with all that blood all over the place and his stomach ripped up like that - ugh!" He grimaced, the blood draining even further from his face. "I realised also that the blood on the dog must be his blood. So, I came back in here and rang the police - well, actually, I was a bit sick in the garden before I could do that, so there were a few minutes delay." He shrugged apologetically. "It's just me and blood - I can't help it."

"It's understandable," said Caine. "You never really get used to it, even in the force." She drew him away from memories of the carnage that was still so fresh in his mind. "But what about yesterday evening, Mr Ford? Or over the last few days - did you see or hear anyone suspicious hanging around outside? You're at home all day - have there been any strangers about the area?"

"No - but then I wouldn't notice, would I?" Ford glanced across at the computer equipment. "I've been working flat out these last few days - right up to half past eleven last night, with my eyes glued to one or other of those screens, so I wasn't looking out of the window much."

"Did you hear anything though? From the Southams? - Any unusual noises."

Ford thought for a moment. "Not really - there were raised voices, but that wasn't unusual with the Southams. They were often fighting with each other. Anyway, I was working on a bit of programming - something I was writing for a client in Ireland, a chemical company, actually - it was high level stuff and it took a lot of brain energy I can tell you - and I must admit that the noise from next door was pretty off-putting. That's the trouble with these modern houses - you hear everything. Well, there's no air-conditioning is there, so in the warm weather you have to open the windows - and it was warm last evening, as you know, well up in the twenties - and these houses are very close together, so you hear everything. Sometimes it's embarrassing." His head was bobbing with nervousness again. "I always used to worry that the neighbours would hear Laura when she started shouting at me..." He paused and bit his lip and Caine thought she saw the wetness of tears in his eyes. He cleared his throat and went on. "Anyway, the sound carries and I don't suppose there's much anyone can do about it."

"And what time was it? - When you heard them arguing?"

"I don't know. Ten o'clock? Ten thirty? It went on for ten or fifteen minutes, I think. I can't be sure." He scratched his chin, took a long drink from his mug. "I was working, had to get the stuff finished last night and e-mail it to my client before the deadline, which was midnight. I just made it."

"And you recognised the voices of your neighbours, Valerie and Bruce Southam?" asked Caine.

He pursed his lips, pulled at his chin, thinking. "Now you mention it - I don't think it was Bruce. He's a big man - his voice is - was - deep, but this was - well, higher pitched. But it wasn't a woman's voice - I could tell that from the contrast with Valerie's - but I don't think it was Bruce Southam's voice. Not now I think about it." He suddenly slapped his knee and giggled. "God! What an idiot!"

"What?" asked Dolby.

"Just me being stupid!" Ford sighed. "I'm sorry - but it couldn't have been Bruce, of course, because he wasn't even home yet."

"What do you mean?"

"I'd forgotten it entirely until you asked if it was him and then I started thinking that the person Valerie was arguing with had a different voice. But now I realise that it couldn't have been him anyway."

"Why not?"

"Because he - Bruce - didn't get home until 11.30. I'd just finished writing up the program and I had just e-mailed my client - you can check the time of transmission exactly if you like, from the computer - anyway, just then a vehicle's headlights swept across the room from the road and I heard a car pulling up outside. I was finished at my workstation and I wanted to stretch my legs a bit, so I went to the window and looked out. Bruce was next door getting out of a taxi. There's a streetlamp on the pavement near his drive-in, so you can see perfectly at night."

"So, you can say it definitely **wasn't** Bruce Southam arguing with his wife an hour or more before," said Caine. "Have you any idea at all whom it could have been? Did you recognise the voice of the other person?"

Ford stroked the wispy growth of hair on his chin and thought for a moment. "It was a man and it was vaguely familiar," he said. "I'm sure I have heard it before, but I can't place it."

"And how long did this argument go on for?"

"I don't know - ten - fifteen minutes."

"Could you hear what they were arguing about?"

"No. You've got to understand that I wasn't concentrating on them. If anything, I was trying to shut the noise out and get on with my work." He paused. "I suppose there was something unusual about it, though...negative rather than positive. Sort of - an omission, if you like."

"How do you mean - an omission?" Caine wondered if the man was being deliberately vague or if this clouding of the issue was merely a normal part of the mystique that so many 'computer people' seemed to enjoy.

"There was something missing from the usual scenario of a Southam row. Valerie - Mrs Southam - wasn't screaming...well, not much anyway."

"How do you mean she wasn't screaming?" Dolby looked up from his note taking, scratching the bridge of his nose with the top end of his biro. "Did she always scream then, when she had a row with her husband?"

"Usually, when they raised their voices and they were shouting at each other, she screamed," confirmed Ford. "I mean, they didn't just shout at each other when they argued - they used to get violent. I would hear things getting smashed, they were throwing things at each other I suppose and it usually ended up with Valerie - Mrs Southam - screaming - and crying." He paused, sighed. "That's another reason why I should have realised she wasn't arguing with her husband yesterday evening. There wasn't any smashing and crashing." He broke off, embarrassed. "I think Bruce used to hit her with his fists."

"You mean he beat her?" asked Caine.

"Yes. I think so."

"What makes you say that?"

"She often had bruises." Ford paused and Caine wondered if he was actually aware that his tongue was flicking from his mouth, licking across his lips. "She would often sunbathe in her back garden" he volunteered at last. "The back gardens here face south west and we get a lot of the sun, when it's sunny that is..." he looked away towards the window. "I sometimes saw her through an upstairs window, if I happened to look out... She didn't wear much - just one of those skimpy bikini things...she had bruises...on her arms and body. Usually, a day or so after they'd had one of their rows. They lasted for weeks. The bruises that is."

Caine nodded. Ford was merely confirming something she - and she was sure Mark Dolby - had already guessed. "What happened after the argument?"

"Nothing. I don't know - I was still working."

"So, you didn't hear anything else from outside - from next door - until the taxi pulled up at 11.30 to let Bruce Southam get out at his front door?"

"No..." Ford pulled at his chin, looked up. "That is - Yes. I did hear something else. The dog was barking."

"When was that, Mr Ford?"

"I don't know - 11.00 perhaps, slightly before. But it wasn't unusual. He sometimes barked when they - the Southams

- were late taking him for his walk." He shrugged. "I didn't attach any importance to it, it was only the dog barking and dogs do bark for all sorts of reasons. I'm only mentioning it because you asked me if I heard anything at all after the argument."

"But the dog didn't bark before the argument?"

Ford shook his head. "No - I don't think so. No. He's usually in the garden and I'd have heard."

"And how long did it go on for?" asked Dolby.

"Ten, maybe fifteen minutes - it had stopped by the time Bruce Southam arrived in his taxi. Then, funny thing, it started up again a few minutes after that - after Bruce had gone into the house. This time it was more frantic - and a bit louder."

"And you saw and heard nothing else unusual?"

"As I said, I think the dog was acting strangely, barking and howling - but anything could have caused that - a fox in the back garden or something - we do get a lot of foxes around here."

DCI Caine leaned forward, closing her hands together, her long slim fingers with their well-manicured nails forming a steeple. "How well did you know the Southams, Mr Ford?"

He shrugged. "Hardly at all. Well, he was very rarely about. He was a workaholic. And when he was there he wasn't what you'd call a good neighbour. Not at all our," he corrected himself, "*my* type."

"And where was your wife yesterday evening while all this was going on?"

"I don't know..." He bit his lip. "We're separated. She went back to live with her parents a few months ago."

"So, she can't vouch that you were, as you claim, alone here working yesterday evening?" asked Dolby.

Ford looked alarmed. "Am I a suspect then? Do you think I killed her - them?"

"We don't know who killed them, Mr Ford. But somebody did. So, your wife moved out - how long ago?"

"I'm not sure that *when* she moved out is relevant," said Ford, "But I have nothing to hide, so I'll answer your question. Laura left me three months ago!"

"Why?"

Ford looked resentful. His face hardened. "I don't know why I should tell you this." They made no comment and he shrugged as if it didn't matter one way or the other whether they knew or not. "O.K., Laura and me - we weren't getting on. She thought I was being unfaithful."

"How long have you been married, Mr Ford?" asked Caine.

He thought for a moment. "Five years, seven months."

"And how long have you lived here in Marazion Road?"

"Just over a year."

"Did the fact that you moved here have anything to do with your marriage breaking up?"

Ford bit his lip. "No. Why should it? It didn't change our way of life. We used to live in Springfied, near Chelmsford, just a few minutes from Laura's parents, so we didn't move that far. They're still only about twenty minutes away. And we're close to our friends. Besides the house is much nicer than the rented flat we had in Springfield. Laura was happy here - at first...

"Did your wife get on well with the Southams?"

There was the slightest hesitation before he replied. "No - well, a qualified 'yes'. She didn't exactly **not** get on with Valerie - Mrs Southam - but they weren't exactly bosom buddies either. As it happens, Laura was out at work during the week, so they hardly ever saw each other."

"And what about Bruce Southam?"

"She couldn't stand him. She thought he was an insufferable pig. And he drank - and stank of tobacco. She doesn't like drinkers and smokers".

"And she thought he beat Valerie up too? Presumably, your wife also would have seen her bruises while she was sunbathing in the garden?"

Again, there was a slight hesitation. "Yes. That was one of the reasons why she didn't like him. The way he beat his wife. That and his drinking."

"But she didn't get on with Valerie Southam either," said Dolby. "Had she no sympathy for her even though her husband was abusing her?"

"No - well, not much. She thought Valerie was a bit of a tart. Mutton dressed as lamb."

"And what did you think?"

"I felt sorry for her," said Ford "She did dress a bit young for her age - she must have been in her mid-forties, I suppose - but she wore very revealing clothes; miniskirts and plunging necklines, that sort of thing. But that still doesn't give her husband the right to beat her, does it!"

"Maybe your wife didn't like Mrs Southam because you were at home all day watching her sunbathe?" Dolby suggested.

Ford bit his lip. His eyes were moist, but they flashed with a quick spasm of anger. He seemed uncertain how to react to Dolby's insinuation. "I don't see what relevance all this has to the Southams being murdered." He said tightly. "I didn't do it, it had nothing to do with me. Or Laura." His eyes were watering once again. "I'm beginning to wish I hadn't phoned you this morning, when I found his body! You're twisting everything I say."

"We're not, and I'm sorry, Mr Ford, if you think that," said Caine quietly. "We are trying to establish the truth. And I would remind you that this is a murder inquiry. If you had not phoned us when you became aware that a murder had taken place you would have been committing an extremely serious offence."

Ford bowed his head. "I know, I know, I just don't see why you have to ask so many personal questions."

"I'm sorry," Caine apologised. She had forgotten what this young man, used to an ordinary and well-ordered life, certainly unused to discovering dead bodies, had been through that morning. "You've been very helpful so far. We won't keep you much longer, but let's just go back to the argument Mrs

Southam was having with some person unknown at about ten o'clock yesterday evening. When the argument ended, did you see or hear anyone leave the Southam's house?"

"Look, I've already told you," Ford said irritably, "I was working at the computer all through that time. I didn't stop until 11.30, so I didn't go to the window to look out, or anything. I am **not** a busybody, I do **not** spend all my life peeping through the curtains and spying on my neighbours."

Caine leaned forward and used her momentum to spring up from the low leather chair. "Thank you - I think that's all, Mr Ford - at least for the time being. But I wonder if you wouldn't mind us just popping in to have a few words with Adam Southam - he is still in the kitchen with Charlie isn't he?"

"No problem," said Ford. He smiled, showing his brilliant set of teeth, obviously relieved they had finished with him. He was flushed with success at having passed, relatively unscathed, through the rigors of his first police interview. "If you'd like to come through," he opened the door to the hall, "Actually, I asked Adam if he would like to give his dog a wash so he might still be out in the utility room."

He led them through the hall into the kitchen. The sink and draining board were piled high with unwashed dishes and crockery and there were empty convenience food packets spilling out of the waste bin. To the right of the sink was a side door that Caine supposed would lead them through to the utility room and garage. Ford put his hand on the door handle and stopped suddenly. He rubbed the downy hair on his chin and his head bobbed nervously on his neck. "I've just remembered." he said. "There *was* something else,"

Dolby, bringing up the rear and looking aghast at the piled, dirty crockery, brought out his notebook and pencil again. "And what might that be, sir?"

"I don't know if it's important, Inspector, Sergeant, but it just occurred to me - Mrs Southam had a caller the other day. I don't know who it was - I didn't even see him, but his car was parked on their driveway for about half an hour one day last week - I forget which day, but it was towards the end of the week - maybe Thursday. Anyway, it just struck me as unusual - I don't think she had many visitors. I don't think either of them had."

"You say you didn't see the driver," said Caine "So how do you know the visitor was a man?"

"Sorry - you're right of course. It could have been a woman I suppose - I just assumed it was a man because it was a big car. You don't see many women driving around in large Mercedes," he finished lamely "- at least I don't think so - they're not really ladies' cars."

"Is there anything else you can tell us about it?" asked Dolby, making a note in his book. "Was it new or old - did you happen to spot the registration mark?"

Ford worried at the hair on his chin with his fingers. It seemed to aid his thought processes. "It was new. At least it looked brand new, but I can't remember the registration. It may have been personalised, but I can't really remember."

"Colour?"

"Blue. Dark blue."

"And you can't recall seeing anyone or anything else that has struck you as unusual over the last few days?" asked Caine.

"No - sorry. Though I did say the Southams didn't seem to have many visitors - that is true, I think, but every now and then I have seen other cars parked on their driveway. Not often, mind. Once a month, maybe."

"What about other visitors on foot, without cars?"

"Susie Neale, of course, one of the neighbours - she and Valerie - Mrs Southam - are - were - bosom buddies. She used to drop in for tea and sympathy nearly every day - I'd hear them in the garden sometimes, talking and laughing."

"Yes, we have met Mrs Neale," said Caine.

"As I say, she's from just up the road - I forget the number, but it's that house with those awful ornamental lions stuck on top of the brick piers at the front end of the drive. Oh! - And there are hideous cast iron lamps on top of the wall as well. Dreadful things! They were designed for big country houses not small, tatty four bedroomed boxes. They're totally out of place," he smiled, "but I suppose they do make it easy to find the house!"

"We won't be able to miss it," agreed Dolby. "Do you know any other people - neighbours - who were close friends of the Southams? We've a lot of background to fill in."

Ford shook his head. "Adam might be able to help you there." He opened the door and leaned into the room beyond. "You there, Adam?"

There was a step down into the long, narrow utility room, which had been rather cleverly squeezed in between kitchen and garage. There was no sign of Adam Southam.

"He must have taken Charlie into the garden," said Barry Ford. "It's a nice day - he's probably drying him out there." They followed him through the utility room and out into the back garden.

Adam Southam was sitting on a wrought iron bench on the small patio area laid out in front of the closed sliding doors that led out of the lounge. Charlie, a black and white Shetland Sheep dog, was perched contentedly on a tartan rug thrown over Adam's knees and the young man was rubbing his abundant fur with a towel. He turned in their direction as they approached around the side of the house then, as he recognised them, turned back to stare over the unkempt lawn.

"Hello, Adam," said Caine. "We'd like a few words."

"Please yourself." He didn't turn to look at them, spoke casually, but with an edge to his voice.

"We need to speak to you, Adam. I know it's hard so soon after your parents' death, but it is important."

He turned towards her and shrugged. She saw that his eyes were slightly red and that he had been crying. His gaze now was steady, but at least he appeared to have felt *something* at the sudden, shocking death of his parents. Perhaps he had felt it very deeply from the beginning but had kept his sorrow well hidden. "No - it's O.K. What do you want to know?" he said. He looked down at the dog on his lap and stroked its still damp fur, running slender fingers along the curve of the mottled, black and white back and up to the head, massaging gently behind the crinkle of Charlie's pointed ears. The animal turned its head, its soft, loyal eyes melancholy, as if it sensed its young master's emotion.

"I'll fetch a couple of garden chairs for you and the Sergeant, Inspector," said Barry Ford. "No reason why you shouldn't be comfortable." His own ordeal over for the time being he was more relaxed.

Barry Ford fetched a couple of plastic garden chairs from a small outhouse built alongside the fence and put them down by the bench.

Caine sat down next to Dolby. "If you're quite sure, Adam, that you're ready to answer a few questions? We can wait until later if you wish."

"It's O.K. I said it's O.K." said Adam irritably, continuing to stroke Charlie's ears.

Caine leaned over and ran her fingers along his fur. "He's a fine-looking dog. How old is he?"

"About seven. We got him when I was twelve. My mother wanted a watchdog because my father used to travel a lot on business. He's quite good in that respect - barks when anyone comes up the path, but he's too affectionate really and I don't suppose he would actually attack an intruder." He smiled, realising what he had said. "I'm talking about Charlie, of course, not my father - I'm sure **he** would quite happily have attacked intruders of any description." He laughed grimly. "My father would quite happily have attacked anyone - and bitten them too!"

"He - the dog - would have barked then if there was someone trying to get into the house last night?" asked Dolby ignoring the young man's flippancy.

"Yes, I'd say so. I wasn't here, of course."

"You often stay out overnight, do you, Adam?" asked Caine.

"I don't live here - next door - anymore," he told her. "I live with a friend, though I only moved out recently. I'd been thinking about it a lot and last Sunday I'd finally had enough of my parents, so I moved out." He sighed. "I suppose I missed my opportunity to get away from them a couple of years ago when I decided not to go away to University."

Caine thought back to her daughter, Alison's, teen age years and the traumas and tantrums they had both been through whilst she had been living at home, before she went up to University. Caine often wondered if those years would have been different if she hadn't lost her husband, Jonathan, so early on. "Things were difficult were they? Between you and your parents?"

"Difficult? You've got no idea. My parents are - were - impossible!" Adam grimaced and held up his hands in mock surrender. "I know - they're dead now and I'm sorry and I shouldn't be saying negative things about them, but it's the truth. They were impossible. They couldn't get on with each other and they were always rowing and screaming at each other."

"You couldn't hit it off with them?" This was Dolby, whose eldest daughter had only just reached her teens and was beginning to flex the muscles of her independence. He was beginning to learn that the physical laws of the Universe, particularly as regards the passage of Time, did not seem to operate in the same way for teenagers as for the rest of humankind. That very morning he had only just managed to get into the bathroom before her, thereby preventing both an embarrassing scene and an extremely late arrival at the scene of the crime.

"No way." Adam told him. "My father, especially."

"Was that why you decided to leave home?" Caine asked.

The young man nodded. "Partly. I just couldn't get on with them. My father didn't like the idea of me moving in with my friend, Philip." He laughed bitterly.

"What exactly happened on Sunday that made you finally decide to leave."

Adam laughed without humour, "It's a long story. Philip does our gardening - he's a horticulturist, works for Budds and

Co. - you probably know them, they're the biggest gardening contractors in East Anglia, or so they claim. Anyway, he does a spot of work on the side, just small stuff. My mother got to know of him because he does the gardening and landscaping for the Perot Estate - I suppose you'd call him the foreman up there; they think very highly of him - and my father knows - knew - the Perots very well. He worked for them for years. They're in insurance or financial services, a combination of both I guess and he was a big cheese in their London Office."

"The Perot family are well known local figures, Ma'am," Dolby explained "They have a big spread out towards Upton Stapleford - must be over three hundred acres including the gravel pits. Charles Perot, the head of the family, is about as close as you'll get to a local Squire in these parts, but they're only recently gentrified." He waved his hand in Caine's direction and explained, for Adam's benefit, "DCI Caine is new to the area, Adam. She's probably never heard of the Perots."

"O.K. Anyway, my father knew Paul Perot - Charles's son and heir - when he was a boy, practically grew up with him," Adam went on. "So, we know the Perot family pretty well - Charles Perot was the one who started the firm in the 1960s - way back before my time, obviously. He's still with the firm as their senior partner or Chairman or something, but he's pretty old now, and I think he's losing it." Adam gave the dog on his lap a playful pat, "I think my parents named this Charlie after him. Mind you, that was probably my father's influence - my mother didn't like the Perots - said they were a stuck-up lot that gave themselves airs and graces they didn't deserve. Said they came up from nothing, which was actually true. Apparently, Charles Perot had nothing when he started out. Personally, I admire him. His Upton Stapleford estate alone must be worth seven or eight million, not to mention the business."

"And how long did your father work for Charles Perot?" asked Caine.

"Yonks! - he knew Charles's son, Paul from their schooldays - they were probably school bullies together!" There was a note of irony in his voice. "They hung about with each other for years and they served in the paratroopers together. Imagine those two fighting for Queen and Country! Can you believe it! Anyway, it was Paul's influence got him the job with Charles Perot's firm when they came out of the army."

"You say your mother didn't like the Perots?"

"No - Florence - we call her "Flo" - Charles's wife. She didn't get on with my mother at all well - there was always an atmosphere between them if you see what I mean and they avoided meeting each other wherever possible. I think my mother hated Flo. Funnily enough, though, Flo seems to dote on me - can't do too much for me."

"How do you mean?"

"She never forgets my birthday, for instance - which is more than I can say for my mother and father - and at Christmas she spoils me rotten. I don't know why she does it, but she always has, for as long as I can remember." He laughed. "I'm not complaining, mind, but maybe my mother resented it!" He stopped, looked at them quizzically. "Sorry, but I've forgotten how we started talking about the Perots!"

"I think you were going to tell us that it was through them that your parents met Philip and asked him to look after their garden," said Caine.

Adam nodded. "Oh yes - sorry, I'm finding it hard to concentrate! Anyway, our garden's obviously only tiny compared with Charles Perot's - I used to do most of it myself before I started full time at Horticultural College, that's what got me interested in plants, I suppose. My mother couldn't tell a cabbage from a carnation so she needed help - and my father not only couldn't, but wouldn't find the time to do any gardening, he positively hated it. Said it was a woman's work or, at best, a job for a country bumpkin - which is another reason we didn't get on, me being interested in horticulture for a career. Anyway, they had to get somebody in to do the garden and Philip came highly recommended."

"And you met Philip - what's his second name by the way? - while he was working on your garden?" Dolby balanced his notebook on his knee and wrote carefully, between sips of tea.

"Chantry - his name's Philip Chantry. No - I knew him before he started to look after our garden. We met up at the Perot's. And, of course, Philip does work occasionally for

Chelmer College. Budds has a contract with them as well. I'm studying horticulture up there as it happens - so we've also met on campus..."

"And you know each other well?"

"Oh yes - we were even thinking of starting up in business together. A Garden Centre, you know - make use of our talents - but we couldn't raise the money."

"So, what happened on Sunday," asked Dolby. "Why did you decide to leave home?"

"Philip turned up on Sunday out of the blue - he usually does a few hours in the evening during the week so as to avoid bumping into my father - they didn't get on and - well, to cut a very long story short, I told my father I was thinking of going to live with Philip. He went ballistic, of course, that's the sort of thing he did, never listened to reason and thought there was only one opinion on everything - his own! He called Phil all sorts of vile names so Phil said he could stuff the garden and walked out. I went with him."

"So, you've been living with Philip Chantry since the weekend and you were at home, with him, yesterday evening and stayed overnight?"

"Yes. Though in fact we went to a party last night and stayed very late. Until about two in the morning."

"So how come you were here so early this morning?" asked Dolby, making rapid notes. "You couldn't have had very much sleep last night."

"I don't need much," said Adam. "I'm at college and I was supposed to have gone in for a lecture this morning. I came to collect some books I needed." He swallowed. "Then, of course, you wouldn't let me into the house...there didn't seem much point in going into college after that." He smiled. "I may never bother to go in again."

Caine's parental instincts came to the fore. "I don't know that that's a good idea, Adam," she found herself saying, "I know it's hard at the moment, but I'm sure you'll want to carry on once you get over your parents' passing. A qualification is always valuable."

"Maybe. But I don't think I'll need it. The way I see it I'm due to inherit over half a million from my Father's life insurance alone, not to mention what's due on my mum, plus this house, of course!" He grinned widely, "At this very moment I'm probably the richest person sitting in this garden. I may even be a millionaire!"

CHAPTER FOUR

"That's a bit callous, isn't it, young man?" said Dolby, clearly outraged. "Your parents are lying dead next door and you're boasting about how rich you're going to be as a result!"

Adam Southam shrugged. "What's the point in pretending? I didn't get on with my mother and father. So far as I'm concerned I'm better off with them dead!"

Dolby drew in his breath and shot a glance at DCI Caine. "You do have a right to your opinion, Adam," she said slowly, "And I dare say what you say is true. But you must realise that in view of the fact that your parents were murdered by some person or persons as yet unknown such statements are extremely unwise!"

Adam smiled grimly. Again, he seemed to have dropped all pretence of grief. "Don't tell me you wouldn't have thought of it yourselves, Inspector! Isn't motive one of the first things you look for? I'm just making it easier for you - saving you the trouble of asking my parent's solicitor for details of their wills. Anyway, I shouldn't think you're going to try pinning these murders on me, are you!"

"We're not in the business of **pinning things** on people, Adam," Dolby told him, gruffly. "But it wouldn't be the first time a man has killed his own parents for his inheritance - and from what you've just said it looks as though you had ample motive in that direction."

"We're simply trying to get at the truth, Adam," said Caine coolly, "That's all we're really interested in. For the time being I think we can stretch a point and be generous. We'll excuse your lack of respect for your parents' death for the time being and put it down to shock." She paused, pleased to see that Adam Southam had turned his handsome young face downwards, towards the animal on his lap, avoiding her eyes, perhaps showing some remorse. Dolby, inwardly fuming at what he considered Adam's callous behaviour and deep in his own thoughts, turned his gaze away from the young man to look down the garden.

There was a long silence before Caine finally spoke. "We'll continue, Adam if you have no objection." He shrugged. "Very well. You have told us, Adam, that you were at a party last night - presumably there were people there who would be able to confirm that?"

Adam looked up again and shrugged. "I guess so - there must have been at least half a dozen people there who knew me. Any number of them will alibi me!"

"Good. We'll have their names in a minute." Said Dolby "And where exactly did this party take place?"

Adam named a local village. "Upton Eccles - in somebody's cottage. A couple of the students were throwing a sort of housewarming or whatever."

"Their names?"

"Jennifer and Dawn. I don't know their surnames. Anyway, their address is "Wisteria Cottage" Church Lane. That's where the party was. It's just off the Market Place, but you probably know that."

Dolby nodded, writing quickly. "What time did you arrive at the party?"

"About 10.00."

"Were you with Mr Chantry all evening?"

"No. He didn't get there until after 11.00. He often works late these light summer evenings, so he told me to go on ahead."

"Did he tell you *where* he was working?"

"No. But I think he must have called in at my parents at some time because I noticed his best pair of secateurs were on the kitchen table - **his** kitchen table - this morning. He told me yesterday morning he'd left them at my parents and meant to collect them sometime."

"And you noticed them there this morning - not last night at any time?" asked Dolby.

"No - is it important?" asked Adam. He looked a little anxious.

"It might be. How did you get to the party?"

"Do you mean did I drive? No. It's not far, a few hundred yards, Philip's flat is also in Upton Eccles and Wisteria Cottage is just at the other end of the High Street, where it runs into the Market Place. So, I walked."

"And what time did you leave?"

"I told you - at about two o'clock. Philip and I walked home with some other guys - one of them lives in the same block as Philip and the other two were staying over." He gave Dolby their names, adding "They're all at Chelmer College. I don't know the addresses of the other two, you'll have to ask the College Secretary."

"I want to talk about your parents now Adam," said Caine, "did they have many friends?"

Adam seemed to resist the urge to laugh, covering his mouth with one of his hands and pulling down on his chin, his teeth clenched together. "No, Inspector," he said finally, "I don't think so. There were the Perots, of course, I suppose they were my father's friends - at least Paul Perot was, he had to be didn't he? They knew each other for so many years. But I suppose it depends on what you mean by 'friends'? It's like Facebook - there's Facebook friends and there's your real friends, people you really know."

"And what about your mother?"

"There was that tart Susie Neale up the road, I suppose. At least they saw a lot of each other. Apparently, they'd known each other for years before they met up again on account of being neighbours."

"And they were friends just because they happened to be neighbours?"

"No, not if you believe Mrs Neale, anyway. My mother never confirmed it - to be honest I wasn't that interested, so I never asked her - but Susie - isn't that a stupid name for a grown woman! - she told me once that she and my mother had known each other very well years and years ago when they were young. They were dancers together or something. Apparently, they met again when they moved onto this estate. Big coincidence."

"Did your mother and father have any other friends?"

"Real friends - no. Acquaintances - Yes - I suppose there were a few people on and off over the years. But not friends - not long-standing friends - apart from Susie Neale and Paul Perot, that is. Neither of them seemed to be able to hold on to anyone for any length of time." He shrugged. "I suppose once the other people got to know what they were really like as a couple they went off them. Let's face it, my father was a pretty unpleasant guy and a boozer, though he would never admit it - and my mother - my mother seemed to be totally spineless. At least, it looked that way to me. Maybe I was wrong though, maybe it wasn't that easy for her to get away from him..." He choked back what might have been tears with a long-drawn-out breath and twisted Charlie's fur between his fingers. The dog growled and snapped at him. He pulled his fingers away and went on, carefully controlling his voice. "She let him do whatever he liked to her. He used to hit her you know! Most of the time she was just covered in bruises! That's why she started drinking herself. It's only been recently, only in the last few months that she started talking about fighting back."

"In what way?" asked Caine.

"She started talking about divorcing him. She didn't tell him, of course, that would have made him beat her up even more. But she did start talking about seeing a solicitor."

"Did she see one?"

"I don't know. She didn't confide in me very often," said Adam bitterly, "She only told me what her intentions were when I came in and found her drunk one evening. She really poured her heart out that night - he'd been really bad around that time - but she never talked to me in the normal course of events. Well, I was only her son, after all!" He sighed, shifted his position on the bench. "I suppose, though, to be fair to my mother, I was hardly about in those days. I used to stay late at college, study in the library, go to friends' houses in the evening - anything to get out of the house and away from them, I suppose. Together they were impossible to live with. No - I can't say I blame people for disliking my parents."

"You obviously didn't like them yourself," Caine said quietly.

Adam used their Christian names for the first time, but without the slightest hint of affection. "No, I didn't. Valerie and Bruce were my parents, but no way were they my friends!"

"What about relatives?"

"I'm glad you used the word 'relatives' rather than 'family'," said Adam bitterly. "There are always relatives aren't there? But that doesn't mean they're family. I have grandparents, if that's what you mean - my father's parents are still alive, though I hardly ever see them. They might as well be dead for all I know. They live in Devon and my father fell out with them years ago." He fondled Charlie, running his fingers over the dog's long, angular head, pulling gently at his ears. "And of course, it is rumoured that I have an uncle I have never seen, living somewhere in the world - God knows where! None of us have seen him since he left university in the sixties and took off for Australia. He may be there still, or he may be dead. Who knows? He hasn't given us many clues over the years!"

"Do you have an address for your grandparents?"

"It'll be in my father's papers somewhere."

"They should be notified of your parents' deaths," said DCI Caine.

Adam Southam shrugged. "I doubt there'll want to come to the funeral. But you never know, they may come to gloat!"

Disgusted by the comment Caine hurried on, now wanting to get the interview over as quickly as efficiency would allow. She did not like this young man. "And what about your mother's family? Are her parents alive?"

Adam shrugged again. He seemed to be doing an inordinate amount of shrugging. Caine found it irritating. It was hard to believe he was as unconcerned as he was trying to make out. "I'm afraid we draw a blank there too!" he said flippantly, "My mother would never discuss her parents with me. Had I been interested enough to find out I would have made my own inquiries I suppose, but I wasn't and so far as I know she didn't even know who they were. I think she was fostered out or something when she was small."

"It seems that your parents didn't have many friends," said Caine, "But what about enemies?"

"I dare say my father gathered a few in the business way of things," said Adam, "Not that I could quote you any. Apart from that I don't really know. I don't think he had anyone who disliked him enough to want to murder him."

"What about your mother?"

"Maybe *she* would - oh, you mean did she have enemies? No - I shouldn't think so. Not murderous ones anyway."

"Did she have any visitors to the house over the last few weeks?"

"I wouldn't know. I certainly haven't seen any, but then I'm hardly ever here, especially during the day."

"Just one or two more questions, Adam," said Caine. "Did your father have any other Christian names, other than Bruce I mean? Something he preferred to be called?"

"Not so far as I know. He always called himself Bruce." He shrugged again, "It's not the sort of thing we used to discuss, not that we've talked much recently. We talked more when I was a kid, I suppose, but even then all he wanted to talk about was football. My father was an Arsenal supporter."

"I think that's all for now, Mr Southam," said Caine. "We shall probably want to see you again, so please let us know if you have any plans to be away over the next few days."

"I hadn't anything planned," said Adam, "Though I shall probably stay at Philip's place for the next day or so, while your people are running all over my parents' - "he corrected himself "**My** house. You've got Philip's address haven't you?" He lifted Charlie from his lap and leaned forward to drop him gently on the ground, then pushed the rug off his lap and onto the bench beside him. He stood up to face the two police officers. "I shall need those books from next door though, so maybe you could arrange for me to go in sometime today?"

Caine nodded. "I'll speak to the scene of crime officer. He'll organise something." She made her way towards the sideway of the house, Dolby following her. "Thank you for answering our questions, Adam - and please accept our sincere condolences. Rest assured we shall do all we can to find your parents' killer."

Adam Southam nodded and smiled and watched them disappear around the side of the red brick house.

CHAPTER FIVE

"What do you think of that young man, Mark?" Asked Caine as they made their way down the side of Ford's house towards the street.

"Adam Southam? To be honest, Ma'am, and if you'll excuse the expression, I find him an unpleasant little buggar."

"I don't mind the expression in the least," Caine assured him," in fact, Mark, I approve of it and I admire you for your restraint. Personally, I'd have called him a diabolical, insensitive and possibly conniving little bastard. I'd like to think my daughter would show some signs of grief if I'd just been killed in the way his parents have. My God! He's a cold fish if ever I met one!"

"Disturbed certainly," agreed Dolby, "but maybe it's his parents that have made him that way!"

They made their way up the drive and away from Barry Ford's house, turning along the road and back towards the Southam's, stopping to watch as a police ambulance backed into the drive preparatory to removing the bodies of the two murder victims. Caine was pleased to note that the crowd gathered in the street to watch the proceedings had dwindled to just three teenagers - two boys and a girl, probably neighbours - who stood on the pavement in front of the house, texting on their mobile phones and gawping at the ambulance. There was no sign of the newspaper reporters. No doubt they would reappear as soon as they got scent of an arrest.

Caine and Dolby acknowledged PC Doyle and walked quickly down the drive to stand at the side of the ambulance. They watched silently as one of the bodies was carried, on a stretcher and concealed in a black plastic bag, out of the front door and into the back of the vehicle.

"Anyway, Mark, returning to the unpleasant subject of young Southam, do you think he's our man?" asked Caine.

Dolby shrugged. "I don't know. He has a sort of motive, but hardly enough to commit two murders - but it's a bit, well - out of his league, wouldn't you think, Ma'am?"

"I wish you wouldn't keep calling me that, Mark. It makes me feel like The Queen, or worse yet The Queen Mother, as was. I'm not *that* old."

Dolby looked flustered. "What? Oh - 'Ma'am'. Sorry - but calling you DCI Caine all the time seems a bit over the top."

Caine sighed. "No, it's me who should be apologising, Mark. I should have told you my preference from the start. Anyway, Ma'am's too formal - you can't call me that - we're supposed to be a team. I don't intend to call you DS Dolby!"

"What do I call you then?"

"Jackie. 'Ma'am' only when there's someone else about. 'Inspector' if you have to be really formal."

"Oh. Right..." He seemed pleased.

She looked at her watch. "It's nearly ten thirty. I'm due back at The Super's office at two o'clock - he wants to introduce me to The Chief Constable. Apparently, he's making a flying visit to Fen Molesey."

Dolby nodded. "Must be his once-a-year day."

"He's planting a tree or laying a foundation stone for a new building in the Town Centre or something. So, I suppose he's dropping into the copshop while he's in the area."

"That figures - he's a bit of a political animal is our Chief Constable. Come to that so is the Super."

"Well, I'm sure he's not coming to Fen Molesey solely on my account," said Caine, "but the Chief says he especially wants to meet me." She started up the drive. "What do you say we take a walk up the road now and have a few words with our friendly Mrs Neale? We need a lot more background on the Southams and I dare say she could help in that direction."

Dolby nodded. "Yes, I'm sure the lovely Susie is busting to spill the beans. Number 27, isn't she?"

"Yes - the house with the rampant lions, wasn't it? But before we go seek her out, Mark, I must admit I could do with a bite more to eat - I didn't have a chance to catch any breakfast this morning."

"I'm with you there," said Dolby. "I hardly had time for breakfast myself."

"So - where do we go to eat? Where's quick and easy and wholesome?"

Dolby thought for a moment. "We may not have to go all the way into town. There's a small cafe on the Industrial Estate in Braxted, just three or four minutes down the road if we drive, no more than ten if we walk."

"Good. We'll walk," said Caine. "The fresh air and exercise will do us good. There's no point in living outside the big city unless you take advantage of the country air."

"We can nip in between those two houses over there," said Dolby, "I think there's an alley that'll bring us out at the back. Then the industrial estate is just a short walk across the park - if you can call it a park."

They set off along the road. In the distance, the sides of the recently erected warehouses of the industrial estate rose gaudily before them.

"Returning to the subject of our mutual young friend," said Caine. "I'm inclined to agree that murdering his parents is a little out of Adam Southam's league. But we don't know what his league is and, as you said yourself, we can't take anything for granted. Patricide and matricide are certainly not unknown in our so-called civilised society."

"No, but if he was guilty he'd hardly call attention to himself by bragging about his inheritance, would he? He'd be purposefully grief-stricken."

"Maybe it's a double bluff. And what about this friend of his? What sort of influence do you think he might be having on young Adam?"

Dolby consulted his notebook. "You mean Philip Chantry? I gather he's quite a bit older than him. Maybe it's a conspiracy and they're involved together. I'm thinking in particular about that handkerchief." He shook his head. "I doubt it, though, it doesn't quite fit - the boy would hardly have shot his mouth off if there was someone else involved. And we weren't exactly putting him under pressure, were we!"

"Hardly. Although it's possible this Chantry person may have been acting alone, to his own advantage. Adam may have known nothing about it. Anyway, whether he's involved or not we're going to interview that snotty nosed insensitive young man again," said Caine "put the wind up him. Innocent or not that is **not** the way you carry on when both your parents have just been brutally murdered!"

They walked on, following a narrow path between two warehouses. "If it wasn't Adam Southam - "said Dolby "and I think we're agreed that he probably wasn't involved - and assuming also that his friend Chantry had no part in it, then we're looking for a third party of some description - probably whoever it was Valerie Southam was arguing with earlier in the evening."

"Yes," Caine agreed. "Ford seemed fairly certain it wasn't her husband and I'm inclined to believe he was being honest - although I'm not so sure about his motives for ogling Valerie when she was sunbathing. There may have been more to that than he was letting on - and his wife probably thought he was having sex with her; I reckon that's why she left him. Anyway, assuming it wasn't Bruce Southam she was talking to we need to find out who it actually was." She paused, thought for a moment, "When we get back to the house, you'd better organise house to house inquiries - see if anyone noticed a man going into the Southam's house earlier on in the evening. Or if there were any strangers hanging about - the usual thing."

They passed between two more warehouses, the high walls of which were painted a cheerful sky blue, the doors bright red. An open van, its back piled high with electrical goods and boxed computer equipment, was being unloaded by a fork lift truck outside one of them. Above the open doors a large logo advertised the **Big Byte Computer Company**. The truck driver nodded pleasantly to the two plain clothes officers as they stood back to let him pass and he manoeuvred his heavily laden vehicle slowly from the road and onto the pavement before entering the vast building. Above them, on tall poles which reached even higher than the roofs of the warehouses, video cameras tracked their progress along the road as they turned towards the cafe.

It was one of the few retail units on the estate, just around the corner from the Computer Company and in the opposite block. There were shops on the ground floor - a chemists, a general store and the retail unit of a computerised printing business, whose offices occupied the floor above. The shops opened onto a wide square, busy with commercial vehicles manoeuvring in and out of the various warehouses and factory premises. The area was buzzing with activity.

Caine was intrigued to see that the cafe went by the name **Fat and Healthy**. "That's a contradiction in terms isn't it! At least someone has a sense of humour."

"Yes - but funnily enough the name's very appropriate," said Dolby. "They do serve the usual high cholesterol fatty foods - trucker's tuck if you like - but they also cater for the local office workers, a lot of whom are women and young girls watching their weight. So, believe it or not, they have a range of vegetarian and health foods on the menu."

"Oh well - there's nothing like hedging your bets."

Dolby held the door open for her and they went inside. The cafe was surprisingly busy for the time of day, most of the tables occupied by men in working clothes. Truckers mainly, in open neck shirts and well-worn jeans, a few office workers wearing ties, but jacketless and with their shirt sleeves rolled up. There were one or two young women at the tables, possibly secretaries snatching a few minutes away from their word desks, their gaily coloured blouses contrasting with the sober white of the men's shirts. Caine felt a little out of place in her smart suit, but Dolby seemed perfectly at home, so she let the feeling pass. The diners, many of them talking animatedly, waving their forks in the air to make their various points, attacked plates piled high with all-day breakfasts. The air was filled with the appetising aroma of freshly cooked bacon, eggs and ground coffee.

"They get a lot of truck drivers coming in," explained Dolby following her across the room to an empty table. "They're coming and going all day with their deliveries and this place has made a good name for itself."

Caine sat down at the table and arranged her handbag on the floor beside her, instinctively looping the strap around one of her feet. "You've been here before, Mark, obviously."

"It's not exactly my regular haunt," said Dolby, sitting down opposite her. "But for one reason or another we've had to pay a few official visits to the area."

"Fertile ground for villains?"

Dolby nodded. "Yes. This place gets a lot of trade and, as you know - where there's money being made there's baddies trying to make away with it."

"Locals?"

"Oh, we get the travelling villains as well as the local bad boys," said Dolby with a smile. He opened his menu. "Strange thing is the estate has one of the most advanced security systems available. Closed circuit TV Cameras, video recording, audible alarm systems linked with the cop shop - but none of it seems to put the villains off."

Dolby looked around for a waitress. On the other side of the room, in the smoking area, a young woman clutching an empty tray was leaning over a table talking earnestly to a bearded man in his late twenties. She seemed to be teasing him about the gold rings - there were four of them - hanging from one of his ears. She was smartly dressed in a white blouse and black skirt of modest length and as he watched she looked in Dolby's direction, made a last remark to the bearded man and made her way towards his table.

Caine ran her eyes down the menu, nodding approvingly. "I must say you've got a nice selection here, Trudy," she said, looking up as the waitress stopped beside her and reading her name from the neatly printed label pinned to her blouse. "I'll have a jacket potato with tuna and sweet corn filling, please. Plus a decaffeinated coffee. Oh and no butter on the potato, thank you." She looked at her watch, then back at her companion. "I know it's early, Mark, but it'll save stopping for lunch. Besides, I'm ravenous."

Dolby consulted the menu again before looking up at the waitress. "I'll settle for a round of cheese and tomato sandwiches, please. And a black coffee, please."

The young girl wrote the order on her pad, smiled pleasantly and made her way back towards the kitchen.

Caine brought her mind back to the events of the morning. "What sort of people live on Marazion Road? I imagine, from the look of the houses, that they're typical lower middle to middle class."

Dolby nodded. "That's about it - I think the developers described the houses as 'executive' type dwellings when they were building them. They call the area 'Little Cornwall' on account of the names of the roads. You've got 'Truro Crescent' and 'Cambourne Avenue' as well as 'Marazion' and a few other Cornish sounding street names. The people are reasonably well to do. Quite a bit of disposable income and, of course, the requisite number of house break-ins." He smiled, his grey eyes twinkling. "Thinking of setting up in Little Cornwall yourself then, Jackie?"

She shook her head emphatically. "No - too modern for me, I'm afraid. I'm more your rustic type. Elizabethan beams and inglenook fireplaces are more my style."

"So, you won't be staying where you are then? Very convenient I would have thought."

Caine had found her present apartment at short notice by visiting a local estate agent just a few weeks before transferring to Fen Molesey. Only three years old and very tiny the flat was a product of the recent redevelopment of Fen Molesey Old Town Centre. So far as she was concerned the only things in its favour were that the lounge window overlooked the gardens of St. Luke's Church Vicarage - a peaceful oasis in the midst of the hustle and bustle of the new shopping area - and that it was within walking distance of the Police Station. Otherwise, it was a modern, cramped, two-bedroomed - in case her daughter, Allison, on one of her infrequent visits, decided to stop-over - shoe box. Architecturally there was nothing about the place that Caine found attractive and she had promised herself that as soon as she was properly in the saddle in her new job she would find somewhere more suited to her tastes. The protracted time she knew it would take from locating such a place to actually moving into it had prompted her to start her search without delay and she was, in fact, already registered with a number of local estate agents.

"Oh no - there's very little around the centre of town that I'd be interested in."

He nodded. "I can understand that. They've really ruined the old town centre recently. Not that there was much in the way of Elizabethan stuff to start with - the Victorians actually put paid to most of that during their spate of building, so consequently the stuff they knocked down for the new shopping arcade ten or so years ago was mostly Victorian. Of course, they have left the Georgian houses on Quay Street, down by the river, but there's precious little else left that's of any age or historical interest."

"You seem to take a keen interest in the local architecture, Mark."

Dolby was about to reply when the waitress reappeared with his sandwich, together with the two cups of coffee. "Just going back for the baked potato." She placed a knife and fork, wrapped in a red serviette, beside Caine's coffee cup and hurried away to the kitchen.

"Oh, that's Lorna's doing - my wife - she's into local history." Dolby sipped at his coffee. "She works part-time at the Central Library and acts as Secretary to the local society. I don't get much time for that sort of thing myself, as you can imagine, but Lorna ropes me in on some of the more interesting stuff."

"So where should I be looking then?" Caine paused as her meal was placed in front of her. "Where am I likely to find a cottage with a bit of history?"

Dolby took a small bite of his sandwich and chewed while he considered his answer. "Notley Seward - where Lorna and I are - isn't bad for that sort of thing. Lorna was very particular and didn't want anything remotely modern, although I'd have appreciated a little less DIY - there is a fair amount of new stuff there. And it's popular with people who've got kids, on account of there's a couple of good schools down that way." He sipped at his coffee, thinking. "And there's more period stuff along the river, down by Birch Medley. Some of it's almost Doomsday Book stuff,"

"Yes, I had a little look at Birch Medley the last time I was down here. Before I started the job," said Caine. "As a matter of fact I'm due to look at a cottage there later on today. I think my appointment's for seven. But what about that village Adam Southam was talking about? Sounded as though there were a few cottages there."

He nodded. "Yes - Upton Eccles. That's a bit to the north east of here, at the junction of this road and the B 1023. About ten minutes' drive. There are quite a few old places about there, some with nice views across to Great Totham and Beacon Hill."

Caine scarcely heard her mobile telephone above the background noise of the restaurant. It was in her bag and she had to lean towards it with her ear cocked before she could be sure it was ringing. "Sometimes I think these things are the biggest curse ever invented," she said reaching down and pulling back the zipper to get into the bag. She found the phone and lifted it to her ear. "Caine." She listened for a moment, frowning, looked at her wristwatch. "Yes, sir - I can be with you promptly at twelve. See you then." She slipped the phone back into her bag. "That was the Super," she said, "I rest my case about mobile phones."

"Trouble?" asked Dolby.

"I shouldn't think so," Caine replied, "I've only just got here - surely I couldn't have done anything wrong yet!" She smiled, cutting into her jacket potato. "No - it seems the Chief Constable's re-jigged his timetable so he'll be calling in on the Super at twelve o'clock instead of two. So, I'm to be in his office at twelve. Sorry, Mark, but it looks as though you'll have to go see Mrs Neale by yourself." He grimaced. "Oh - you'd rather I saw her?"

"No - not really…"

"I must admit she does look like a bit of a man-eater. But you're a big boy Mark - I'm sure you'll cope. Or shall I ask PC Doyle to go along and chaperone you?"

"No thanks, boss!" He looked down at his plate and played with the remains of his sandwich, moving it around between two of his fingers before lifting it to his mouth. "As you say - I'm a big boy and I'll cope!"

"Attaboy!" She smiled. "Me - I'm due to meet the sheriff at High noon. I just hope the Clancy brothers don't show up."

*   *   *   *   *

*   *

Superintendent Edward Hansen shook Caine's hand firmly and waved her to a chair. "I am so sorry to have kept you waiting Detective Chief Inspector - so sorry - do please accept my apologies - important call, you know." According to the French carriage clock in the glass fronted display cabinet behind the Superintendent's desk it was three minutes after twelve - he had kept Jacqueline Caine waiting for just three minutes; not exactly the crime of the century. "Chief Constable's on his way, he's just a few minutes late. Can't be helped, but he did say he would particularly like to meet you."

Hansen eased his six feet four-inch, seventeen stone bulk down onto the swivel chair behind his desk. He was dressed in what Caine assumed was his Sunday best, well cut business suit, white double cuffed shirt showing heavy gold cuff links, striking blue tie decorated with tiny yellow motifs that seemed like they should be familiar to her but weren't. He beamed across the desk at her "So here you are - Jacqueline. First Lady DCI in the Fen Molesey Division - shows how forward looking we are. Chief Constable likes that, you know! Feather in our cap." Caine smiled inwardly. The Superintendent obviously didn't realise that, in the same breath, he was acknowledging how backward the Division actually was. He leaned forward, his hands clasped together and resting on the surface of the big rosewood desk. "So - how are we getting on? What's this I hear about a double suicide up at that 'Little Cornwall' housing development? Nasty piece of business apparently."

"Yes sir, very unpleasant," Caine confirmed. "But it wasn't a double suicide. At first, it did look as though the wife had killed the husband with a kitchen knife and then took an overdose, but we soon realised..."

Hansen interrupted her. "Ah! Classic!" He wasn't really listening. His mind was on other things, probably how best to make political capital out of the Chief Constable's impending visit. No doubt they would be out playing golf together this afternoon, planning the future of the Fen Molesey Police Force against the background of the eighteen holes. "All wrapped up in a few minutes, then I suppose, Inspector. So, you can move onto something else." He boomed his laughter. "New time new crime I always say!" He's been away from the action for far too long, thought Caine.

"No sir," she was determined that he was going to listen to what she had to say, if only as a matter of principle. "It turns out, sir, that it's not as simple as that. We're pretty sure they were both murdered by a third party – so, I'm afraid we have a full investigation on our hands."

He grunted unhappily. In these days when ever scarcer resources must be spread ever more thinly to meet a seemingly ever-growing demand full investigations were always bad news. They tended to work out expensive and, it seemed, the last thing the Police Authorities wanted was to spend their hard fought cash on crime investigations. "So, who are they?" asked Hansen. Caine looked puzzled. "The murdered couple, Inspector! The victims!" barked Hansen, who seemed to have forgotten that Caine was supposed to be visiting his office for mere social reasons. "Who are they?"

"Their name was Southam, sir. Mr and Mrs Bruce Southam. The wife's name was Valerie." Caine couldn't imagine what possible purpose there was in the Superintendent asking the question. The chances of him knowing the Southams was negligible. But she remembered that Hansen had come up through the ranks of detectives - maybe he still imagined himself as a sleuth and was doing a little armchair detecting whilst waiting for the Chief Constable to arrive?

"What else do we know about them?"

Caine searched her memory for some other facts that might, conceivably, be of interest to the Superintendent who was, she was now convinced, using the Southam case merely to make conversation. Surely, there could be little more to it than that? She was the first female Detective Chief Inspector to be appointed to the rank in Fen Molesey and in spite of the hype and protestations of delight she wasn't sure how popular the move had been with her superiors. She had not expected they would make it easy for her - the powers that be never had at any point in her career - and she accepted Hansen's apparent enthusiasm for her appointment with a healthy dose of cynicism. But she had hardly been in the saddle long enough for him to be looking for faults. "Sir, Southam was something in the insurance world, I believe," she told him lamely. "Apparently he was a Director or Senior Partner in a firm run by some local businessman - name of Charles Perot."

She seemed to have struck a chord with the Superintendent. His head jerked up and his eyes flashed with interest. "Yes - that would be Paul Perot's old man. I wondered where I'd heard the name before - 'Bruce Southam' - yes, I knew it rang a bell. Used to be a keen golfer - used to see him a lot at the club up till a year or so ago. Big man, moody, but a good golfer. Didn't play with him but saw him perform and met him in the Clubhouse later. Didn't take to him, though. Don't think many did. Good player by all accounts but a moody beggar, bombastic - not a popular man to make up a foursome, if you see what I mean, although he did know how to play. If my memory serves me correctly Southam was supposed to be a well-known figure in the insurance world - a key man so to speak - particularly good at selling policies apparently, or whatever they do with insurance nowadays." He rubbed his chin thoughtfully. "But Paul Perot now - you wouldn't know this as you're new to the patch - he's an important man in The County. He'll be quite cut up about

Southam's death, I should think - could affect the Perot's business very badly - so you'd better be careful what you say to the media."

Caine found herself increasingly irritated by the large man behind the desk. Was it possible that he had known the connection between the murder victims and the Perots all along? Could this be why he had pumped her with questions? To lead, in a subtle way, to this admonition concerning the media? And what did it mean exactly, this warning 'to be careful what she said to the media? Or was there more to it than that? Was Hendry instructing her, in a subtle way, to compromise her investigations into the murders, in case the Perot business interests were damaged by her findings?

CHAPTER SIX

Mark Dolby had no difficulty finding Mrs Neale's house. Just as Barry Ford had indicated, the two stone lions were crouched menacingly at the top of their red brick piers at either side of the driveway. There, too, were the mock carriage lamps, three of them, fashioned from cast iron and ranged along the top of the twenty feet or so of wall that fronted the garden. They were wired for electricity and the glass panels in the fronts of two of them were cracked, a fact which did not surprise Dolby in the least as, standing as they did on the top of the wall, which was itself no more than four feet high, they were obviously vulnerable to the tender loving care of local vandals (even the so-called respectable areas had vandals nowadays, Dolby reflected). Two black wrought iron gates bridged the gap between the brick piers and guarded the entrance to the drive, which was paved with red brick and led down to the garage at the far side of the house. A Ford Ka, nearly new, red paint work polished to a high gloss, was parked in front of the closed garage doors. Dolby pushed open the gate and approached the front door. He found the doorbell and pressed it, waited as the sombre tones of some obscure fugue - possibly Bach - resounded through the house.

"Oh - it's you." Mrs Neale's greeting was not welcoming. She made no attempt now to hide her Estuary accent. Her blue-grey eyes were tired, and her cheeks puffed as if she had been crying and as she swung the door open, she dabbed at her cheeks with a small white handkerchief, stained red where she had smudged it across her lipstick. She merely glanced at Dolby's ID card, stepping back into the hall to let him pass. "You'd better come in."

"I'm sorry to trouble you, Mrs Neale," said Dolby. She cast a weary glance at him over her shoulder as she led the way through into the lounge, wobbling slightly on her high heels as though not in full control of her legs. He was surprised at the way she looked. Just a short while ago, when he had seen her on the Southam's driveway, she had appeared confident, eager to get involved in whatever was going on. True, Adam Southam's innuendoes had dampened her spirit, but not to any great extent and she had stridden defiantly off, back to her house. Now she looked worn and dispirited, as if she had spent the last hour or so weeping. Perhaps here was the first sign of grief from someone who knew the Southams?

The lounge was brightly lit by the sunshine streaming in through the net curtains at the window, but there was very little dust on the surfaces of the TV set and Blue Ray Player that stood one above the other on a black metal stand in the corner, or on the coffee table and fawn leather settees that furnished the room. A tall glass-fronted unit containing some pieces of china, cut glass and porcelain - Dolby recognised some well-known Lladro pieces amongst them - stood against the wall. Further along, partially concealed in a narrow alcove was a bookcase stacked with hardbacks and a number of leather-bound volumes, their spines etched with gold leafed titles. There was a packet of cigarettes on the coffee table, next to an onyx cigarette lighter and an ashtray, but otherwise the room was free of clutter. Dolby wondered if the Neale's had domestic help or if Mrs Neale herself was responsible for this surprisingly neat and tidy room. She waved him to one of the settees and sat down opposite him. Now that he could examine her more closely, he noticed that the top buttons of her orange blouse were still undone, revealing the top of her lace brassiere and that her mini-skirt rose up her thighs as she crossed her legs. For a moment he imagined a similar meeting that might have taken place between her and Adam Southam, a scene which might well have given the boy the impression that she was trying to seduce him. But she was not trying it on with Dolby, flattering as it might have been for him to think so, for the brashness had gone from her demeanour and she was subdued, almost like a little girl who had done some heinous deed and was now filled with remorse. Mrs Susan Neale, Dolby concluded, was merely a woman with poor dress sense who had chosen to ignore - or had not the whit to notice - the passage of the years.

He broke the silence. "As I say, I'm sorry to have to ask you questions at this time, Mrs Neale, but in the circumstances, you will understand, I'm sure."

"She *was* murdered then." It was a statement, not a question, delivered in a toneless voice. "Did *he* do it?"

"If you mean did Mr Southam kill his wife - frankly, we don't know what happened yet. But we are fairly certain that there was a third party involved..."

Her hand leaped to her mouth and she interrupted him with a little cry. "Oh! You mean someone else killed her?"

"**Them** - somebody else killed **them**, Mrs Neale. That's the way it looks. We need to find out as much about Mr and Mrs Southam as we can. That's why we're going to need your help."

"Call me Susie, everybody else does," she leaned forward to pick up the packet of cigarettes from the coffee table. "Fancy a ciggy?" He shook his head. She took a cigarette from the packet and placed it between her lips, leaning forward again to retrieve the lighter. He could see that her hand was shaking. "I don't usually smoke in the house," she said, flicking the lighter open and bringing the flame towards the cigarette. "Norman, my husband, doesn't like it." She inhaled deeply, blowing the smoke up into the air with a sigh. "Actually, I'm supposed to have given it up - smoking, I mean. Me and Valerie, we were having a go at stopping, a sort of joint effort."

"So, Valerie had given up as well?"

She inhaled again. It was a few seconds before she replied. "Yes - she was doing much better than me. Hadn't had one or bought any fags for three weeks, or so she said." She leaned forward to flick ash into an ash tray. "Norman was keen for me to give up, you know, he says it's no good for me and he's right - and we don't want the kids to start on it, neither of us." She inhaled again, seemed to be justifying her actions to Dolby. "Norman said it's OK for me this morning. Just this once. In the circumstances of what's gone on - not that I knew it was murder until you said. I just thought it was, you know..." She let her words fade out, shook her head as if still unable to believe that her neighbour and friend was dead. "Sorry, I haven't offered you a drink - do you want a cup of tea or something?"

"No thanks, Mrs Neale." He thought she was going to pick him up on her name again, but she shrugged and drew deeply on her cigarette. "I've had my mid-morning cuppa, thanks." He took his notebook from his pocket and flicked over the pages. "Now, if you don't mind, I would like to ask you a few questions."

She relaxed a little, uncrossing her legs and shifting her bottom on the seat, pushing herself backwards to lean wearily against the back of the settee, showing a good deal of leg.

"How well did you know Mrs Southam, Mrs Neale?"

"I was her best friend, and she was mine." The words came in a rush and there was an edge to her voice, which had lost its dullness. Her eyes were sparkling with tears and the tiny handkerchief appeared in her hand again. She dabbed deftly at her cheeks.

"You go back a long way, then?"

"Oh yes - me and Val we've known each other over twenty years. Not continuous, like, but when we first met, we must've been in our teens. Least ways, I was - she was a bit older than me."

"Where?"

"Where did we meet?" She inhaled, holding the smoke for a long moment before exhaling and reaching forward to crush the cigarette in the ash tray. It was only half finished. She sighed. "I really shouldn't smoke like this. I've been trying to cut down and I haven't had a fag for over a week - not until today." She remembered the question. "We was dancers together, me and Valerie - some night club in town - Soho." Her eyes strayed down towards her legs. "I had really good legs in them days - outstanding - and a good figure too. Course, that was before the kids came along. Play havoc with a girl's figure kids do, but you men wouldn't know anything about that, would you?"

"You said before, Mrs Neale, that you hadn't known Valerie continuously - so at some stage you must have lost contact with her."

"Yes. That's right. We didn't see each other for years."

"What happened? Where did she go?"

"It was me that went, not Valerie. Well, first anyway. We was both dancing in this night club in Soho at the time, called *The Red Dragon* or some such stupid name - it was in Frith Street and we were both working there when I got this offer of a job belly dancing in Turkey. I know it sounds daft, but the money was good and I didn't like the way things were going at *The Red Dragon*, so I took it."

"How do you mean you didn't like the way things were going?"

"Drugs. There were a lot of people there who was getting into hard drugs - dealing and that - and it wasn't my scene. I know I smoked, but I never done drugs." She reached for the cigarette packet, picked it up, but then changed her mind and put it down again. "The word on the street was that Bobby Roberts was moving in on the place - and that meant nasties!"

"Bobby Roberts?"

She smiled. "Before your time, Sergeant. Bobby was one of the big gangland bosses of the time. Heavily into drugs, not to mention murder and all sorts. He'd have your throat cut as soon as look at you. That's what they said, and it may have been true, though it's not the way I saw it at the time - it wasn't till later I learned the truth. I knew his daughter once and she was okay and they seemed like a nice family, then - really pulled the wool over my eyes, they did. Anyway, your lot - the police - finally got something to stick on Bobby and his goons a few years later and he got sent down for life. But, like I was saying, he was moving in on *The Red Dragon Club,* so it wasn't the place to be."

"How about Valerie? Was she on drugs?"

"I don't know. I don't think so - not seriously - a bit of grass now and then - but she didn't mainstream or anything. There was a lot of people in the club that did, though and there was a lot of dealing going on even before Bobby Roberts muscled in on the action."

"So, you went to Turkey and you lost contact with Valerie?"

"Yeah. Excuse me," she got up suddenly and crossed over to the display cabinet, kneeling down to open one of the wooden fronted cupboards beneath it. "It's in here somewhere." She moved various things about inside the cupboard. "Ah! here it is." She returned triumphantly to the settee with a large unopened box of chocolates, tearing at the cellophane wrapping with her long-painted fingernails. She sat down, looked across at him apologetically and giggled nervously, the weariness still in her eyes. "I know I shouldn't, my figure's going anyway, but it's better than smoking and I've got to do something. Norman says it's comfort eating and I suppose he's right. It's been a bit of a shock, what's happened today!" She crumpled the wrapper in her hand and dropped it on to the seat beside her, at the same time pushing her fingernail under the lid of the box and easing it upwards. "**Terry's All Gold** these are - my favourites." She leaned forward with the open box held towards him. "Would you like one?"

He shook his head. "No thanks. I'm not too keen on chocolates myself. You go ahead. But you were telling me about Valerie Southam."

She bit into one of the chocolates, savoured the taste for a moment before continuing. "Mind you I wasn't out there for long - in Turkey I mean - before I found out why the money was so good. It wasn't really dancers they was looking for - they wanted girls that was easy, girls that would - you know - jump into bed with any bloke that shoved money down their cleavage. Anyway, I wasn't into all that. I didn't mind dancing in practically nothing on stage and that - well, I had a good body in those days..." she looked down at her legs again and he followed her eyes noting the thickening around the thighs and the rolls of fat around her waist that her short, tight skirt accentuated. Her legs were still pretty good, but the chocolates wouldn't help to improve matters. He tore his eyes away - her figure was no affair of his. He brought his attention back to her words. "I didn't mind showing off my body," she was saying "but there was no way I was going to do what they wanted me to. Especially out there - you never know what you might catch in them hot countries and they've never heard of safe sex."

"And when you came back to England Valerie had left **The Red Dragon**?"

"Well, it took me a few months to get out of Turkey - they weren't going to make it easy for me were they, those men that arranged for me to go out there in the first place. It got a bit nasty for a bit, I can tell you, but luckily I met Norman out there - he was there on business - and he took a bit of a fancy to me and asked me to marry him. I said yes provided he would help me get out of there and he did." She giggled at some secret memory; her horror of the events of the morning suspended and took another chocolate from the open box on her knees. She bit into it with relish. "Are you sure you wouldn't like one?" He shook his head.

"Please yourself - all the more for me! Anyway, by the time I got back to London Valerie had disappeared. I couldn't find out where she went to."

"You couldn't trace her through her parents?"

"No - she told me her mum and dad had snuffed it when she was a little kid." Susie paused to pop another chocolate into her mouth, chewed at it before carrying on. "No, Valerie told me she'd been brought up by an Uncle and Aunt. She hated them, or so she said. And she didn't have any other family - not that she let on about anyway. I don't think they were very good to her, her Uncle and Aunt, which is why she left home and took up dancing. She didn't have a good start in life," mused Susie, "maybe that's why she stuck with Bruce for so long."

"How do you mean?"

"Maybe he wasn't so bad in comparison. After all, if you're not used to things being good maybe you don't know what you're missing."

"I suppose that could be true. But going back to those early years, you don't know why she left that particular night club? Did she get a job with one of the others?"

She shook her head. "I asked around, but nobody seemed to know what had happened to her. Mind you, there was some trouble with drug-busts by the fuzz - sorry, the police - at the *Dragon,* especially after Bobby Roberts appeared on the scene, so maybe she'd had enough and got out before things got too hot." She bit into yet another chocolate, this time breaking it and leaving one half held between her fingers. "Anyhow, I didn't look for her, did I?" She swallowed and popped the other half into her mouth, then licked traces of chocolate from the ends of her fingers. "I had Norman then and he wanted to get married." She looked around the room and smiled. "I wasn't really that keen at the time, you know - I only really wanted him to get me out of trouble in Turkey and, of course there was the age difference. He's a lot older than me, but it didn't seem to matter at the time. I suppose I got to like him and it didn't turn out too bad did it? At least he treats me like a human being."

"And presumably you heard nothing else of Valerie until you met again some years later?"

"No. Mind you, there was some rumours about her at the time, when I got back."

"How do you mean?"

"Well, I didn't know if it was true or not, not then," she studied the card showing the variety of chocolates in the box and then lifted another from the moulded plastic tray. She held it poised in front of her mouth ready to be snapped up. "I mean, there was no way of telling if it was true or not, was there? Not then. But it probably explained why she wasn't at the club anymore."

"If *what* was true?"

"Sorry, I'm going on a bit aren't I! Anyway, the point is there was an old girl there Martha Harney - we called her Marty - we always joked about that, reckoned she'd nicked the name from that Mata Hari, the spy, just to give herself an air of mystery, you know. Anyway, old Marty used to be a stripper when she was young and she was also probably a street tart - a bit of rough, if you know what I mean - but by the time me and Valerie got to know her she was just the old hat girl that looked after the cloakroom. She'd lost her figure ages before, of course and she must have been in her late fifties by then - she must be over eighty by now. She's living in an old people's home just outside Chelmsford - Valerie and me went to visit her a couple of times a few months back. Valerie's kept in touch with her and goes to see her quite often." Susie Neale sighed. "Valerie was quite close to Marty back in **The Red Dragon** days. She wasn't a bad old dear, I suppose, bit of a mother figure really, some of the girls used to confide in her about their men problems, that sort of thing. She knew a thing or two about men I can tell you!"

Dolby wasn't sure he wanted the full and intimate details of this woman, who was probably quite incidental to the subject he was investigating. He cut Mrs Neale short. "So, what did this Martha Harney tell you about Valerie?"

"Well, she reckoned Val didn't leave **The Red Dragon** because of the drugs trouble, but because she was expecting." She popped the chocolate into her mouth, chewed on it and swallowed quickly.

"She was pregnant?"

"Yeah. Marty looked after her for a bit when they kicked her out of the night club on account of her being pregnant."

"You heard nothing from Valerie herself though?"

"Not a dicky bird. She had my address in Turkey - I gave it to her when I went out there in case she wanted to join me if things turned out all right."

"But they didn't."

"Like I said it all went wrong. I did write to her a couple of times before I came back - to let her know what was going on - but she never replied. So, in the end I just forgot about her and got married to Norman." She giggled and bit into another chocolate. "Of course, he didn't want me to go on with the dancing, not after we were married. Between you and me I think he was jealous of other blokes looking at my body. He was a lot more - you know, *physical* - in those days." She hurried on, seemingly unabashed by the intimate revelation. "Well, he understood I had to do something with myself, so he paid for me to learn hairdressing. I enjoyed that, worked in a unisex salon in Chelmsford High Street for three or four years before the kids started to come along." She smiled and chose another chocolate. "He's all right is my Norman, a bit boring at times, especially recently when he's been working so hard, but I suppose he has given me a good life and we've got a lovely house in one of the best areas, so it can't be that bad can it?"

"And when did you meet up with Valerie again?"

"Oh - it was when we moved here." She looked down at the chocolate box on her lap, closed the lid slowly. "She didn't have much of a life with that Bruce, you know. She deserved better than him. And, you know - it surprised me when I found out what sort of life she had with him. When she was young she was a fighter, never let anyone put one over on her!" When she looked up there was genuine grief in her eyes

Dolby felt sorry for her. "When you moved here, to Fen Molesey, she was living here already? In this street?"

"Oh no - her and Bruce moved in a little bit after us - a few months, I suppose. This was seven or eight years ago. I couldn't believe my eyes when I bumped into her in the street. It was such a coincidence her moving in as my nearly next-door neighbour - just out of the blue after all those years that we hadn't seen each other. It was amazing, although I suppose she was coming back to her roots - she said she'd been brought up in Essex - as a matter of fact quite a few of the characters we knew from **The Dragon** was Essex bred and I bump into them again now and then - but who'd have thought Valerie and me would end up living so close together? And she hadn't changed a bit - well, naturally, she'd lost a bit of her figure, but that's natural isn't it!"

"You renewed the friendship?"

"Yeah - course. We soon became good pals again."

"What about your husband? Did he get friendly with Mr Southam?"

She laughed briefly, without humour. "What? My Norman and that Bruce Southam? No - Norman couldn't stand the man. Neither could I come to that. He was a pig."

"But you got on well with Valerie?"

She sighed, opened the box to look at the rapidly diminishing rows of chocolates, but resisted the temptation to select yet another one. "Yes, we got on very well. Mind you - that Bruce didn't like her having any friends. He treated her like dirt - it made me very angry to see it. He didn't love her - he only ever loved himself if you ask me. We still saw each other though, Val and me, talked about old times and that sort of thing."

"Did she tell you why she'd left *The Red Dragon*? That she was expecting a baby?"

"She wouldn't talk about it. I mentioned what I'd heard from the old girl - Marty whatsit, but Val just exploded, she went ballistic and screamed and shouted at me - said the old girl was a nosy Parker and didn't know what she was talking about, which I thought was a bit funny as Valerie still kept in touch with her. I decided it was just nerves made her say that. Then she just went all quiet and weepy and she wouldn't talk about it anymore. In the end I gave up." Susie resisted the urge to take another chocolate and pushed the box away from her to the other end of the settee. "I didn't say nothing to her, but I reckoned maybe she'd lost the baby and didn't want to talk about it." She pursed her lips, looked across at Dolby with a scowl. "You men don't understand how a thing like that can affect a woman!"

"So, there's no chance her son, Adam, could have been that baby?"

"No - course not!" She giggled like a fourteen-year-old. "Not unless she was carrying him for five or six years! She wasn't an elephant you know!" She pulled herself together, stopped giggling and said seriously. "No - he's only about nineteen is Adam - if it had been him he'd be well into his twenties by now, wouldn't he. Besides, Valerie never actually let on that she was having a kid then. For all I knew it could have been a figment of the old girl's imagination - and she weren't exactly bright that Martha! - so I didn't believe Valerie had had a baby." She paused, looked at him hesitantly as if uncertain she should go on. "I was wrong though."

"What do you mean you were wrong?"

"I mean that when she wouldn't talk about it I assumed she couldn't have had a kid when she was working at *The Dragon*."

"You mean there *was* a baby? But I thought you said..."

"No, I said she went mad - angry - and that she never wanted to talk about it. So how was I supposed to know what was true and what wasn't? Anyway, it turns out she did fall pregnant when she was working at *The Dragon* and she left there not only because she didn't like the drugs scene - they was dealing in a big way, she told me later - but because she was afraid for the baby."

"But what about the father? Presumably it wasn't Bruce Southam's?"

She raised her eyebrows scornfully. "Course not - she hadn't even met him then, had she! She said she didn't know who the father was, but I don't know if that was true or not. Anyway, even if she had known she wouldn't have been able to prove it - they didn't have them DNA tests in those days did they - and she was sleeping around quite a bit at the time, even though she did have a sort of a steady boyfriend."

"How do you mean - sort of steady?"

"You know - on and off all the time." She giggled. "They had rows. She used to pull the petals off the flowers he sent her when they'd had a row and made up - they was always carnations, nothing else, that's all he ever bought her and she used to sit there pulling off the petals and saying 'he loves me he loves me not', that sort of barmy thing."

"Did you ever meet him?"

She shrugged dismissively and looked away. "I suppose I met him a couple of times then, that's all. It must have been just before I went to Turkey."

"And I assume he didn't want to know about the baby. What happened to it?"

"Valerie had her adopted. It was a girl. Afterwards Val was upset, she said, she never wanted to talk about it."

"So how did you find out?" asked Dolby.

"She told me. Well, she swore me to secrecy in case *he* found out, her old man."

"But why did she suddenly tell you after denying it for all those years?"

"Her daughter got in touch," said Susie dramatically. "Suddenly, out of the blue Val had this letter from this long-lost daughter saying she'd traced Valerie as her natural mother and could she come along and see her? Val was in a bit of a two and eight about it I can tell you. Well, anyone would be, wouldn't they?"

"What did she decide to do?"

"Well, she didn't know *what* to do did she? - she asked me what she should do, but I couldn't really help her could I - I mean, you can't unless you've been in that situation yourself and I certainly hadn't."

"So, she did nothing? She just ignored the letter?"

"Yes, she didn't know what to do so she didn't do anything. As I say, she was afraid Bruce might find out about the kid. As she said to me, she didn't want that problem and she hoped if she ignored it it would go away. But then they visited her. Just a few weeks back."

"*They*?"

"Yeah, the daughter - Karen I think her name is - and her bloke. She was shacked up with him Val told me, and they were living somewhere in Rainham, so it wasn't far to come. Val said the man was horrible - rough, you know, a bit of a low-life. And he threatened her."

Dolby leaned forward in his seat. "How do you mean he threatened her?"

"Turns out when he realised Karen's mum was married to a bloke with money he wanted a slice of it. So, he asked Val for cash - made up some sob story about how short of money he and Karen and the two kids was - yeah, Val had grandchildren she'd never seen or even knew about! - and when she refused to give them the dosh he threatened to do her over."

"Did you get his name - or their address?"

"No, I don't know his name - but I think Val kept the original letter so there'll be an address on that if you can find it." She stopped speaking suddenly and her hand flew to her mouth. "Do you think he done it then, the murder, this bloke of Val's daughter's?"

Dolby shrugged his shoulders. "I don't know. But you're sure about this, he actually threatened her? Valerie wouldn't have made it up, would she?"

"Why? What reason would she have for making it up? No - she was telling me the truth that time, I'm sure of it. I think she was frightened of the bloke."

"Why didn't she come to us about it?"

She laughed dryly. "What? Come to the cops? I suppose she might have, eventually, but it was only about ten days ago that it happened. When they called on her and asked for the money. I dare say she didn't know what to do - whether to pay them or not."

"Well, I wish she had come to us," said Dolby, pursing his lips with exasperation. What did people like Valerie and Susie think the Police were there for? Traffic duty and rescuing pussy cats from tall trees? Still, it was too late for Valerie Southam and at least Mrs Neale had had the good sense to tell him about it now. "You'd better tell me more about Valerie."

"What else do you want to know?" She eased herself up off the settee, smoothing her skirt and wobbling slightly on her high heels as she got her balance. "Are you sure you won't have a cup of coffee? - I'm making some anyway, so you might as well." She crossed the room towards the door. "Come into the kitchen. We'll have it in there. I always find it's easier to think things out when I'm in the kitchen."

Dolby got up and followed her.

Like the other parts of the Neales' house the kitchen was clean and sparkling. There was the smell of newness about it and Dolby sniffed appreciatively. It was a big room, and there was a snug area with a pine table and chairs at the far end, leading out onto a conservatory furnished with Lloyd Loom style furniture and potted plants. The walls of the kitchen were lined with fitted cupboards faced with light grey board that was so clean it must have been scratch proof and smear proof. He wondered if Susie Neale walked about all day wearing plastic gloves.

"Nice kitchen," he said. "Looks brand new."

Susie Neale filled a cordless kettle at the sink and switched it on, turning back towards him. "It is new. Norman, my husband, runs a double glazing and fitted kitchen company. At any rate he's one of the directors." She smiled proudly. "The firm did the job for us, of course. He's not a bad bloke, I suppose, my Norman, he only ever wants the best for me and the kids. Not like that Bruce Southam and the way he treated his family!"

"You didn't think much of Mr Southam did you, Mrs Neale."

She opened one of the wall cupboards and took out two cups and saucers, putting them down on the work surface. "I know they say you shouldn't say bad things about dead people," she said, "But I told you - he was a pig with a capital 'P'."

"Surely he must have had some redeeming features," said Dolby. She looked at him incredulously. "There must have been some nice things about him," he exclaimed. "After all - why did Valerie marry him?"

"Search me. He was well off, of course, but money isn't everything. And in any case she never saw much of his money did she?" Susie Neale swept her arm through the air encompassing her magnificent new kitchen. "You've been in their place - did you see anything like this there? And did you see their lounge furniture - if you could call it that? I wouldn't give it house room, myself. They should have chucked it out years ago - it's not much better than orange boxes." She shook her head. "No - he had money, but he didn't spend it on her, or the house, did he! Why do you think she had to go out to work?"

"She had a job?"

"She was a part-time receptionist up at that posh hotel over in Faulkbourne. She told me she did it for the interest and because she liked meeting people, but I never believed her. Bruce was always tight with his money and he kept her short, so that was her real reason. He wouldn't let her go to the hairdressers regularly or buy any nice clothes, or shoes. She had to have me do her hair for her because I didn't charge her - well, she used to buy me a box of chocolates now and then. That was the sort of man he was - really mean! So, she had to go out to work - it was the only way she could afford anything nice." Susie leaned across the table towards Dolby. "He didn't know, of course. She never told him - she never dared tell him or he'd have knocked her into next week."

"Why? Surely there's nothing wrong in a man's wife doing a part time job to earn a little extra!"

"You are wet! But then you're a man! Don't you see - it would have been a challenge to his macho-ness wouldn't it! Anyway, he'd have gone spare if he'd known and Valerie didn't want that, did she. Besides, it wasn't true - he did earn enough, more than enough by all accounts - only trouble was he never let her have any of it, aside from her housekeeping." Susie Neale walked angrily over to the double drainer sink unit. She wrenched the hot tap on and thrust her hands under the running water. "That's the sort of bloke he was! Lived in the nineteenth century, the chauvinistic pig!"

"I can see why you're angry," said Dolby, "But what do you suppose made him like that?"

She finished washing her hands and wiped them on a towel. "What makes any man like that? Perhaps they're born with a mean gene. I don't know, I'm not a head doctor, am I? Personally, I think the drink made it worse and by God that man could drink!" She took a coffee jar from one of the cupboards and spooned coffee into the cups.

"He drank a lot then?"

"You're kidding! I can't think of a time in the last few years when I've seen him without a glass in his hand. Except, that is, when he drank straight from the bottle." Dolby searched her face for signs of a smile but decided she had made the last comment in all seriousness. "He was always drunk. Your lot should know that, Sergeant."

"How do you mean - my lot?"

"The Police. Bruce Southam had a record didn't he."

Dolby stared at her. Perhaps this was the connection he was looking for, something that would lead on to a motive for the killings? "Did he? I'm sorry, but we don't know all the villains in our patch by sight and name, Mrs Neale. There's too many of them for that! Anyway, I wasn't aware Southam had a criminal record – we've not had time to look him up yet."

"Maybe not criminal," Susie shrugged. "Not like your burglars or muggers or drug dealers - not that sort of criminal.

More important than them, I think, much more serious than them."

He realised she was enjoying her temporary advantage over him and smiled indulgently. "So, what did we have him for, Mrs Neale?"

"Drunken driving. Just over a year ago. He's just got his licence back, if you don't mind - like he didn't nearly kill someone when he was the worst for drink. Wrapped his car round a tree he did! I reckon your lot should have put him away and thrown away the key."

"You may be right," said Dolby. She was echoing very closely his own views on drunken drivers. He sighed. "But it's not 'our lot' that does the sentencing - unfortunately, Mrs Neale, all we do is catch the villains, we don't try them or sentence them."

"Well, it would've been better for Valerie if they'd locked him up. At least he wouldn't have been able to hit her whenever he had a drop too much, which was practically every night if you ask me."

"We thought that's what he was up to," said Dolby casting his mind back to the bruises on the dead woman's body.

"I don't know why she put up with it. I'd have left him years ago." The kettle boiled and she poured hot water into the cups.

"I'll have mine black, please," said Dolby.

She reached into the refrigerator for a carton of milk and poured some into her coffee cup, stirring it with a spoon and carrying the two steaming cups over to the table. "Sit down, Sergeant. Do you take sugar? Or I've got some of those sacca-whatsit things somewhere. Oh, and there's biscuits." She traced her steps back to one of cupboards and took down a biscuit barrel.

"No thanks," he shook his head and lowered himself into one of the pine dining chairs.

She came and sat opposite him, putting the biscuit barrel on the table and undoing the top. "Help yourself." She stirred her coffee. "Val and me used to have coffee together sometimes," she said sadly. "In here. It's funny to think we won't be doing that ever again." She lifted her cup and looked across at him. "She was a bit of a funny cow, sometimes, though - no disrespect to her, I liked her a lot, but sometimes I just couldn't understand her."

"In what way?" He sipped the almost boiling coffee carefully.

"She didn't seem to want to do anything to stop Bruce from beating her up - not at first she didn't, anyway. Right from the minute I realised what was going on - and it didn't take me long I can tell you! - I was on at her to do something about it. I even told her to go to your lot, you know, the police - but she always said no, that she deserved it." Susie scowled. "deserved it? What a load of cobblers that was, but I dare say she got that from listening to one of them stupid head shrinkers - some of them are real potty, pottier than the pottyist if you ask me."

"She'd been to see a psychiatrist? Why?"

"Not recently. It was years ago, before I ever knew her. When she was having trouble with that uncle and aunt I mentioned. I think she was just disturbed, but you know the social services, they'll send you to a head shrinker soon as look at you!"

"You say at first she didn't seem to want to stop the beatings - do you mean you finally got through to her and she was going to do something about it?"

She shrugged, sipped her coffee. "I dunno if it was me carrying on at her that did it. I don't rightly know what it was, but about a year ago she suddenly starts saying 'yes' I was right and she would do something about it. She said she'd leave him."

"But **did** she actually do anything about it?"

"She talked about going to a solicitor, but I don't know if she did. She didn't say. Sometimes she talked about it, but at other times she went **schtoom** on me. I think she was afraid of him finding out that she was even thinking about divorcing him."

"So, for seven or eight years - ever since you met up with her again - Valerie was telling you she accepted the fact that she was a battered wife? And she wasn't prepared to do anything about it?" She nodded. "And then about a year ago she started to talk about doing something positive, even to the extent of leaving him?" She nodded again. "So, what happened to make her change her mind?"

She took a large gulp of her coffee and fished a biscuit from the barrel. "I dunno - I really don't, but maybe..." She stopped and shook her head. "No - I'd have known, wouldn't I?" She bit into the biscuit.

"Known what?"

"It's only a feeling I've had, mind," She replied, crunching, "but I have thought, sometimes, that she might have found another man."

CHAPTER SEVEN

"You think she might have had a lover?" asked Dolby. Susie Neale nodded. "But surely, as you say, if you were on such close terms with her you wouldn't just *think*, you would *know*."

She shrugged. "It was just a feeling - a hunch. I know we were very good friends, but she wouldn't necessarily tell me everything, would she? No more than I would tell her if I was having an affair." She lowered her eyes and looked away. "*You* don't tell your friends *everything*, do you?"

"I think she would. She seems to have shared a lot of other things with you."

"Maybe she was scared he - Bruce - would find out. She may even have been scared what Bruce would do to him - to her lover."

Dolby rubbed his chin thoughtfully. "Maybe. It is possible, I suppose."

"I think it's quite likely," said Susie Neale. "I know if I had a husband like Bruce Southam and a new man came along who was kind to me and considerate and thought about me instead of himself all the time - you wouldn't see me for dust!" She looked away again. "And she was a passionate woman was Valerie. We're only human us women - nobody's perfect."

Dolby finished his coffee and stood up, going to the window and staring out over the back garden. He turned to face her again. "And you're telling me, Mrs Neale, that you just had a feeling she was having an affair? It was nothing more than that." He shook his head slowly. "Sorry, but I don't buy that - there must be more to it than that. We don't have feelings out of the blue, for no reason. There's always something that triggers them off. Did you ever see her with another man?"

She hesitated. "No." She was playing with her small handkerchief again, twisting it in her fingers. "I don't know if this is important - I don't know anything anymore this morning, I can't think straight. But..." She hesitated again and he had to prompt her. "Well, once or twice there was a car parked on her drive and I saw a man getting into it. As if he'd just come out of her house and was about to drive away."

"Did you recognise him?"

"No."

"But you saw his face?"

"No - I didn't see his face. He was bending forward to open the car door and then he turned slightly towards me as he got in, the way you do, so I only really saw him properly from behind."

"And you saw him just the once?"

She leaned forward with her hands gripping the edge of the table, speaking slowly as if she was trying to recapture the incident in her mind and recount it to him. "I saw the car on Valerie's driveway twice - both times in the afternoon - but I only saw *him* - the driver - once. I was going by in my car and his car was facing down Valerie's drive - as I say, his head was bent forward to open the car door and then he turned slightly so I could see a little bit of his face - but it was only a split second, so I only really caught a glimpse of him."

"What did he look like?"

She shrugged. "I don't know - I didn't have time to see very much. I remember now, I was driving past to pick up one of my kids from school to take her to the dental clinic or something and I was in a hurry. I didn't think about it at the time. It was only a man and a car."

"O.K. Fine, but was the man you saw tall, small, fat, thin? - You must have seen that much at least. Think, Mrs Neale, it could be important."

"Tall - he was tall. And he was wearing a dark suit."

"What build was he?"

"Thin - well, tall and thin, but he had broad shoulders."

"Did you notice the colour of his hair?"

"Yes, but I only saw him for a second. It was salt and pepper - that's what we used to call it in the salon - brown but with some silvery grey bits. And he looked smart - you know, he was wearing a good suit. Oh, and there was a white handkerchief in his top pocket. I remember that 'cos my Norman always wears a hanky in that pocket and it's really unusual to see men do that nowadays. You don't see it very often."

"What about the car? Can you describe it?"

She shrugged. "It was a big car, I think, expensive looking. I don't know much about cars - Norman looks after that sort of thing."

"What sort of car does your husband drive?"

She thought for a moment. It was clear that she really did not know much about motor cars. Dolby guessed that the Ford Ka parked on the drive was probably hers, but that her husband had probably chosen it for her. "Oh - yes - a Jaguar - Norman has a Jaguar, but I don't know what sort. I'm not well up on that sort of thing."

"Was the car you saw on Valerie Southam's drive bigger or smaller than your husband's car?"

"Bigger. It looked bigger. Higher anyway. Norman's car is harder to get in and out of because it's so low down."

Dolby had not expected a full and complete specification of the vehicle, but this was hardly very helpful. "Anything else? I don't suppose you got the registration number, and what about the colour? And was it old or new?"

"I didn't really notice the colour," Susie Neale looked flustered as though she had let him down. "And I don't know enough about cars to say how old it was. I didn't see it very well." She paused, smiled wanly. "But I did notice that it was clean! It was nicely looked after."

Dolby looked around at the gleaming kitchen surfaces. Yes, she would notice that wouldn't she, he thought wryly. The vehicle in question may have absolutely nothing to do with the investigation, but even if it did he wouldn't get very far if he put out a search for a **big clean** car with no other description. Anyway, he told himself, by now it could be dirty and that would upset any search he might institute. He was about to make a cynical comment when her face suddenly lit up.

"I remember something else about the car. There was a sticker in the back window - you know one of them advertising things."

"What did it say?"

She hesitated, deflated again and shook her head. "Sorry - I didn't have time to read it. Anyway, it might have nothing to do with anything - he might have been a salesman calling to sell the Southams something!" She looked hurt.

"O.K., Mrs Neale - it was a big car, but you can't remember the colour, it was clean and there was a notice in the back window, but you don't know what it said. Fine. Thank you." Dolby shrugged helplessly. It wasn't much to go on. He returned to the kitchen table, sat down and flicked through his notebook looking for his notes on the interview with Barry Ford. "Let's come back to the subject of the mysterious car some other time, Mrs Neale, maybe some more details will come to mind. Let's talk about young Adam Southam for a bit. How well do you know him?"

Her cheeks reddened. "You don't believe what he said out there do you? The lying little tyke! It's obvious he was making it up!"

Dolby looked at her short skirt and the way her bosom thrust itself towards him through the straining fabric of her blouse. "Maybe there was a misunderstanding…"

"I'll give him bloody misunderstanding, the snotty little buggar!" She got up from the table "He was just making trouble for me!"

"Why would he do that?"

"He doesn't like me. Anyway, it's obvious to anyone who knows him that he was making it up!"

"Why?"

She sighed. "Do I have to spell it out to you, Sergeant? He doesn't like women - he's gay! Didn't you realise that?"

Dolby shook his head uncomfortably. "No - anyway, it's not relevant. The only thing we're interested in is who killed Valerie and Bruce Southam. We need to build a picture of the Southam family. That's why I need to ask you about Adam. Tell me about him."

She eyed him defiantly. "What's to tell?" She shrugged and sniffed, wiping the handkerchief over her nose. "He's a snotty nosed little kid who happens to be the son of a friend. I've hardly spoken to him for two years or more. I hardly see him. You can see he doesn't like me though - and I can't say I'm that keen on him really. Mind you, I didn't say it to Valerie - you wouldn't to a friend would you? - but I don't think he's a very nice kid."

"How did he get on with his parents?"

"He hated his dad…"

"What about his mother?"

"He was Okay with Valerie - when he was young they were quite close, but recently she wasn't very happy with him. She told me she was worried about him making friends with that gardener of theirs - I forget his name..."

"Philip Chantry."

"Yes - that's him. You have been doing your homework, Sergeant. He's a good gardener, works for that big company, Budds and Co. I think it's called. Anyway, Valerie was concerned because this Philip guy is also gay - she was worried in case Adam was the same. It's obvious he is, of course - to me anyway. I told her not to be stupid. If he is he is and that's all there is to it."

"Did she actually fall out with Adam though?"

"No, I don't think she fell out with him - she tried not to. She actually did love him you see and at the end of the day it didn't really matter to her what he was; whether he was straight or gay he was still her kid, I suppose. It was different with her husband, though. I think he took it personally - it was like Adam was only saying he was gay to hurt Bruce's stupid pride and damage his macho image. Bruce was like that, he only cared about himself."

"Did Valerie tell you what happened last Sunday?"

"The row you mean? Yes, she told me on Monday. She said that gardener, Philip, was there and he had a flaming bust up with Bruce. Apparently, Adam took Philip's side and walked out on them. He told Valerie and Bruce he was leaving home to shack up with Philip, or something. Valerie was very upset."

"I imagine she was. She must have thought she had lost her son."

Susie Neale looked at him over her long eyelashes, her eyes sad. "That was bad enough," she said, "But it wasn't the worst of it for poor Valerie. Bruce blamed her for everything and that night he beat her up real bad."

"Valerie told you that?"

She nodded. "Mind you, I didn't need telling. She had a black eye and bruises on her face. You could see what'd happened a mile off. I told her she was mad to stay with him and she ought to get out before he killed her."

"When did you last see Valerie, Mrs Neale?"

"Monday afternoon. I knew she worked up at the hotel Monday and Tuesday mornings and I was going to be busy chauffeuring Hilary, my second oldest daughter, yesterday afternoon," she stopped, looked at him quizzically. "It was Tuesday yesterday, wasn't it?" she laughed nervously. "Sorry, now I don't know what day it is! Anyway, I had to collect Hilly from school and take her to have her teeth seen to yet again - I'm sure them private dentists invent decay in people's mouths just to get the extra money out of them! - And I wanted to ask Valerie a favour, so I popped in on Monday at about three o'clock. It was then I saw her bruises and told her she was crazy."

"And she'd been to work in the morning, bruises and all?"

"Well, she'd made up, so they weren't quite so obvious and she wore a pair of dark glasses to hide her black eye. She said she was going to tell the people at her work that she'd walked into a door, but I don't know if anybody actually asked."

"And what was this favour you asked her to do for you?"

"Oh, I just wanted her to record something for me on the telly. Norman was using our recorder for his football and the timing of the film I wanted to see clashed with that. They were both starting at half past ten - different channels, of course and we've only got the one recorder, we're a bit behind the times I suppose. Would you like to know what film it was?"

"I don't know if that's necessary, Mrs Neale."

She ignored him and went on enthusiastically. "It was *"Chicago"* - you know that musical with Catherine Zeta Jones and Richard Gere - oh and that Renee Zellweger - she's really good isn't she!" She was obviously a film buff and Dolby expected she would go on to tell him the names of the composer, lyricist, producer and choreographer, but she contented herself with - "And don't you think the dancing is terrific. Anyway, I was really keen to see it, but Norman and me had to go out to dinner with the MD of his firm and the other directors, so I'd have missed it if Val hadn't recorded it for me."

"And that was the last time you saw Valerie alive?"

She nodded. "We had our little natter, like always - mostly about them bruises on her face. It was then she told me about Sunday and how Bruce nearly had a fight with Adam - a right barney she said it was, they nearly hit each other - and then Adam stormed out of the house with his friend, Philip, saying they was going to live together whatever Bruce thought about it. She was really upset. I told her what I thought about her husband and asked her to do the honours on the recording. Then I left at just before four o'clock to be home in time for the kids."

"What about Bruce Southam? When did you last see him?"

"I haven't seen him to talk to for months, but I did see him last night as it happens. It was about half past eleven and me and Norman drove past Val's house on our way home. There was a taxi just turning in the road and Bruce was at his front door searching in his pockets for his keys. He looked like he'd had too much to drink. In fact, he was so pissed he just fell into the house once he'd got the door open."

"And did you see anyone or anything else? Anything that struck you as suspicious?"

She shook her head. "No, nothing. Bruce's taxi had just turned around in the street - Norman says they always drive like they're the only ones on the road - so he, Norman, was driving quite slow, just in case - Norman's a very careful driver, but then he does a lot of miles, does Norman. Anyway, there was no one else about so far as I could see."

"And there were no cars parked on the Southam's drive?"

"No. There was nothing on their drive at all. Certainly not the big car I told you about earlier."

"Mrs Neale, one last question and then I'll be off. Did Mr and Mrs Southam have any enemies?"

"**She** didn't, Sergeant, not so far as I know, but I shouldn't be surprised if **he** had lots, especially in his business dealings." She grimaced. "He was **not** a nice man!"

Dolby snapped his notebook shut and stood up. "Thank you, Mrs Neale, it's been very helpful. If we need anything further we'll be in touch." She led him out to the hall.

"Well, thank you, Mrs Neale for your co-operation," He stepped out onto the porch. "We may need to speak to you again, in which case we will be in touch."

CHAPTER EIGHT

Detective Chief Inspector Jacqueline Caine drew her Ford Focus into the kerb opposite number 19 Marazion Road, behind the three other police vehicles that were still parked there and sat thinking for a few moments before switching off the engine and reaching under the passenger seat for her bag. She checked the clock on the dashboard and saw it was nearly two o'clock. For a moment longer she sat back in her seat, drumming her long fingers impatiently on the steering wheel. She could only conclude, once again, running the events of the last two hours through her mind for the third or fourth time, that the meeting with Superintendent Edward Hansen and the Police Chief Constable, Sir Frederick Barnett, had been a total waste of time. She had never been a political animal and so far as she was concerned the cosy chat over tea and biscuits in Hansen's office, whatever purpose it had served for the two Senior Officers, had succeeded only in drawing her away from her investigations into the Southam murders. To her that was a far more important and pressing matter than the revisiting of her past record by her superior officers. It seemed now that the meeting had consisted largely of Sir Frederick making patronising comments, sycophantically echoed by Hansen, on her '*marvellous achievements*' as a female officer in the police force. The implication had been, of course, that they rated those achievements as '**marvellous**' only because they judged the average woman officer's abilities far below those of the average man's. Caine wondered whether this heralded a re-play of her career with the Walthamstow CID and, with a grunt of frustration, pushed open the car door and stepped out into the road.

She crossed to the Southam's house, noting that PC Bailey was now serving a lone vigil at the top of the drive, and nodded to him. "Good afternoon, Bailey. Is DS Dolby inside?"

He returned her greeting. "Yes, Ma'am, I think you'll find him in the front room."

Caine entered the house by the front door, which was ajar, and pushed open the door to the lounge, once again noting the shabbiness of its furnishings. Dolby was sitting at the open bureau at the far side of the room, going through an untidy mound of papers that spilled out of the cupboard and onto the pull-down flap of the bureau he was using as a desktop. There were more documents on the floor at his feet, arranged in neat piles. Through the door at the far end of the room she glimpsed WPC Doyle seated at the dining table and working her way through a pile of similar documents. She nodded to the young policewoman, who smiled back.

Detective Sergeant Dolby looked around as Caine entered the room. He smiled and waved his hand to take in the papers. "Hello, boss, I'm just going through Valerie Southam's personal papers to see if there's anything that might cast some light on last night's events." He nodded towards the other room. "There's an awful lot of stuff to go through, plus, of course, anything that might be on their computers and smart phones; so PC Doyle is giving me a hand." He pushed a pile of what looked like bank statements to one side and stood up. "How did the meeting with the Super and Sir Frederick go?"

Caine scowled. "Don't ask, Mark. Supers and Chief Constables are strictly taboo subjects this afternoon. I'd rather talk about something more pleasant, like a double bloody murder." She dropped her bag onto one of the armchairs and crossed the room to stand beside him, running her eyes over the pile of papers. "Valerie didn't throw much out did she?"

"No - and you should see the pile Wendy's looking through in the other room. She must have been quite a hoarder must our Valerie. But some of it actually makes interesting reading."

"How so?"

He returned to his task and finished stacking a thick wad of official looking papers on the flap top. "Valerie had her own bank account." He explained. "These statements go back a couple of years. There's not much in this particular account, but she also had one with a building society. I think you'll find *that* a lot more interesting." He reached into one of the small drawer compartments at the front of the bureau and handed her a small red booklet. "Here's the passbook."

Caine took the little book from him and opened it, moving it closer to her eyes and squinting. "Sorry," she said irritably, "I'll need my glasses for this. Why do they always print this stuff so small?" She rummaged in her bag for her spectacles, found them and positioned them on her nose. She scanned quickly through the first few pages and whistled with surprise. "There's an enormous amount of money in this account, Mark." She ran her finger down the last page. "Regular deposits of cash - three times a month and five or six hundred pounds at a time. That does seem rather a lot for a suburban housewife to be salting away, doesn't it? Generous husband do you think?"

He shook his head. "Hardly - according to her friend Mrs Neale, Bruce Southam was a miser so far as his wife was concerned." He indicated with a sweep of his hand to encompass the worn contents of the shabby room. "He doesn't seem to have been much different in buying things for his house either, does he? So, those cash deposits certainly weren't coming from him."

"So where *were* they coming from?"

"At the moment I've no idea. Incidentally, Mrs Neale *also* said Valerie had a part-time job with a local hotel, as a receptionist - you can see there are regular receipts for that in her bank statements."

Caine nodded thoughtfully. "Do you think perhaps Valerie was transferring part of that money from the bank into the building society?"

"I don't think so," said Dolby. "Her salary payments were made into the bank by direct transfer and the deposits in the building society account were all in cash. So, assuming it was the same money being transferred from the bank to the building society she would have had to have drawn the cash from the bank in the first place so as to deposit it again. That would be a weird way of carrying on and anyway the withdrawals from the bank don't match the deposits in the building society - so the bank withdrawals were probably just for spending money." He shook his head. "No, so far as I can see, Jackie, she kept her hotel wages separate from the stuff in the building society and there's no relationship between the two accounts."

"So, it looks like the building society may have been a nest egg of some sort."

"It looks that way," agreed Dolby.

"But where was all that other cash coming from?" asked Caine. Still holding the passbook she sat on the arm of one of the armchairs and flicked through its pages. "Interesting. She's been making those deposits for years." She riffled quickly through the pages again, frowning. "That's strange - there seems to have been one entry a month up until about eighteen months ago - and after that there are *three*. Different amounts, but three regular deposits of cash."

"Meaning?"

"I don't know - I can only surmise. Possibly, that she was getting money from three different sources every month. And it was in cash. Which, so far as I'm concerned, always makes it suspect!" She peered into the passbook again and ran her index finger down the columns of figures. "And there are hardly any withdrawals, which accounts for the large balance that's still sitting in there."

"All of which is part of young Adam's inheritance," Dolby reminded her. "Though he may find there's a bit of a complication in his expectations." She raised her eyebrows. "I'll fill you in on that in a minute."

"Anyway, that's academic," said Caine, "the important question is - where did that cash come from? More to the point, from whom did it come - and why were they paying it to her and why in cash?"

"Blackmail?" suggested Dolby.

"If so, it looks like there were *three* victims! Busy little Valerie!"

"Well, she wasn't always your ordinary common or garden suburban housewife, you know. According to Susie Neale she had something of a colourful background. They both had."

Caine closed the passbook and placed it back on the flap of the bureau. "Speaking of whom, tell me how you got on with the fair Susan."

"Mrs Neale? I think her bark is worse than her bite." He smiled. "She was a bit heavy going, I must admit. Living in Marazion Road she thinks she's really arrived - a classic case of *nouveau riche*. Her husband's something in double glazing, director of a company or something and she was bending over backwards to look like the contented housewife - but if you ask me she's a bundle of nerves."

"How do you mean?"

"It looks to me like Valerie Southam's death has knocked her for six. For instance, she was supposed to have given up smoking - she and Valerie were making a joint effort, but there was Susie today smoking her head off."

"Understandable I suppose – I wonder if Valerie had a comparable excuse!" She smiled grimly, remembering the cigarettes beside Valerie Southam's bed.

He grinned, his mind obviously on the same thing. "Anyway, the news of Valerie's death must have hit her hard, because this morning she went straight back on the fags. Then, believe it or not, she dived straight into a box of chocolates and practically scoffed the lot. In short, she strikes me as a psychological mess!"

"Well, there's no law against eating chocolates. Not yet anyway, we coppers have enough to keep us busy. So - did she make eyes at you?"

He laughed. "No - I didn't even get a nibble of her chocolate fondant, though I must admit she did offer. But seriously, she looks like a tart, but I honestly don't think she even thought of flirting with me. Maybe I'm not her type."

"So, you don't think there's anything in Adam Southam's allegations of sexual harassment?"

Dolby shrugged. "No. According to her Adam Southam's gay, so she would hardly have tried it on, would she! I think Susie dresses provocatively without even realising it and it just got his goat! She used to be what I think they call an 'exotic dancer', way back in the early nineties when she first met Valerie. They both were, apparently. And our Susie hasn't got out of the habit, she still dresses - or maybe I should say undresses - as if she was on a Soho stage." He gave Caine a brief summary of what Susie Neale had told him about her background. "Anyway, I think young Adam was just being mischievous. He probably has a very vivid imagination. If he wasn't gay I'd say he'd been having fantasies about her."

"I don't suppose it matters much what happened between them," said Caine. "He's not a minor so he can do what he likes and so can she for that matter. But going back to Susie Neale's background, you say she was a dancer in a nightclub and that's where she met Valerie Southam?"

He nodded. "It was back in the nineties and she was in her twenties. What was the place called now?" He pulled his notebook from his pocket and flicked through the pages before continuing. "Oh yes, **The Red Dragon Club** in Soho. I think she said exactly where it was, but I didn't get it down."

"Frith Street," said Caine. Her voice was unsteady.

"You know it then?"

"Yes, but it was a very long time ago." Her eyes closed, the blood draining from her cheeks and she turned her face away from Dolby's inquiring eyes. Hearing that name again, just out of the blue, came as quite a shock. For over twenty years she had shut out the memory of **The Red Dragon** and of that dreadful night when Jonathan - her husband of only a few weeks - had been brutally murdered. Somehow, she had sensed he was involved in a dangerous mission, although he had never so much as hinted at it. But his manner had subtly changed and she had picked up on it. The more than usual tenderness, the long and lingering kiss in the hallway as he set out, the plea for him to be careful. Now it all came back to her in a rush. The solemn telephone call from the officer in charge, the scramble to get to the hospital and the agonising wait outside the operating theatre until finally the surgeon delivered the grim news that nothing further could be done. Then, the long and fruitless investigations, the search for Jonathan's and the other officer's assassins, for the cop killers, as the newspapers had called them, she had buried the memory in over twenty years of hate for the unknown assassin, over twenty years of sublimated revenge and now it all flooded back in the chance repetition of an absurd name. **The Red Dragon**. It was a coincidence, nothing more, she told herself. Susie Neale and Valerie Southam had been in their early twenties at that time, unimportant strip-tease girls and surely had had nothing to do with Jonathan's death.

"Are you all right?" asked Dolby, his voice reaching her as if from a great distance.

Caine opened her eyes, hoping Dolby could not hear the loud thudding of her heart. "Sorry, Mark - it's not something I talk about very often." He kept his silence while she composed herself. "It's closed down now, that Club," she could not bring herself to say the name, **The Red Dragon**, "but it was on Jonathan's, my husband's, patch when he was with the Met. Drug squad, he was..." she hesitated. "He was shot to death there one night."

Dolby did not know what to say. "I'm sorry!" was all he could think of.

She smiled weakly. "It's okay. It was years ago now, of course, not that the pain goes away. The worse thing is we never got to find out who did it." She sighed, visibly pulled herself together. "Just one of those things!" She coughed to cover her momentary lapse of attention. "It could have been about the same time Susie and Valerie were there. I don't know - it's such a long time ago. I can't recall seeing either of them, but I only actually went into the place once. According to Jonathan there were a lot of drug raids there over the years, before they finally forced it to close down."

"I'm sorry, I didn't realise..." said Dolby, looking wretched.

"How could you realise?" said Caine. "I've only been here for forty-eight hours and, in any case, it's not something I talk about very often. It's just coincidence it happened to come up."

She shook her head and sighed. "Let's get back to the matter in hand, Mark."

"Maybe drugs *are* the connection we're looking for," suggested Dolby after a long silence. "Maybe that's the connection with Valerie's mysterious paymasters. Perhaps she had something on someone from way back and was blackmailing them?"

"I suppose it's possible. It's a small world and people have long memories. Sometimes they come back to haunt you." She paused, asked in a tired voice. "What else did the Neale woman have to say?"

"A lot. She was a veritable mine of information - though I don't know how much of it will be of any use to us." He went on to give her a brief account of his interview with Mrs Neale.

"Quite a story," said Caine. She had walked to the window to look out at the front garden. Now she turned quickly towards him. "So, the long-lost daughter and her hubby actually threatened her?"

"Yes. Seems they had big eyes on Valerie's money - or more likely Bruce's seeing as how they probably didn't know Valerie had any cash of her own. She may or may not have paid up, Susie Neale didn't know, but if Karen and her man friend had violence in mind then that must put them in the frame as hot suspects."

Caine nodded. "The thing is how do we trace them? There must be hundreds of Karens living in the Rainham area.

And she and her man friend are not likely to show up again now that the Southams have been bumped off and they're bound to be under suspicion."

"Unless, of course, they're going to make a bid for the inheritance," said Dolby. "That's what I meant by possible complications in Adam Southam's expectations."

"I suppose that is a possibility," said Caine. "Although they would have to be absolute bloody cretins to show up asking for a share in the Southam's estate if they *were* responsible for the murders." She paused thoughtfully. "You mentioned a letter...?"

"Yes, according to Mrs Neale there was a letter from Karen to Valerie. With any luck we may be able to find that."

Caine looked towards the various stacks of paper that Dolby had sorted through. "You obviously haven't come across it yet. We'll have to keep looking. What else did Susie Neale have to say?"

"Quite a bit." Dolby outlined the rest of his interview with Mrs Neale.

"So, Valerie Southam had a mysterious visitor. It could be," surmised Caine, "that

this guy is the body to the mysterious 'other voice' Barry Ford says he heard last night, arguing with Valerie before the murders."

"We can certainly work on that assumption, but our best chance of establishing who he is would be if somebody saw him going into the house, or coming away again," suggested Dolby.

"Speaking of which, has the house to house come up with anything?"

"Not yet. One or two of the neighbours say they may have seen the car on occasions, but there was nothing definite. What we could really do with is a nice nosy neighbour, who spends all her or his time looking through the curtains, but they seem very thin on the ground in Marazion Road. Anyway, our lads and lasses are still knocking on doors, so something might crop up."

"Are forensics still here?"

"Yeah, they're still going over the place." Dolby told her. "Mostly upstairs and in the kitchen."

"What about Adam Southam - where is he at the moment?"

"He's gone over to Upton Eccles to see his friend Chantry. Do you want to get him back for another session?"

She shook her head. "No - not yet, but it might be useful to see him again to see if he has any ideas who Valerie's mysterious visitor might have been."

"He did say he hadn't seen anyone," Dolby reminded her.

"I know, but I think we'll keep our options open on young Adam."

"We've got to check out his alibi, of course," Dolby agreed. "And that initialled handkerchief still bothers me - we ought to have a few words with Philip Chantry about that. How about if I go up to Upton Eccles and check them both out? I can get Adam's alibis cleared up while I'm there."

"Yes, okay. You know, Mark," she went on thoughtfully "I suppose it's just possible this may be a burglary that went wrong. We should get Adam Southam to check there's nothing valuable missing from the house."

"Yes, I suppose we should," agreed Dolby, "but as Susie Neale told me - and it's quite obvious from the state of the house - Bruce Southam didn't like parting with his money, so I don't suppose there's much that's of any value here except Valerie's wedding ring. And that was still on her finger when we saw her body." Dolby paused, thoughtfully. "Also, none of the drawers and cupboards have been rifled. If it was burglary you'd expect them to be wouldn't you? But I suppose it's just possible the thief didn't realise there was nothing here worth pinching. Perhaps he broke in and Valerie stumbled on him. He hit her - too hard - and killed her. Then he panicked when he realised what he'd done and, when Bruce turned up, he also had to be disposed of."

"Yes, but it's extremely unlikely," mused Caine. "A person who goes to the trouble of wiping all his prints before he leaves the scene of the crime - **and** stuffs his victim with brandy and pills to make it look like a suicide - doesn't sound like the panicky type to me, nor an opportunist burglar for that matter. We won't rule it out entirely at this stage, Mark, but I'm inclined to think the cash in the building society is our best lead towards a motive so far. Blackmail may well be the key. But then, of course, we've got this mysterious daughter who just popped up from nowhere. She and her heavy-handed boyfriend may be involved, so that's also worth following up." She paused thoughtfully. "Still, you can check out the burglary scenario when you see Adam, just in case we've missed anything."

"It'll probably be a waste of time," said Dolby. He got up from his chair and went over to pick up the man's jacket that was still draped over one of the armchairs. "I'd forgotten. This is Bruce Southam's jacket." He opened it out and looked at the label. "Size XL - from the look of his body I reckon that would be his size. When I found it his wallet was laying on the floor by the chair, just as it is now. It may have fallen out of the pocket when he threw the jacket over the chair." He picked up the wallet and flipped it open. Caine could see the edges of several credit cards peeping from their slots in the leather compartments and the bulge of a wad of bank notes. "There's at least two hundred pounds here in notes and five or six different credit and charge cards. I don't think any burglar would have left this lot behind, unless he really was panicking!"

Caine nodded. "You're probably right, Mark, but you'd best check it out anyway."

Dolby nodded. "Right, will do." A sudden thought occurred to him. "Oh, by the way, Jackie, talking of robberies there was a break-in at that computer and electrical goods warehouse last night." Caine looked blank. "You know, near the cafe where we had our brunch this morning."

"Oh, that one." She laughed. "Weren't you commenting on the state-of-the-art security systems they've just installed? Just goes to show doesn't it, the villains will always have a go no matter what. Did they get away with much?"

"I don't know. The usual sort of stuff that's easily fenced, I believe. Some Smart TVs, a few computers and Smart Phones and some bluray recorders."

"Oh good," Caine looked pleased "That could be handy, Mark. It just so happens I need a blueray machine in my new flat. I'll have to drop into the local pubs and see what's going down. I might be able to get one dirt cheap!"

She caught the flicker of concern that crossed Dolby's face. "Mark, please, I'm joking." She turned back to the piles of paper on the bureau flap. "Getting back to the paper chase you've set yourself on, have you been through the contents of Valerie's handbag yet?"

He shook his head. "No - I think it's upstairs isn't it?"

"Yes, if my memory serves me correctly it was on a chair in her bedroom." She stood up. "I'll go up and get it. I've a hunch that's where the daughter's letter'll be - unless, of course Valerie threw it away in disgust."

Dolby looked at his watch. "It's just gone two thirty - all right if I slip over to Upton Eccles now? Check out those details on Adam Southam's alibi and maybe speak to him and Chantry? To tell the truth I'm going boss eyed going through all this paper! Still, Wendy's on the case and I've always found her to be very thorough." Caine nodded. "Okay, I'll just tidy this stuff before I go. I'll be in touch." He paused. "Oh, by the way, I've asked Wendy Doyle to take herself out to the Faulkbourne Manor Hotel to interview the staff there. Valerie's work mates might have some interesting background on her."

"Okay, fine." She left him shuffling through the wad of papers he had taken from a drawer at the foot of the bureau and made her way out of the room and into the hall. The house was gloomy, quiet but for the occasional subdued voice of one or other of the police officers working at their tasks in the various rooms. She went up the stairs and turned towards Valerie Southam's bedroom. The door to the bathroom along the hall was open. On impulse Caine entered the small room. The door to the bathroom cabinet gaped wide and cartons and plastic medicine drums were strewn about on the floor and in the wash basin and bath, suggesting that somebody had opened the cupboard in a hurry and cast them aside in their haste to find something. There was a dark smear on the cupboard door, close to the handle. Caine slipped her glasses onto her nose and peered closer. She thought it might be blood.

She crossed the hall into Valerie Southam's bedroom. Her body had been taken from the bed, but nothing else in the room had been disturbed. Caine stepped carefully around the brandy bottle on the floor - which would no doubt soon be taken away for closer examination by the forensic officers - and retrieved Valerie's handbag from where it was hanging on the back of the chair. The bag was of black leather, heavy and bulky, with a top that flipped over to secure to the front by means of a metal press stud. A fine layer of grey powder, dusted on to it by the fingerprint officer, still adhered to its surface. Caine blew the dust away and carried the bag over to the window. The curtains were still drawn, but it was lighter there. She released the stud and opened the bag, to reveal a number of zippered compartments. The first one contained a small purse, heavy with coins, a bank cash card and thirty pounds in five and ten pound notes. In the second there was a wad of papers, folded over unevenly. Caine looked through them carefully. A few money-off tokens for groceries, a book of second-class stamps, a shopping list scrawled on a scrap of paper in a childish hand that Caine guessed was Valerie Southam's. In amongst these miscellaneous items, pushed carelessly in between the other papers, was an A4 sheet, folded many times. She opened it out to its full size. It was a letter from a local firm of solicitors, typed on de-luxe quality bond. Caine read the letter quickly and nodded to herself. Here was confirmation that Valerie Southam had been prepared to leave her husband and would have done so very shortly if another, more sinister fate had not overtaken her. She refolded the letter and replaced it in the bag, turning her attention to the remaining compartment. It contained a small address book.

She flicked through the pages to the letter 'K'. A tiny scrap of paper fell out and she caught it as it fell towards the floor and held it up to the light. It was the corner of a lined page, probably torn from an exercise book and when she peered closer, she could see there was an address scrawled across it in a small, spidery hand. The writing seemed vaguely familiar and thinking for a moment that the two had been written by the same hand she found herself comparing it with the writing on the shopping list she had found in the other compartment of the bag. The two hands were similar, but certainly not identical. She read the address again - **23, Ridge Buildings, Rainham, Essex.** Evidently, Valerie - hoarder though she was - had not wanted to hold on to the letter from her long-lost daughter, Karen. Perhaps she had been upset by it - by the sudden shock of her rejected baby's voice calling to her down the years. Maybe it was a letter heavy with accusations, sowing guilt in Valerie's heart. Whatever it had said, Valerie had not welcomed the letter. She had ripped it up, but perhaps made a last-minute decision to save the address; just in case she ever changed her mind and wanted to respond to her daughter's overtures.

Caine opened the address book and replaced the small scrap of paper between the 'J' and 'K' sections, replacing the book in the handbag before retracing her steps out of the room.

CHAPTER NINE

Driving almost on autopilot, his mind filled with the events of the morning, Dolby turned into the busy B road. The first few hours working with DCI Caine had not, after all, turned out quite as difficult as he had feared. She had certainly not 'taken over' the case as he had anticipated but seemed happy to let him contribute to their joint effort in his own way, even suggesting that he carry out the interview with Mrs Neale on his own and raising no objection to his suggestion he should drive out to Upton Eccles to see the Chantry man and check on Adam Southam's alibi. No, he was not unhappy with the way things were working out with DCI Jacqueline Caine.

His thoughts turned to the murdered couple. Someone had wanted them dead. Was the motive blackmail and had death been the price of their silence? The cash in Valerie Southam's bank account – three deposits every month - had come from somewhere; was it possible she had been blackmailing **three** people? It seemed unlikely, but what other explanation was there?. Maybe her husband had been aware of what was going on, so the killer – or killers - had felt compelled to eliminate them both. But who could it have been? Someone from Valerie's past? Someone she had met again after a very long period and about whom she had important and damaging information? Or was it a new acquaintance - her new man friend, for instance, the man who had driven his Mercedes car onto her drive? If he was her *friend - and* if he actually existed? The neighbour, Barry Ford's, information that he drove a top of the range Mercedes certainly put him in the income bracket where he could afford to meet her demands for money.

Dolby's mind swung back to the theory that the killer was an old acquaintance. Was there a tie-up with the **The Red Dragon Club**? That train of thought led him straight back to Jacqueline Caine's revelation that her late husband had been murdered in an undercover operation involving drugs. Was it just a coincidence that she, Valerie Southam and Susie Neale all had some connection with the Club? And then there was Valerie Southam's illegitimate daughter who had popped up out of nowhere, with her partner, just a few weeks ago. They had allegedly made threats against her long-lost mother. Did that put them in the frame as possible murder suspects?

Still driving mostly on instinct, he turned right, off the B road and into the lane leading to Upton Eccles, slowing the car and carefully following the twists and turns of the lane that was now taking him between fields of corn. There were few vehicles ahead of him, but a few hundred yards before he entered Upton High Street the market day traffic slowed almost to a standstill and he admonished himself for not having thought out his route before starting his journey. If he had continued on to the A12 he could have entered the village from the north and come into Church Lane, his destination, without touching the centre. For even here, in this tiny Essex village, the traffic situation was becoming impossible. It was market day in Upton Eccles, of course, and although, nowadays, the market amounted to little more than two or three dozen stalls purveying local produce and crafts, it would still take him more than ten minutes to manoeuvre his way through the other vehicles, around the marketplace and into Church Lane.

Eventually he turned off and edged his way along the rows of vacant vehicles and parked in front of a row of seventeenth century thatched cottages beside the ancient church. Wisteria cottage was a short walk up the lane.

Dolby was a frequent visitor to St. Peters Church, Upton Eccles, or at least to the vicarage, a big square house to the east of the imposing old building; Lorna, his wife, had developed a close friendship with the Reverend Peter Pavitt, the Vicar, and his wife, Margaret. Like Lorna the Pavitts were keen local historians. An acquaintance that had started when Lorna met them at the Local Historical Society's gatherings had blossomed into a comradeship marked by frequently exchanged visits to their respective homes for tea and historical talk. Unlike many husbands who might have pleaded pressure of work as an excuse to avoid these gatherings Mark Dolby was interested in the custom and folklore of the area - which was very close to where he had grown up - and attended their little social get togethers as often as the non-social hours of his work permitted. Consequently, Dolby knew Wisteria Cottage well. He had never been inside it but had frequently admired it from the outside as he and Lorna drove past. It was one of two detached cottages, the other going by the name of Arbour Cottage, which lay in what had once been church land, set back from the road where Church Lane widened out and only a hundred or so yards from the Church.

In spite of the yellow lines and waiting restrictions which had invaded even this once quiet backwater of the village there were parked cars on either side all the way up the lane. He walked in the centre of the road and, as he drew nearer to Wisteria Cottage, angled off towards the low wicket fence that bordered the property. According to the Reverend Pavitt the cottages had been built in the late seventeenth century, but they were well preserved, having been re-thatched only recently. Wisteria, the plant that had given the cottage its name, was much in evidence, growing in profusion on the walls and winding its way along the eaves.

A nearly new red Alfa Romeo Sports car, its top down, was parked on the short drive in front of the cottage and he walked around it to the front door, which had been recently repainted dark green, as had the wooden frames of the leaded light windows. A large brass door knocker in the shape of a frog adorned the centre of the door. He knocked loudly and stepped back.

A woman's voice floated out to him from inside the cottage. "Hang on, please, I won't be a moment."

It was two or three minutes before a young woman of about twenty-five came to the door of the cottage, easing it open a few inches on a safety chain. His first impression was that she was beautiful. Her fine skin, tinged with a blush of rose, glowed healthily without the assistance of makeup. Her nose was short and straight and perfectly in proportion to the oval of her face. Her eyes were large, soft and brown, questioning. Through the small gap between the door and the jamb he could see that she was dressed in a white towelling wrap, the belt tied tightly around her waist, pulling the thick luxuriant material close to her slim body. There was a matching towel wound like a turban around the top of her head, but a few strands of long blonde hair had escaped its confines and hung wetly down against one of her ears. It was obvious that she was wearing very little besides the towel and dressing gown.

"Hello! Do I know you?" she asked.

Dolby stepped back, a little embarrassed and fumbled for his warrant card. "Detective Sergeant Mark Dolby, Fen Molesey, CID. I'm given to understand that two young ladies - Jennifer and Dawn - live here."

She smiled attractively, showing prominent dimples and white, even teeth which stood out starkly against the healthy pink of her complexion. He was glad when she reached out and took the warrant card from him, scrutinising it slowly - after all, it might have been anybody knocking at her door and, only partially dressed as she was, she was certainly vulnerable. Satisfied that he was who he said he was, she returned the card to him and released the chain to fully open the door.

"Do come in, Sergeant." She stepped back into the room. "I'm sorry to have kept you waiting. I was taking a shower."

He followed her inside. The front door opened directly on to the living room and he realised that Wisteria Cottage was larger than it appeared when viewed from the front. The room was sparsely furnished with dark, old wooden furniture of good quality, very much in keeping with the exposed beams that ran across the ceiling. The upper floor was reached by means of a wrought iron spiral staircase cut into one corner of the low ceiling, a recent modification, he felt sure. It was untidy. There were dirty glasses on the small occasional tables, together with a number of discarded paper plates, some with pieces of what he thought may once have been black forest gateau clinging to them. Others were caked with discarded lumps of soft cheese and broken pieces of French stick bread. Items of women's clothing lay on the backs of the chairs where they had been carelessly discarded and odd ladies' shoes were strewn about the floor. Slung across one end of a dark red leather chesterfield was a large blue canvas ruck sack, with a few items of clothing spilling out of its open top.

The young woman followed his eyes and smiled apologetically. "Sorry the place is in such a state, Sergeant. The girls haven't cleared up yet." She shrugged prettily and held out her hand. "No matter - they'll do it later I suspect. I'm Phyllida Ormsby, by the way. My friends call me Philly." Her grip was firm, her hand still warm from the shower. "I'm afraid Jenny and Dawn are out at the moment, Sergeant. Maybe I can help instead, but I warn you I am in a bit of a hurry. Please sit down, won't you?"

She indicated the heavy leather chesterfield, herself reclining into one of the two single seater settees. As he sat down, she crossed her long, shapely legs beneath her and pulled the hem of the dressing gown across to hide all but her calves and ankles. "Now, what can I do for you, Sergeant?"

He cleared his throat. "I understood that the cottage was being rented to the two young ladies, Jennifer and Dawn. Sorry, I don't have their second names."

"That's okay," said Miss Ormsby. "And your information is correct. Jenny and Dawn will be looking after the place while I'm away." She glanced around the room and giggled. "They haven't done very well so far, have they!" She looked suddenly serious. "I hope they're not in trouble with the police."

"No - no - nothing like that. Do I take it then that they're renting the place from you, Miss Ormsby?"

"Philly, please. Yes. They have the place on one of those whatsit leases - you know the official thingies whereby they don't get sitting tenant's rights or whatever. Daddy was most insistent I did the thing properly."

"I think you mean a shorthold tenancy."

"That's the thing. Daddy's solicitor looks after all that stuff for me. I shall probably be away for a year, but I might let Jenny and Dawn stay longer, depending on how they look after the place. It's big enough for the three of us," She wrinkled her nose and looked around the untidy room. "I wouldn't bother to rent the place out myself, but daddy insisted. Said it's far better from an insurance point of view to have the place lived in than empty for a whole year." She shrugged. "I suppose he does know what he's talking about - he should - he's a big cheese in one of those enormous multi-national insurance companies."

"You're away for a whole year then?" He nodded towards the ruck sack perched at the other end of the chesterfield and wished he was ten years younger. He had trekked Europe and America in his gap year from University and had never been able to recapture the sheer freedom and complete lack of responsibility he had felt. "Going back-packing?"

She smiled. "It's not a holiday if that's what you mean, Sergeant. As a matter of fact, I'm off to Indonesia on a field trip - an expedition, really, I suppose. We're going to some little-known areas of the islands to investigate the flora and fauna."

"Sounds remote!"

She grinned. "Middle of nowhere! No joke if you're not partial to grub soup or worm casserole, I can tell you. You can't leap into your car and drive to the nearest Tescos when you run out of corn flakes. A lot of the time we'll be pretty well out of touch with civilisation."

"No telephones then?"

She shook her head. "Even mobiles aren't much use out there - they can receive digital satellite broadcasts, of course, but it's restricted - there are lots of hills and mountains to get in the way of the transmissions." Her eyes sparkled enthusiastically. "It's a case of really getting back to nature."

"Sounds exciting."

"Sounds, yes - I suppose it is really - but it's no picnic. I was out there in the rain forest a couple of years ago and it can be pretty hellish what with the heat, humidity and insects. They have moths as big as bats, you know and some of their spiders could swallow a domestic cat." She laughed at his expression. "It is beautiful, but primitive and it makes you appreciate the mod cons all the more when you get home. There were times I could have killed for a hot bath or to walk into a tiled shower room and turn on the hot water - and I dare say it'll be the same this time!"

Dolby knew next to nothing about the string of thousands of islands that make up the Indonesian Archipelago and he was fascinated that this young woman, who looked to him no more than a frail slip of a girl, could be venturing out there on what sounded like a very hazardous expedition. "But what makes you want to go out there?" he asked, "If that's not a rude question."

She laughed again. "Not at all - most people think I'm nuts until I explain it to them." She stood up, pulled her dressing gown around her and then unwound the towel from her head allowing her long blonde, still damp hair to fall freely down her back. "I'm sorry, but I am in a bit of a hurry, but I can answer your questions while I'm dressing, so long as you don't mind shouting." She made her way across the lounge, lingering at the entrance to the corridor. "But, in answer to your question I'm going because I'm a botanist and we need to find out much more about the plants down there in Indonesia. A lot of them are unclassified and they may have uses we've never dreamed of."

"I think I've read about that. Some of the plants in the rain forests can be used for the extraction of medically efficacious products. Isn't that right?"

She nodded. "Yes - look, I'm sorry, but I have to get dressed. I won't be a tick." She started off down the corridor, pulling her gown off as she went, leaving him with a receding rear view of her flimsy and provocative black lingerie. She turned off into one of the rooms and called out to him.

"Ask away, Sergeant, I can hear you if you shout."

"Okay," Dolby called out dubiously. He had never considered himself prudish, but he felt more than a little uncomfortable alone here in the cottage with this decidedly attractive, almost naked, young woman. She herself had shown no signs of being in the least bit embarrassed by her state of undress and he found himself wondering if she made a habit of receiving visitors in her dressing gown and brief lingerie. He acknowledged it as a mean-spirited thought, but he wondered what her neighbours, the Pavitts, would think and if the Vicar and his wife could possibly have seen her open the door to him in her dressing gown. He dismissed the thought. You couldn't see the front door of the cottage from the Vicarage, you couldn't even see the cottage. Anyway, nothing had happened between them or, for that matter, was likely to happen. He marshalled his thoughts, got up from the hard leather chair and faced down the corridor to call out his first question.

"Can you confirm there was a party here last night, Miss Ormsby?"

It was a cue for her to switch on her hairdryer.

Momentarily she switched the dryer off in order to call out her reply. "Sorry - I didn't hear you - you'd better wait until I've finished with the dryer before you ask me anymore." The hair dryer went on again.

Dolby smiled to himself and walked idly about the room while he waited for her to finish drying her hair. His eye was caught by a group of framed line drawings that hung on the wall opposite the fireplace. He went closer and saw they were of vintage motorcycles their riders standing proudly at their sides, decked out in thick leather riding gear. He read the label on one of the frames. He recognised the name Harley Davidson, but the expression "WL45 side-valve 'flathead' Vee-twins" meant absolutely nothing to him and he wondered why a young girl like Phyllida Ormsby would adorn her walls with such pictures. The answer came to him a few moments later when he noticed a group of photographs on the bay windowsill. There was one of Phyllida with an elderly man and woman - Dolby presumed they were her parents - and a young man who might have been her brother. Another of her holding the bridle of a large chestnut pony; a third dressed in climbing gear, smiling, her teeth white against the bronze of her face, her sun goggles pushed up onto her hair, which she was wearing in a tight ponytail. Her slim body was obscured by thick, padded weatherproof anorak and trousers, her feet were encased in heavy climbing boots. She was standing in the snow at the summit of a mountain with a range of peaks fading into the distance behind her and she was holding up a small flower which drooped faintly yellow petals towards the camera. One of her field trips, perhaps? His eyes flickered across to the fourth photograph and there she was again smiling at the camera, this time in black leathers astride a heavy, powerful looking motorcycle, her crash helmet resting in front of her between the gleaming chrome and black rubber of the handlebars.

"Admiring the rogues' gallery, I see." He had not registered the fact that Phyllida's hairdryer had stopped whirring and he swung round at the sound of her voice as she entered the room. She had changed into tight, figure hugging jeans and a lurex knit halter top that left her arms and shoulders bare and she was carrying a pair of trainers in her right hand, whilst with the other she ran a silver backed brush through her long blonde hair. She dropped the trainers to the floor where she stood and went over to look in the mirror above the fireplace. "I see you're admiring my Rapide."

"Er - sorry!" He apologised. "Your rapid what?"

She laughed. "My Rapide - the motor bike," she explained proudly. "It's a Vincent 1000 Series C Rapide - an original. It's nearly forty years old and it's still going strong. It goes like a bomb - but perhaps I shouldn't be saying that to a policeman!" She laughed again and he could tell from her enthusiasm that she was talking about one of the loves of her life. He watched as she gathered the ends of her long tresses together, folding them upwards into the beginnings of a ponytail and then letting them fall gracefully back as she turned to face him. "You men are all the same aren't you - you get gobsmacked at the thought of a girl riding one of those *mean machines*!"

He had to admit he was surprised. The bike looked far too big for a slight girl like her to control. "Sorry, I don't know much about them. But it is a nice-looking bike."

"*Nice*! It's one of the best. And one of the few left in the world." She gathered her hair together at the back again and with that dextrous skill all women and no men seem to possess, effortlessly threaded a rubber band around it.

"It must be expensive to run."

She shrugged. "Not really. The parts are expensive - I have to get them specially made sometimes - but they hardly ever wear out, so it isn't so bad. And the petrol consumption's almost as good as a modern bike - so long as you keep the speed down – which helps with the environment." She crossed the room to pick up her trainers and sat on the edge of the chesterfield while she put them on. "And servicing's no problem so long as you know a bike enthusiast who runs a garage. I use Mike Thompson down in the Isle of Dogs - I've just finished an environment project down there in docklands - he did a full service for me only yesterday and he only charged eighty-seven quid. That isn't bad is it?"

He shrugged, not knowing the answer to her question, which he assumed was rhetorical anyway. "You use the bike in town then?"

"Yes - it's the ideal transport for getting through the traffic. I keep it at my London flat - it's not worth taking the car in." She looked up from tying her laces. "What about those questions? And by the way, what's it all about? Why did you want to see Jenny and Dawn?"

"I'm afraid I'm investigating a double murder, Miss Ormsby."

She looked shocked. "They're not involved, are they? I mean it's not one of their friends or relatives who've been murdered is it?"

"As I said before - it's nothing like that," Dolby assured her. "Miss Ormsby, was there a party here last night?" He looked around the room at the still uncleared mess. He need hardly have asked.

"Yes - as you can see, there was."

"Were you here?"

"Yes - at least, when I got in at just after midnight it was still going strong. I took the train last night from my London flat and picked my car up at the station. Actually, I was a bit surprised when I got here."

"Why is that?"

"Well, the girls hadn't said they were having a party."

"You mean they didn't tell you?"

"Oh - it's not the way it sounds, Sergeant. No - you see I was supposed to set off for Jakarta last week, but the trip was postponed - something to do with the visas. Anyway, I stayed in London and didn't speak to Jenny or Dawn until last night. That's why I didn't know about the party. I didn't mind, though, I was a bit tired when I got in, but I couldn't possibly have got any sleep with all the noise going on, so I just joined in. It was fun." She smiled. "There were lots of quite hunky guys as a matter of fact."

"Do you happen to know a young chap named Adam Southam?"

"Adam? Oh yes, I know Adam."

"And was he one of last night's hunky guys by any chance?"

She laughed. "No, he was not." She said emphatically.

"He wasn't here then?"

She laughed again. "Oh yes - he was here - it's just that he wasn't one of those *hunky* guys. Sorry, I shouldn't really have made a joke of it, but Adam Southam certainly is not a hunky guy. Not so far as I'm concerned anyway!" The big brown eyes flickered questions at him. "But why are you so interested in Adam? Is he one of your suspects? It's not him that's been murdered is it?"

He answered her last question first. "No. It's his parents. They were killed last night, I'm afraid, in their house." She looked shocked, the colour draining from her cheeks. He answered her other two questions obliquely. "I have to eliminate all possible suspects - that's why I need to know where he was last night."

"Good Lord - his parents. I hardly knew them, of course, but why would anyone want to kill them?"

"That is exactly what we're trying to find out, Miss Ormsby. Have you any ideas?"

She shook her head. "As I say, I hardly knew them."

"How well do you know Adam?"

"Hardly at all - I did go out with him once, believe it or not. Yes, I know he's too young for me, but it was a parent thing, you know."

"Your parents encouraged you to go out with him?"

"Well, we met at the Perots - you know, Charles Perot and his wife Florence - they've got that big place out at Upton Stapleford - daddy knows Mr Perot quite well - actually it's his son, Paul who runs the show now - and anyway they invited us over one day last summer. They had a barbecue out in the grounds by the big house and Adam was there with his father - I think Mr Southam works for the Perots - Sales Director or something, I'm not much good with business matters. But it was

Florence, Charles's wife, who tried to encourage us to go out with each other. Absurd at our age differences, of course." She was at the age, Dolby reflected, where a few years' difference is looked upon as significant. "But I suppose she thought something might happen later - when Adam gets a bit older. She couldn't have been more wrong, of course."

Dolby nodded. He could not imagine this beautiful and vivacious young woman having much in common with Adam Southam. "How long did your relationship last?"

"It was hardly a relationship - we only went out together once," said Phyllida. She laughed again. "And that was mainly to keep old Mrs Perot happy. Adam really was hopeless. The only thing we had in common was horticulture, but then Adam's supposed to be interested in formal gardens, whereas it's the sheer botany - the scientific bit if you like, the more exotic stuff - that turns me on. Besides, he's a wimp. Can't ski, can't climb. Scared of going on a bike - wouldn't even ride pillion. We had nothing in common at all." She used her hands to emphasise her point. "Whichever way you look at it, he was - and is - pretty hopeless! Anyway, he's gay - so we were hardly going to hit it off, were we?"

"I guess not. But why do you say Adam's **supposed** to be interested in formal gardens? He either is or he isn't."

"I think **he** thinks he is because he's in love with Philip Chantry." She giggled and put her hand to her mouth in mock remorse. "I know I shouldn't say it like that - especially in the circumstances and I do feel really sorry for poor Adam, losing his parents so suddenly..."

Dolby interrupted her. "I wouldn't waste too much sympathy on Adam Southam, Miss Ormsby. *He* doesn't seem to be very upset by their deaths. To tell you the truth I was shocked at his apparent apathy and at one point I thought he was actually *glad* his father had been killed."

"How dreadful." She wrinkled her nose in disgust and then softened her expression. "Perhaps he's still suffering from shock," she suggested. "I don't know, but I shouldn't really have said that because there's nothing wrong with Philip Chantry - he's a nice guy, but he's as gay as a carnival in Rio. Anyway, Philip's into horticulture so Adam thinks *he* ought to be into it, if you see what I mean." She paused thoughtfully. "They do like each other, you know, but I'm not altogether sure they'll stay together for long."

"Why is that?"

"Well, Phil's got these ambitious notions about starting up his own garden centre and Adam wants to go in with him. But they haven't got the money - it'll cost a lot to buy or lease the land, as you can imagine, and Phil's got next to nothing behind him. I think he'll drop Adam the minute some fancy guy with cash comes along." She stopped as a sudden thought struck her. "But of course, that could be Adam now, couldn't it? He must be inheriting quite a lot of money from his parents."

Dolby consulted his notebook. "You say you arrived just after midnight - was Adam here then?"

"Yes - although it may have been a few minutes before I spotted him." She went over to the ruck sack and looked inside thoughtfully. "I must make sure I haven't forgotten anything. It's the devil of a job to get things out there."

"So, you wouldn't know what time Adam actually arrived?"

"No, sorry, I wouldn't." She turned towards him again and threw her hands upwards in a gesture of helplessness. "That probably means my evidence - if you can call it that - is useless. I hope you're not going to arrest me for wasting your time, Sergeant."

He smiled. "No. I don't think so." He flicked quickly through his notebook. "I think you've given me some useful background material. Thank you very much. When did you say Jennifer and Dawn will be back?"

"I didn't, but they shouldn't be long now. That reminds me, I mustn't forget my multi-purpose, underwater, 250 atmospheres pressure, tell-you-the-time-anywhere-in-the-world electronic chronometer." She picked up the large black timepiece from the occasional table and strapped it around her wrist and then peered at it to check the time. "Well, Sergeant, I have to be off now, so I'm going to have to throw you out."

"That's quite all right, Miss," said Dolby. "Good luck with your expedition. I hope you discover a lot of new plants they can name after you."

She laughed and began the process of zipping up and securing the many pockets of the backpack. "Yes - the plant world is just waiting for Phyllidus Ormsbius - hey! That sounds good!" She glanced up towards the front window. "And that sounds like the girls arriving - your journey may not be wasted after all."

"It certainly hasn't been wasted!" He thought as he walked over to the front door and opened it. Two girls that he presumed must be the students, Jennifer and Dawn, were chattering merrily to each other as they propped their bicycles up against the wall of the cottage. They looked up as Dolby stepped from the porch and into the front garden. "Thanks again for the very pleasant talk," he called back into the cottage. Phyllida waved and disappeared down the corridor towards the bedrooms. Dolby took out his warrant card and walked, still smiling, towards the two students.

CHAPTER TEN

Jacqueline Caine, deep in thought and still holding Valerie Southam's handbag, walked back across the landing towards the stairs. Now she had the address of Valerie Southam's daughter, Karen, she and DS Dolby would be able to pursue their inquiries with her and her boyfriend. It might lead somewhere, but Caine had her doubts. It did not seem very likely that Karen and her friend had visited the house the night before and murdered the Southams. It was hardly a productive way of extorting money from them and, as DS Dolby had pointed out, whoever was responsible for the killings had not even taken the cash from Bruce Southam's wallet. Certainly, from what Susie Neale had told Mark Dolby, Karen and her boyfriend were not exactly cash rich and they certainly would have taken it. The answer might still lie in their direction though, Caine mused - the man had apparently threatened Valerie. But there was still too little to go on. If she and Dolby were to understand what had happened and solve the crime, they must continue to build up their picture of the Southam's way of life.

Caine stopped at the head of the stairs and stood leaning against the balustrade, thinking. They had learned quite a lot about Valerie by going through her private papers, but apart from the fact that he had been generally disliked, they knew very little about her husband, Bruce. Perhaps the identity of the killer was to be found in *his* background rather than Valerie's? Although she had moved in questionable company in her earlier years, if Caine and Dolby were wrong about their blackmail assumptions and *if* the cash deposited in her building society account had been acquired by some more respectable means than blackmail, *then* she seemed recently to have led a fairly blameless life. Bruce Southam, on the other hand, if he treated other people in the same way as he treated his wife, might easily have made powerful enemies over the years. Perhaps, among them, there had been someone prepared to murder him and his wife; but if so, why? There may be some clues amongst his personal papers. But first they had to find them. There was a chance they would be downstairs amongst the things that PC Wendy Doyle was going through, but Caine doubted this, it did not seem likely that Bruce would keep his personal papers in the same place as his wife's. The Southams had not had that sort of marriage.

Caine crossed the hall and pushed open the door to another of the bedrooms. On her earlier, brief, look around the first floor of the house she had decided that this, the fourth and smallest bedroom, had been used as Bruce Southam's study. The room was much the same as she had seen it that morning, the only visible change being the light residue of grey dust on the various surfaces, left after the fingerprint man had done his work. It was a small room and there was just enough space for a desk top computer, placed in front of the window, an office swivel chair in front of it and a two-drawer filing cabinet to one side.

The computer would have to go to the Division technical department for examination so, for the time being, Caine examined the contents of the filing cabinet. There were a few files in use, all of them related to Bruce Southam's work and Caine flicked quickly through these before discarding them. There were also various files devoted to household accounts, correspondence and Bruce Southam's private bank accounts and credit card statements. Caine flicked quickly through the accounts and correspondence and pushed the papers back into their respective files, extracting the pile of bank and credit card statements and sitting down on the swivel chair to examine them more closely. Bruce Southam had been earning an extremely high salary, that much was obvious from the bank statements and - apart from normal household expenses - he had rarely spent much. There was a large sum of money in his current account and, as you would expect with someone apparently well up in the insurance and financial world, he had a lot of additional cash invested in various tax savings or exempt schemes and in the stock market. The certificates of his holdings were scattered through two or three different files. But there was nothing out of the ordinary, no regular payments apart from the mortgage and direct debits, no tell-tale cash movements either in or out of his accounts that might point to extraordinary - perhaps illegal -

financial activities. The situation might, of course, prove different when the contents of Southam's computer had been scrutinised.

With a last look around Bruce Southam's study Caine closed the door and went along the hall to his bedroom. The couple had slept apart and she wondered at whose instigation this arrangement had been made; it may, of course, have been mutual. There was evidently no love lost between Bruce and Valerie and perhaps this separate sleeping arrangement had suited them both. The room was relatively tidy. There was a pair of men's slippers arranged neatly by the side of the double bed, which had not been slept in, but apart from a pair of socks rolled into a ball and deposited on top of the light oak chest of drawers there were no other items of clothing lying around. Beside the socks, in a cheap wooden frame, was a small colour photograph of Bruce Southam. There were no other pictures in the room. The chest of drawers, which was wide and deep, and fashioned from solid wood, stood in front of the central window of the room, which looked out over the front of the house. On the far wall stood a matching oak wardrobe. There was a digital clock radio on the small bedside cabinet, together with an empty glass. Both were still grey with fingerprint dust as were the various surfaces about the room.

Caine realised she was still carrying Valerie's handbag and dropping it on the bed she moved across to the chest of drawers. She looked more closely at Bruce's photograph. It looked recent. He was wearing an open necked shirt over which was a well-cut sports jacket of light material, probably a mixture of wool and cashmere. It was a three-quarter length photograph and grey flannel trousers could be seen beneath the jacket. He held some sort of trophy in his hands and he was looking well pleased with himself, as if he had gained some major award and was posing in his moment of triumph. It was probably not relevant, but Caine made a mental note to make inquiries as to what the trophy was for.

She turned her attention back to the chest of drawers, the first of which was filled with underwear - evidently thrown in carelessly and in no particular order. The next contained jumpers and an occasional piece of underwear which may have found its way into that drawer by mistake. They were expensive clothes, but none of the drawers revealed anything else of interest and Caine walked around the bed to the wardrobe. She was about to reach out to pull the door open when she noticed a small dark smear on the polished wood, just below the handle. She peered closer. A small area of the wood was stained a reddish brown and as her eyes followed down the line of the door she spotted a similar stain, standing out against the grain, on the edge of the plinth on which the top part of the wardrobe rested. There was a similar mark on the beige carpet. She nodded thoughtfully to herself and made a note to mention the stains to the forensic team. She pulled open the wardrobe door and peered inside. Bruce Southam had not stinted himself on shirts, at least a dozen of which hung from a rail inside. They were expensive, one hundred per cent cotton – a nightmare to iron - and, beside them Caine counted five business suits, hand stitched, in sober fabrics, clerical greys and dark blues; they had obviously been custom made for Southam by a bespoke tailor and, just as obviously, they were extremely expensive. In addition to the suits there were half a dozen sports jackets and casual slacks suspended on hangers from the other end of the rail. As she pushed one of the suits aside to see if there was anything on the floor of the wardrobe, the jacket swung open to reveal a fancy dark silk lining with a label bearing the legend "House of Journee" surmounting the letters "XL", which Caine assumed must signify the size of the garment.

Caine closed the wardrobe and stepped back to take a last look around the room. It was fairly featureless, showing nothing of the personality of the man who had slept in it. Certainly, it held no secrets. She picked up the handbag and made her way downstairs again. When Caine went back into the lounge PC Doyle was still seated at the table in the dining room surrounded by stacks of paper.

Caine sat down at the table and nodded towards the piles of papers. "Anything interesting cropped up amongst that lot?"

Doyle shook her head. "A lot of it's just junk mail that Mrs Southam obviously couldn't bear to chuck away. I can't think why she's kept most of it. Mine usually goes straight in the bin." She reached over the piles of paper to pick up what looked like a card index box. "I got a bit excited when I found this though, it was hidden away in the back of a secret drawer in the bureau," she said, opening it to reveal a number of small photographic slides. "I thought they were going to be a real find, well, slides are unusual, aren't they? - nowadays - I thought they might be pictures of something special, but the ones I've looked at so far seem to be just ordinary family photos, at least so far as I can see - there's no slide viewer." She shrugged. "I don't think they're very good quality, anyway."

Caine took the box from her and looked inside. There were three dozen or more slides in there and she picked a couple of them out and held them up towards the light. As PC Doyle had said, although very indistinct, they appeared to be ordinary family snaps. She replaced them in the box and closed the lid.

"There are a lot of ordinary photographs too," said Doyle, taking the box from her and replacing it on the tabletop. "Mrs Southam seems to have let things get into a real muddle."

Caine reached over to pick up a pile of photographs, of various sizes, that Doyle had stacked up at one end of the table. She flicked through them cursorily, not quite knowing if she was looking for anything in particular or even if she would recognise anything significant if she happened to come across it. The pictures were of people she did not recognise because she had never seen or known them. "Other members of the family, probably," She suggested. "No chance of recognising anybody, I don't suppose."

The young policewoman found a few prints that she had obviously looked at earlier and laid to one side for possible future reference. "There's some here of the murder victims, I think," she passed one of them across. "I think that's him - Mr Southam - when he was younger, although I'm not absolutely certain. The young chap next to him might be his son, Adam, except it was taken a long time ago. It's obvious when you look at their flared trousers - and aren't those jackets something else!"

The picture showed a youthful Bruce Southam standing beside another young man. Behind them was the rail of a ship and beyond that the wide vista of the sea. Bruce's features were unmistakable, even down to the broken nose, but it was the face of his companion that caught Caine's eye. It could have been Adam Southam standing there beside his father, except that Bruce was obviously too young, then, to have had Adam. And the clothes they were wearing were nineteen seventies, right down to the flared trousers and the long jackets with wide collars and reveres - Adam had not even been alive when this photograph was taken.

Caine nodded. "Yes, trousers like that were all the rage way back then," She adjusted her glasses and peered more closely at the slightly faded photograph. The younger man did slightly resemble Adam Southam, although it was obviously not him. "It isn't Adam - it can't be, he's too young. Maybe it's Bruce's brother. According to Adam, Bruce did have, or maybe has, a younger brother, but he left home a good many years ago. Hasn't been seen since, not by his family at any rate."

"Yes, I suppose so, although he doesn't look much like Bruce," said Doyle. She passed over another print. "I haven't got a clue who this is, but don't you think she's lovely? I wish those nineteen thirties fashions would come back again!"

It was an old, sepia print showing a beautiful young blonde woman, in an unmistakably nineteen thirties costume. She was posed in front of the Arc de Triomphe in Paris, a typical tourist, but it was a good photograph, sensitively taken. Caine studied the picture closely for some seconds, not because she felt it held any significance to the case, but simply because she was captivated by the beauty of this unknown female whose large intelligent eyes seemed to burn into hers. Tearing her gaze away, Caine turned the picture over and read the words "**Love, Emma. 24th July 1937**" written in a thin sloping and childish hand on the back. For a split second she had the impression that she recognised the handwriting, but she threw off the thought, reminding herself that the picture was over ninety years old, the lady depicted in it unquestionably long dead.

"She is lovely." She nodded her agreement and stood up. "But I'm quite sure she has absolutely nothing to do with the murder of Bruce and Valerie Southam, unless of course, she came back to haunt them." She indicated the pile of documents, "If you should find anything amongst that pile of paper that looks as though it might be of some relevance, then please bring it my attention. And, when you've finished going through all that I'd like you to get as much information as you can on Mrs Southam's background. Go back as far as you can. I want to know where she was brought up, where she went to school, who she worked for, when and for how long, who her friends and enemies were. Right down to the shade of her tights. I want to know what sort of a woman she really was! Same for her husband – except, of course, for the tights." The young policewoman did her best to hide an involuntary groan. Caine softened her tone. "Sorry, Wendy, I know it can be a bloody bore, but it's by plodding through most of the routine stuff that we most usually get results, so keep at it. I'd be particularly interested if you find anything to give us a clue as to how Bruce Southam spent his money. He had plenty of it and he couldn't have saved it all!"

Caine was about to continue when PC Bailey came into the room from the lounge. "I've got Mr Southam and another gentleman outside Ma'am." He said apologetically "He says he'd like a word with you."

Adam Southam was waiting for her out on the porch. Beside him stood another young man, tall and thin, in his mid-twenties she supposed, and wearing faded blue jeans, mud scuffed about the splits on the knees. The jeans were topped by a vivid yellow T shirt, also a little mud spattered. He bobbed, hiding his obvious nervousness, shifting his weight from one foot to the other. Caine wondered if his obvious tension was brought on by a natural timorousness or if his timidity was caused by the proximity of so many police officers.

"This is Philip Chantry, Inspector," said Adam. Chantry gave a shallow bow and reached out to shake her hand. "Charmed, I'm sure." His manner was exaggerated, his voice high and affected. His grip, however, was surprisingly firm. "We could have hoped to have met in better circumstances, of course. What a dreadful, dreadful thing!"

Caine nodded. "That's for sure, Mr Chantry." She turned to the younger man. "I didn't expect to see you again today, Adam."

He shrugged. "I decided you were probably right and I shouldn't give up my course. I've come for those books."

"I'm glad you talked some sense into him," said Chantry. "It would be such a waste to give up his studies now, after all, he's very nearly finished this part of the course and it would be such a pity for him to miss the exams."

Caine frowned. "I was speaking more long term, Adam. I didn't mean you should continue your studies right this minute. In view of what's happened it would be perfectly understandable for you to have a few days or even weeks break. I'm sure the college would be pleased to come to an arrangement."

"Oh, Adam will be all right, Inspector, don't you fear - he's an intelligent lad, aren't you, Adam." He patted the young man's shoulder affectionately. "Besides, he's got me to look out for him now."

Caine turned to the Police Constable. "If you wouldn't mind, Constable Bailey I'd like you to accompany Mr Southam while he picks out the textbooks he needs." She returned her gaze to Adam. "I assume they're in your room, Adam. We'll need a note of them and I would ask you not to remove anything else without clearing it with me first." The young man nodded. "After that, if you think you're up to it we'd like you to make a positive identification of your parents." He nodded again, swallowing hard but setting his jaw determinedly. "You'll arrange transport, please, Constable." She turned her attention to Philip Chantry, "In the meantime, Mr Chantry, I'd like a few words with you, if you wouldn't mind waiting here for a few moments while I just have a quick word with one of my other officers."

"No problem, Inspector," said Chantry. He stepped aside to let her pass.

Caine went back inside and walked quickly through to the dining room. PC Doyle looked anxiously up from her pile of papers. "A few minutes respite from boredom, Wendy" said Caine with a smile. "Will you please give DS Dolby a ring and tell him there's a slight change of plan. Adam Southam and his friend Philip Chantry have turned up here, so I'll question them about last night. But if he'd like to take a trip over to Rainham and talk to Mrs Southam's daughter Karen and her man friend, I'd be most appreciative."

Doyle nodded. "Yes, right - has DS Dolby got Karen's address, Inspector?"

"No, just as well you mentioned it, Wendy. Hang on." Caine opened Valerie's handbag and found the scrap of paper on which Valerie's daughter's address was written. "Number 23, Ridge Buildings, Dagenham Road, Rainham." Doyle wrote it quickly into her notebook and reached for her mobile telephone. "Thanks." Caine consulted her wristwatch. "Oh and tell Mark I'll see him back at the station tomorrow morning. I have an appointment to have a look at a house in Birch Medley at seven o'clock this evening and I don't suppose I'll have a chance of getting back to the station between times. He knows where he can reach me."

Caine retraced her steps to the front door. Adam Southam had gone off with PC Bailey. Philip Chantry was waiting for her in the front garden. She was faintly amused to find him crouched down beside one of the flower beds, pulling up weeds.

"Sorry to keep you waiting," she said, "But I can see you've been putting the time to good use."

"Don't like to see my good work going to waste," he leaned forward and pulled at one last weed before rising to his feet. "As of Sunday, it was no longer my problem, but now…who knows?" He shrugged and crushed the weeds in his hand prior to throwing them into the wheelie bin, which stood at the side of the garage.

"Perhaps we can talk out in the back garden, Mr Chantry." Caine suggested.

"No problem, Inspector. I'm always happier out in the open."

They made their way around the side of the house and walked across the patio to two white plastic chairs that faced out onto the back garden. "Please sit down," said Caine. She pulled one of the chairs around so that she sat opposite, facing him, a few feet away, her legs crossed. She turned her head to look across the sunlit garden for a few moments before bringing her gaze back to his face and continuing. "This is familiar ground for you, of course, Mr Chantry."

He turned to look out over the lawn, smiling with obvious satisfaction. "Oh, you mean the garden. Yes, I am rather proud of it - it's not much, of course, but getting that man Southam to spend even a little of his money on rescuing it from the state of utter desolation I found it in, was quite an achievement I can tell you. Quite an achievement!"

"How long did you know the Southams, Mr Chantry?"

"Oh, I don't know - two, three years, something like that."

"How did you get on with them?"

"You probably know by now that I didn't get on at all well with *him*," he said, wrinkling his nose as if it had been assailed by an offensive odour. "When we're young we're told not to speak ill of the dead - especially the recently dead - but Bruce Southam has got to be one of the exceptions. He was an insufferable pig, a bigot of the first order, Inspector!"

"He didn't approve of your friendship with Adam?"

"No, he jolly well did not! But then his type don't approve of anything that isn't Anglo Saxon white and sexually straight, do they? Not that he had anything to be so high and mighty about! He had no accomplishments in life except a big bank balance. And to me money's not that important!"

"Oh, but that's not strictly true, is it?" said Caine. "You have your ambitions too, don't you, Mr Chantry. A little money doesn't harm your chances of getting what you want in life, does it?"

"I take it, Inspector that you're referring to my ambition to own my own garden centre? God knows where you heard it from, but it's no secret. I'm always looking about for likely investors and there's no harm in that. It's an honest business and a jolly sight nicer than many other things people get up to."

"And you wanted Adam Southam to go into partnership with you on this garden centre venture?"

"Well, yes - we had discussed it, Inspector. We got on well and he does want to make his career in horticulture. It would have been a very good move, I think."

"But you never got past the discussion stage?"

"No. Frankly, Inspector, we couldn't afford it." Chantry stopped, ran his hand nervously across his chin. "I hope you don't think, Inspector that I - that Adam and I - no, no..."

"It is a possible motive Mr Chantry, and I am not in a position at the moment to discount any plausible theory to explain why the Southams were murdered." She paused thoughtfully,

"But coming back to Bruce Southam's dislike of you - I presume that his main objection was your friendship with his son. Is that not so?"

"Of course. It's obvious what the problem was. He made it quite clear he didn't like me the first time we met. It wasn't hard to guess why, Inspector."

"You still did his gardening, though. Why? If you disliked the man so much?"

"It wasn't just *his* garden," said Chantry. "It was Adam's - as you know he's interested in the trade himself, would like to go into it. I like him and it seemed like a good idea to help him along with a bit of free tuition and experience. And, of course, there was Mrs Southam - Valerie - she was okay even if her old man wasn't!"

"You got along well with her?"

"Oh yes, she was fine. She didn't mind that I'm gay, although to be perfectly honest I think there was the teeniest weeniest bit of concern on her part that Adam might be." Chantry smiled thinly. "I suppose there often is with mums, isn't there - always thinking about the possibility of having grandchildren one day, I suppose - and if your only son's gay the chances of achieving that little ambition in life are somewhat diminished! I must admit I did have that same problem with my own parents, until they realised that my sister and two brothers were quite capable of providing all they could ask for in that direction."

Caine nodded. It was an aspect of life that had never really occurred to her before. Her daughter had always been precocious with boys and she had never doubted that when Alison finally settled down, she would soon be presented with grandchildren. She could understand that those faced by a different set of circumstances might be upset by them, but she had always been a believer in allowing people to lead their own lives, provided they did so within the bounds of decency and, of course, the law.

"When did you last see the Southams, Mr Chantry?"

He rubbed his chin thoughtfully, "Sunday, this Sunday." He paused, moving his hand up to massage the side of his nose with his index finger. "I'm sure you've heard by now about the little argument I had with Mr Southam that afternoon. The neighbours will have heard and Adam's probably told you anyway." He sighed. "I suppose it makes it look bad for me, doesn't it? Having a flaming row with the man just a couple of days before he's found brutally done to death! I can assure you, though, Chief Inspector, that I had nothing, absolutely nothing to do with it!"

"And you haven't been back here since Sunday?" He nodded. "How often would you normally have come here to do the gardening?"

"Once a week normally. Usually on a Tuesday evening from about four o'clock. I'd come across from the Perots and put in a few hours here."

"But you didn't come yesterday as usual?"

"No - I told you - I had a bust up with Bruce Southam on Sunday - well, we almost came to blows - and I told him he could keep the rotten few quid he was paying me. You won't see me dead here again, I told him!"

"Did you keep any gardening tools here?"

"A few small things, Inspector, nothing big. I used the Southam's own mower for the lawn." He indicated with a sweep of his hand, "Well, it's not exactly a big spread, is it? - hardly needs a sit-on mower!" His eyes narrowed. "But is that relevant? Valerie and Bruce weren't killed with a pair of garden shears were they?"

"Not so far as we know," said Caine. "Did you take your tools with you on Sunday, when you left?"

Chantry glanced out over the garden and scratched the side of his nose before answering. "Yes - I did. There was no way I was going to leave anything of mine in that man's house!"

"Do you drive a vehicle, Mr Chantry?"

"Yes, I have the use of a firm's van to carry the heavy machinery about, the big mowers and the like. Most of my work's over at the Perot estate so I leave the big stuff there mostly. I also use my bike a lot, though, whenever I can, for short journeys, when there's not too much to carry. It's environmentally friendly, Inspector and we all have to think of these things nowadays, I'm sure you agree."

"Well, I wouldn't disagree," said Caine. "Now, as I understand it, after you had your argument with the Southams on Sunday you left and Adam Southam went with you. Is that right?"

"Yes. We had talked about him moving in with me and Sunday seemed like a good time to go ahead." Chantry leaned forward in his seat and said intensely. "You must understand, Inspector, that he wasn't happy at home. His parents, well..." he raised his hands in despair, "they did not get on with each other and I'm afraid poor Adam was in the middle of it all. Not a happy place to be, Inspector, I can assure you."

"So, you took pity on him and offered him a place to stay?"

He looked hurt as if there was a hidden inference in what she had said. "Well, yes - that is what happened. I'm extremely fond of him, Inspector."

"And you were with him last night?"

"No - that is, not the whole evening. We'd been invited to this party - two girl students, friends, not far from where I live in Upton Eccles were having this housewarming or cottage warming, or whatever people warm nowadays. I told Adam I was working late at the Perots, so he should go on and I would join him there later. Which I did, at just after eleven o'clock."

"So, at eleven o'clock, you would have been at the party, with Adam?" He nodded. "And presumably a lot of people would have seen you there and could confirm that?"

"Yes, it must have been about eleven. And we stayed until about two o'clock this morning, Inspector."

Caine stood up. "Thank you, Mr Chantry. I think that's all for the time being." She stood in the bright sunshine for a few seconds, looking out over the small garden, walked slowly up the narrow path of circular paving stones to stop beside the big lavatera plant. "I must say you have made a good job of the garden. It's very pretty."

CHAPTER ELEVEN

It was well past five o'clock before Detective Sergeant Dolby turned off the A13 into Rainham. The traffic had been heavy, even though he had avoided the obvious route from the A12 and around the M25 which, as predicted by the doomsayers, was now a slowly moving 'parking lot' for most of every day and almost grid-locked at peak times. Instead, he had cut across country, only to find a large number of other drivers with the same thought, and he had finally resigned himself to a slow meander through the back lanes. Still, he consoled himself, a compulsory spell inside a slowly moving car was at least a period of comparative peace during which he could ruminate and draw his thoughts together. Old Charlie Walker had often said that to him - "leave yourself room to think, Mark and if you ever have to commute don't waste the time on the train or in the car - use it to sift your thoughts, file away all those notions and ideas that have occurred to you during the day and let your subconscious mind get to work on them." It worked. It was surprising how many ideas came together to form solutions once you shunted them away into your mental processing system.

The two students boarding with Phyllida Ormsby had confirmed that Adam Southam and Philip Chantry had been at their party from at least eleven o'clock onwards, although their recollection had been anything but clear. When Dolby asked about Adam and Philip they had protested there had been an 'awful lot' of people there, and yes, Adam and Philip had been there, but no, they wouldn't know the exact time they had arrived or, for that matter, when they had left. And yes, it was possible either one of them might have nipped out for a few minutes without them noticing, they could even have been gone for as long as an hour for all they knew. They certainly hadn't had time to notice two, rather uninteresting persons, at their party. They were far too busy doing other things - what, Dolby could well imagine, having been at student parties himself back in the dim and distant past. But he was left with the inescapable conclusion that, considering the short distance between Phyllida's cottage and Marazion Road Adam and, possibly, Philip, could have got there, murdered Adam's parents and then got back to Upton Eccles before the party was over. Adam and Philip's alibis, therefore, were anything but watertight and Dolby spent an extra ten minutes with the girls taking down a complete list of the people who had been at the party - at least he hoped it was complete, the two girls had been astonishingly vague about the whole thing. He would now have to get corroboration from those on the list before he could eliminate Adam and Philip from the inquiry.

Ridge Buildings was a tall block of flats - one of three - set amongst a sea of mid-fifties council dwellings. The area was run down, the houses for the most part in dire need of repair and the building itself, built of concrete sections adorned with peeling red and blue paint, was cheerless even in the bright sunshine of the brilliant June day. It was noisy, being close to the A13 Rainham by-pass and the common areas between the buildings was dotted with groups of children playing ball games or just being as loud as possible. It took him nearly ten minutes to discover which of the high-rise dwellings was the one he wanted, for the illustrated plan of the area, thoughtfully put up by the Council at some distant period in the past, had been rendered illegible by the application of thick layers of extremely imaginative graffiti. With some trepidation for the safety of his car when he left it, he approached what he thought was the correct block, and slipping through the entrance doors, made his way into the dimly lit lift lobby. Letters carved deep into the side of a concrete wall - the only method of preserving them against the onslaught of latter-day vandals - confirmed that this was indeed Ridge Buildings and a wall plan told him that number 23 was situated on the sixth floor of the twelve-story block.

He walked over to the lifts fully expecting them to be out of order and heaved a sigh of relief when, at his pressing the button, the "lift coming" light glowed - he had been on the go all day and the last thing he needed was a walk up six flights of concrete steps. After a very few seconds the doors opened and a middle-aged woman stepped out into the lift lobby. Her head was covered with a knotted scarf and she was carrying a couple of shopping bags and a large handbag. She fixed him with a stare that combined suspicion with a certain amount of fear, probably the way she looked at every strange man she met when stepping out of this lift. He smiled at her, he hoped reassuringly. Visibly alarmed she scuttled past him, making for the exit doors as quickly as her legs would carry her. He sighed sadly and walked into the lift. His nostrils were assailed by the inevitable smell of urine. He pressed the button for the sixth floor and tried not to breathe through his nose as the doors closed and the car mounted slowly up the building.

Number 23 was as featureless and lacking in character as all the other flats in the block, except that there was no front door. It was clamped firmly to the top of a mobile work bench and a carpenter - an elderly man with grey hair and arms that would have done duty on an orang utan - was working on it, shaving away with a wood plane. He was watched, fascinated, by a tiny snot-nosed little girl - Dolby guessed her age at about three - who delighted in picking up the rolled wood shavings and chewing on them before spitting them out on to the floor. Dolby had no way of knowing that this was number 23, except that he had looked at the numbers on the doors of the other three flats on that floor - which were 21,22 and 24 respectively - so he asked if his assumption was correct.

"How should I know?" said the man belligerently, as if the lady of the house - or flat - had not served him any tea for at least a quarter of an hour. "Look on the door - that's where the numbers usually is."

Dolby sighed. "There isn't a door, is there! At least, if there is one it's the one you're working on and that hasn't got a number on it has it?"

"Course it ain't!" said the orang utan, placing the plane carefully on the floor without seeming to bend down. He selected a chisel from his tool kit at the same time kicking a pile of shavings in the small girl's direction. "'Ere you are, Emma, darlin'!" he said with the manner of a grandfather speaking to his infant granddaughter. He turned back to Dolby. "It's new this door is, so I ain't put no number on it yet 'ave I!"

Dolby gave up trying to get any sense out of the man and walked through the doorway into the flat. He passed through a dingy corridor, by a tiny bathroom filled with dank smelling laundry and dirty nappies and into a small lounge. A young woman in her early to mid-twenties knelt on the carpet beside another small child of perhaps eighteen months. They were playing with building bricks, the young woman gently coaxing the child to hold one of them in its hand and place it on the growing pile in front of them. The room was surprisingly well furnished with a couple of well-worn settees, a pinewood coffee table and a wide screen Smart TV with the inevitable satellite control boxes and blue-ray machines. Dolby wondered, not for the first time, how people living in these sorts of surroundings could afford such state-of-the-art pieces of consumer equipment. He dismissed the answers to this question for fear of being side-tracked away from his murder investigations and turned his attention back to the young woman. She seemed completely absorbed in the baby and had not realised Dolby had entered the room.

He coughed apologetically and she looked up, then started back in alarm as she saw a strange face. The child, sensing her discomfort, started to wail and she gathered her - or him - in her arms and stood up.

"Sorry - the door was open," said Dolby, "that is, there isn't a door so I came in without knocking." He reached into his pocket for his warrant card and held it up. "I'm Detective Sergeant Mark Dolby, Fen Molsey CID. I'm looking for a lady named Karen."

The young woman rocked the baby, trying to quieten her (Dolby had decided it was a girl). "That's me. What the 'ell do **you** want?" She was small and dark, fat, and dressed in a cheap, badly fitting, blue track suit. Her hair was almost black, cropped short and she had a number of silver rings threaded through her ears and another through her nose. Her small oval face was heavily made up, but the powder did not hide the dark, puffy bruise around her left eye, the white of which was shot through with threads of blood.

"Can I sit down?" She shrugged, which Dolby took to be a 'yes'. He sat on one of the sofas and took out his notebook. "I apologise for just walking straight in, but in the circumstances…" he looked towards the passageway and the sound of sawing that came from the direction of the front door.

"Doesn't matter," said Karen. The baby was quiet again and she put her carefully down on the carpet. "The bloody council've taken long enough putting in a new door and when the bloke turns up to do the job yesterday afternoon it's the wrong size ain't it. Bloody typical that is!" Her accent was East End Essex that some people called 'estuary'. "And the geezer didn't find that out until they'd taken away the old door - if you can believe it, we 'ad to 'ave a curtain strung across the bleeding doorway last night and that's bloody dodgy round 'ere I can tell you. Anybody could've got in - they're a bloody load of tea leaves round 'ere they are. I wasn't too pleased last night neither when Jason said 'e 'ad to go out and leave Emma and Jacintha and me alone 'alf the soddin' night. I asked 'im not to, of course, but 'e says 'e's got a special job on and 'e can't let his bleedin' mates down..." She stopped, realising that maybe she was talking too much. She lapsed into a brooding silence.

"But the council have obviously sent someone back to finish the job today," Dolby prompted.

"Yeah, well, 'e's a clueless bleeder too if you ask me. 'E's been 'ere 'alf the day cutting lumps out of the bleedin' door to make it fit. We've 'ad soddin' sawdust everywhere. I wish 'e'd 'urry up and get the job done and then buzz off!" She sat down on the settee opposite. "Well, what do you want?" She asked impatiently.

"I believe you've been in contact recently with a Mrs Valerie Southam of Marazion Road, Fen Molesey?"

Karen's eyes narrowed suspiciously. "Oo says so?" she asked. Then, quickly "I've never 'eard of 'er, ooever she is."

"That's funny, because you wrote her a letter a few weeks ago, Karen. We have it and it has this address on it." Her lips were pursed, and she looked away from him. He read from his notebook. "23, Ridge Buildings. We also have reason to believe that you claim to be Mrs Southam's daughter, although you haven't seen each other since you were fostered out just after you were born."

"All right, so I wrote 'er a letter, but it was mostly Jason's doing. 'E's my bloke, 'e put me up to it. *I* didn't want nothing to do with 'er, the stuck-up bleedin' cow!"

"What exactly did he put you up to then?"

She shrugged. "The 'ole lot. You know - when 'e found out I'd been adopted as a kid and I didn't know who my real mum and dad was, 'e says why not find out? Might do you a bit of good 'e says, though we all know who 'e has in mind to get something good out of it, don't we? So, I made inquiries and this woman Valerie Southam turned out to be my mum. 'er 'usband wasn't my dad, though, she didn't marry 'im until years after she 'ad me - and got shot of me."

"And you wrote to her..."

"That was Jason's idea too. 'E said to write and ask 'er for money - well, we need it, for the kids, this ain't no way to bring up kids and they've got plenty, them Southams - my real mum and 'er old man. Jason said she should be pleased she's got grandkids she don't know nothing about..." she gave a little laugh, half amused, half tragic. "But she didn't bloody care - she didn't even bother to write back, did she!" She fell silent again, brooding.

Dolby prompted her. "So, what did you do then?"

She looked across at him, her eyes angry. "What do you fink? We went and saw 'er didn't we. We didn't take the kids, just in case it got rough. And do you know, she didn't want to know me - she denied everything, that I was her kid, everything!" She stopped, curled her lip. "But I know better, 'cos that's what the papers say, the official papers. She can't argue with them, can she? And even if she did, I could go and 'ave a DN-soddin' test!" She paused to catch her breath. "So, what's she up to now, getting the Bill involved? We didn't do nothing, Jason just told 'er what 'e thought of 'er and then we skedaddled off out of their soddin' 'ouse!"

"And made a few threats apparently," said Dolby. "Or so we've been led to believe. Anyway, he did frighten her, apparently."

"So, she's put in a complaint and I suppose you've come round 'ere to charge me with some fancy crime I didn't commit! What's with the woman? We didn't do nothing 'cept ask for what's our due!"

"She's been murdered," said Dolby. Karen looked startled, as if she had not heard him correctly. "She and her husband, Bruce Southam, were murdered last night, in their home."

She stood up; her hands pressed to her mouth. The baby, presumably Jacintha, who had been playing happily on the floor, seemed to sense her mother's alarm and started to cry again. Karen bent down and scooped her up in her arms. "It weren't Jason," she said. "I know he said them things to 'er, but 'e didn't mean it. 'E wouldn't do a thing like that – 'e's not a violent man!"

"That's not what that bruise on your left eye tells me, Karen!"

"That wasn't 'im - I had a bleedin' accident, walked into a soddin' door didn't I!"

Dolby had met it too many times before - the seemingly infinite capacity some women have to defend the men who brutalised them. Here it was a case of like mother like daughter, he thought ruefully. He sighed. "Pull the other one, Karen! It beats me why you women put up with it!"

The young woman stood still in the middle of the room, holding the baby close to her bosom as if for comfort, her eyes staring. She ignored Dolby's comments. Her brain seemed to be churning slowly towards the solution to some unnamed problem. "'Ere!" She said suddenly. "That's why your lot picked 'im up this afternoon ain't it - and I thought it was for that video and computer job 'e'd done - but it's not is it? You're going to bleedin' pin a murder case on 'im ain't you."

Dolby stood up hurriedly. "What do you mean that's why my lot picked him up? What are you talking about, Karen?"

She looked daggers at him. "As if you didn't know! You're going to charge my Jason with murder ain't you! You just came 'ere to try to make me spill the beans on 'im. Well, I don't know nothink!"

Dolby felt as if he didn't know anything either. "Are you saying, Karen, that the police - my lot as you call them - arrested your partner, Jason, this afternoon?"

"Yeah! They was 'ere about two hours ago," she said belligerently, "Two blokes from Fen Molesey nick. They took 'im away with 'em, said 'e was wanted for questioning or something, you know, to 'elp with their bleedin' inquiries!"

*   *   *   *   *   *

*

Detective Constable Dave Milligan pressed the button on the remote-control unit and the combined TV and DVD player on the desk in front of him crackled into life.

"It's all on here, Mark," he said, "Plain as the nose on his face - and he has got a bit of a hooter."

Mark Dolby sat down beside DC Milligan and tapped his fingers on the desk impatiently, waiting for the picture on the screen to settle. The moment it had become clear to him that Karen's boyfriend, Jason, was not there he had set off on his return journey from Karen's flat, feeling more than a little irritated at what he considered was a wasted journey. Ironically, while he, Dolby, had been making his way to Rainham, Jason had been sitting in the back of a police car with DC Milligan on his way to Fen Molsey police station. A quick telephone call had established that Milligan had brought him in for questioning about the Braxted Industrial Estate computer store robbery that had taken place the night before.

"And you're telling me that he didn't bother to wear anything over his face when he got out of the van to do the job?" said Mark. "Couldn't he see the place was crawling with CCTV cameras?"

"Search me," said Milligan, "Perhaps his nose got in the way! You'll see in a minute. I'll give it a touch of the fast forwards." He pressed a button on the remote control and the picture speeded up, finally settling into a view of a floodlit night scene. Dolby recognised the industrial estate he and DCI Caine had visited that morning. The pictures had been taken from the top of one of the tall camera masts at the corner of the block housing the **Big Byte Computer Company** and the road along which he and DCI Caine had walked that morning was clearly visible. The road was empty but for a car parked some way away and as the two police officers watched the screen a small white van drew up in front of the computer company premises. A short, stocky, bearded man got out on the driver's side. Another man, taller and thinner, emerged from the other side.

"Which one of those is Jason, Dave?" asked Dolby. "And by the way I still don't know his surname."

"He's the taller of the two," said Milligan, "the one on the passenger side of the van. His name's Garvey. Jason Garvey. The other one is Gary Oldham. They've both got records as long as your arm and I can tell you they're a couple of ugly customers. I'll just zoom in on them for you." He touched a slider control on the remote and the camera appeared to zoom in on the two men so that their heads almost filled the screen. Now Dolby could see that Oldham, the smaller man, had pulled a thick black stocking over his head. Garvey was attempting to do the same thing but was having trouble with the stocking with the result that his prominently nosed face was clearly visible in the centre of the screen. "Gotcha!" said Milligan, freezing the frame. "You'd think with a hooter like that he'd have put a cardboard box over his head, wouldn't you? And what about that ring through his nostrils - talk about gilding the lily!" He swung round in his swivel chair to face Dolby. "Anyway, that's Jason Garvey for you, delivered to your door by the FM CID, so there was no need for you to rush over to Rainham for him!"

"I wouldn't have if someone had told me what was going on," Dolby protested. He peered more closely at the screen. "Funny, I'd swear I've seen that bloke Oldham somewhere before. Recently." He scratched his head. "No, I can't think where, but it'll come to me. Anyway, you're sure these two were pulling a robbery?"

"We've got a fairly shrewd suspicion," said Milligan with a grin. "We've got the whole lot on CCTV, Oldham and his mate Garvey getting in through the door - with a key mind you - disarming the alarm - they must somehow have got hold of a key and the alarm code number - we don't know how yet - then we've got some lovely snaps of them carrying the stuff out to the van, locking up and driving away. Plus, the fact that we picked Oldham up inside a little lock-up garage in Rainham stuffed to the roof with the fruits of last night's labours. Yes, I'd say we have an open and shut case here!"

Dolby nodded appreciatively. "How did you get on to them so quickly?"

"Oh, that was the result of another of Oldham's brilliant moves," said Milligan, grinning widely. "The van was stolen."

"It wasn't local, though, was it? I noticed there was a company logo and address on the side - somewhere in Rotherham, Yorkshire, wasn't it?"

"Yeah - but don't be misled by that. The owner of a small corner shop not two doors down the street from Oldham's girlfriend's flat in Rainham bought it at an auction a few weeks ago. Apparently, they're cheaper up North, so he goes up there for his motors and buys them in the auctions. Bit dodgy if you ask me. Anyway, he didn't have time to repaint the sign on the outside and the minute we realised the address of the van's owner was a couple of doors down from Oldham's lady friend we thought it was worth a little look. Gary's shacking up with her at the moment while he's out on temporary leave from one of Her Majesty's luxury hotels - so we sent a couple of guys over there and what do you know? Who should they bump into in one of the lock-ups at the back of the flats?"

"Gary?"

"Yep - young Oldham up to his neck in stolen DVD Players and computer equipment."

"So how did you get on to Jason?"

"It didn't take much to match his face up with those of Gary's known accomplices." Said Milligan, "His conk was a dead giveaway!"

"So, we know that Jason Garvey was over in Braxted last night, not five minutes away from the Southam's house" mused Dolby. "What time did the break-in take place, Dave?"

Milligan glanced at the digital clock in the corner of the screen. "It's on the recording - twelve twenty-eight. So, you reckon Garvey may have been involved in the murders?"

"It's hard to say," said Dolby. "But we do have reason to believe he made threats against Mrs Southam. What's his form?"

"Oh, a little bit of this and a little bit of that," said Milligan, consulting a thick file on the desk in front of him. "Including robbery with violence and a bit of grievous bodily harm. He's one of your usual small-time crooks, who doesn't mind kicking somebody's head in when the need arises. We seem to breed a lot of them in these enlightened days."

"What about his friend?"

"Gary? Much the same. Went down for a couple of years for kicking a small shopkeeper's teeth in for the sake of a couple of hundred quid. I understand he's well known to the Rainham boys and girls for his love of fenceable consumables. Videos and computers are right up his alley. I don't know about murder," he rubbed his hands together. "But at least we've got them for theft."

"What about the van?"

"They ditched it somewhere. We're still looking for it. They probably swapped over into another motor at some point before bringing the stuff home. But it's a side issue, just something else to go on the charge sheet."

Dolby picked up a pencil from the desk and rolled it abstractedly between the palms of his hands. "Maybe murder isn't Garvey's usual MO, but it could be they paid the Southam's a visit to soften them up and things got out of hand."

Milligan shook his head doubtfully. "I doubt it, Mark. Working the poor woman over is definitely they're MO, but I doubt they'd have the savvy to fake her suicide."

Dolby stood up, yawned and stretched. "Anyway, I wouldn't mind having a go at young Jason if that's okay by you, Dave." He looked at his watch. "But not tonight. As it is I've got a lot of paperwork to do before I leave. You are keeping him in overnight I take it?"

Milligan nodded. "They'll be up before the beaks tomorrow morning, so get in early if you can, Mark - unless we can reasonably prove they had some involvement with the murders we may have to let the buggars out on bail. Theft isn't heinous enough to keep them locked up, things ain't what they used to be, you know!"

"Right. See you in the morning." Dolby left the room and made his way down the corridor to the office he shared with three other detective sergeants. The room was empty, and he walked around to his desk and sat down, pulling the pile of papers towards him. There was a message at the top asking him to ring Mrs Susie Neale and giving him her number. He lifted his telephone receiver and punched out the numbers on the keypad, listening with the speaker to his ear as the telephone rang in the Neale's house. Susie answered.

"Mrs Neale, it's Detective Sergeant Mark Dolby. You left a message for me to ring you."

"Yes, thank you for ringing back, Sergeant. There's something I thought I should tell you. It may not be important, but just in case it is." She paused.

"You'd better tell me then," he prompted impatiently.

"It seems silly!" she stopped speaking yet again and he was tempted to urge her to get on with it and say what she had to say - the pile of paperwork on his desk was not getting any smaller and he had a home to go to. Finally, she continued. "It's about that telly recording, Sergeant." For an instant Dolby thought she was referring to the CCTV footage he had just been watching with DC Milligan. He wondered what on earth she could know about a security video taken at the Braxted Industrial Estate in the middle of the previous night.

"Sorry?"

"Chicago - the movie…"

For a moment he still did not know what she was talking about and then it clicked. "Oh, right, the film you asked Mrs Southam to record for you. What about it?"

"It's not finished. It's stopped halfway through."

"I'm sorry, Mrs Neale, but I just do not understand why that might be important."

"I think Valerie must have stopped the recording halfway through. I just thought it was a bit funny, that's all," she went on hesitantly. "It's not like Valerie. She's never done that before - I mean, she has done recordings for me before, but this is the first time she's stopped it before the end."

"Do *you* think this has any significance, Mrs Neale? I must admit that it doesn't make much sense to me."

"Well, no - but I just thought - maybe - when she was attacked - it got turned off accidentally like. Oh and…"

Dolby broke the long pause. "Was there something else, Mrs Neale?"

"It's just that…" She began hesitantly and then stopped again.

"What is it, Mrs Neale? I am rather busy you know, so if there's something you want to say please say it."

The pause went on a little longer before she finally spoke again. "No - no - I'm sure it's nothing. You won't be interested." She hung up before he could make any further comment. Dolby replaced his receiver and returned his attention to the depressingly high stack of paper on his desk.

CHAPTER TWELVE

Jacqueline Caine drove into Birch Medley at just before seven. According to the estate agent's instructions Lime Tree cottage, the property she was going to view, was off the High Street, along a narrow lane aptly called Willow Walk. The streets were quiet and the whole ambience, once she entered the short, narrow High Street, was one of sleepy indolence, as if the village had taken a siesta and not bothered to wake up afterwards. One or two of the local inhabitants, their faces weather beaten, the flesh of their arms nut brown from the sun, ambled about the place with, seemingly, no sense of urgency or purpose. The windows and doors of the little cottages that lined the way lay open as if to encourage a small breeze to ripple through them in the almost still heat of the early evening. In the small front gardens, the heads of giant sunflowers undulated on their long stalks and white blossomed Wisteria clung to the cottage walls and dripped gracefully from arching branches. Cats basked in the sun on thatched roofs and, outside front doors, contented dogs lay in furry curled balls. Caine slowed her car almost to walking pace and enjoyed the peace, gently turning the steering wheel to the left as she came abreast of the entrance to Willow Walk, hardly noticing the slight bump and rock as she drove from the relatively well-kept tarmac of the village's main street onto the liberally potholed surface of the unmade road. She drove past a large, square Georgian House boasting the name 'Medley

Grange', and for a few moments the lane was so narrow that the side of her car was only inches from the herring bone brickwork of its orchard wall. Apple tree branches, heavily laden with their still unripe fruit, hung down over the lane and wild campion and cornflowers brushed the sides of the car.

After a hundred feet or so the lane widened out again and, following the agents' instructions, she looked to her left to find the wooden entrance gates of Lime Tree Cottage. The agent was waiting for her in his car, which was parked on the circular driveway in front of the house and as he heard her approach, he pushed open the door of his vehicle and clambered out. Caine drove slowly through the open gates, the wheels of her car crunching on the gravel, bringing the vehicle to a halt beside the "For Sale" notice, nailed to a wooden stake driven deep into the earth of one of the garden's front borders.

"Daniel Carmichael," said the agent, striding towards her, hand outstretched. He was late middle aged, tall and broad, with sparkling eyes and the bright, enthusiastic manner of a man who enjoyed what he did.

She got out of the car and shook his hand and then she stood looking up at the house. Set well back from the road it was a chalet bungalow, extended to a gable at one end. The thatch of the roof had recently been renewed and the frames around the leaded light windows were recently painted. Now she had switched off her car engine it was quiet in the garden, save for the gentle murmur of running water coming from the stream that ran to one side of the grounds, about thirty yards from the house. She stood for a few seconds enjoying the moment, drinking in the relative silence, not realising that she had momentarily closed her eyes.

"Are you O.K. Mrs Caine?" asked Carmichael anxiously.

She opened her eyes and laughed. "Yes. Yes, I'm fine. I was enjoying the peace - I can tell you I have had one hell of a day!"

He nodded understandingly. "Yes, I can imagine." She did not think he could. Although she supposed all jobs must have their stresses and strains, somehow problems arising from appeasing difficult house seeking and vending clients could not compare with those of solving a double murder. "It is very peaceful here," he went on, "I always say there are precious few places that can compare with Birch Medley so far as stillness is concerned. And we all need a little stillness in our lives – although we could have done without the pandemic last year. Still, I suppose it's all part of the natural balance." He smiled and took a set of keys from his pocket. "Shall we go inside?"

The inside of the house, entered by means of a heavy oak door, was even quieter than the garden and the rubber of their heels sounded hollowly on the parquet flooring. Lime Tree Cottage was set well back from the road and the nearest trees - a group of tall Limes - were a long way off down the bottom of the garden, so that none of the early evening light was shut off from the interior. Caine stood for a moment in the hall, beside the clear glass double doors that led into the drawing room, in the centre of a shaft of bright sunshine that poured through the first-floor hall window and flowed down the stairs to envelop her. The feeling was good. The house had a friendly, warm atmosphere that made her feel comfortable. Jonathan would have liked this place, she thought.

Afterwards, when the enthusiastic Daniel Carmichael had gone off in his red BMW, having promised to communicate her offer to the vendor that very evening, Caine stood quietly in the back garden and gazed out over the fields. The feeling she had had when she stepped through the front door into the house was still with her. It was well over twenty-five years since Jonathan had succumbed to an assassin's bullet, but she still felt him with her at such times. It was as though, whenever she had to make a long-term decision affecting the essential quality of her life, he was there, at her shoulder, giving her strength. The cold, rational side of her mind told her it was foolish to have these feelings, that Jonathan was gone, that he had ceased to exist when he was slain in that dark Soho alley - and yet the thought that he was here, beside her, gave her comfort, gave her an inner strength that, nowadays, she seemed to need more and more often. Perhaps it was foolish to have such thoughts, but it was even more foolish to talk about them. Professional suicide. When she was younger and confided in people, they had either laughed outright or behind her back, or taunted her, saying that if Jon was there, with her, why didn't he tell her the identity of his murderers? Consequently, for years, she had not mentioned these feelings to anyone.

She walked slowly around the side of the house, back to her car. The bungalow was perfect. A retreat from reality, almost, it was so quiet here. Could she afford it? She had offered as low a price as she dared and even that had been stretching her budget. She told herself she had to afford it, that no other property in the area would suit her so perfectly.

She climbed into the car and switched on the ignition, taking one last chance to peer up at the property before turning out into the lane and making her way back to the High Road. The village was much busier now, the locals were beginning to gather outside the pub on the other side of the road and she waited at the T junction while a number of cars swept by some of them turning into the car park opposite. One last vehicle came slowly towards her and she was mildly surprised to see that it was a late model Bentley, finished in metallic silver. Not the sort of car you would expect to see in such a small village. But then, of course, there were plenty of gentry and well-to-do farmers around, the vehicle might even belong to the owner of the rather grand house next door to Lime Tree Cottage - what was it called? Medley Grange. But the Bentley did not turn off to make its way past her and down the lane up which she had just driven; it continued its slow journey towards the B1022 to Maldon. She waited for it to pass. It was not as clean as it had at first seemed - the bonnet was grey with dust and the front tyres and wheel arches were splashed with dark reddish mud. When it had passed, she seized her opportunity and pulled out in the opposite direction, making her way back towards the centre of Fen Molesey.

It was nearly nine o'clock when Alison rang.

"Hi Mum! It's me!" She was her usual lively self. "Guess What!" She invariably started her seemed - the bonnet was grey with dust and front tyres and wheel arches were splashed with dark reddish mud. When it had passed, she seized her opportunity and pulled out in the opposite direction, making her way back towards the centre of Fen Molesey.

telephone conversations like this, without giving Caine more than a split second to think of a reply. "Lyall and me *can* make it this weekend - flying visit mind, we can only stop over on Friday night. But it'll be great to see you!"

"Oh, yes, that'll be lovely, darling. Will you be staying over?"

"Yeah, but we're taking you to some posh country house

"Mum, you haven't forgotten, have you? I'll bet you have."

Her daughter's voice was impatient hotel for dinner - so we've taken rooms there. Save you the bother."

"Oh, right!" Caine was still searching her memory.

"I should know you by now shouldn't I! - you *always* forget!"

"Of course, I haven't forgotten, darling" But she had. Her mind had been too full during the last few weeks. She had had a new job to worry about, house hunting and the temporary flat search and now the double murders this morning had driven all thoughts of what was to happen at the weekend clean out of her mind. Not that that was any excuse, after all Alison was her only daughter and she ought to find the time for her. But it had always been the same. The job did come first. It had had to. It was what put the bread on the table.

She looked quickly across at the calendar hanging from the handle of one of the kitchen cabinets - she had been in here making a quick snack when the telephone rang - and gave a sigh of relief. She had entered something for Friday, but the date alone had reminded her what tomorrow was. "Happy birthday for tomorrow, darling - I hadn't forgotten!"

"Liar!" said Alison, but without the slightest hint of anger. As a small child she had resented her mother's obsession with her work, but now that she had an interesting job of her own, she understood what a hold it could have on a person's time. "I'll bet you haven't got me a card yet - I know, you're saving it to give to me on Friday evening. In case it gets lost in the post." She chuckled and Caine knew that it was all right. Her daughter was not the sort of young girl - she corrected herself, young **woman** - to upset herself over trivialities. Alison went on. "What's new? There was something in the paper this evening about a murder in your part of Essex. Is it one of yours?"

"I'm afraid so, darling."

"Messy was it? The paper said it was messy!"

"Never you mind, young lady. I've told you before that no murder is nice!"

"No, but I'll bet it's interesting! Oh Lord! I hope it's not going to muck up our arrangements for Friday evening."

"No, of course not - well, I don't think so. The FM CID can manage without me for a few hours, I think. We're still going shopping for your present, aren't we?"

"Oh, Mum - was that on Saturday? Sorry, we have to rush back to Town. I must've forgotten. But the arrangements for Friday - I told you I couldn't get the whole day off, but I'll be away from the office by five-ish and in your neck of the woods by about 6.30. Could you pick me up at Chelmsford station? Lyall will be coming down later from somewhere else, I think he said Cambridge. Anyway, he'll meet us at the hotel. It's called the Layer Marney Country House Hotel, or something weird like that. Do you know it?"

"No, I'm afraid not - you know I've only been in the area for a few days. I didn't even have time to get my feet under my desk before those two homicides came in. But don't worry, someone here'll know where it is - and there's always the SatNav."

Alison gushed on. "Well, it's supposed to be really cool mum, the Hotel. It's got a sports centre with a pool and a jacuzzi. You'll love it. And apparently they've got a fabulous restaurant with one of the best cellars in England - Lyall's very keen on having a good wine with the meal - and the food's on us by the way - well, it's on Lyall actually - he said that as it's my birthday he'd be delighted to foot the bill and I didn't say "no, don't be silly", because he's got literally pots of money and he won't even notice. Did I tell you he was a Director at F.B?"

"FB?"

"Foggarty Bleu!"

Although it sounded more like a weather forecast Foggarty Bleu was one of the biggest and successful advertising agencies in the UK. Alison had gone into advertising when she left university four years before - she had fallen into it really. Like so many other young people entering the world of self-sufficiency she hadn't known what she wanted to do, but she had landed on her feet and now she was in charge of some sort of creative team at Hogg Willoughby Fenton - or HWF as it was known - one of the other trendy UK agencies. Now Caine recalled a little more of what Alison had told her about her boyfriend. He was something of a highflier in the advertising world, some sort of whizz kid who had flitted from one agency to another over the past fifteen years - he had to be in his mid to late thirties, thought Caine, which was not pleasing to her considering Alison was only twenty-five. She hoped her daughter would not get too fond of Lyle. These mercurial types often treated their women in the same way as they treated their jobs. They screwed what they could out of them and then left them to move on to more important bodies.

"And how's the job, darling?"

"Fab, mum - it's really interesting at the moment. Jim Fenton's given me this fantastic chance to have a go at a new client - well, they're not clients yet, but they soon will be when they see my proposals for their new campaign. You've heard of Ashby Foods haven't you? - Well, everybody has, they're all over the telly at the moment - well, they're really pissed off - sorry mum! - they're really fed up with their present agents - they've spent Millions, but they haven't increased their turnover by a bean, in fact it's gone way down - the people they're with, TP I think, just haven't got the image right – so, they're looking for a new agency. If I can get their account for HWF I'm bound to get promoted! And Lyall's a real sweetie, he's helping me put the proposal together."

"Isn't that a little strange, dear? - I mean he works for another agency, doesn't he?"

She could almost see her daughter's disdainful shrug at her ignorance of the advertising industry. "Yes, but FB don't touch *food* products, mum. They're all high tech - you know, computers and mobile phones and TVs, that sort of thing. They don't know anything about food," she giggled, "except to eat it, of course - they know how to do that all right!" She went on to change the subject without the slightest pause. "How's the house hunting, mum?"

"I've hardly had time," said Caine. She had been thinking about Lime Tree Cottage ever since she had driven away from Birch Medley, but she did not want to let the thing get out of proportion. The place was ideal for her, but it was expensive, and she had only looked at it once. But an opinion from her daughter would not do any harm. "I did see somewhere this evening…"

"And you liked it, I can tell from your voice! Where is it? What's it like?"

"Hey! Slow down! I've only seen it once - and it's expensive," said Caine. "I'll tell you what, you can have a look at it on Saturday."

Alison was hesitant. "I don't know, mum - sorry - but I don't think I'll be able to manage it. Lyall and I have to get away early on Saturday morning! Tell you what, I'll try and get down again next weekend without Lyall. Just for the day. How's that?"

"If you could, darling! I would like your opinion."

Alison sighed. "I know, it's rotten of me, but Lyall and me have to get back for an Advertising Art Exhibition in the afternoon and then there's this dinner party in the evening - influential people, you know. But I can't wait to see the new house," She changed tack. "Look, I've got to go now - I'm working on that proposal. See you Friday evening - I'll ring you when I'm on the train and tell you what time it gets into Chelmsford. Love you!" She hung up.

Caine smiled to herself and put the telephone receiver back on its rest. The microwave oven had 'pinged' while she was talking to Alison and she opened it to retrieve her ready-meal - some sort of Indian dish, consisting mainly of chicken with curry - and carried it into the small lounge. She squatted down in one of the armchairs with the plate on her knees and switched on the television set. The news was still on and she watched it while she ate, her mind only half on the various items that flashed across the screen, the other half thinking through the events of her day and what tomorrow might bring. She was pleased with her progress with Mark Dolby. She had had her doubts, quite naturally, he had been an unknown quantity and she had been worried that he wouldn't take very easily to working with a woman. Some men couldn't, especially in The Force which, in spite of the progress made in the last two or three decades, was still so male dominated. But it looked as though it was going to work out all right with Mark. As for solving the Southam case - well, they really hadn't enough to go on yet, but Dolby's sifting through Valerie Southam's papers had been very useful. She wished she could say the same for the work she and Wendy Doyle had done during the afternoon - there really hadn't been much amongst those other papers and photographs and, at times, she had felt as though they were wasting valuable time.

There was something on the television now about a scientific expedition to Indonesia and she turned up the sound. A group of young scientists - zoologists, geologists and botanists - were boarding a plane at Heathrow bound for Singapore and Jakarta intent on discovering new minerals and plants in the Pacific archipelago. Caine smiled. That, she supposed, was another form of detective work.

CHAPTER THIRTEEN

"It's not right," grumbled Jason Garvey, "getting an innocent bloke up at six o'bleedin' clock in the morning to give 'im the third soddin' degree! And listen, mate, you can use all the police brutality you bleedin' like, but I'm not saying nothing until I've 'ad me early morning cup of tea." He sat down heavily, barely interrupting his tirade and shivered slightly. The air was cold and damp in the large, grim interview room so placed within the building that it never got any direct sunlight. "And another thing, Mr Copper, it's effin'' freezing in 'ere! The service in this nick is non-bleedin' existent, you'll never get your Michelin ratings up 'til you pull out your soddin' fingers and start thinking about your poor bleedin' customers!" In spite of his easy turn of phrase he looked only half awake. His eyes, which seemed to have been dropped at random on either side of his huge hooked and be-ringed nose, were deeply hooded. Dolby suspected he was not long off a drugs trip. Garvey yawned, leaned back in his chair and crossed his arms and legs, staring defiantly across the interview table at the Detective Sergeant.

Dolby chuckled inwardly. Villains like Garvey possessed an irrepressible sense of the ridiculous. They used it to bolster their confidence in times of stress and he had no doubt that, at this moment, Garvey was stressed. Very stressed indeed. He had been kept in the cells overnight and DC Milligan had given him something to think about the night before by implying that he wasn't being held only on a breaking and entering charge, but for something far more sinister. An offence quite outside Garvey's usual form; but he had not told him what. Dolby nodded at Milligan, who stood just inside the door of the room. "OK, Dave, we may as well humour our guest. It's not a bad idea to order up some tea and biscuits, is it?" He returned his gaze to Garvey. "You're used to being waited on I suppose. Karen gets up at six in the morning to make your tea for you, otherwise you give her a good beating. Is that the way of things, Jason? Oh - and before you answer you can cut out all the effing language or before you know it you'll be effing your mouth off in front of the Magistrates this morning - it's not going to help your case any to sound like an effing villain as well as look like one! Just a word of advice."

Garvey's face reddened, but the thought of tea seemed to mollify him. "Sorry, Guv'nor!"

"Anyway, for your information, Mr Garvey, it's not six o'clock - it's seven thirty and if you think I enjoy being here talking to you at this time in the morning you've got another think coming!"

"Well, how am I supposed to know what the f…bleeding time is when your lot took my bleeding watch away?" whined Garvey. "What was I gonna do? 'Ang meself on the strap? And I didn't ask you to come 'ere did I? Anyway, who are you? I 'aven't seen you before 'ave I?"

"No, I suppose they usually entertain you down at the Rainham nick," said Dolby. "You probably know them all by their first names by now. Well, for your information I'm Detective Sergeant Dolby and I'm with the Fen Molesey CID. You've already had the pleasure of meeting my colleague, Detective Constable Milligan. Now let's get on with it." He leaned across and switched on the recording equipment, repeating the details of his identity into the microphone and adding Garvey's name and the date and time of the interview. "Now, Jason - I can call you Jason can't I? - you're going to tell me what you know about Valerie and Bruce Southam, aren't you?"

"Who?" In spite of his feigned puzzlement Garvey was wide awake immediately.   "Don't tell me you don't know them, Jason. You and your girlfriend, Karen, came down here to Fen Molesey to see them a week or so ago."

"No, we never. We've never been to their 'ouse. Who told you that?"

"Never you mind, Jason. Case the joint did you? Saw something you couldn't keep your thieving little hands off."

"No I didn't - there weren't nothing there.." Garvey said indignantly, stopping in mid-sentence, as he realized what he had said. He scowled. "Well, there was nothing worth pinching anyway. Living in an 'ouse like that you'd think they'd 'ave some decent gear, wouldn't you, but oh no!" He shrugged. "I've never seen a bigger load of crap. Anyway, so what if I was there? I didn't take nothing."

"I'd just like you to tell me what went on when you met Mr and Mrs Southam."

"Why? What am I supposed to 'ave done?"

"Oh, come on, Jason," said Dolby, "I think you already know that." There was a knock on the door. "Ah, here's the tea." He waited while the tray bearing the tea and biscuits was laid on the table between them. "Chocolate digestives - how many Michelin points do they rate, Jason?"

Garvey ignored the flippant question and scratched the side of his large nose, working around the big brass ring that made him resemble a bleary-eyed bull. He turned his head to look at the recording equipment fixed to the wall at the side of the table. "I dunno what you're talking about. Anyway, I don't know nothing about the geezer - Mr Southam or whatever you'd like to call him - I only met 'is wife. Turns out she's Karen's mum. We went there because, by rights, she ought to be interested in 'er daughter and grandkids. Anyone who says different don't know the meaning of the word 'family'."

"Oh, please," said Dolby with mock weariness, "it's too early in the day for social philosophy, though I must say that's pretty rich coming from someone who's not married to the mother of his two kids." He had done his homework and felt confident he knew almost as much about the man sitting opposite him as did Garvey himself.

"We're still family even if we ain't married," retorted Garvey. "Anyway, what's all this about? Ten minutes ago your mate over there was trying to pin a thieving rap on me, now you're asking me about Karen's mother. What's she got to do with it?"

"I'm asking the questions here, Jason, you're answering them. So, what did you say to Mrs. Southam when you and Karen met her?"

Garvey reached across the table for his cup of tea, ladling three spoons of sugar into it and stirring the steaming brown liquid slowly. He reached across and took a biscuit, breaking it in two before placing one of the pieces into his mouth and chewing reflectively. He put the cup down and stroked the stubble on his chin. "Nothing much, I don't suppose. Can't really remember what I said to tell the truth." He scratched the side of his nose with a dirty fingernail.

"You don't really expect me to believe that, do you, Jason?" asked Dolby. "You took the trouble to travel all the way from your place in Rainham to the Southam's place here in Fen Molesey to ask your partner's long-lost mother for money and now you're telling me you forget what you said to her. Come on, Jason, pull the other one."

Jason Garvey took another gulp of tea and chewed on another biscuit. Then he wiped his mouth with the back of his hand and resumed his nose scratching. "Well, I suppose we talked a bit about 'ow tight things are - told 'er we were short of the readies you know and 'ow 'ard it is for the kids." He interrupted his nose scratch to pick up his teacup again. "And we asked 'er if she could 'elp out like, you know for the kiddies' sake." He stared defiantly at Dolby, rolled his eyes across the room to implore Milligan's sympathy. "She's the grandma - she's entitled to 'elp out, ain't she. There's nothing wrong in asking for 'er 'elp is there? It ain't against the law!"

"No, but threatening her unless she pays up - now that *is* against the law," said Dolby. "That's extortion."

Garvey's eyes narrowed and he took a large gulp of his tea, choking slightly as the hot liquid went down. "I didn't threaten 'er. I didn't do nothing like that! I wouldn't!"

"That's not what your file says," Dolby pointed out, tapping the buff folder that lay on the table. He opened it and flicked through the printouts. "According to this you're not the least bit impartial to a spot of gbh."

"It ain't true! You ask my Karen," he said this with the assurance that his live-in cook, skivvy and mother of his children would not dare utter a word in contradiction. "She knows what I said, she was there!" His eyes narrowed. "Who told you anyway? I bet it was that bitch, Karen's mother - I can see 'er little game. Get the police to cart me and Karen off and she won't have to do nothing to 'elp 'er poor little grand kids. That's what she's up to! Getting us put away!"

"Hardly," said Dolby. "If she went down that route she might have ended up getting landed with the kids on a permanent basis."

"Anyway, she's lying!"

"Yes, you're right there, Jason. She is lying. In the morgue."

Garvey stared at him and rubbed his ear as if he hadn't heard properly. "What? What do you mean she's in the morgue? She ain't dead is she?" He rubbed at his chin with his hands, one of his fingers snaking up to scratch at the side of his nose again.

Dolby's laugh was filled with irony. "As if you didn't know. She was murdered last night, along with her husband." He leaned over the table, stabbing at Garvey with his index finger. "Where were you last night, Jason?"

Garvey pushed his chair back to get further away from the table. "I ain't saying a word more until my brief's 'ere. Bleedin' Ada! You drag me in 'ere on some trumped-up fievin' charges and you end up trying to pin a murder rap on me! I want my lawyer! I've got a right to a bleedin' phone call!"

Dave Milligan came across to the table. "You had your call last night, Jason and your brief hasn't turned up, has he! Obviously, he's tied up - he probably has dozens of client's like you, they must keep him too busy to fit you in."

"'e said he'd be 'ere," said Jason defiantly, taking a dirty red handkerchief from his jeans' pocket and wiping it around his neck as if he suddenly felt very hot in the cold, sunless room. "And I didn't tell 'im it was a murder rap yesterday. I didn't know did I? Anyway, I ain't saying another word until 'e gets 'ere."

Dolby stood up, stretched and yawned. "We know where you were for part of last night, Jason. We've got a lovely mug shot of you on video. So, we know you were in the area when the murders took place." He stroked his chin, "let's see, the Southam's place in Marazion Road must be - what? - five minutes away from the Braxted Estate, where you did your little bit of thieving. Probably less. So, there was nothing easier than for you to nip across to Marazion Road and do a bit of threatening while you were in the area." He leaned over the table towards Garvey. "Only, things got a bit out of hand, didn't they, Jason, you hit Valerie a bit too hard and then her old man turned up unexpectedly, found you in his house beating up his wife. It wouldn't have done to have him as a witness, so the Southams both ended up dead!" He straightened up. "So, while you're waiting for your solicitor, Jason, you'd better do a bit of thinking." He walked to the door, beckoning Milligan to follow him. "I don't know if he is involved in the Southam killings, Dave," he said to the Detective Constable in a low voice, "but we can't discount anything at this stage. See what you can get out of him about his movements before and after the robbery and see how his story and Gary Oldham's tie in together. If there's the slightest deviation between them me and DCI Caine'll want to know about it."

"Right," said Milligan. "I'll run them both through the mill this morning and let you know if anything turns up."

"Thanks, Dave." Said Dolby. "He's all yours for the time being." He turned and walked off along the corridor, checking his watch as he went.

It was just after eight o'clock when he got to his office. There was a note on his desk telling him DCI Caine had called and asked him to drop along to see her as soon as possible. He stopped in the corridor on the way and got himself a cup of coffee from the machine. Up here on the third floor they did not enjoy the luxury of popping next door to the canteen - suspects being questioned in the basement interview rooms got better service than the officers on the third floor, he reflected. He sipped at his coffee as he walked slowly along the corridor and up the stairs towards Caine's office, turning over in his mind the interview he had just concluded with Jason Garvey. He **could** be their man. He had been in the area and he and his mate Oldham had histories of violence. The boss would be interested in what he had to say about those two.

"Lovely morning, Mark," she said, smiling as he came into the office. "Draw up a chair." She lifted a file from her desk. "The initial post-mortem on the Southams has arrived - I must say the forensic and pathology boys and girls are pretty quick off the mark."

He put his plastic coffee cup on her desk and pulled over a chair. "They do the job when they have to," he agreed. "But I dare say they're not under as much pressure as the boys in the Met. A murder around these parts is pretty rare - a double is even rarer, of course - so there's a certain amount of curiosity value. What have they got for us?"

"There's not a lot we hadn't already guessed," said Caine, turning slowly through the pages of the report. "But it confirms Valerie Southam died from a blow to the head, not from an overdose."

"So, the pills and brandy were to cover up the fact she was beaten to death rather than took her own life?"

"It seems that way, Mark. But let's go through the report." She found her place on the page. "Bruce Southam - cause of death – multiple stab wounds - time, anything between 11.30 pm and 12.30 am. - give or take the usual margins" Caine laid the file on her desk. "The stabbing was obvious - but they go on to say the wound to the jugular was probably the first that was struck, implying that whoever was using the knife knew exactly what he - or she - was doing. Unless, of course, they were very lucky. It was probably a "he" because some of the other wounds, to the body, penetrated the rib cage and, in a big man like Southam, must have been delivered with a considerable amount of force. And there were more than a dozen other wounds on the body, which seems to indicate the killer either wanted to make sure of the job or went berserk."

"Perhaps a bit of both," suggested Dolby. "Unless it was pre-meditated or the bloke's a butcher, the sight of all that blood would have unbalanced him." He grimaced. "But then it would anybody. He might have reacted like that even if it was premeditated. Thinking about it beforehand isn't the same as actually doing it."

Caine nodded. "Yes, this blood thing is interesting though, isn't it. There was so much blood the killer must have got it all over him. So, he either left the house with his clothes awash with gore or he took his clothes off and stashed them somewhere in the house. But it's unlikely he went out naked, or in his underclothes, so he might have taken some clothes from Southam's wardrobe."

"We haven't found any blood-stained clothing in the house," said Dolby, "or anywhere around it. So, the killer must've taken it with him. He probably also used the shower, but there were no wet towels hanging about so he must have taken them away as well."

"Yes, too much chance of leaving his DNA" said Caine. She paused thoughtfully, turning the pages of the report. "As I said before, this confirms that Valerie died from a blow to the head, not from drugs. By the time the drugs and alcohol were in her body she was already dead. And there was no sign of sexual interference, so it wasn't a rape that went wrong."

"Any ideas on the weapon the killer used on her?"

Caine shook her head. "Nothing conclusive, Mark. Apparently, it was some sort of blunt instrument. Her skull wasn't very thick it seems, so it didn't take much of a blow. It's surprising that with all those beatings he gave her her husband didn't send her on her way years ago." She returned to the report. "There's something else here - forensics found traces of alcohol - probably brandy - on the flesh around Valerie's chin and neck, down her throat and on other parts of her body. Most of it had evaporated, of course, but there were faint residues."

"Meaning?"

"Probably, that when she was drinking the stuff she missed her mouth and slopped it all over herself."

"So, she was already drunk?"

"Either that or whoever killed her tried to force it down her throat after she was dead. Naturally, they had a hard time - she couldn't swallow it, so it came back out again!" Caine made a face. "Disgusting, but I suppose murder is disgusting whichever way you look at it!"

"So," mused Dolby, finishing his coffee and throwing the plastic cup across the room into Caine's wastepaper bin. It missed and he got up to retrieve it, dropping it into the bin from closer range. "They hit her first - with whatever weapon it was - and killed her, then they tried to make it look as though she'd taken an overdose."

"Yes, it looks that way," agreed Caine. "Hoping the bruises on her body and face caused by Bruce's beatings would mask the bruises they inflicted. But what they didn't expect was for Bruce to arrive home when he actually did. If I had to guess at it I'd say that Bruce came home unexpectedly and stumbled on the killer in the kitchen, they had a fight and the killer grabbed a knife and stabbed him to death. Then, he made it look as though Valerie and Bruce had had a fight. That's the way he set it up. You can imagine it, can't you. Bruce hits Valerie, she decides she's had enough and grabs a knife. She lashes out at him. Bingo! - One dead hubby."

"Then, full of wifely remorse," suggested Dolby, picking up the thread, "she goes upstairs and tops herself with the help of some brandy and pills. Taking good care to take the murder weapon with her and leave it generously covered with her fingerprints. The brandy glass had a nice little bit of blood on it too, of course, put there by rubbing it into the blood beside Bruce's body."

"Which would have worked very nicely, thank you, if the killer hadn't carelessly left his fingerprints all over the place," agreed Caine. "When he realised what he'd done he had to wipe everything clean. But he overdid it and there were no fingerprints left at all, not even the ones from normal use of door handles and such like. The other thing he forgot was to splash blood over Valerie's body. She was pristine clean when we found her, apart from the bruises and even if she had showered, where are the soiled towels?" She paused to read a part of the report again. "The other curious thing, Mark, is that the pills Valerie is supposed to have taken were *not* Ergotamine - the ones she was taking for her migraine, or so we thought - we'll have to check it with her doctor, of course. The forensic people haven't been able to identify the drugs they found in her body yet, but their guess is they were some other powerful pain killer. Apparently, there was no sign around the house of any bottles or containers they might have come from."

Dolby rubbed his eyes and yawned. "That is interesting. Oh, by the way, I forgot to mention it, but I had that Neale woman on the phone yesterday evening telling me that the video Valerie taped for her - *"Chicago"* the movie - was cut short. I mean, the whole film hadn't been recorded when the recorder stopped."

"Is that significant?"

"She didn't know - neither did I at the time - she just thought it was funny peculiar because it was the first time Valerie had let her down on a recording - apparently she'd done it for her before and it's been okay, no problems.   But this time the recording stopped short. Why? The thought just occurred to me - what if the reason the recording stopped was because there was a struggle in the bedroom and the button on the remote control got knocked by mistake and switched the video recorder off?"

Caine nodded slowly. "If that is what happened, Mark, it could help fix the time of Valerie's death pretty precisely, because we can check the exact time the broadcast went out. Good work." She ran her eyes over the last page of the report. "The only other points the forensic people make is that the blood on the handkerchief we found under the bed - the one with the mysterious "P" on it - was Bruce's, which comes as no surprise as his blood was everywhere. But that doesn't prove it was his handkerchief, so it might belong to the murderer. Also, they found one or two other things around the house that *don't* match up to the victims - the odd human hair, a few fingerprints in the less obvious places that our killer overlooked in his wiping efforts, that sort of thing. They may belong to Adam Southam of course. The Forensic lads and lasses need to investigate that possibility further before they can comment. There's just a chance one of the hairs or prints may belong to somebody else - somebody who had no business being in the house. In which case we might have something. We should hear further from them within the next couple of days." She closed the file. "Now, I think we need to fill each other in on yesterday afternoon's events. Did you manage to see those two girl students?"

"Yes. They confirmed that Adam and Philip Chantry were at their party," said Dolby, "but as far as the girls were concerned, they could have gone out and come back again at any time and nobody would have noticed. Certainly, they had the opportunity to go out and kill Bruce and Valerie and then get back in good time. The place is no distance away from Marazion Road. The girls say they didn't really notice what Adam and Philip Chantry were up to, which isn't surprising really, considering they had a party in full swing."

"Anything else?"

Dolby shook his head. "No but I have taken down the names of a lot of other people who were there - maybe one of them saw something. I'll get Wendy to follow them up. Incidentally, I also had a long chat with the owner of the cottage the two girls are staying in - a Miss Phyllida Ormsby, - but she really couldn't help much, although interestingly enough she knows Chantry and Adam Southam. She met Adam at the Perot's. It's interesting how that name keeps coming up isn't it? But what about Adam and Philip Chantry? I believe they came back to the house yesterday afternoon."

Caine nodded. "Yes. Adam wanted those study books he was looking for yesterday morning. I sent him off to give us a positive ID on his parents' bodies - that's confirmed, by the way, not that there was any doubt."

"What about Chantry? Did you get anything useful out of him?"

"Nothing much, except I'm convinced he's lying about not being at the Southam's on the evening of the murders. He was there all right. He's well known in the area and one of the neighbours interviewed during the door to door says she saw him cycling along Marazion Road at some time after nine o'clock. She can't be any more specific than that, but Chantry was heading towards the Southam's house, that's definite. That ties in with Adam's comment that he saw Chantry's secateurs on Chantry's kitchen table at breakfast on the morning after the murders."

"And that implies Chantry picked them up from the Southams' place on the night of the murders," agreed Dolby. "So why did he deny being at the house?"

Caine shrugged. "Perhaps he was afraid we'd pin the murders on him."

"And what do you think, Jackie? Do you think he did it?"

"Chantry and Adam do have a motive," said Caine. "With the cash young Adam is going to inherit they could easily set up their nursery business - as it happens, Chantry seems a good enough horticulturist to make a go of it, so it's not just pie in the sky. And from what you've said they may have had the opportunity to carry out the murders. And then there's the "P" handkerchief that may belong to Philip Chantry. That's persuasive. Yes, they both have motive and they both have opportunity and Adam seems peculiarly unaffected by his parents' deaths. But did he - or they - do it? I don't know. I honestly don't know. My instincts tell me 'no', their motive isn't strong enough - but I've been wrong before - sometimes..." She had been riffling idly through the pages of the postmortem report and now she closed it and pushed it to the other side of her desk. "Did you get to see Valerie Southam's long lost daughter in Rainham?"

"Yes, not that she was much use. I felt quite sorry for her, actually. She's living in a high rise out at Rainham with two tiny snot nosed kids and her boyfriend Jason, who obviously knocks her around, although she wouldn't admit it. Funny thing was, though, that while I was on my way out there to see her, DC Milligan was dragging Jason in for questioning here at FM." He explained the circumstances concerning Jason Garvey's arrest. "So, within the time frame of the murder he wasn't five minutes away from the scene of the crime. How's that for coincidence?"

"I don't believe in coincidences," said Caine. "He probably spotted the computer warehouse as he was driving past with Karen on his way to see Valerie Southam the other week and he couldn't resist going back and having a go at it. That would explain why he was so far off his normal beat, but it does not explain why he chose to do the job so close to the time Valerie and her husband were being murdered."

"Yes, he could have done it. He could have dropped in on Valerie - accompanied by his charming friend Gary Oldham - they both have records for violence, by the way - and given her a working over. Just to soften her up, maybe, get her to come across with some money. And maybe they hit her that little bit too hard."

Caine pushed her chair back and opened the window blinds again. The sun was already high and the temperature in the office was rising rapidly. She slipped the metal fastenings and pushed one of the windows open, letting in the sounds of the traffic. "If they'd beaten her up, Mark, she would have screamed blue murder or made some sort of noise. Her neighbour, what was his name? - Ford, Barry Ford - he would have heard something."

"Not necessarily," said Dolby. "He kept telling us how he was so tied up with his computer programming that he wouldn't have noticed what was going on outside."

"But he did hear the argument next door," said Caine. "And he also said he heard nothing else out of the ordinary that evening, apart from the dog barking." She turned away from the window and sat down again.

Dolby frowned. "You're assuming, of course, that Ford is a reliable witness. Me - I'm still a bit suspicious of the reason he gave as to why his wife left him. He may have been involved with Valerie Southam himself - he certainly admitted to ogling her when she was sunbathing."

"I take your point, Mark," said Caine, "but ogling a woman is a long way off murdering her - and if you think he may have tried it on with her and then got nasty when she refused him, just think what sort of a man he is. I think it's highly unlikely he'd have enough confidence with women to do that sort of thing and we have no proof whatsoever that he did."

"So where does that leave us?"

"Well, pinpointing the time of death could be very helpful - it might eliminate somebody - hell, we're over run with suspects at the moment - so I think you should follow up that lead on the DVD recording. Get the disc back from Susie Neale and take it from there. Apart from that we've got the blackmail possibility with Valerie - three in fact! - let's see if we can take that any further."

"What about Bruce Southam's work colleagues? It's quite possible they may know something about him that could lead us a bit further along the road. Whoever it was killed them didn't force an entry, so the Southams knew them. It could have been somebody from work - Bruce probably had as many enemies there as he seems to have had everywhere else."

Caine tapped her fingers impatiently on the edge of her desk. "Yes, we really do need to find out what made that man tick, Mark. Valerie's also a bit of a puzzle. Sad upbringing, disreputable youth and then marries well to a man who has his foot in the door with one of the most influential families in the area. I wonder how she managed that?"

"Well, I wouldn't say it's that unusual for an exotic dancer to marry well - if you can call it that," said Dolby. "A lot of the aristocracy used to marry 'actresses' as they called themselves."

"Bruce Southam wasn't aristocracy, but he was well connected, particularly with the Perot family. If, that is, the Perots are what they've been painted."

"They are," said Dolby. "They're certainly in with the County lot and they own land that must be worth a pretty tidy sum."

"And they seem to have our Super, Eddy Hansen, dancing to their tune as well. You know, he told me to watch what I said to the Press in case it upsets the Perots!"

"What? The Super?" Dolby shrugged as if Caine's revelation was no surprise. "I dare say he belongs to the same golf club as Paul Perot!" He looked at his watch. "I suppose we ought to set up a meeting with Perot - find out a bit more about his relationship with the Southams."

"Yes, I'd particularly like to know how Bruce's demise is going to affect the Perot business. By all accounts he was one of their key men. Insurance isn't it?"

Dolby nodded. "They run a big brokerage plus they're into financial planning in a big way. Rumour has it they were hit very hard by the Lloyds debacle a few years back and, of course, by the financial crash of 2008, but I couldn't say how badly. We've not had to run any checks on them before and even now I'm not sure it's necessary."

"Let's go at it gently then. At the moment there's no real connection between Bruce Southam's place of work and the two murders - and the way the Super was rushing to Perot's protection I don't want to tread on any toes unless I have to. We'll speak to Paul Perot though. And, yes, let's interview the people Southam worked with. You don't happen to know where their offices are do you?" Dolby was about to answer when the telephone rang. Caine picked up the receiver. "DCI Caine." She listened for a moment. "He's quite sure about that? She didn't tell him where she was going?" She paused and listened again. "Right, tell him to go back to his house in case she turns up. DS Dolby and I will be straight over - we'll see him there." She replaced the receiver and reached under her desk for her handbag. "That was PC Doyle," she told Dolby. "She's over at the Southam house, still going through all those papers." She pushed back her chair and stood up. "Apparently, Susie Neale's husband has just turned up - he claims Susie went out last night and he hasn't seen her since."

CHAPTER FOURTEEN

Norman Neale was a short man, grey haired and, Caine judged, a good many years older than his wife. By the look of him he had spent most of the previous night pacing the rooms of his house, waiting anxiously for his wife to return home. He met them at the porch with the Bach fugue from the doorbell still ringing in their ears, flinging the door open angrily. "It's about time! Where have you been? It must be a good half hour since I spoke to that young policewoman and told her about my wife." His face was drawn; his eyes bloodshot and he had not shaved that morning. His chin and short neck were black with stubble, his check sports shirt open at the collar, his tan trousers unpressed and baggy as if he had either spent the night in them or dressed hurriedly during the few minutes before they arrived.

"We got here as quickly as we could," said Caine. It had only been twenty minutes, but she could see the man was distraught and she did not want to argue with him. They had taken longer than they should, for the traffic in town had been heavy and they had traveled in Dolby's own car, blue lights switched off.

"Well, you'd better come in, I suppose, now you're here" said Neale. His accent was full blooded East End of London. He led them through into the bright and well-furnished lounge. They were only just through the door when Neale turned on them suddenly, causing Caine, who was immediately behind him, to step back. "I'm sure this is all to do with those bloody people being murdered," he said. "I told her not to get involved with that woman!"

"I think you should calm down, sir!" said Caine. "Just sit down and tell us what the situation is."

Instead, Neale nodded at the three-seater settee, indicating that they should sit down and made his way over to the cocktail cabinet where he proceeded to pour a large whisky into a heavy cut glass tumbler. "I won't offer you anything." he said with an attempt at playing the attentive host. "I know you're on duty," He came back to sit opposite them in one of the single armchairs.

"Perhaps you'd like to tell us what has happened," suggested Dolby.

Neale frowned and took a heavy swig from the glass, closing his eyes as the amber liquid poured down his throat. "I don't **know** what's happened, do I? That's why I've sent for you. You're the police aren't you? I just want you to find my wife!"

"I'm sure she'll be back with you safe and sound at any moment," said Caine, although she was not at all sure she believed her own words. She had told Dolby only that morning that she did not believe in coincidences and she did not. There was almost certainly more than coincidence in the fact that Susie Neale had disappeared so soon after her friend and neighbour had been murdered.

"It's easy for you to say that" Neale was saying, "but how do you know she'll be back safe and sound? You don't know my Susie - she's not the sort of woman who stays out overnight." He took another slug of the whisky and stared belligerently across at the two police officers. "It's all your doing - what with all the police activity around here! Why aren't you doing something useful right now - why aren't you out there looking for her?"

"For a start, because she's an adult woman and she's been missing for less than twenty-four hours" said Caine, frostily. Neale's comment on the recent police activity left her stunned. What did he expect them to do when a double murder had been carried out just a few houses up the street - one of them sadistically and brutally perpetrated - stay away from the area? Not carry out an investigation? She could understand Neale's concern for his wife's safety, but she still thought there might be an everyday, harmless explanation as to why Susie Neale had not returned home the previous night. "It's quite possible, Mr Neale, that she went somewhere last night - to a friend or something - and stayed overnight. She may have forgotten to tell you where she was going, or she may have told you and you've forgotten."

"That's a nice thing to say I'm sure!" He gulped down the last of the whisky and then stared down at the carpet for a few seconds before running his hands through his thinning grey hair and looking across the room at them. His eyes were pained. "I'm sorry! It's getting to me. Me and Susie haven't been apart for years. I just don't know what to do!"

"If you'd like to tell us about it," suggested Dolby again, "Just tell us what happened - when you last saw her - what she said - anything that might help - then leave it to us."

Neale got up and went back to the cocktail cabinet to replenish his glass before he spoke again, moving slowly now, his brow furrowed with thought. "Okay, I was home yesterday afternoon at about four thirty on account of the fact that I had an evening appointment, so I thought I'd leave the office a bit early. I often do that in my work."

"Which is?" asked Caine. Dolby had mentioned it in the report of his interview with Mrs Neale, but she wanted confirmation.

"I run a double glazing and fitted kitchen company. I've got a couple of fellow directors and we employ quite a few staff now. But the work's like that, some of it's in the evening, though I don't normally do evenings anymore - only when it's really necessary. Anyway, there was the chance of a big job coming up, a very big house out in Dunmow, all the windows and a conservatory on the back. I couldn't get them to go to a kitchen as well, but the estimate for the windows and conservatory came to more than forty thousand quid and they signed the contract yesterday evening." He smiled for the first time during their interview, enjoying the memory. "Anyway, I had to be out there at the punter's place in Dunmow by seven thirty, so we ate early, with the kids, at about half past five and then I set off at a quarter to seven. Susie, my wife, was here when I left, but when I got back there was no sign of her."

"How old are your children, Mr Neale?" asked Caine.

He thought for a moment as if trying to remember. "Hilary's fourteen and Jennifer's twelve. They're both at Upton Grange." The most expensive private school in the area. Neale did not want them to give them the impression he was not a successful man.

"Did they see their mother go out?"

"No, but they weren't here, you see. They've got friends not far away, school friends in Truro Crescent," he waved his arm in the vague direction of somewhere outside as if indicating the exact location. "Their friends are sisters, like Hilly and Jenny - they're about the same ages - so they went over there. They go there quite often and the other kids come here as well. Anyway, I dropped them off on my way out to Dunmow and their friend's dad, Mr Turnbull I think his name is, he brought them back safe and sound at about nine thirty."

"And Susie - Mrs Neale - wasn't here when they got back?" Dolby was making notes.

"No. She must have gone out after us. Her car's not there. She must have taken it."

"Did any of the neighbours see her go?" asked Caine.

"I don't think so. To tell the truth, I don't really know." He took another slug of his whisky. "It's not the sort of thing you ask the neighbours is it - have you seen my wife? Did you see her leaving last night? It doesn't sound right, does it? It'll only set their tongues wagging."

"But did she say anything to you about going out, Mr Neale?" asked Dolby. "She didn't mention she was going over to a friend or anything?"

Neale shook his head. "No. Susie doesn't go out much in the evenings. Well, normally speaking I'm at home you see - it's only when something really special comes up, like that order last night that I go out. Usually, we spend the evenings together, especially now that the girls are getting a bit older. Of course, we do go out together quite a lot, but Susie hardly ever goes by herself." He shrugged. "I don't stop her, of course - not like that Southam bloke used to stop his wife - kept her on a very short length of rope he did, or so Susie tells me - but my Susie, she doesn't need to go out of an evening, does she, if she wants to go out she can go out during the day, can't she!"

"And she didn't leave a note? Any indication as to where she was going?"

He shook his head. "Nothing. She's got a mobile so I tried ringing that, but all I get is the message that it's switched off." He put down the whisky glass and cradled his head in his hands. "I don't know what to do next."

"Did she take anything with her? Clothes, a suitcase? Anything to indicate that she was expecting to be away for a few days?" asked Caine.

Neale shook his head again. "I have checked, but there's nothing missing so far as I can see. Her handbag, that's all. She didn't take any extra clothes or anything, not even her overnight vanity case she uses when we go for weekends away."

"What was she wearing?" asked Dolby.

"Oh - I don't know - I'm not much good at these things. You don't notice do you, not unless you have to."

"Men don't," said Caine. "Your daughters will have. I shouldn't be surprised if they can tell us exactly what she was wearing. Always assuming she didn't change before she went out. You say nobody saw her leave?"

"I don't think so," said Neale. He stood up and walked across the room to stare through the window.

"Has anything unusual happened between you during the last few days?"

He turned to face them again. "Between us…What's that supposed to mean?"

"I'm sorry, but we have to ask these questions," said Caine. "We're just trying to jog your memory. I don't necessarily mean anything personal between you - she may have said something that has some bearing on where she's gone. Her parents, for instance, could she have gone to see them?"

"She doesn't have any parents. They died a good few years ago. And to save you asking, she don't have any family either - apart from me and the kids - she was an only child. Like me. We don't have any family, so she can't be with them.

Besides, if she was I'd have had a phone call by now telling me she's safe. But there's been nothing."

"And she wouldn't be with friends?" asked Dolby.

Neale shook his head yet again. "I've already phoned round anyone she might have been with, but nobody's seen her."

"What about new friends?"

He hesitated. "She didn't make new friends without me knowing about it. She would have..." he stopped in mid-sentence and rubbed at the stubble on his chin. "No, she hasn't mentioned any new friends, but now I come to think of it she did mention something about bumping into someone she hadn't seen for years. An acquaintance or a friend or something."

"When was this?" said Caine.

"Two or three months ago. I don't know, maybe more."

"And...?"

"That's it. That's all she said. She didn't mention any names or anything - at least I don't think so."

"Not even if it was an old girl friend or an old man friend?"

He grimaced. "It wouldn't be a man would it - she wasn't like that." He thought for a moment and then shrugged. "Well, I suppose it might have been. I can't honestly remember now. I must have been doing something at the time - I think I was working on a complicated quotation for some windows, or something." His face flushed as though he had been caught out doing something he shouldn't. "To be honest, I don't think I was really listening - I thought it might have been something to do with that Southam woman and I don't suppose I was interested."

"So, we don't have much to work on," said Caine. "What about the children? Would she have talked to them about it? By the way, where are they?"

"They're at school," said Neale gruffly. "I thought it best. Couldn't have them sitting around the house and worrying like me. I got one of the other mothers to take them." He sighed. "But I don't suppose they know anything. I asked them if their mother said anything to them about going out last night and they said 'no'. I could see they were upset, so I pretended she must have told me where she was going, but I'd forgotten." He shrugged. "There wasn't much else I could do, was there? I didn't want them worrying."

"No, you're right. We might want to speak to them later," said Caine. "In the meantime, if anything occurs to you let us know." She nodded to Dolby and they stood up.

"So, what are you going to do to find Susie?" said Neale anxiously. "Are you going to make up a search party?"

Caine shook her head. "No - it's too early for that sort of thing, Mr Neale. We'll make a few inquiries in the area, but it's really only been a few hours and I honestly think she'll be home before the end of the day. These things do happen, you know, your wife is an intelligent adult, free to come and go as she pleases. She probably just forgot to tell you where she was going. Try not to worry."

He grimaced. "Easier said than done! But I hope you're right and she turns up soon. Frankly, I don't believe she will." He turned away to look out of the window again and then burst out "My Christ, Inspector! Two people were murdered in cold blood just down the road, less than forty-eight hours ago and one of them was a friend of my wife's! And you're telling me she's all right. I just don't believe it!"

"It's no use thinking like that, sir," said Dolby. "It doesn't do any good. We all hope she'll turn up safe and sound during the next few hours."

"Before we go, Mr Neale," said Caine "I wonder if you could help us - your wife had a DVD being recorded by Valerie Southam on the night of the murders. I believe it was of the film *"Chicago"*. It was in Valerie's machine when she was found, but apparently she was recording it for your wife. It was returned to Mrs Neale, but we do need to have another look at it. Have you any idea where it might be?"

Neale flushed with indignation. "Isn't this a bit ridiculous?" he said bitterly. "My poor wife is out there, perhaps dead or kidnapped or something and all *you're* interested in a DVD disc!" He stopped, breathed heavily and turned away. "All right," he said, a little calmer, "I suppose you must have a good reason for wanting it. I'll see if it's over there with the others." He strode across the room to the television set under which was a satellite control box and a blueray player. There were a number of discs lying on top of the recorder and he looked through them, reading the labels. "This must be it," he said, picking one of them up and bringing it over to them. He handed it to Dolby. "I hope it helps! Now, for God's sake get out there and do something to find my wife!"

Back in the car Dolby drummed his fingers on the steering wheel. "What do we do, Jackie? Do we take Susie's disappearance seriously?"

Caine made a gesture of helplessness. "It's too early to know, isn't it! Her vanishing at this point in time may be connected with the Southam murders...but on the other hand it may not - she might simply have decided to leave her husband."

"She's picked a good time for it," grunted Dolby. "Right in the middle of an investigation into her friend's murder. It might seem suspicious to some." He sighed. "But I agree, it's too early to do anything constructive."

"I'll get Wendy to pop in later on, when the two daughters are home and see if she can get a description of what she was wearing," said Caine "always assuming she hasn't turned up by then."

"Right. What now? Do we go see the Perots?"

Caine shook her head. "While we're here we might as well go back into the house and see if we can find out anything else about the Southam's background. We've a lot to fill in in that direction and I think Wendy could do with a bit of help ploughing her way through all that paper. We may be wasting our time, but I want to know where that cash in Valerie's building society account was coming from."

"Right." Dolby opened the car door. "It might be an idea, though, to phone Paul Perot and make an appointment. I gather he's a busy man. I'll set that up if you like."

"Fine. Do it. And, Mark, we also need to have a chat with the people in Bruce Southam's place of work - they'll know him better than most I should think. Ask Perot for the details when you speak to him and set something up with them."

CHAPTER FIFTEEN

At just after seven o'clock the following morning Caine took a telephone call from Detective Sergeant Dolby. Mrs Neale had not returned home the previous day and was still missing when he rang the Neale home a few minutes earlier.

"Mr Neale is distraught, and it sounded like the two daughters were in tears. We're going to have to do something, Jackie."

Caine thought for a moment. She looked across at the kitchen clock. "As you know, I'm due to see Paul Perot at half past eight; I may be able to get across to the Neale's place before then."

"No, you won't have enough time. If you go you can't just walk out again at your own convenience. You're the big cheese in the case so far as Norman Neale is concerned and he'll want your undivided attention. I've already organised it for Wendy to go over straight away and I'm not due at the Perot Offices in the City until eleven o'clock, so how about if I pop across in a few minutes and report back to you. I'll make your apologies."

"As long as we're seen to be doing something." Her voice dropped. "I don't like it, Mark - It's thirty-six hours now. I'm worried about Mrs Neale. I can't help feeling there's got to be a connection with the Southam murders."

"You and me both, boss. I'll speak to you later."

Caine drove as slowly along the B1022 towards Upton Stapleford as the fast moving traffic would allow, looking out for the signpost to Upton Stapleford House and the lane which Mark Dolby had informed her would bring her on to the Perot Estate. He had warned her there was a sharp bend in the road only about fifty yards before the turn off and she came upon the sign suddenly, a rather ancient board announcing "Upton Stapleford Gardens" and bearing the emblem of a '*garden of special merit*', awarded by the Royal Horticultural Society. She slowed and indicated a right turn, waiting patiently while the stream of traffic traveling in the opposite direction rushed by. She checked the time on her dashboard clock. It was just after half past seven, leaving just half an hour before her appointment with Paul Perot. He had taken a rather aggressive attitude and insisted on an early meeting, claiming he had an important business meeting in Chelmsford at nine, and there was no way he was going to postpone it, even if the police did wish to discuss the murder of one of his employees. So, their meeting would have to be eight o'clock, take it or leave it. Dolby, who had made the telephone call, had supposed he could have been bloody minded and insisted on a later meeting, but he had seen no point in antagonizing the man. Caine, for her part, had made a mental note to take no nonsense from Perot during the interview, neither would she arrive early for the appointment - he would no doubt keep her waiting if she did. Besides, she had decided to leave home early to give herself a little time to look around the gardens, about which Mark Dolby had been very enthusiastic. They were, apparently, a popular local attraction and she would enjoy a few minutes peace to start the day.

Upton Stapleford Gardens, Dolby had informed her from his vast store of local knowledge, had been set up by Paul Perot's father, Charles, in the mid nineteen eighties, a short while after he had bought the property. In those days there had been a thriving industrial plant, High Point Quarry, on the site. Situated on high land in the South East corner of the Estate it had overlooked the Blackwater estuary and the neighbouring town of Malden. Anglia Aggregates, the company established in the nineteen twenties to exploit the mineral wealth of the site, had also been bought up by Charles Perot as a part of the deal for the land and, according to Dolby, the company had since brought in a fortune for the Perot family. To compensate for the dereliction of the land caused by the gravel quarrying Charles, a keen gardener, had set out to create a model garden which he had opened to the public. Now, after more than forty years, the gardens were mature and the trees planted in Charles' early years rose majestically on either side of the wide, now frequently pot-holed drive. The gates leading on to the land, standing between twin notices stating that this was a 'Private Estate' and that there were no public rights of way except by permission of the landowner, were wide open and looked as if they had not been used to keep people out for years. Set back from the road and almost hidden by a massive chestnut tree that loomed over the structure, was an old stone lodge house and as Caine swept in past the gate she saw a thin spire of dense black smoke rising up from a large bonfire set in a corner of the garden. A short wiry, red haired man stood beside it, feeding twigs and clumps of tree foliage into the flames. He looked up as she drove into the lane and came lumbering towards her, carrying a long-handled woodsman's axe. He was frowning.

"G'Morning!" he said gruffly, as he reached the small wooden gate and came through into the lane, the axe dangling at the end of an arm that was so long for his short body that the blade brushed against the ground. He was probably in his late fifties Caine judged from his weather-beaten face. "And what might you be doing here at this time of the morning?" He asked.

Caine stopped the car and spoke through the open window. "Police," she said, releasing her seat belt so she could delve into her pocket for her warrant card. She held it up. "Detective Chief Inspector Jacqueline Caine, Fen Molesey CID. I have an appointment to see Mr Paul Perot."

"Oh, right," he nodded, seeming almost disgruntled that she was a legitimate visitor and that he would have to let her pass. "Bit early aren't you?"

As he spoke a middle-aged woman appeared around the side of the lodge house and came towards them. Her greying hair was coiled into a tight bun on the top of her head and the flowery apron tied with a white cord about her middle emphasised her portliness. She carried an empty washing basket. "Morning!" She peered at Jacqueline Caine through a pair of dark tortoiseshell glasses at least twenty years out of fashion. "You must be the Police Lady Mr Paul's expecting. Bit early, aren't you?"

"Detective Chief Inspector Caine." Said Caine again, waving her warrant card. "Yes, I am a little early, but I thought I'd take a look at the gardens while I'm here. I take it there's no objection to that?"

"You're not expected until eight o'clock," said the woman, "so you can look all you want. The gardens are open at this time of year, although if you ask me they're at their best in the Spring or Autumn."

"How often are they open to the public?"

"Thursdays through to Saturdays during the Summer," said Mrs Thompson.

Her husband grunted. "You don't mean Summer, woman! We opens in March - that's the Spring that is - and we closes in September, that's the Autumn so far as I'm concerned! Though it's a mystery to me why Mr Perot don't put his foot down and close it altogether!" He grunted his disapproval and, seeming to lose interest in the visitor, moved back into the garden of the lodge house to tend his bonfire.

"Why should the Perot's close the Gardens?" asked Caine. "I had the impression it was quite an attraction to local people."

"It is," agreed Mrs Thompson. "But it's devilish expensive to keep going - why there's all the new plants that go in each season and the trees to be looked after and all that grass to be kept short. You know, they have to use a gardening company from Chelmsford to keep proper track of it, my Jake can't do everything, what with all the other things that need doing around the estate."

"Couldn't they charge a little more to the public, for entrance? I'm sure I wouldn't mind paying a few pounds to go in, provided the gardens were well maintained and they seem to have a good reputation."

Mrs Thompson laughed. "They don't charge nothing to the public. Not a bean. When old Mr Charles started out making the garden he said he'd never make a charge to the public and he's stuck by his word all these years. But now things are different and Mr Paul, his son whose taking over the business, he won't put up with that much longer. Between you and me, I don't think he can afford it now what with all the money they lost when the banks and that went."

"They were hit by the economic downturn?"

"I don't know about that, but they did have a lot of trouble a couple of years back and Jake said something about the banks - I don't understand it myself, but I do know they've been strapped for cash for a few years now."

Caine nodded towards the lodge house. "Do you live here?"

"Yeah - me and Jake are what you might call old retainers for Mr Perot. Been with him here on the estate for more than thirty years now we have." The woman put the plastic clothes basket down on the floor and moved forward, extending her hand. "I'm Bernice Thompson and that's Jake, my husband."

Caine reached through the window and squeezed her hand. "So, you know the Perot family very well."

"What? There ain't a blessed thing we don't know about the Perots," said the woman.

Caine nodded thoughtfully. A few minutes talking to Mrs Thompson might throw up some useful information. She switched off the car engine and climbed out. "Perhaps you can tell me a little about the estate, Mrs Thompson."

"Depends on what you want to know." She looked suddenly evasive. "I am a busy woman you know and I'm right in the middle of my washing."

"I suppose you and your husband must get through quite a bit of clothing," said Caine. "Considering the sort of work you do."

"You don't know the half of it," said Mrs Thompson. "It's not just for me and Jake that I does the washing for neither - there's the whole family."

"You mean you wash for the whole of the Perot family?"

"Oh yes - there's nine of us if you count that Hendry woman," said Mrs Thompson "not that she's family mind you..."

"Who is she then?"

"The young nurse that looks after old Mr Charles. He's a sick man that's for sure, but I don't know why I have to fetch and carry for **her**!" She stuck out her lower lip aggressively. "But of course, she's got Mr Paul right where she wants him **and** he insists I treat her like everybody else on the estate. Jumped up little Madam, she is, no better than she should be, but Mr Paul favours her above all of us, including his own missus." She paused reflectively. "Not that it's difficult to see why when you look at her - he always has had an eye for the pretty ones has Mr Paul!"

Jake Thompson, who had obviously been following their conversation, called irritably across to his wife, "Stop gossiping, woman. The Inspector don't want to hear none of your gossip."

"On the contrary, Mrs Thompson, I find it all very interesting," Caine assured her. "So, there are nine people living on the estate?"

Mrs Thompson shot a look of triumph in the direction of her husband and answered Caine with alacrity. "That's right, there's Mr Paul and his missus, Mrs Jessica, they live in the big house now. Mr Charles and Mrs Perot, Paul's parents, they moved out into one of the bungaloes a couple of years ago, on account of Mr Charles being on the poorly side and not being able to climb the stairs any longer." She nodded, going through a mental roll call of the inhabitants of the Perot estate, almost ticking them off on her fingers. "Then, of course, there's Mr and Mrs Parr - she's Mr Charles's daughter - they're in Beacon Cottage, the first place you come to on the drive. And last who should be least, but isn't, if you get my meaning, there's the

Hendry creature, that gets all the privileges - not that I envy her the task of looking after Mr Charles. He's had a stroke, the poor dear and he's got a bit of that Alzheimer's. Going downhill quite rapid he is too, I'm afraid, and Mrs Florence, his wife, she can't cope anymore, so I suppose he needs a nurse nowadays. And of course, that Hendry woman also does a bit for Mrs Parr."

"She's sick too, then?"

"In a wheelchair she is. Paralysed on account of a riding accident a good few year ago now. I suppose having Hendry there is a help to her husband, poor Mr Jamie. Credit where it's due, though, he does most of the fetching and carrying for his missus, being as how she can't manage very much herself. There ain't many who would've stuck by her like he has." She leaned forward, dropping her voice almost to a whisper. "Well, it's not a proper marriage really, is it? What with her being paralysed from the waist down - can't be can it?"

"It must help, though, you doing the washing for everybody," said Caine, "and I suppose you do other things."

"Oh yes, me and Jake accounts for most of the daily chores around here, what with Miss Ursula being disabled and Mr Charles's wife, Florence, being very elderly now. The only one of 'em that's capable nowadays, of course, is Mr Paul's Missus, Jessica, but you won't get no work out of her. Much too la-di-da she is, and too busy rushing around the countryside making a name for herself in the bridge fraternity! County Champion she was a couple of years ago, though it beats me as to how anyone can spend hours and hours every day of their lives playing about with a handful of cards."

Caine looked towards the bonfire. The smoke was getting a little less black now. "Rather early for a fire isn't it?"

Mrs Thompson shrugged. "Don't matter much around here do it. Our nearest neighbours are Mr and Mrs Parr and they're nigh on a quarter mile away!"

"I was just wondering what you've been burning," said Caine. "When I came along the smoke was really thick and black."

"Oh, that'll be the old clothes Mr Paul left for us to get rid of," said Mrs Thompson. "That's where the dark smoke'll be coming from." She turned and walked back towards the house. "Sorry, but I've got to get on, that washing won't get itself done!"

"Right," Caine said to her receding figure. "I think I'd like a closer look at that fire if you don't mind." She walked quickly through the gate and across the garden towards the fire that was still burning fiercely, although the smoke now was a light grey. Jake Thompson looked up defiantly as she came closer.

"You be careful of them flames," he warned. "You go too close and I won't be responsible."

"Don't you worry about me, Mr Thompson," said Caine. "Your wife tells me you've been burning old clothes."

He shrugged. "That's right. They was only fit for burning, they was in such a grotty state! It was Mr Paul gave them to me and told me to get rid of 'em and I just do as I'm told."

"Does he do that often?" Thompson looked blank. "Does he often give you clothes to burn, Mr Thompson?"

"No."

"Why now? What was wrong with them? Why didn't he just give them to charity?"

"Like I said, they was grotty. Filthy. Way past dry cleaning they was."

"Were they his?"

"What? Mr Paul's? No - they were his father's - old Mr Charles's. He used to use them in the garden. Had them for years, but he won't have no more use for them now seeing what a state the poor man's in."

"And what sort of clothes were they?

"Old shirts, jumpers, a few pairs of really old trousers, that sort of stuff. I didn't take inventory, but they was nothing special."

"Did you have a good look at them before you burnt them, Mr Thompson?"

He shrugged. "Depends on what you mean by a good look."

"Were they stained?"

"Yeah - I said. They was covered in mud and filth."

"Not blood?"

"What do you mean blood? Where would they get blood on 'em from?"

"Never mind where it came from Mr Thompson, just answer the question - was any of it blood?"

"Not so far I know. I don't suppose you could tell though, what with all that other dirt and stuff on them."

"O.K. But did you recognize them as being Mr Perot's? Did they seem to be the right size for him?"

"Beats me if they were or they weren't. I didn't recognise them - I told you they was covered in mud and filth. He didn't bother to have them dry cleaned or nothing when he used them - they was only for the garden and when he got out there amongst his shrubs and weeds he couldn't have cared less about keeping himself clean. As for the size - how should I know what size they was? I didn't look at the labels, did I? I wasn't going to try them on myself was I?" He laughed bitterly. "And as for whether they fitted him - they might have done once, but the way the poor man's lost weight these last few years while he's been suffering they wouldn't go nowhere near him nowadays!" He frowned. "Why are you so interested in them anyway? They were only old rags not even fit for a scarecrow!"

Caine didn't answer him. She reached over for a garden rake that leant against the hedge and pushed the end of it into the fire, turning over the ashes at the bottom. There was no sign of any cloth, it all had all burnt down to cinders. She pulled the rake from the flames and rested it against a bush. "And when did Paul Perot give these clothes to you and ask you to burn them?"

"The day before yesterday," said Thompson. "I didn't get around to it yesterday or you'd have missed all the fun!"

Caine wondered what he meant by his last comment, but decided he was just being facetious. She stared into the flames for a few seconds. If there had been anything of interest amongst the clothes Thompson had just incinerated, it was far too late to make any use of it now. She shrugged. Probably there was nothing in It. She turned on her heel and walked back towards her car. "Well, thank you for your time, Mr Thompson." she said as she started the engine. "I assume the gardens are straight ahead."

Thompson, who seemed relieved she had stopped questioning him about the clothing and had followed her out into the lane, nodded sagely. "Just straight up - and when you get to the fork in the road you take the left-hand track." He paused. "Unless, of course, you wanted to go up to the quarry."

Mrs Thompson had come out of the house again and stood beside him. "You wouldn't want to go there," she said, "Not to the gravel pit face any way. That's nothing but an awful mess, especially now it's all overgrown and the workings have flooded. But if you're interested in the view from High Point - that's above the quarry workings - that's worth seeing on a day like this."

"Yeah - that'd be a treat this morning," Thompson agreed. "You'll get fine views clear to the Blackwater Estuary and beyond." He looked at his watch. "You've got time to get up there if you wants to."

"So how do I get there?"

"You takes the track on your right instead of your left when you gets to the first fork and then it's the left hand one when the road divides again a bit further up. You can't really miss it - and there's signs - that puts you on the top road and you just winds your way up from there."

"But you take care of yourself up there," warned Mrs Thompson. "It's fenced off, but there's a sheer drop off the edge, straight down into the old quarry - about sixty foot down it is into the water! We've had a few suicides up there over the years, I can tell you, but you'd know all about that being with the police, wouldn't you."

"And Mr Perot's house? Is that just straight up the drive from here as well?"

Mrs Thompson nodded. "Yeah - they're all on this road - you just follow it through. First property you come to is Mr and Mrs Parr's - that's Beacon cottage, you'll see it off on your right as you go by. It's called Beacon on account of it being quite high up - I suppose they used to light beacon fires up there in the old days. The road takes you right past the cottage and then it swings around again to go past the Manor House - that's Mr Perot's place. You can't miss it."

"This track here, you see, was built as a crescent," explained Jake. "It curves around from here in a horseshoe shape that takes you right back to the road, so you can get onto the estate from either end. The houses, where Mr and Mrs Perot and the others live, are just off the track. They're fenced off of course so that when we have people visiting the gardens the family can get a little bit of privacy."

The lane narrowed down to a single track, with passing places and then it widened again and she found herself driving through an avenue of limes. Beyond them, spread out on either side, on wide undulating lawns, were tall oaks, chestnuts and sycamores interspersed with rhododendron bushes and flower beds that were riots of colour. In the distance, a dark sentinel against the sky, stood the grey rocky ridge of High Point.

She came to the fork in the lane. There was a finger post barely visible amongst tall bushes, indicating that Upton Stapleford House was off to the left, whilst the other route - entered via a sharp right turn - led to the disused quarry below the escarpment of High Point. Caine checked the dash-board clock again and decided she had enough time in hand. She would take the Thompson's advice and go up to the quarry for a look at the scenery. Although she had lived on the Essex borders for most of her life she really had not taken much interest in the countryside, living out her life and career in the urban sprawl of the metropolis. Now that she had finally moved out into the countryside she had promised herself she would take more interest in her rural surroundings. She had never seen the Blackwater Estuary either, closeup or from a distance. Now was the time to rectify that situation.

She turned off to the right, following the lane that ran between high hedges, now neglected and overgrown, deeply rutted by the passage of heavy vehicles that had for years travelled this route laden with gravel. She came to another fork in the road and took the narrower of the two tracks, the one on the left, which was heavily overgrown through lack of use and that, she assumed from the Thompsons' directions, would take her around the side of the ridge and up to the head of the quarry. The other track, wide enough to take trucks and heavy vehicles, she surmised must carry on to the working faces of the quarry itself and to the lake that had formed in the man-made bowl at its base. The track became even narrower and closed in on her, brambles and branches rubbing against the side of her car as she wound up the side of the hill, following the tight twists and turns. It was not the sort of road where one would welcome a vehicle coming in the opposite direction, but the quarry had been worked out long since and there was no longer any industrial activity either down at the work- face or up here above the workings, so there was no sign of any other traffic. Even the noise of the busy B road, now a half mile or so behind her across the open fields, was lost in the low drone of her own car's engine. After three or four minutes on rough and rocky surfaces which she hoped would not damage the car's axles she emerged on to a plateau where the track turned into a wide-open space, the ground grey with powdered gravel. Here and there the thin layer of clay that covered the plateau showed through, a dull terra cotta red. Scrawny bushes, clinging to life in the poor soil alongside the chain link fence, were discoloured by the mineral dust that hung in the air, kicked up even now by the contact of her car's tyres. On a windy day this dust would be blown everywhere and even in the relative stillness of this early June morning it was already settling on the bonnet of her car and powdering the windscreen. She stopped in the middle of the open space and got out, walking slowly across a layer of scree towards the heavy-duty wire fence guarding the edge of the sheer drop down to the disused quarry. Beyond it she could see over the fields and meadows towards the sea. Here, at the head of the quarry, she was at the highest point for miles around and the Blackwater Estuary, a good seven or eight miles away, lay spread before her, the blue of the distant water brilliant in the early morning sun.

There was an old workman's hut towards one end of the flat, grey space on which she had parked. It was derelict, its roof open to the sky, the battered door hanging on its hinges. An old water butt at one end of the decrepit structure still oozed water from some recent rain, its bottom two or three inches stained red by the heavy clay on which it stood. Apart from the tyre marks her car and some other recently visiting vehicle had made in the dust, there was no evidence that anyone had been up here for years. Glancing a few feet along the fence she saw, with some surprise, that the wire had been cut, upwards from the bottom, in two roughly straight lines about three feet apart as if a flap had been cut in the fence, twisted upwards to let someone through and then bent back down again. Her inquisitive mind drew her towards it and she noted that it had been recently made, for the broken ends of the wire were still shiny. A tiny piece of red fabric was clinging to one of the jagged edges. She remembered Mrs Thompson's remarks about suicides and shook her head dolefully before turning and walking back to her car, taking one last look at the vista before climbing in and switching on the engine.

Caine drove back down the hill and, leaving the track where it met the drive, turned off towards Upton Stapleford House. She came upon it after a few minutes. It was set well back from the estate road, high up, emerging suddenly through the avenue of limes. She turned into the wide forecourt through a pair of ornate metal gates, set in a high red brick wall. The house was a large, square structure, Victorian and, Caine judged, renovated by Charles Perot when he had bought the estate in the nineteen seventies. After forty years it was in need of more work. She parked well away from the double garages, which were at one end of the forecourt, and walked across to the front door, her medium high heels crunching loudly on the gravel. On either side of the door were a set of large, low windows and, standing in the porch after she had rung the bell, she could see into the rooms. They were large, with high ceilings, expensively decorated and furnished.

The door was opened by a tall, middle aged woman who introduced herself as Jessica Perot. Obviously, an early riser she was already fully dressed in a neat, well-fitted suit. Her long blonde hair was carefully brushed and sculpted around the oval of her face. Her eyes were large and blue and, at the moment, far from friendly. "I believe my husband's just finishing his breakfast," she said, frowning. "You are rather early you know - it's only just eight o'clock."

"Exactly as your husband requested," Caine assured her, stepping into the hall. "I would have preferred it later myself."

She was shown into the room at the front left of the house, one of those she had seen through the porch window. There were a number of antique settees and armchairs dotted around and a grand piano over in the corner by the wide French windows leading out onto the gardens. The floor was wood block, highly polished and one of the walls, before which stood an antique secretaire, was lined with shelves containing leather bound books, their titles etched with gold lettering. In the opposite wall was a large, ornate cast iron fireplace, polished a shiny black, with a mirrored Victorian over mantel occupying the wall above. A brass faced bracket clock stood on the mantel shelf, showing the correct time of just after eight o'clock.

"I'll tell my husband you're here, Inspector," said Mrs Perot, indicating that Caine should sit wherever she liked.

"Before you go, Mrs Perot," said Caine, "I am here to investigate the murder of one of your husband's senior employees and his wife - Mr and Mrs Bruce Southam - you've probably heard about it. I'm trying to build up a picture of what they were like. I wonder if you would mind answering a few questions about them? It would be most helpful."

Jessica Perot regarded her coolly. "Not at all, though I really don't see how I could possibly help. Of course, we were all very shocked to hear the news of their deaths. Dreadful affair! I hope you'll track down the killer very quickly." She waved her hand again vaguely in the direction of one of the armchairs. "But do please sit down, Inspector. I'll just go and tell my husband where he can find us when he's ready. I'll only be a few moments." She moved away towards the door. "Have you eaten, by the way, Inspector or can I ask Mrs Cooper to bring you anything? A cup of tea, perhaps, or coffee."

"A coffee certainly wouldn't come amiss," said Caine, "Thank you."

"My pleasure," Jessica Perot smiled for the first time and left the room. Caine could hear her high heeled shoes clacking on the wood floor as she made her way down the hall to the back of the house. A door opened and there were voices murmuring, then the heels were again clacking on the wood floor and she came back into the room, closing the door behind her.

"Your coffee will be along shortly," She sat down, "as, hopefully, will my husband. Of course, he's up to his nose in the Financial Times at the moment. He never misses reading it over breakfast, says it's essential for his business and, of course, it's a good excuse to ignore me." She crossed one elegant leg over the other and laid her finely manicured hands on the arms of the chair. "Now, what can I do for you, Inspector?"

"How well did you know Mr and Mrs Southam, Mrs Perot ?"

"Hardly at all, really." She gave the impression they were the sort of people with whom a sensible person would not mix. "I met them on one or two occasions - one would, as he - Bruce Southam - was one of my husband's key men in the company; and, of course, they lived so close that we could hardly ignore them. Paul, my husband, knew Southam from way back in his youth, I believe they may even have been at school together. But I never really took to the Southams. Especially her - she used to be a strip-tease dancer you know."

"That hardly makes her fair game as a murder victim," Caine observed.

Mrs Perot frowned. "What I mean is that Mrs Southam wasn't my type. Frankly none of us here really liked her - not that we saw much of her anyway, but on the few occasions we did meet we were very unimpressed. Florence, Paul's mother - positively hated her."

"Have you any idea why?"

Jessica Perot waved her hands again, vaguely. "Not really. Something must have happened between them, though, because she actually introduced Valerie to Bruce Southam, so she must have liked her then. That was years ago of course - how old is that son of theirs? Adam isn't it? - About nineteen I think, so they must have been married for about twenty years. Anyway, I dare say that if Florence hadn't introduced them they would never have married - not each other, anyway."

"Which may have been a good thing for Valerie," said Caine. Jessica raised her eyebrows questioningly. "We have very good reason to believe that Mr Southam physically abused her, Mrs Perot."

There was a knock on the door and a sprightly, grey haired woman in a bright blue apron entered. She carried a tray laden with a pot of coffee and two sets of bone china cups and saucers, together with matching sugar bowl, milk jug and a plate of biscuits. She looked around the room inquiringly seeking a place to unload her burden.

Mrs Perot indicated the low coffee table that lay between herself and the Inspector. "Thank you, Mrs Cooper. If you'd like to put it down on the table. I'll pour." She waited until Mrs Cooper had left the room and then leaned forward to pick up the coffee pot. "Mrs Cooper doesn't live on the estate," she said, pouring coffee, "She comes up to help out most mornings. Mrs Thompson, the live-in help, finds it very hard to manage by herself." She leaned across the table to hand the coffee cup to Caine. "Help yourself to milk if you want it, Inspector, biscuits also." She poured her own cup and then sat back, ignoring the biscuits. "It doesn't really surprise me that Southam was beating her. He wasn't a likeable man." She stirred sugar into her coffee. "I really can't see what Paul saw in him. I never could."

"Can you think of anyone who might have wanted to kill the Southams, Mrs Perot?"

She shook her head. "That is a rather melodramatic question, Inspector, like something out of an Agatha Christie mystery. But no - nobody springs readily to mind, although I do believe *he* wasn't well liked by anybody."

Caine sipped her coffee. "And can you tell me where you were on the night of the murders, Mrs Perot?"

"When was it exactly? Tuesday evening?" Caine nodded. "At least that's a little easier to answer than in the films where the police ask someone to tell them where they were on a certain night three or four years ago. I've always thought such questions singularly unreasonable. Do policemen ask them in real life?" She stopped to take a sip of coffee. Caine did not attempt an answer. Mrs Perot carried on. "I was playing bridge that evening. As a matter of fact I was at Fred Barnett's house. His wife is a very keen and a very good player. She was my partner for the evening." She smiled. "I don't suppose I could have a much better alibi, could I? Sir Fred was there, by the way. He poured me a drink before the game started."

"You mean Sir Frederick Barnett, our Chief Constable I suppose?" Jessica Perot nodded, smiling. "No, you couldn't have a much better alibi than that, Mrs Perot." Caine finished her coffee and leaned forward to place her cup on the table. "And how long were you there, at Sir Frederick's house?"

The door opened to admit Paul Perot. He was tall, about six feet Caine judged. His hair was dark, luxuriant and he wore an obviously expensive navy-blue pin striped suit. His shirt was white and his blue and white spotted tie matched the handkerchief that peeped from his breast pocket. His face was familiar, but Caine could not think where she might have met him before. "Good morning," he barked rather than spoke, not bothering to come across the room and shake her hand or introduce himself, but going straight to one of the upright chairs, carrying it into the centre. He sat where he could see the two ladies and crossed his arms. "You've got exactly twenty-five minutes of my time, Inspector."

His wife smiled thinly and ignored him, answering Caine's earlier question as if he was not there. "I left here at just after seven, Detective Inspector, and the journey takes about twenty minutes - so, I suppose I arrived at Fred's house at about twenty past seven, or just after. And I was there until just gone eleven and got back here at about eleven thirty." She smiled again. "Will that do?" She rose from her chair. "Now I'll leave you in the tender loving hands of my dear husband, Paul." She turned towards him as she left the room. "Are the markets down again this morning, dear? It always depresses you, doesn't it! Ciao!" She closed the door quietly.

Perot consulted a scrap of paper he had been carrying in his hand. "I made a note of your name when your Sergeant telephoned - Detective Chief Inspector Caine," he read slowly.

"You've just joined the force here at Fen Molesey I understand. Bit of a shock for the troops is it, working with a woman?"

"Not at all, Mr Perot - you **are** Mr Perot? I think they've taken it entirely in their stride." She decided to cut the small talk and go straight into the questioning. "As Sergeant Dolby told you yesterday on the telephone, we're investigating the death of one of your employees and his wife - Mr and Mrs Bruce Southam. They were murdered on Tuesday night. Where were you on that night, Mr Perot?"

He answered easily. "I was in my London flat, Inspector."

"The address?" She took a small notebook and pencil from the jacket of her suit and prepared to write it down.

"68, Antigone Wharf, E14."

"Docklands?"

He nodded. "It's a renovated warehouse overlooking the Thames."

"And you often spend the night there?"

"It's convenient for the office. That, by the way, is in the City, just off Fenchurch Street. I'm not there every night, of course. I stay only when it's necessary."

"You normally drive in from here?"

"You might say that. My brother-in-law, James Parr does the driving. At least he's useful for that much!" The comment was made casually, but Caine detected a hint of anger in his voice. "I have a parking space at the office, of course and James drives me in in the morning and back home again at nights."

"A useful arrangement."

"Well, it usually suits everybody, except when he dithers - he's a born ditherer is James - he did that morning, Tuesday. Had to drop into the Pharmacist to get a new supply of Ursula's pain pills and darn me if he hadn't mislaid the bloody prescription. Took him ten minutes to find it and it was in his pocket all the time. Made me late for a meeting!" Perot threw up his hands in despair. "But he's here on the premises and he might as well make himself useful by driving me, he's worth damn all to us in the office otherwise!"

"Mr Parr works for you then?"

"I suppose you might call it that," said Perot, unsmiling. "I call it one of my dear father's acts of charity."

"You paint a quite different picture of your brother-in-law than Mrs Thompson."

"Bernice? What did she have to say about James?"

"She was impressed by his loyalty to his wife - your sister, Mr Perot. I understand she's a paraplegic."

Perot smiled ruefully. "Loyalty? I call it guilt myself."

"Guilt?"

"She had a riding accident over fifteen years ago. James was with her. If you ask me, he was the cause of the accident. Now he looks after her, fusses around her like a mother hen - but it's not loyalty, it's guilt - and fear. He knows if he doesn't treat Ursula properly he'll lose my father's support and be out of a job. He lost my support years ago - his father may have been one of the founding Partners of the firm, but James hasn't inherited his business acumen. I'm not quite sure what he *is* good at to tell you the truth, except, of course, his famous wood carving. His pieces do have a certain panache, I suppose, but so far as business is concerned he's a non-starter." He sighed. "Yes, James does work for the family firm - he has an office and a desk and a secretary - but let's leave it at that shall we?"

Caine shrugged and moved on to the next item on her mental list. "And what time did you get to your flat on Tuesday evening?"

"About ten thirty, I suppose. It could have been slightly later."

"What were you doing before then?"

"I had a business meeting. And dinner of course."

"Where did you dine and at what time?"

"There's a Chinese in Limehouse - The Junk - it's only a walk away from the flat. I'm often there - that evening I got there at just after nine and left at about ten thirty."

"Right, thank you." She made a quick note. "And would you like to tell me with whom you were doing business?"

"No - as a matter of fact, Inspector - I wouldn't. The matter was private - that is, it was sensitive from a business point of view." He leaned forward conspiratorially and rubbed his chin with one hand, his index finger reaching up to stroke the side of his nose. "Strictly between you and me, Inspector, my company is pursuing a possible merger. Naturally, I am not at liberty to divulge with whom we are talking."

"On the contrary, I think you'll find that you are not at liberty to withhold that information or any information at all," said Caine. "This is a murder inquiry, Mr Perot. But I'll let you think about that. For the time being please tell me what you know about Mr & Mrs Southam."

Perot scowled and folded his arms over his chest again. "It depends on what you want to know, Inspector. Bruce Southam and I were at school together and it's no secret that we served alongside each other in the forces for a short while. Then, he came to work for me in the family business. We were acquaintances - no, friends, I suppose - for years." Perot stood up and walked across the room to the French windows, turning back to Caine to finish what he was saying. "You probably will have learnt by now that Southam was one of the key men in my organisation. He was responsible for a good deal of the business undertaken by the Company." He paused to look out of the window and then turned back to face her. "They say that nobody is indispensable, Inspector, but frankly, I'm not sure how we're going to replace him."

"What business are you in, exactly?"

"Insurance and financial services," said Perot.

"And what did Bruce Southam do for you?"

"He was our top Salesman. Our Sales Director, actually."

"He was also an alcoholic," said Caine. "Were you aware of that, Mr Perot?"

"Nobody's perfect," said Perot. "People with special talents often develop unacceptable behavioural patterns. Perhaps it's their very unacceptable traits that give rise to their talents. I don't know, but what I do know, Inspector, is that being an alcoholic does **not** make a person useless. Bruce Southam was far from useless."

"What about Mrs Southam?"

"What about her?"

"How well did you know her?"

"Hardly at all."

Caine raised her eyebrows. "Come, Mr Perot, she was married to one of your closest acquaintances - sorry, friends - for over twenty years and you hardly knew her?"

"That's right. She wasn't my type. We met socially a few times - usually when the business needed boosting and we put on a special dinner party, or whatever sort of gathering was appropriate - but that was all. I hardly knew her, but I may say that I didn't like her."

"Your mother, Florence Perot - didn't get on with her either, I believe."

"No. Why should she?" Perot moved back to the chair he had previously occupied and sat down. "She had no reason to like her so far as I know."

"And yet she introduced her to Bruce Southam before they were married," said Caine. "Why would she do that if she didn't like her?"

"Don't ask me," replied Paul Perot. "My Mother has never said. Maybe the woman - Valerie - deluded her - you know, used her wiles to get around her knowing she had influence with Bruce - he was a good catch in those days, quite a prize for a **strip tease artiste**." He emphasised the words sneeringly and nodded as though he had tumbled upon the truth. "She married well, did Valerie Southam."

"Did she?" asked Caine reflectively. "Were you not aware that Bruce beat her up regularly?"

Perot shrugged as if the information was not known to him but was of absolutely no consequence anyway. "No, I wasn't. I hardly ever saw the woman."

"When was the last time you did see her?"

"Oh, some while ago, Inspector."

"And you can't be more precise than that?"

"I do not keep a diary of when and where I meet everybody who happens to cross my path, Inspector."

"And what about Bruce? When did you last see him?"

He smiled thinly. "That's a little easier, Inspector. Tuesday, as a matter of fact. At the office."

"Did you notice anything unusual about him?"

"Unusual? No. Should I have?"

"No. I mean, was he acting strangely, as if anything was on his mind?"

Perot smiled again, more broadly. "You mean as if he was aware he was going to be murdered that night? Don't be absurd, Inspector."

"I did not mean that!" said Caine tightly. "Whoever killed him and his wife must have had a reason. Did he discuss any problems with you, as a friend, that might give us some clue as to what exactly happened on Tuesday night?"

"No, he did not, Inspector." He stood up again and looked at his watch. "I have only a few minutes, Inspector, so I do wish you would get on with your questions and let me get on with my business." He swept his hands out as if to indicate the large room and its expensive contents, the house and the grounds that were visible through the windows. "This place does not pay for itself you know."

Caine ignored the comment. "So, Bruce said nothing to you about any problems he may have had? In spite of the fact that you were life-long friends and he was a key man in your organisation?"

"You are making the assumption, Inspector, that there **was** a problem. For all you or I know there may not have been. The murderer may have had a quite different motive." He stopped, eyed her critically as if turning over something in his mind, sat down again and crossed his legs. "Perhaps I should tell you, also, Inspector, that your assumption that we were still friends may not be correct - strictly speaking."

"What do you mean? Either you were friends, or you weren't."

"Let's just say that the bond of friendship may have been a little strained of late." She was about to interrupt him, but he held up his hand to stay her words. "I will explain. You mentioned earlier that Bruce was an alcoholic. I was, of course, aware of that. In the early days it didn't bother me over much, but towards the end - well, frankly, Inspector, it was becoming an embarrassment. Work wise that is. Other people were beginning to notice."

"And it was affecting Bruce's work, his sales results?"

Perot nodded. "Embarrassingly so. I was considering telling him to book himself into some sort of Clinic for alcoholics, to dry himself out. And I was worried about his sales figures and the impact their reduction was having on the business." He paused. "But I didn't kill him, Inspector."

"At the moment I am not saying you did," said Caine. "But tell me, Mr Perot? Why did you ask your caretaker, Jake Thompson, to burn certain items of clothing a couple of days ago?"

Perot had not expected the question and he took a few seconds to answer. "Oh, those? They were just a few of my father's old things. He'll never use them again - not in his state - so I asked Jake to dispose of them. They were so incredibly filthy that burning them was the logical thing to do. Nobody else would have wanted them. Why? Is it suddenly a crime to throw old clothes onto a bonfire?"

"It depends on which old clothes they were," said Caine. "It just so happens that we have been wondering what happened to the murderer's clothes. There was so much blood at the scene of the crime there was no way he walked out of Bruce Southam's house still wearing them."

Perot laughed humourlessly. "And you thought they were the clothes Jake was burning? Be reasonable, Inspector, what possible link could there be between my father and the two murders? The old man hardly knows what day it is, let alone how to go out and commit a double murder. You really are scraping the bottom of the barrel!"

"I have only your word that the clothes Jake Thompson burnt **were** your father's." Caine reminded him. "Jake couldn't identify them as his. They might have been yours. And you must admit it is a coincidence that you asked him to dispose of some old clothes the very day after the murders?"

Perot flushed angrily. "That's all it is - coincidence. Now, how much longer are you going to keep me?"

Caine glanced across at the bracket clock that stood on the mantel shelf over the fire. "You promised me twenty-five minutes, Mr Perot. We still have a few left. Tell me about your father. He seems to have been a very remarkable man in his time."

"He was - but very much *in* his time, Inspector." There was a note of pride in his voice, but also of frustration. "We all owe him a lot, those of us who live on this estate. He built up the business with his own hands and was responsible for developing the estate and the gravel business - AA - Anglia Aggregates was one of the most profitable extraction businesses in the country in the fifties, sixties and seventies. Most of the new roads and motorways built at that time were built using Anglia's grit. Yes, he did a good job there. There's only one thing I'd fault him on and that is that he was too soft."

"How do you mean, too soft?"

"You're a woman, you probably wouldn't understand," said Perot.

"I'm a Detective Inspector as well as being a woman." Said Caine. "Try me."

"Well, it took him a long time to go in for the kill," said Perot. "Businesswise I mean, he'd often dither over making a decision, particularly where cutting out the deadwood was concerned. Invariably all that dithering wasn't good for the business."

"I believe he's had a stroke and has handed the business over to you now?"

"I wished!" He laughed bitterly. "Yes, I suppose in the day to day running of the business he lets me get on with it, but he's never given up completely. Even now, when he's losing his marbles - he had a stroke, you know and there's a touch of

Altzheimers - even now he's not letting go completely. I can't seem to make him see that we need to cut out the deadwood to survive." Perot shook his head ruefully. "What with losing the profits from AA and the problems we had with Lloyds - we were big Names, you know - followed of course by the latest shenanigans in the financial world, we can do without paying big salaries to the hangers-on. I keep telling him we must cut our clothes according to our cloth, but he won't hear of it. Keeps going on about them being family or, indeed, *having* families and you can't do that to family! Yes, he was a remarkable man, but it's time he stood aside and left it to me! In fact, I'm thinking it's high time I arranged Power of Attorney over his affairs." He looked pointedly at his watch and stood up. "Now, if you've no further questions, Inspector, I really must be getting off to that meeting."

Caine remained seated. "There is just one question, Mr Perot. You haven't told me yet who you were talking to on the night of the murder."

A flash of anger crossed his face, "I've told you before, Inspector, that I cannot divulge that information!"

"And I have told you, Mr Perot that this is a murder investigation. You will have to tell me sooner or later, so it may as well be sooner. Then - and only then - will we be able to eliminate you from our inquiries."

"I'm under suspicion, then," said Perot. "So be it. I'm not giving out that information, Inspector, not yet anyway. It really can't be helped." He stood up and moved pointedly towards the door." But I wish you joy, Inspector, in proving that I killed Bruce and Valerie Southam."

CHAPTER SIXTEEN

The news came in just before Detective Sergeant Mark Dolby left the Neale's house. Susie Neale's car had been found abandoned in the car park of a public house on the borders of the village of Birch Medley. There was no sign of Mrs Neale. Dolby went to his car and rang Jacqueline Caine on her mobile, catching her as she left the Perot house.

"Does her husband have any idea why she would have been at that Pub - what was it called again, Mark?"

"The Bald Griffin. No. According to him he'd never been there with her, although he remembers stopping off there on his travels for a drink, with one or two of his colleagues."

"And there are any signs of violence?"

"None," said Dolby. "Forensic are hauling the car in for examination. Apparently, the doors were closed, but not locked and the keys were still in the ignition when they found it. And Mrs Neale's handbag was stuffed under the front passenger seat."

"Anything missing?"

"Not so far as we know. There was cash and credit cards in the bag, so it doesn't look like robbery."

"And there's no sign of Mrs Neale," Caine said with a sigh. "This is not looking good, Mark. We're going to have to start searching for her. How long do you think you'll be in London?"

"Three to four hours, I reckon," replied Dolby. "The Perot office is in the city, just off Fenchurch Street, so I'll be going down by train. I don't know how many people I'll have to see; I'll be playing it by ear. Would you prefer me to postpone the visit?"

Caine thought for a few seconds. "No, you go ahead as planned. I've just finished with Paul Perot, so I'll get things moving on Susie Neale when I get back to the station. I don't know yet whether we'll be treating this as the same investigation, or even if I'll be handling it. The only link with the Southams is the fact that Mrs Neale knew them."

"There must be a link somewhere!" Dolby insisted. "It's too much like coincidence!"

"I think so too, but that doesn't prove anything. By the way, did Wendy manage to get anything from Susie's daughters as to what she was wearing?"

"Yes, you were right there, boss. The girls knew all right. Wendy has all the details. A red trouser suit or something." He looked at his watch. "I'll have to get moving if I'm to catch the train and be in the City by eleven. I'll keep in touch."

The journey to Liverpool Street was quick and uneventful. Dolby had not visited the station for a good many years and with all the design and building changes that had taken place since he was last there it took him a few moments to get his bearings. It was about a quarter to eleven when he stepped off the platform and on to the concourse, making his way through the ever-present crowds, up the stainless steel escalator and out into

Bishopsgate. He turned right, away from the Broadgate Centre and up Bishopsgate to cross the road at the traffic lights on the corner of Camomile Street, turning left and then right to work his way through the back streets towards Cullum Court which was just off Fenchurch Street. During the journey he had been turning over in his mind the latest news about Susie Neale's disappearance and now he walked slowly through the busy streets, sifting through the many details he and Jacqueline Caine had so far gleaned concerning the deaths of Bruce and Valerie Southam. Somewhere in amongst all those facts there must be something linking the double murder with Susie's disappearance. But what? Was she still alive? He had no idea. Except for the fact that she had been on extremely friendly terms with Valerie he did not know how she fitted in to the rapidly growing jigsaw puzzle, of which, so far, they possessed only a few of the pieces.

He turned into Cullum Court and looked for number 6. The entrance was on the other side of the road, next to the entrance to an underground car park and he crossed over and pushed through a revolving door into a vast marble and glass reception hall. The area was dominated by a massive cast iron sculpture of an animal, possibly a bird, suspended from the high ceiling by almost invisible steel cords. So far as he could tell this fantastic creature had three sets of wings but no legs - and eyes and a beak at **both** ends of its body. He stood for a moment looking up at it. The uniformed security guard behind the reception desk saw his puzzled look and followed his line of sight. He grinned understandingly.

"Don't worry about it, sir. Nobody here knows what it is either! Except, of course, that it was expensive!"

That, thought Dolby, was probably very true. Any business that rented an office in this block would need a sizeable turnover. He wondered how well the Perot's business was doing.

James Parr looked quite taken aback when Dolby asked him the question. "I really don't know anything about that side of the business," he said, shaking his head nervously. "You should have let me know and I would have asked our Accountant to have some figures ready."

Parr was a tall, thin bespectacled man who answered the police officer's questions slowly and tremulously. At his behest, so that he could continue to smoke during the interview, they were standing on the balcony which opened out from his office. In the ten minutes that Dolby had been questioning him he had consumed - or, more accurately, half consumed - four cigarettes and was now reaching, hands shaking, into his pocket for the black and silver packet. He extracted the fifth, lifted it to his lips and lit it with a pocket lighter. He was curiously fastidious with the ash, which he almost continuously tapped from the end of the cigarette into an ash tray balanced precariously on the stainless-steel railing.

"Don't worry, I'll ask him when I see him," said Dolby. "Perhaps you'd like to tell me where you were on Tuesday night."

"The night of the murders?" Dolby nodded. "I was at home." He was speaking slowly and with care as if he found it difficult to enunciate the words. "With my wife."

"Doing what?"

"I should tell you, Sergeant, that Ursula, my wife, is severely disabled." His hands shook as he flicked at the lighter and lifted it towards the cigarette that hung from his lips. "Accident - years ago!" His face flushed with confusion as he remembered his cigarette was already alight and he brushed a lock of unruly greying hair from his forehead with his other hand. "Consequently, she's paralysed from the waist down and confined to a wheelchair. We are very restricted in what we can do. We don't often go out."

"So, you were doing what? Watching television, surfing the net?"

"If my memory serves me correctly, we were reading," said Parr. "Until nine o'clock. Then I helped Ursula get to bed. After that I stayed up for a couple of hours and did a little work in my workshop."

"Oh really, and what might that be, Mr Parr?"

He took off his glasses and polished them on his handkerchief with a slow, circular motion. "I carve wood, Sergeant. It's just a hobby. It helps me relax." He stubbed out the fifth half smoked cigarette, crushed it in the ash tray and reached for the black and silver packet once more. "I went to bed at about eleven thirty I believe."

"Your wife can verify that, can she?"

Parr shook his head. "No, I'm afraid not, Sergeant." He smiled weakly; the first time Dolby had seen him smile. "We sleep in separate rooms. As I've told you she is not a well woman and it wouldn't be fair for us to share a room. I'm a light sleeper myself, you see, and I would keep disturbing her, although she is usually on sedatives to minimise the pain. She still gets a lot of pain you see even though it's been years since the accident." Parr sighed. "So, you see, Sergeant, I really can't help you very much at all."

"Oh, I don't know, you may surprise yourself," said Dolby. He was not being entirely flippant. Clues and vital information that could break a case often came from the most routine, even boring inquiries and, if he was honest with himself, he found James Parr one of the most boring people he had ever met. He seemed to lack the verve and energy needed to make even his own life interesting. "How well did you know Bruce Southam, Mr Parr?"

"I've known him most of my life," said Parr. "But not well. We were never what you might call friends. In fact, I think you might say there was a high degree of animosity between us."

"You didn't like him?"

"To be honest, I hated him. He was a braggart and a bully - I'm sorry to speak ill of the dead, Sergeant, but I believe that is what he was."

"And what about Mrs Southam? How well did you know her?"

Parr drew deeply on his cigarette and choked, coughing on the smoke. "Excuse me!" He caught his breath and continued; his words punctuated by throat clearings. "I didn't know her at all well, really. We did meet on a couple of occasions, sort of social cum business gatherings. As you probably know, the Southams lived just a few miles from Upton Stapleford where we Parrs and Perots 'hang out'." He gave a nervous little giggle as if he had said something funny. "Before he had the stroke my father-in-law used to host gatherings up at the big house. I ran into Mrs Southam there a couple of times. Nowhere else, though, no, no, we never met anywhere other than US..." He laughed nervously. "We call it US in the family - Upton Stapleford you see, not the United States!"

"OK. So, when did you last see her?"

James Parr drew on his cigarette again and then crushed it out in the ash tray. It was less than a quarter finished. The man must be financing the tobacco industry practically single-handed, thought Dolby. Parr coughed again and turned his head away. "It must be months ago. I really can't remember."

"Thank you, Mr Parr." Dolby consulted his notebook. "Now I would like to have a few words with your Accountant, Mr Brian Walker. Where can I find him?"

Walker was a short, plump man in his early thirties. He was in his shirt sleeves when Dolby entered his office. There were dark sweat stains under his armpits and he moved quickly to put his jacket on.

"Don't worry about your jacket on my account, sir." said Dolby. It was an extremely hot day, but the offices were air conditioned and seemed cool to him. He held out his warrant card. "Detective Sergeant Mark Dolby, Fen Molesey C.I.D. I'd like to ask you a few questions about Mr Bruce Southam. As I'm sure you know he and his wife were murdered earlier in the week."

Walker nodded. "Yes, a dreadful business, Detective Sergeant. I'll answer whatever questions I can." He sat with his jacket on, although it was obvious he was uncomfortably hot. He had been working at his computer when Dolby entered and now he pushed the keyboard away and waved vaguely at one of the two guest chairs.

Dolby sat down and took his notebook from his pocket. "Thank you, Mr Walker. How did you get on with Mr Southam?"

"O.K. Fine," said Walker. "As you've probably been told, he wasn't the easiest man to get on with, but I did O.K."

"He was a key man in the Company," said Dolby. "A high-income earner?"

"He brought a lot of money into the company, if that's what you mean. Although..." Walker stopped uncertainly. "I'm not sure I should tell you this, it may or may not be relevant, I don't know, but his earnings on behalf of the company have dropped considerably over the last twelve months."

"Why?"

"I don't really know. I suppose there's been more competition in the marketplace. The industry has had a bit of a shake-down in the last few years. But I don't know that that has affected Bruce Southam unduly. It hasn't been that." Walker made a gesture of helplessness. "He's just seemed to have lost it in the last year or so."

"You mean he may have had other things on his mind?"

"Yes." Walker seemed reluctant to go into details. "He may have."

"Like what?" urged Dolby.

"I don't know." He shrugged. "That is, I do know, but I don't know that I should be telling you this, it may or may not be relevant." He frowned. "Well, you probably already know, anyway. Southam was drinking too much. He was banned for twelve months for drunk driving not long ago."

"But do you know *why* he was drinking? Was there something worrying him?"

"No - that is, I don't know why he was drinking, and I don't know if there was anything worrying him. I wasn't close to the man. He was a hard man to get close to and, quite frankly, I wasn't even inclined to try. He was just a working colleague and I got on with him when I had to. But I think he always did drink a bit - maybe it just got worse. But the point is the drink was beginning to affect his work. And - as you know - he was our Sales Director, so the way he behaved was important to the company."

"And the Company was suffering as a result?"

Walker nodded. "This mustn't get out. Most of the staff don't know about the bad figures and our business contacts certainly haven't got an inkling, although…" He spread his hands and sighed. "Southam upset one of our biggest accounts only a week or so ago. UI - Universal Insurance. He went to a meeting in their offices and he was blind drunk. Apparently, he said a lot of things he shouldn't have. They've been considering their position ever since."

"I see. So, they may not do business with you anymore?"

Walker nodded again "Worse than that - they were going to take an interest in the Company - make a huge investment that we're badly in need of. And when word gets out that they've pulled out - and it will, it's an incestuous industry and you can't keep these things quiet forever - it'll be curtains for us, or at very least a massive downsizing. Paul - Mr Perot - was due to go and see Universal on Tuesday - the night of the murders as it happens - in Norwich - to pour oil on troubled waters, that sort of thing, smooth things over. He insisted on taking Southam with him, said he'd have to apologise - but when UI found out Bruce was included in the meeting their Chairman, Sir Charles Ormsby, threw a fit – apparently. he was the butt of a lot of the sick jokes Bruce made the first time he upset them. Anyway, they called the meeting off at the last minute."

"Sorry if I misheard, but did you say Sir Charles Ormsby?"

"Yes. Why?"

"No reason. I thought I'd heard the name before, that's all." Dolby paused, thinking. "So, Mr Perot had good reason to be quite miffed with Bruce Southam?"

Walker pulled a large white handkerchief from his pocket and wiped his brow. "Yes, he is - was - pretty miffed at him - he has good reason to be - but not enough to kill him! I mean - I don't think he would!"

It was Dolby's turn to shrug. 'You can never tell,' he thought. 'It's a funny old world.' He asked, "Where were you on Tuesday night, Mr Walker?"

"Me?" Now Walker looked alarmed. "You're not suggesting…? No, of course not." He laughed nervously, "Just conducting your inquiries, I'm sure. I was at home, Detective Sergeant. I left the office at about seven, took the train to Tunbridge, where I live, and was at home, with my wife and kids, all evening."

"What else do you know about the Southams Mr Walker?"

"As I said, not much. I've never met her - Mrs Southam - and I only knew Bruce from a business point of view. He wasn't the easiest person to get to know."

"And the Perots - they're an interesting family. How long have you known them?"

"Not long," said Walker. "I've only been here for just over a year. I've never even met the old man, Charles. What exactly do you want to know? Couldn't you ask Paul Perot?"

"I don't think so. I need background. Unbiased. Let's say 'unexpurgated'. There may be nothing in it, but Bruce Southam seems to have been around the Perot family for a long time. Whoever killed him, for whatever reason, may be connected or they may not. Or, one of the Perots may know something, even without realising it." Dolby shrugged. "Call it being nosey if you like, but we're trying to build a picture, or a series of pictures that fit together."

"Pitcher's the man you want then," said Walker. He gave a little laugh. "Excuse the pun, but that's his name. Pitcher. Bernard Pitcher. Used to have my job here at Parr Perot. He was here for thirty years or more, saw the firm grow up from nothing. He'll tell you everything you want to know, I'm sure." He smiled. "The man can surely talk! I spent a month with him when I started here, before he left and I used to go to the loo just to get a few minutes silence. I've got his address and phone number somewhere." He turned to his computer and clicked the mouse a few times, moving it around on its pad. He peered forward as the details he was looking for came on to the screen. "I'll print it out." He clicked the mouse two or three times more and Dolby heard the printer, at the far end of Walker's desk, whirr into action. After a few seconds a sheet of paper spewed out of it. Walker picked it out of the tray and passed it over.

"Brentwood, Essex. Not far from Fen Molesey, I believe. Pitcher's got a bungalow there."

After a few minutes with Paul Perot's secretary Dolby took the lift back down to the marble vestibule and, under the eagle eyes of the strange, sculptured bird, found his way out on to the street. He was about to cross the road on his way back towards Liverpool Street Station when a large blue car swung across his path, making its way into the underground car park. Dolby stepped back and let it pass, following it with his eyes. It was a blue Mercedes, clean and well looked after and as its tail swept past him he saw there was a stick-on notice fixed to the back window. It proclaimed "*Bikers do it on two wheels*" and there was a mildly amusing caricature of a leather clad motorcyclist roaring around a bend, the wheels of the cycle spinning madly, throwing up spray. He hadn't had time to see the driver of the car, but his mind registered its license plate number - PPA 1. He stood for a moment, scratching his head and thinking. He had seen that car before somewhere, but he couldn't think where.

Dolby caught a train to Fen Molesey, retrieved his car from the car park and set off for Brentwood. Pitcher's bungalow was situated somewhere in Great Warley, a few minutes away from the main town and he found it quickly from the details Walker had given him. It was a small bungalow, set well back from the road in a well-kept garden and as he pushed open the wrought iron gate an elderly lady, on her knees before one of the herbaceous borders and working at the soil with a small trowel, looked up inquiringly.

"I'm afraid we're not buying anything today, young man."

He stopped on the path, a few feet from her and smiled. "I'm not a salesman, Madam. Are you Mrs Pitcher?" She nodded and he showed her his warrant card. "Detective Sergeant Mark Dolby, Fen Molesey C.I.D. I wonder if I might have a few words with your husband?"

"Oh - he's not in trouble, is he? I keep telling him he drives much too fast!"

"Nothing like that, Mrs Pitcher. He's not in any kind of trouble so far as I know. I just need to ask him a few questions."

She struggled to her feet. "I'm afraid he's not in, Sergeant, but you'll probably find him at the bowls club. He's been there practically every day since he retired. He'll either be there or in the pub opposite. The Castle and Keys, I think it's called." She gave an unhappy little snort. "Bernard says he enjoys a little drink after a game." She pointed up the road, "Turn left at the junction and then first right. It's not far."

Her directions were good and a few minutes later Dolby found himself buying Bernard Pitcher a pint of bitter in the Castle and Keys, directly opposite the local Bowls Club.

Pitcher was smartly dressed in a dark blue blazer, with pocket handkerchief, a crisp white shirt and a pair of light grey flannel trousers. His hair was thick and white, his face ruddy from the sun and, Dolby decided, he must have been in the pub frequently during the morning as his breath smelt distinctly of beer. And as Walker had said, Pitcher talked incessantly. He had hardly paused to catch his breath since Dolby located him in the Bowls Club and introduced himself. Pitcher had suggested they go across to the pub to get away from 'the noisy throng' gathered in the Tea Room.

Dolby did not mind the older man's propensity to talk the hind leg off the proverbial donkey. Some of his colleagues held the belief that the investigating officer should keep strict control of a questioning session - for Dolby's part he was often content to let the person he was interviewing talk about everything and anything. For one thing it relaxed them and, for another, they often found themselves telling him things they originally had no intention of mentioning. Dolby let Pitcher have his head and just listened.

"Do you play?" Pitcher asked, presumably referring to bowls. Dolby shook his head and led the way to a table at the back of the saloon bar. Fortunately, the Castle and Keys was one of those hostelries that served food all day, for it was now well past two o'clock and he hadn't eaten since breakfast. He bit into a cheese and tomato sandwich while the older man talked on.

"You should, Sergeant, you should. I know some people call it an old man's game, but it's not I can assure you. It's not. People of all ages play bowls - some of the youngsters are very good at it you know - it takes years of practise mind, you can't just pick it up overnight, good Lord no! And it's not a mere game either, oh no, it's a skill. You need a good eye and a good sense of balance in your delivery arm."

He paused to sip from his beer and Dolby took the opportunity to say something himself, although his mouth was half full of cheese and tomato. "I believe you worked for a company called Parr Perot Associates, Mr Pitcher..."

The mere mention of the name was enough to open Pitcher's vocal floodgates. "Good Lord, yes! I was with the firm for nearly forty years. Left them only a year ago." His lip curled distastefully. "Would have been there today if it hadn't been for that Paul Perot, though." He drew on his beer. "Got rid of me first opportunity he had."

"But your wife said you were retired."

Pitcher laughed ruefully. "That was the excuse he gave. Okay, so I had a little angina trouble, but it was nothing much. The doctors had it under control. I was only sixty-six, good for many years yet! But that Paul Perot wanted all the oldsters, as he called us, out of the firm and as soon as he managed to elbow his father out of the way, out came the long knives!"

"But you were there a long time, Mr Pitcher. And you were due for retirement."

Pitcher snorted. "It **was** a long time, Sergeant. Not that Paul was impressed by that. You would have thought that after all those years they'd have given me a bit of a golden handshake, but not a bit of it! A clock! That's what they gave me when they kicked me out - and it wasn't such a horologist's delight either, I can tell you! Horrible brassy little thing that doesn't even keep good time." He took another long draught of his beer.

"But the job couldn't have been that bad, Mr Pitcher," said Dolby, taking advantage of the short interruption in Pitcher's flow. "Not if you were with them for forty years!"

"No, I suppose not," Pitcher reflected. "But things were different in those days. Let's see, I must have been in my mid-twenties when I started with PPA. Just qualified as a chartered accountant I had, and I answered an ad in the paper. Charles Perot had just started out on his own with old Alfred. Alfred Parr. They'd just set up Parr Perot Associates, although in those days it wasn't a limited company."

There was a brief interruption in the flow of words whilst Pitcher took another long draught of beer from his glass. Dolby took the opportunity of breaking in with another question. "Would that be any relation of James Parr?"

Pitcher nodded vigorously, still swallowing. "Yes, James or Jamie as they all call him - that's Alfred's son. I'll tell you about that in a minute. Anyway, it must've been back in the sixties, when Charles and Alfred got together. Alfred was still pretty vigorous and a power in the business in those days, of course. It wasn't until the late nineties, or maybe it was early in the two thousands that he started to lose interest - well, his wife died somewhere around then, and he didn't want to go on, so he asked Charles to buy him out. That must have been two or three years after Paul, Charles's son, came into the firm."

"You say that as if it made a big difference."

"You bet it made a difference." Pitcher leaned forward and stabbed at the table with his index finger, making his point. "Paul was trouble even in those days. Charles had a problem keeping him under control even then. Paul thought he owned the place. Even started to tell *me* how to do my job! Wanted me to travel pretty close to the wind on the statutory regulations, I can tell you, but I wasn't having any of it!" He took another quick gulp of his beer, continuing to grip the handle of the tankard as he continued. "Of course, he immediately stuck his oar in on the question of how much Charles should pay Alfred on the buy-out. If it'd been up to him Charles would have been quite generous, but there's always been a mean streak in Paul. He's got the killer instinct in more ways than one."

"He persuaded Charles to pay Alfred less than he was entitled to, to buy him out of the business?"

"Yes, but how do you value these things? There's a hell of a lot of good will has to go into the calculation and because of that you can play around with the figures as much as you like. Paul did a lot of playing about, and all I can say is they paid Alfred a lot less for his share than he should have got. In my opinion, that is. They knew what he'd put into the firm and what the prospects were for the future - and so did I, that's why I'm saying they under paid him!" Pitcher banged the tankard emphatically down on the tabletop. "They short changed Alfred Parr, no doubt about that! Mind you, I think he knew, but he let them get away with it because he wanted to safeguard his son's future."

"James already had a job with the firm?"

"Yes, but they had to promise there would always be a place for him at Parr Perot, you see. Maybe that's why Paul forced down the amount of the pay-out. He never has liked Jamie and he certainly hasn't been a great asset to the business."

"Why couldn't Jamie look after himself?"

Bernard Pitcher chuckled. "You've got to be joking! Have you met him, Sergeant?" Dolby nodded. "Perhaps it didn't come over to you, but he's been spoon fed ever since he was a toddler. He's got about as much moral fibre as a packet of cornflakes and the business acumen of a paper bag. Added to that he hasn't got a competitive bone in his body. All right, he went to public school and he got himself a third-rate degree at one of the red bricks, but he'd never be able to get himself a decent job - not one that's worth having, anyway! It seems to me he's always been totally dependent on someone else - first on his father and then on the Perot family." Pitcher drank some more beer before carrying on. "Mind you, he must have a little bit of cunning in him."

"How do you mean?"

"Well, he married Charlie Perot's daughter didn't he?"

"The disabled lady?"

"Yes, Ursula Perot, but she wasn't always disabled. Up until she had the riding accident about fifteen years ago she was a beautiful woman, a keen sportswoman. She's still beautiful, mind you."

"How do you suppose he managed to marry her then, Mr Pitcher, if he's such a hopeless case?"

Pitcher shrugged. "When I think about it, maybe it wasn't native cunning. Maybe he was being led by the nose even then. You see, rumour has it they were childhood sweethearts, him and Ursula. Well, they grew up together - they all lived on the Perot estate even in those days, not that it all belonged to Charles then, of course. Alfred Parr had a goodly portion of it and his family lived there too, so the kids were in each other's pockets. By all accounts Paul and Bruce Southam - they went to the same school, you know, that's where they got to know each other - anyway, they bullied young Jamie something rotten - he's two or three years younger than Paul and physically he was no match for the older boys. It seems that Ursula took pity on Jamie and they fell in love." Pitcher grunted disdainfully. "It sounds like romantic nonsense - like something out of Mills and Boon, I know, but it's true none the less. Anyway, by all accounts the parents wanted them to get together, so the Parrs and the Perots were quite pleased. In those days, of course, before Alfred's wife died, they were trying to build a business dynasty, so the whole thing made sense." He finished his beer. "You going to have another one, Sergeant?"

Dolby shook his head. "I'm driving," he said.

Pitcher stood up. "You sure? I'll just get one for myself then." He went off towards the bar, swaying slightly, leaving the policeman deep in thought.

"Alfred Parr, I take it, is no longer alive?" Said Dolby on Pitcher's return.

Pitcher sat down and nodded, smiling. "I know what you're thinking, Sergeant. You're thinking Jamie must have inherited a small fortune when his father died, so why is he so dependent on the Perots?" He sighed. "Well, he might have. The only problem was that Alfred married again - a woman considerably younger than himself I might add, a bit of a tart if truth be told. I never met her myself, but that was the consensus of opinion of those who did. Anyway, she made sure Alfred got through most of his money before he popped his clogs - they were on cruises all over the world most of the time. Spent a fortune. And what there was left she managed to persuade Alfred to leave to her. So, so far as I know, Jamie ended up with next to nothing."

"But if he was so concerned that Jamie was well looked after why didn't he leave him anything in his will?" asked Dolby. "It doesn't make sense."

"It does if his new wife convinced him the Perots would look after his son," said Pitcher. "Anyway, I'm only telling you what I've heard. But it's got to be true, because if Jamie had money of his own he wouldn't continue to go in to work every day would he? He told me once he hated the work and he hates being beholden to Paul Perot - he drives him to the office most days you know, like a hired hand, which is all he is, I suppose - but, can you imagine having to kow-tow like that to the man who bullied the life out of you when you were a boy? And on top of that he has to look after his invalid wife." He nodded sagely, "and here's another thing you might find interesting, Sergeant, although you may have thought of it yourself. Jamie and Ursula might have been madly in love with each other when they got married way back in the good old days, but it's not much of a marriage now, I'll wager!"

"I don't follow you."

"Well, think it out for yourself, Sergeant. Here's a man in his early forties with the normal sort of animal urges - and there's his wife, paralysed from the waist down - nudge, nudge, wink, wink, know what I mean - they don't get it together, do they?"

"I don't think that is any concern of ours, sir," said Dolby sternly. "It's not the sort of thing people discuss. Besides, you can't be sure about it."

The other man sneered. "Can't I just! It's obvious to anyone with any savvy. Jamie Parr's got the urges all right! Damn it! He's only a young man, even now! And you can't say he's not like that - he nearly got done a few years ago for interfering with one of the young girls in the office. Luckily, Charlie managed to smooth it over, said it must have been a mistake, but he knew what was going on. Read Jamie the riot act. Told him he had to keep his thing in his trousers no matter what, and he wouldn't have his son-in-law playing around!" Pitcher laughed mockingly. "Of course, that was in the days before the affair of Clinton's trousers, when playing around suddenly became respectable." He picked up his glass and took a long swig. "Anyway, it proves that he wasn't getting enough of it from his wife at the time and I can't see that anything would have changed in that direction."

"Well, I'm not so sure," Dolby told the other man, "from what I've heard, Jamie Parr is very attentive to his wife. He looks after her like a ministering Angel."

"Well, yes, he might," said Pitcher. "Maybe he does still love her, but he's still got the other imperatives hasn't he! He's still a man with natural urges! Besides, it's probably guilt makes him look after her - that and the fact that he'd be for it financially if he didn't. Old Charlie wouldn't stand for him ratting on Ursula, not if he got to know about it. And Paul would certainly kick him out lock stock and barrel if he thought he was playing away from home. It's not *do as I do* with him, it's *do as I tell you*."

"I can see that, but where does the guilt come into the equation?"

"It's obvious isn't it! I wasn't there at the time, of course, but rumour has it he was almost totally responsible for his wife's accident. That's why he feels guilty!"

"It's possible," agreed Dolby. He disliked the way Pitcher would happily undermine another person's character on the basis of what appeared to be unsubstantiated evidence. But at least the man was talking freely.

"Going back to what I was saying about Jamie playing the field," said Pitcher, "Charlie had a bloody nerve there, didn't he, putting him in his place! Talk about the pot calling the kettle black!"

"You mean Charles Perot was also playing around with other women?"

"No - not Charlie - he's never been the type. Straight as a die is Charles Perot, ever faithful to his wife, Florence, so far as I know. His son, on the other hand, isn't so particular, in spite of the fact he's been married for yonks. But that's Paul all over. Not a man of much principle, our Paul - fickle as you like!" He laughed. "Not that Jessica, his wife, cared. She was always at it herself was Jessica. Posh bitch, but her knickers were up and down like Tower Bridge."

"You mean Paul and his wife both carried on like that? And it was common knowledge?"

"Present tense, Sergeant, so far as I know. I may not be with PPA anymore, but I keep in touch. Paul and Jessica both still carry on, or so I'm told, and they don't care who knows about it." Pitcher laughed suggestively. "Well, the insurance industry in the city is a close-knit club. Everybody knows everybody else and you can't keep any secrets. Jessica knew what Paul was up to from day one - *before* day one, probably - and she wasn't very particular who she hopped into bed with herself." He smiled lecherously and winked at Dolby. "She's a good-looking young woman is Jessica."

"And Paul doesn't mind?"

"Why should he mind if he's doing the same sort of thing? But it isn't Jessica he has to watch out for."

"How do you mean?"

"He has to be careful who he strikes up an alliance with, hasn't he! Well, he can't jump into bed with the wives or daughters of his best clients, can he? Although, I did hear tell he got into trouble once for bedding the daughter of one of PPA's biggest customers!" Pitcher chuckled at the memory. "That caused quite a ruckus, I can tell you, but I don't suppose he learned his lesson. His type never does. Anyway, him and Jessica have a marriage of convenience - he married her for her money, her daddy was worth millions. I don't think love was ever involved; Paul wouldn't know the meaning of the word!"

"You must have known Paul from an early age."

Pitcher took a swig of beer and turned the question over in his mind. "I suppose he must have been a lad of about ten when I first met him. Not a likeable lad - even in those days he was going about with Bruce Southam. They were both a couple of tear-a-ways and they had a vicious streak in them. You could tell when they played competitive games - they weren't there to play, they were there to win, and they didn't care who got hurt in the process. I'm surprised they didn't end up being charged by your lot!"

"I don't believe either of them have any sort of police record," said Dolby, "Although Bruce Southam was suspended from driving on a drink driving charge, but that was quite recently."

Pitcher shook his head. "They wouldn't have police records, would they? I'm pretty sure that whatever trouble they got themselves into Charles would have bailed them out - he knew a lot of the top people in the county by then, of course." He drank down some more beer. "When they left University, they both of them joined the paras - which would suit them, of course, they'd learn how to put the killer instinct into action in a practical way! They did three- or four-years beating people up for Queen and Country and then by all accounts they got mixed up in something *really* smelly and got drummed out."

Dolby leaned forward. "What exactly?"

Pitcher shrugged. "I don't know. It's rumours again. I do know there was a bit of a rumpus going on around when they were in their early twenties; they were in the paras and it was something to do with a girl, something pretty vicious, but they walked out of it smelling - not exactly of roses, I suppose, but they walked out of it unscathed, nevertheless. Although, come to think of it," he continued thoughtfully, "whatever it was probably rebounded on Paul in later years when he almost got the nomination as the local Tory MP."

"What happened?"

"Nothing earth shattering - the usual scenario, I suppose, the local party started off keen and then, when they did some digging into his background, they must have unearthed something they didn't like - something that could have embarrassed the Party, you know and they very politely told him to sling his hook."

"He seems to be accepted now, though," said Dolby.

"Oh yes, this was ten or fifteen years ago. He's had time to lubricate the wheels since then. But he'll never get anywhere with his political ambitions." Pitcher stretched and yawned. "Still, the business must keep him pretty busy."

"I know you've been gone for a year," said Dolby, "but you keep in touch. What's your impression of how the business is doing?"

"I've heard things aren't good," said Pitcher. "Sad really, but they seem to have gone downhill since Paul took over from his father. Not that it's entirely his fault. The financial services industry, insurance, banks, you name it, has been in turmoil and it's hit the Perots pretty badly. And when they had to close the aggregates business it was disastrous for them - that more or less paid for the running of the estate - after that they had to find the money out of the earnings from the insurance business, which wasn't - I should say isn't - easy."

"So, Bruce Southam's death will be an additional blow financially," said Dolby. "I understand he was one of the firm's biggest earners."

"Blow?" said Pitcher. He looked puzzled. "It won't be a blow - far from it - it's probably the best thing that could have happened to the firm - if you ignore the fact that Bruce Southam had to be murdered to achieve it."

"Sorry, I'm not following you."

"Obviously nobody's told you about the Top Earner's Policies. The firm has them on all its high earners. You know **key person** policies."

"And what exactly are key person policies?"

"Insurance Policies. Personal indemnities. PPA took them out on all its high earning employees," explained Pitcher. "If any of them die or are unable to work for whatever reason the insurance company pays out cash direct to the company. It helps tide the company over while they either get the person concerned back on his feet or, of course, replace him."

"And how much would the insurance company pay out on Bruce Southam?"

Pitcher stared into his beer. "I don't know what the current situation is, of course, but when I was looking after the policies his one was worth, say - "he paused again, knitting his brows in thought, "if my memory serves me correctly..." he paused and thought again, "...subject to checking the policy you understand - and bearing in mind when I was there he'd had two or three really successful years - well, I should think, something in the region of two million pounds."

CHAPTER SEVENTEEN

The proprietor of The Bald Griffin, irritated at being called away from serving at the bar, shook his head vigorously when Jacqueline Caine showed him Susie Neale's photograph. "No, sorry. If she did come into the bar I don't remember seeing her. Of course, we've been busy every evening this week and she could easily have come in without me noticing her. Anyway, what's she done?"

"Nothing, so far as we know," said Caine. "She didn't return home on Wednesday night and her husband is concerned for her safety. Actually, so are we - it's her car outside in your car park, up at the top end. She seems to have abandoned it." She turned to the proprietor's wife, a large bosomy woman with too much make-up. "She was wearing a red trouser suit. We estimate she would have got here about seven thirty on Wednesday evening, although we can't be sure of that."

The woman echoed her husband's words. "The face doesn't ring a bell with me and I don't remember serving anyone wearing a red trouser suit. But maybe one of the other staff served her. Or maybe she was with someone else and she didn't come to the bar herself. I don't know." She paused and scratched her ear thoughtfully. "You say she probably got here at about half past seven. If she was that early why would she park there - right at the other end of the car park?"

"Why shouldn't she?"

"Well, we're hardly full up at seven thirty and the car park would be half empty. Why park right at the back there, behind the trees?"

"I don't know." Caine returned the photograph to her bag. "But aside from exactly where she parked, what you're saying is, she might have parked and gone off somewhere else. But where would she have gone on foot?"

The proprietor, a small rotund man with ruddy cheeks and a round face, frowned helplessly. "Dunno. Into the village, I suppose. But why walk it when you're already in your car?"

"She may have met someone," suggested his wife. "Maybe she arranged to meet someone in our car park and then went off with him. He might have bought her a drink in here before they went, but I can't remember seeing her."

"I suppose there's no point in asking if you took note of the other cars in the car park?"

"You suppose right, Inspector," said the wife. "We'd like to help, but you've got to understand that this is a very popular meeting place in the summer - we've got a good reputation and our customers come a good distance. There's dozens of people coming and going all evening and this Wednesday was no exception, although, as I say, we weren't that busy at seven thirty when she's supposed to have got here."

"And of course, we're behind one or other of the bars for most of the time," added her husband, "Serving. So, we're not out in the car park taking notice of who's parking where and who's meeting who, if you see what I mean. You'd do better asking our customers if they saw this woman - maybe she was there when some of them were parking. They might have seen something." He looked across to the crowded bar again. "Now, if you wouldn't mind, Inspector, we really do have to look after our customers!"

"If you'd like to leave a picture of her, we could ask around our regulars and see if anyone saw her," suggested the wife. "That might help."

"I might do that," said Caine. "Thanks, anyway. One of my officers will be in touch. Oh, and sorry for dragging you away from your customers!" She walked across the saloon bar and out into the bright sunshine, blinking as she came into the light. It was just after mid-day and the car park was busy. The Bald Griffin was a well-run, popular pub purveying a variety of real ales and a wide range of pub grub and she was sure that whatever time Susie Neale had driven into the car park on Wednesday evening there must have been a lot of people about. Caine walked towards Susie's Ford Ka that was still parked over in the corner of the plot, on the other side of the tall, mature chestnut tree that towered over the area cordoned off by the blue and white incident tape. Now she thought about it she realised it was a curious place to park when there must have been plenty of other spaces closer to the Pub. What had induced Susie Neale to park so far away?

She walked across the car park. There were one or two curious sightseers hanging around the Ka, watching the tall figure of Sergeant Briggs, the fingerprint man, who now was crouched down beside one of its open doors dusting for prints. He and his colleagues from the forensic department had been examining the vehicle for nearly two hours now and soon it would be hoisted on to a police transporter truck and taken to the laboratories for further scrutiny. So far, the forensic team had come up with nothing interesting or unusual inside the car itself. Outside, they had found the tiniest spot of blood on the shingle beside the driver's door, so small that the forensic officer had almost missed it. But he said it could have come from anything or anyone - animal or human. What made it interesting was that it was where Susie would have got out of the car - and it might possibly have fallen from her body if, at that point, she had been wounded or attacked. But it might not be her blood and it would have to go to the laboratory for tests before they could be certain. Also, if she had been attacked as she left her car why had nobody seen or heard anything? And where was Susie Neale now?

It had taken DCI Caine some time to convince Superintendent Hansen that he should spare some extra manpower to look into Susie Neale's disappearance. After all, he had argued, she was a grown woman and well capable of looking after herself. She had probably sneaked off for a dirty mid-week break with a boyfriend, was his opinion. He had practically told Caine to come back when there was a dead body. It had only been her insistence that Susie's close association with the murdered Southams should be taken seriously that, in the end, had persuaded him to release a little extra resource and she knew that if she didn't come up with something interesting very quickly, even that assistance would be swiftly withdrawn.

Had Susie met someone here, in the car park, and gone off with them, as the publican's wife had suggested? It seemed a likely explanation. She had not walked down into the village, which was a few hundred yards away down the winding lane. At least, it was unlikely, as there was a dozen or more cottages between here and the High Street. Wednesday had been a pleasant evening when people were out and about, some of them even working in their front gardens. And nobody had seen Susie going by - a couple of PCs had spent the last hour and a half calling on the occupants of the houses and the few shops in the village, asking questions, and nobody had seen Susie - either alone or with somebody else - or heard anything unusual. But where else could she have gone? Caine walked to the edge of the car park and looked across the open countryside that lay beyond. Surely Susie had not left her car here and set off across the fields? There was no evidence to suggest she had. There had been some rain over the past few days, not very much and mostly during the night, but enough so that her shoes would have left some impression in the soft earth. But an hour's combing of the area by one of the constables had found no signs of anybody, Susie Neale or anyone else, leaving the Bald Griffin Car park to walk across the fields.

Caine opened the door of her car and climbed in. She sat quietly, thinking. Whatever had happened to Susie Neale she had not been robbed. Her handbag had been found stuffed under the front passenger seat and, so far as the police had been able to tell, nothing had been taken from it. Her credit cards were still there and there was over seventy pounds in cash still in her purse; so, too, was the car's key. Why would any woman get out of her car leaving her handbag under the seat with the car key still in it? Reluctantly Caine admitted to herself that the latter was possible. After all, dozens of vehicles were stolen every week from people who carelessly left their keys in the car when they got out. But she was certain that Susie would not have left her handbag behind, not voluntarily - why had Susie done this? There seemed only one possible reason - and it also explained why she had parked in this particular spot, such a long way from the pub. She had recognised the person she was meeting and he - or she - had arrived first and parked here, calling her over to park beside him when she arrived. They had been close enough to her car so that she had not had time to think about her bag before getting out to greet them. But why had she not gone back for it immediately afterwards? Whoever she was meeting they had somehow prevented her from going back for her bag. How had they accomplished that? Perhaps, if the blood on the shingle was Susie's...? Caine shivered, in spite of the brightness of the sunshine streaming in on her through the car windows. Whatever had happened here in the car park they - Susie Neale and the person she was meeting - had left in the other person's vehicle.

Caine suddenly realised she was hungry and looked at the clock on the dashboard. It was almost one o'clock. She had bought a tuna sandwich and a bottle of orange juice in the pub and now she removed them from the paper bag and tore the cellophane wrapping from the sandwich, taking a quick bite before reaching behind her for the Southam Murder file.

Caine skimmed quickly through the pages. Valerie Southam had been born in August 1974 and brought up by foster parents in Southend on Sea, Essex - there were no details of where she had actually been born, just a note that following the birth she had been taken under the care of the local authority and put into a Children's Home. She had attended a comprehensive school and left at the age of fifteen. After this the details became even more vague. Evidently, the normal means of tracing her movements - through her national insurance number and tax records - had not yielded much information, probably due to the fact that when she had worked she had not often paid national insurance or income tax - there was no mention, for instance of the time she had spent as a dancer at **The Red Dragon Club** and her records for the roughly seven years from fifteen to twenty two were full of large gaps. Finally, she went legitimate again, taking a job as a hairdresser in a Fen Molesey salon called Cutie-Cuts. Then, in quick succession, she had been a doctor's receptionist (W.B.Beard, M.D., The Grange, Maldon), a shop assistant at a Chelmsford branch of Boots The Chemist, some kind of office assistant in a commercial photographic records firm called Microcell Limited, a "demonstrator" for a company called "Midas Magic Gadgets" (probably, thought Caine, demonstrating widgets at exhibitions, such as the Ideal Home) until she had settled down as a housewife, marrying Bruce Southam when she was twenty four. Her marriage details were clearly recorded as were those of her son, Adam's, birth, and Caine was interested to see there was a note giving brief details of her earlier confinement, when she had had her daughter Karen. *'Subject gave birth to a daughter at University College Hospital 22.8.92 whilst resident at 42, Ramilles Mansions, Old Compton St., W1. Name of father not recorded. Child subsequently fostered'*, was all it said. Finally, bringing the record right up to date, there was a mention of Valerie's job as a receptionist at the Faulkbourne Manor Country House Hotel, just outside Maldon.

There really was not much to go on, thought Caine, nothing to indicate why Valerie Southam and her husband had been murdered - or, for that matter, why her best friend, Susie Neale, had vanished only a day or so later. Caine finished her sandwich and, leaving the bottle of orange juice unopened, started the car and set off back to FM Central.

Mark Dolby came into her office at just after four o'clock. "I think I may have something for you, Jackie." He said, looking pleased with himself. "But first I'm going to get a coffee. Can I get you one?"

Caine nodded. "Thanks, Mark. Black with one sugar." She had been reading through the file again, turning over something that was nagging at her mind. "But make it quick will you please, Mark, my daughter, Alison, is up from Town this evening with her boyfriend - it's her birthday and we're eating somewhere posh, apparently at his expense," she brushed a fringe of hair away from her eyes. "I suppose I should have had a haircut for the occasion, so the least I can do is get away early to tart myself up." Mark hovered in the doorway waiting for her to finish. "But I want us to compare notes before I go. And I hope you've got something significant to tell me because, to be honest, I feel like we're getting nowhere fast on this case."

He was back in a couple of minutes, balancing two reinforced plastic cups in one hand and a pile of biscuits on the other. "I raided the canteen on the way up," he explained, dropping the biscuits on the table and handing her one of the cups. He sat down. "I see you've been reading Wendy's report on Valerie Southam. Not much light there so far as I can see."

"Doesn't seem so." She closed the file and took a sip of the hot coffee. "I saw Paul Perot this morning, as you know. It's really curious - I've obviously never seen him before, but there's something familiar about him."

"Like what?"

She shrugged. "I wish I knew. It's just that he reminds me of someone. On a subliminal level - there's nothing definite, he just reminds me of someone, but I can't pin it down. I don't even know if it would help if I could - it could be just a TV personality or something equally inane. It's been bugging me all day. It's a bit like this whole case - I've been going round and round in circles on it all for hours and I still feel like I'm getting nowhere. So - please tell me you have something that might help!"

"As a matter of fact, I have," said Dolby. "A motive. A very good reason why the man we're looking for could easily be the same guy that's doing your head in with doppelgangers!"

"Paul Perot?"

"The same." Dolby nodded, smiling. "You know he heads up quite a big insurance and financial services operation in the City? Well, it transpires they're in quite a bit of financial trouble - and they just happen to have some sort of insurance cover on their top people that pays out if any of them pop their clogs or stop producing results for any other reason the insurance company considers legitimate." He paused to sip at his coffee. "Naturally, Bruce Southam was one of their top men, if not *the* top man - so, he's top of the list - and he has, of course, recently stopped being productive."

"How much are they paying out?"

"The policy's for Two million quid."

Caine whistled. "He must have been a good salesman!" She crunched another biscuit. "So, Perot's firm gets two million out of Southam's death?"

Dolby nodded. "Apparently. Always assuming we can't prove Perot did the evil deed himself, of course. So, as far as I'm concerned, that makes him our number one suspect."

"It's certainly a bloody good motive to kill someone." She took another sip of her coffee. "Perot didn't even mention this. Who spilled the beans to you?"

"Perot's firm's ex-accountant. Chap by the name of Bernard Pitcher. Retired, or more accurately kicked out of the firm not so long ago, but he was with them for nigh on forty years. Knows Paul and his father Charles very well. Seems a reliable sort of person too, although I have to say that he quite obviously doesn't like Paul Perot. What did you think of him?"

"He wasn't exactly Prince Charming and he didn't exactly bend over backwards to co-operate. As I say he didn't say a word about this insurance policy. And so far, he hasn't come up with a convincing alibi - says he has one, but he won't supply any of the details so we can check it."

"What *did* he say?"

"Nothing of any substance. According to him he was at a business meeting in the City on Tuesday evening, discussing merger plans with some big insurance outfit who are thinking of putting money into his business. But he refused to tell me who they are on grounds of business confidentiality."

"Ah now, that is interesting!" Dolby smiled conspiratorially, stretched his arms above his head and crossed his legs. "According to his new accountant those people backed off and the meeting was cancelled. The name of the company was -" He dug into his jacket pocket for his notebook and flicked quickly through the pages. "UI - that stands for 'Universal Insurance'."

"Why did they cancel?"

"Interestingly enough because of Bruce Southam. He had a meeting with their top brass a week or so ago and he turned up drunk. And, coincidentally, Sir Charles Ormsby, the Chairman of UI and the guy Southam apparently targeted for his insults and innuendoes, turns out to be the father of Phyllida Ormsby who lives in Upton Eccles and happens to be the owner of the cottage where Adam Southam and Philip Chantry went for their party on Tuesday evening. Interesting or what?"

Caine finished her coffee and leaned over to drop the empty cup into her waste bin. "I'd call it incestuous. This case is going that way, Mark, everyone seems to know everybody else. And most of the buggers are suspects!" She tapped her long slim fingers on the desktop. "So, Bruce really cocked things up for Paul Perot?"

Dolby nodded. "Handsomely. All the more reason why Paul should bump him off so as to collect the insurance money, I'd say. It's a sort of poetic justice. Shall we pull him in for further questioning?"

Caine shook her head. "Not for the time being. We haven't got enough on him yet and after what the Super said the other day I don't want to start making waves before we're sure of our ground."

Dolby nodded. "I suppose it's wise. He's bound to have a sharp brief working for him. That type always does. Do we have anything else on him?"

Caine frowned uncertainly. "As it happens we might have, although it's circumstantial and we can't prove anything. The evidence, if that's what it was, has gone up in smoke - literally." She told him how she had found Jake Thompson burning the old clothes. "But I had no way of knowing if they were linked to the crime. Perot said they were his father's old gardening clothes, but who know?" She looked at her watch. "I think we might just take another trip over to Upton Stapleford to see the Perot family tomorrow morning. Would you like to ring Paul Perot and tell him to expect us? Organise it for some time in the morning, preferably ten o'clock."

Dolby nodded. "I think there are some answers up at Upton, if you follow my drift. Any further news on Susie Neale?"

"Nothing. Forensics have taken her car away for examination, but they're not hopeful of finding anything else. It seems likely she met someone in the pub car park and went off with them - it doesn't look good. She left her handbag in the car; no woman would do that unless she was being coerced. Still, where there's life there's hope - and so far as we know she's still alive!" She pushed back her chair and stood up. "I'm off - hopefully I'll have time for a shower before picking Alison up at the station. Keep in touch, Mark and I'll see you at the Perot's tomorrow morning."

Dolby followed her out of the room. "Have a nice evening, Jackie and wish your daughter 'happy birthday' from me. I'll make that call to Paul Perot now and let you know if there's any change of plan." He walked back along the corridor to his own room. Once again, the colleagues he shared it with were all out, probably indicating, he thought, that the crime rate in Fen Molesey was running along nicely. As he sat down his telephone rang.

"Hallo, Mark - Dave Milligan. Thought you might be interested. We've found that van."

Dolby thought for a moment before he realised which van the Detective Constable was referring to. "You mean the one Garvey and his mate, Oldham, used for the computer and electrics heist? I don't know that my Guv'nor and me are interested in that case anymore, Dave. Garvey's too stupid to be involved in the Southam murders."

"I wouldn't argue with that," said Milligan. "Except..."

"Except what?"

"Maybe you should come and take a look. I'm out at Breckon Woods where Garvey and Oldham abandoned the van after they'd transferred the loot to Oldham's old banger. They pulled it well off the road and drove into a coppice of trees. A man out walking his dog spotted it a couple of hours ago and called it in."

Dolby looked at his watch. "I still don't see what this has to do with the Southam case, Dave - it's Friday evening and I had thought I might actually see my family and introduce myself to my wife and kids this weekend. I'm not driving all the way out to Breckon Woods on a Friday night unless there's something a lot more interesting than an empty van to look at."

"But that's the point," said Milligan, relishing the moment. "The van's not empty. There's a black sack in the back - and guess what's in it..."

"You tell me, Dave," said Dolby wearily. "I've had a hard week."

"Only some old clothes and a couple of towels." Said Milligan. "And before you say anything else, Mark - they're not just any old old clothes - they're covered in blood."

CHAPTER EIGHTEEN

Caine was waiting at the station pick-up point as Alison came out of the station. She was clutching one of those long canvas holdalls that reminded her mother of enormous colourful sausages - this one was bright red with blue piping - and made her wonder how any clothes could come out of them without creases. Like most young people, however, this did not seem to bother Alison. Somehow, she managed to look good even in creased and wrinkled clothes - an ability her mother envied. Now she was dressed in a smart, navy, short-skirted business suit that showed off her figure to great effect and as she opened the car door to throw her bag on to the back seat she pulled off the light-weight jacket with the yellow embroidered breast pocket, loosened the fine silk scarf about her neck and undid the top two buttons of her white blouse to expose the frilly lace of her brassiere.

"Phew! It was bloody hot on that train, mum!" She leaned over to kiss her mother then lapsed back with an exhausted sigh, pulling the seat belt across and pushing it down into its latch. "Sorry the train was late - something on the line apparently."

"Don't worry about it, darling - as a matter of fact I was almost late myself." She had been halfway home before she remembered she had not yet bought a birthday card for her daughter and she had frantically doubled back to catch one of the corner shops. It had taken her a good ten minutes to find a card that was at all suitable - for that read 'something funny', Alison couldn't abide the ones full of silly, sentimental words that she described as 'ugh!' "I had to tear myself away from the office - it's been a very busy day - then my number two rang me just as I got into the flat. I'm afraid we'll have to go back to my place so I can finish myself off."

"You don't need to mum, really - you look great!" Caine dismissed her daughter's comment as filial loyalty. She felt far from great. It had been very hot all day. Her make-up was a mess, her blazer was creased, her skirt felt like a rag and she hadn't had time to strip off and take a shower when she got home. Not two seconds after she had opened the door to go into her flat Mark Dolby had rung her with the news that a bundle of blood-stained clothes had been found hidden in an abandoned van. They might be those worn by the murderer in the Southam case - only **might** he had warned, they couldn't be certain at this stage. They would know as soon as the lab tests had been had carried out. The other interesting thing was that the van in which the clothes had been found was the one used by Jason Garvey to rob the computer and video warehouse. Did she think that meant Garvey was involved in the murders? She told Mark Dolby to sleep on it - they would discuss it in the morning. No sooner had she finished that call than Alison rang to say she was on her way and expected to be at Chelmsford station in half an hour. Caine had checked her watch, calculated it would take her all of that time to drive to Chelmsford during the evening rush hour traffic, grabbed her handbag and set off back to her car; only to arrive at the station to the announcement that the service was 'suffering delays of up to half an hour, due to 'something on the line'. She had spent the next forty minutes sitting in her car hot, bothered and watching out for marauding traffic wardens. What made her even more exasperated was that she had even forgotten to write out the card she had gone to all that trouble to buy for Alison. She would have to do it back at the flat, before they went on to the hotel, and give it to her at dinner.

"There's time, Alison, if you're worrying about being late for that boyfriend of yours. What was his name - Lyall? My flat's on the way to the hotel. According to the directions I've been given it's only a few minutes out of town - Layer Marney used to be a Manor House or something owned by the local squire and it's literally a stone's throw from Fen Molesey. Anyway, all I want is to just have a quick shower and then throw on some fresh clothes." She unconsciously took one of her hands from the steering wheel to brush away her fringe for the umpteenth time. Her hair she could do nothing about, except wash.

"I'll join you then, mum - I might just as well change at your place as at the hotel." Said Alison. "And don't worry about Lyall - he's usually late for appointments - he says that whoever he's meeting will be glad to see him no matter what time he arrives!"

Then he's a conceited beggar, thought Caine.

It was an opinion she had no inclination to change when she finally met Lyall Keating in the bar of The Layer Marney Country House Hotel. She and Alison had arrived at more or less the agreed time - eight o'clock - and Alison, now looking fresh and made up, casual but cool in a loose-fitting trouser suit, had just had time to take her bag up to her room and get back down again when he arrived. Lyall Keating was handsome in a classic way, Greek almost, with raven black hair, light olive skin that spoke of Mediterranean ancestry. He was immaculately dressed in a navy-blue suit that was well cut and expertly pressed, belying the fact that he had just driven down from Cambridgeshire on a hot summer's evening.

He looked at his gold Rolex as he strode across the room to meet them. "I'm so sorry I'm so late, Alison, darling!" he caught Caine's daughter in a swift but firm embrace, kissing her on the lips and then swung her away to confront her mother, reaching out his hand to snatch hers up with an exaggerated flourish and kiss it. "And this must be your mother - I'm delighted to meet you, Mrs Caine - I've heard so much about you! Alison is very proud of your achievements you know!" His looks may have been Mediterranean, but his voice was pure English upper middle class.

"Oh, really, I wonder what they can be!" said Caine.

He squeezed her hand and practically clicked his heels in his enthusiasm, not giving Alison the opportunity to introduce him. "I, of course, am Keating - Lyall Keating."

Alison would probably castigate her for it if she knew, thought Caine, but she could not help feeling that her daughter's boyfriend was behaving like an overbearing 'Hooray Henry'. She fully expected him to hand her his business card, pointing out that he was a Director of the largest advertising agency in the United Kingdom, second only to God's. Instead, he raised his hand to catch the eye of the barman and asked. "Can I get you another drink? What are you having?"

Caine was about to answer him when another man, tall, about her own age, with prematurely silvered hair, entered the room. He stopped and, with a quick glance about him to examine the faces of the other people congregated at the small tables and at the bar, nodded when he saw Jacqueline Caine and came swiftly in her direction. He stopped a few feet in front of her, smiling, seeming not to notice Alison and Lyall, his eyes fixed on her alone.

"Jackie - Jackie Caine - It must be over twenty years, but you've hardly changed. I'd recognise you anywhere!"

Someone once said that faces may change, but voices never do. Jacqueline Caine recognised both his face and his voice, although now there was a distinct North American twang to the latter.

She had not seen Christopher Stone for well over twenty years - a quick calculation told her it could be as many as twenty-five - and she could hardly remember the last time they had met. He had arrived at the door of her tiny flat in Walthamstow, looking flustered and excited and asked if Jonathan, her husband, was in. She, Jacqueline, had been preparing to go out and she had called to her husband and left Christopher to find his own way into the lounge, where Jonathan was relaxing and watching television. She never found out what they had discussed that night, but she suspected it was something to do with drugs. Jonathan was working undercover at the time, and that evening was just two nights before he had been gunned down in the course of his duties. Christopher, she knew, managed a Casino and entertainment set-up in Brentwood at the time, a perfectly respectable place so far as she knew, but Jonathan had hinted that there was mounting concern that establishments of this sort were being targeted by drug cartels eager to expand their illegal 'markets'. She had surmised that Stone was passing some sort of information on to Jonathan, information which had resulted - Jacqueline Caine believed - in the police raid in which Jonathan had been murdered. After that Christopher Stone had disappeared. It was rumoured he had left the country, his life under threat from one of London's leading drug barons.

She was surprised to see him here, in Fen Molesey, after all these years. "Christopher! I almost didn't recognise you." She laughed. "It must be the moustache. You always said you were going to grow a moustache! I'm not sure it suits you, though!"

He smiled. Caine had never been sure about the way Christopher Stone smiled. His cheeks creased into dimples and he showed his teeth, but his eyes seemed never to follow the mood, they remained cold, grey and aloof, cynical, as if his early experiences had soured his entire outlook on life. He moved forward and kissed her lightly on the cheek, then turned inquiringly towards Alison and Lyall.

"My daughter, Alison," Said Caine, "We're here to celebrate her birthday this evening - and this is her friend, Lyall Keating. Alison, Lyall, this is Christopher Stone an old acquaintance. We haven't seen each other for more than twenty years!"

Alison smiled widely and made a gesture which Caine took to be a minimal excuse for a curtsy. Keating, looking none too pleased at the way this tall stranger had burst in upon their little group and hijacked his womenfolk just at the point where he had meant to take control of them himself, offered his hand in the direction of Christopher Stone and announced gruffly, "Lyall Keating, Creative Director of FB Fogarty Bleu." Caine wondered at his use of the professional title in a purely social context. Did he need it to boost his confidence? More to the point, did Christopher Stone have even a clue what he was talking about when he mentioned "*FB Fogarty Bleu*"?

Unperturbed, Stone grasped the other man's hand and shook it vigorously. "Christopher Stone, proprietor of the Layer Marney Hotel." Keating withdrew his hand hurriedly, his face colouring as if he had been bested in some strange battle of wills and was unable to think of an adequate rejoinder.

"Well, you always wanted to be a chef, Christopher" said Caine, surprised herself at his revelation that he was the proprietor of this splendid hotel. She quickly filled the small silence that had descended between them. "It looks like you've more than achieved that - I hear this place is renowned for its excellent dining facilities."

Stone laughed with false modesty. "Oh, I've only had the place for three and a half years, but I think I've stamped my mark on it!" He put his arm around her shoulder and gave her a squeeze, a little too possessively Caine thought, but she said nothing. "Look, why don't you have your meal on me tonight - to celebrate our meeting again."

Caine hesitated. "Really, Christopher, I'm not sure..."

"Nonsense - everything's on the house. It's the least I can do, bumping into you again after all these years!" He bowed with mock grace. "I'm so glad - and I wonder, as I seem to have the evening free, if I could join you?"

Caine found herself nodding. "Well, of course, yes we'd be delighted..." She did not know how she could refuse.

"Excellent!" Stone smiled broadly and waved at the barman. "A bottle of our best Dom Perignon, Charles - bring it to table number seven." He turned back to Caine's group. "Jackie, Alison, Mr Keating - may I call you Lyall? - I'm going to treat you to the best meal you've ever had anywhere - anytime."

For a fleeting moment Jacqueline Caine wondered why Stone was being so generous - and whether she had done the right thing in accepting his generosity. She hardly knew the man and she wasn't sure she wanted to know him any better. Her association with Stone all those years ago had been entirely through her late husband. She had met him on two or three social occasions, in larger groups, but she had hardly spoken to the man and could scarcely describe him as a friend. An acquaintance, certainly, but a friend? Hardly. He had not, in those days, seemed particularly friendly towards her. Maybe, now, he was trying to extend his circle of friends? He had obviously been in the area for over three years, but sometimes it is hard to establish social contacts, especially if you have been out of the country for well over twenty years. On the other hand, come to think of it she, herself, was just about to move into the area; it could do no harm to make a new friend or acquaintance, could it? She acquiesced. Stone led them off towards the dining room. Lyall Keating opened his mouth to say something, thought better of it and stepped aside to let Caine and her daughter walk in front of him.

Table number 7, Caine noted, had been set for three, but at a snap of Stone's fingers his extremely efficient staff had set an extra place and a fourth chair had appeared, as if from nowhere.

They had ordered their hors d'oevres and main courses before Caine had the opportunity of asking Stone her most pressing question. "Where did you get to all these years, Christopher? And why?"

He regarded her across the table, over the elegant arrangement of red, yellow and white carnations and she thought the hardness in his eyes softened just a little when he raised his champagne flute. She noticed that his fingers were short and fat, an incongruity in a man so tall and lean. "Ever the inquisitive police lady," he was saying with a smile. "Always asking questions; but before I answer that one let's drink a couple of toasts - first of all to the young lady," he turned to Alison, "Here's to a very happy birthday and many more to come and" he turned back to face Jacqueline Caine, "to 'renewed friendship'" The four of them clinked glasses and drank. He put his glass down and considered her question for a few moments. "I was in the States for nearly twenty years," he said. "You know why I went there - you must have known what was going on. I had to get out when Bobby Roberts realised that I'd been informing on him and sent his goons after me. I came back to England again about three and a half years ago, when the news reached me that he had died."

"Who was this Bobby Roberts, then?" asked Alison, sipping her champagne.

"He was a gangster - leader of a drugs ring," said her mother. "He was most active in the early nineteen eighties and nineties."

"If you knew about him why didn't you arrest him and put him away?"

"Would that it was that easy," sighed Caine.

"That was all part of what I was working on, I suppose," said Christopher, reaching for the champagne bottle and lifting it from the ice bucket. He topped up their glasses before continuing. "Putting him away, I mean. Roberts managed to move in high circles even though he was a big-time crook and I suppose the reason I got involved was to help bust his racket. Of course, he didn't like the idea of that - not one little bit! Unfortunately, as your mother will tell you, Alison, he got to find out what I was trying to do and, so I'm told, he took out a contract on me."

"He was going to have you killed?" Alison asked, unable to keep the enthusiasm from her voice. "It's just like a movie!"

"Unfortunately, it was more real than that," said Christopher. "I got out fast, I can tell you."

"Your father, on the other hand, Alison, was not so fortunate. They got him," said Caine bitterly, taking a large gulp of the chilled champagne to cover her emotion and stem the tears that pricked the back of her eyes even now, more than twenty years after the event. "I always knew Roberts was behind Jonathan's death, Christopher, but we never came anywhere near proving it." She looked across at him, her eyes accusing. "You leaving at the time you did, just disappearing like that, didn't help! We didn't know for certain, of course, because Jonathan didn't let on what was going on, but we thought you might have had vital evidence that could have convicted Roberts!"

He threw up his hands in a gesture of surrender. "I'm sorry - believe me, I am - really sorry. But what I had wasn't concrete evidence, Jackie - it would never have stood up in court, not after Roberts's lawyers had had a go at it! I was working on it, but I didn't have enough. I'm sorry!" He sighed. "Look, I just couldn't hang around waiting to be dumped in the Thames wearing a pair of concrete overshoes - Roberts was determined to get me. Neither could I let anyone know where I was going, or he'd have sent his goons after me. I just had to drop out of sight until the heat was off. I had to vanish!" He shrugged. "So, that's what I did!"

Caine looked about her, her eyes running over the large dining room which must have seated at least sixty people very comfortably at the large tables, each laid with its glittering array of silver cutlery on a snow-white tablecloth, with a perfect arrangement of red, yellow and white carnations at its centre. The carpet was thick and sumptuous, the high, vaulted ceiling with its crystal chandeliers and hand painted, gold leafed cornices spoke of wealth and opulence. "You seem to have done very well for yourself, Christopher, for a man who ran away from his responsibilities."

Stone looked hurt. "Don't say that, Jackie. All this has nothing to do with the fact that I ran away from Bobby Roberts and his thugs. Good God, woman, it was more a long time ago! I worked hard to get where I am today - I started in the States way back then, with something really small. I'd always had leanings towards being a chef and it was a good way to hide out - nobody would have thought of looking for a chef when they were searching for an entertainment manager would they? So, I started off cheffing for someone else, then after a few years I set up on my own. I was lucky, I made a bit of money and when I came back to England, after Roberts went to meet his maker, or more likely his maker's chief protagonist, I sold up and came back to England. I spent a long time looking around the country before I settled for this hotel. I had a bit of money, but not that much! There is a mortgage on this place you know!"

His face coloured and he stopped speaking abruptly as the team of waiters descended on the table to serve the hors d'oeuvres. The food was artistically arranged on enormous bone china plates which they expertly placed in front of each diner. Food properly in place they hung anxiously, each at the shoulder of the person they had served, until Stone, their Lord and Master, nodded his approval, when they vanished as if at the wave of a Magician's wand.

"This is splendid," said Lyall, looking pleased for the first time since Stone had joined the party. He lifted a small piece of pate de foie gras, balanced precariously on a slice of melba toast, to his lips and popped it into his mouth, his jaws working in appreciation. "Delicious."

Alison was making appropriate noises over her Parma Ham. Stone gave a satisfied nod and looked across the table at Jacqueline Caine. She was taking no interest in her food but gazing over Stone's shoulder at something that was happening behind him. He turned. A group of four people - two men and two women - were walking across the room behind a waiter, towards a corner table. Stone turned back and smiled. "I see you're showing an interest in Paul Perot and his guests, my dear. Do you know him?"

"We have met," said Caine. She looked across at him, continued sternly. "And please don't refer to me as 'my dear', Christopher. We weren't that well acquainted even in the old days and we certainly aren't now. Besides, being addressed as 'your dear' makes me sound old and I certainly don't *feel* old!"

"You always were hard to get on with," said Stone, with a pained expression.

She smiled sweetly, feeling she had made her point. "It's you, Christopher, you don't know how to treat us modern ladies, we're far too independent for your liking, that's the problem, we want to be our own people, not some man's little lap dog - or should I say, 'lap bitch'. We want to go our own ways and do our own things - but all is not quite lost, Christopher dear, we still like to think we can attract a man when we want to." She lifted her champagne glass. "Let's drink to the continued fraternisation of the sexes, shall we, each on their own exclusive terms?"

They drank. Stone cut into his Swedish herring and pushed a portion across the plate to coat it heavily with sour cream before lifting it to his mouth. He chewed appreciatively for a few moments. "I take it your interest in Perot is professional? I understand it was one of the directors of his business who was murdered the other night. Does that mean it's your case?"

"Mmm!" This was an affirmation of the quality of Caine's creamed avocado as much as an answer to Stone's question. She chewed thoughtfully for a few moments before answering in more depth. "One of the directors of the company, yes and his wife. And yes, it is my case."

Keating leaned forward keenly. "This sounds interesting. Somebody been murdered?"

"It's been all over the papers, silly," said Alison. "Mummy's the detective in charge of the case."

"Oh, any luck then?" asked Keating, smiling widely. "Know who-dun-it yet?"

"We do have some ideas," said Caine carefully. "A number of people are helping us with our inquiries."

"And I'll bet yon Perot is one of your suspects," said Stone with a smile. "Bit of a dark horse he is. Always has been, mind."

Caine looked up from her spoon, which she was sliding effortlessly through the flesh of the fruit on her plate. "I can't comment on whether or not he's a suspect Christopher, but do you happen to know him?"

He nodded, placed another piece of herring into his mouth and wiped his lips delicately with his napkin. "As a matter of fact, I've known Paul Perot for most of my life - not as a friend, you understand, he's a few years younger than me, but as a sort of distant acquaintance. We were at the same school."

"Of course, I'd forgotten you were brought up near here. So, you knew Perot as he was growing up? What was he like?"

Stone finished his herring and arranged his knife and fork carefully on his plate. "Your interest is purely professional?"

She nodded. "Purely. I'm only interested in Perot because he happens to have known the murder victims. When we're investigating a crime, we like to get to know something about the background of our victims and those who were close to them. We often find motive in proximity if you follow my drift. Personal detail of that sort often turns out to be very important to an investigation."

Keating nodded shrewdly. "It's a well-known fact, Chris, that most murders are committed by people who know the victims. Isn't that correct, Mrs Caine?"

"So, I have heard," agreed Stone. "Of course, Jackie, I ask only in your own interests," he was almost going to add 'my dear' but stopped himself just in time and smiled across at her. "Perot is a bit of a ladies' man. Oh, I know he's been married for years, but I can assure you that hasn't stopped him playing the field. His wife, Jessica, doesn't really care what - or should I say 'who'? - he does. That is Jessica by his side, by the way, she's the ideal dinner companion when he wants to charm a business prospect. She loves her food and she can't resist the victuals we serve here - by rights she should be fat as a house, but just look at her figure! Obviously, it doesn't attract Paul any longer, but she has plenty of other admirers I can assure you." He returned his gaze to Jacqueline Caine. "Anyway, he's a typical ladies' man and I understand he treats them very badly once he's got what he wants out of them."

Caine smiled. "This sounds a little like the pot calling the kettle black. As I recall it, Christopher, and if I remember rightly what Jonathan said about you, you were a bit of a lady killer yourself back in the old days."

Stone smiled and shrugged. "One might say those were the days, Jackie. Unfortunately, my charms seemed to be lost on you. Anyway, I thought you ought to know - Paul Perot can be very charming, Jackie, especially when he's after something."

"Meaning me, I suppose?" said Caine, raising an eyebrow quizzically. She laughed dryly. "Have no fears on that score, Christopher. I interviewed your friend Paul this morning in connection with the Southam murders and I found him far from charming. I'm quite safe, I can assure you." She laughed again, "Besides, I'm probably too old for him. His type usually go after the dolly birds." She glanced meaningfully at Keating, but he missed the look and continued to eat slowly, his eyes on his plate, savouring each mouthful. "Tell me what Perot was like at school, Christopher."

"Oh it's '*show me the child and I will show you the man*' time is it?" asked Stone, leaning back in his chair and considering his next words. "He and Bruce Southam were bosom buddies of course in those days - I knew them at Boarding school. They would have been eleven when I first ran into them. I left when they were about fourteen, I suppose. I was - 'am' I guess - a few years their senior."

"And what were they like?"

He shrugged. "They were schoolboys. They hated lessons. They were keen on sport. Keen on girls. And keen on cruelty and anything connected with it."

"They liked pulling the legs off spiders?"

"Probably. But they were more into pulling the legs off other kids - at least, they would have been if they could have devised some way of doing it without being found out. They were bullies, Jackie." He half turned to look in Paul Perot's direction. "Have you met Paul's brother-in-law, James Parr, during your investigations?"

"No, but I know of him. My number two interviewed him. I expect I'll meet him tomorrow when we continue our inquiries. Why?"

"Oh, it's just that he was their main victim at school - they bullied him unmercifully, at least during the time I knew them."

"But why would they do that? Parr practically lives with Paul. He married his sister for Christ's sake!"

"Don't ask me to explain it, Jackie, I'm just telling you how it is - or was, certainly in those days. You'll have to ask Parr himself if you want reasons! Or even Paul Perot, although I don't suppose he'll give you an answer - he's more likely to shout 'foul!'

and call for his lawyer. Anyway, I understand Paul and Bruce went on to use their undoubted talents in the infliction of agony and cruelty by going into the paratroopers and learning how to inflict injury and death in a more professional manner."

"Did they see any action?" asked Keating.

"I think they did a term or so in Northern Ireland if that's what you mean. But they saw plenty of action of another kind here in England, or so I'm told. Spent a couple of years living it up, tearing around the countryside on high performance motor bikes and bedding every available woman - and some not so available - within ten miles of their barracks! They finally went too far though and got kicked out of the service, or so I've heard." He shrugged. "That's about all I can tell you about them. Except that Perot seems to have lived his reputation down and is quite a figure in the county Establishment nowadays - mind you he owes most of that to his father's influence in establishing those gardens of his out at Upton Stapleford. The people who matter look upon it as a very useful and public-spirited service."

Caine peered across the room at Paul Perot and his party. "Who are the couple with them tonight?"

Christopher Stone half turned in his seat and looked in the same direction, as if to double check before answering. "That's Charlie Ormsby and his wife - Sir Charles and Lady Ormsby to be precise. Ormsby is a big noise in insurance. That's Perot's business, of course."

"Funny - I thought they'd fallen out," said Caine, almost to herself.

*   *   *   *   *   *

*

It was only when she stood up at the end of the meal that Caine realised just how much drink they had had. Christopher Stone had obviously ordered his staff to keep the champagne flowing during the evening, and the discussion around the table had been so lively and interesting that she had hardly noticed her glass being topped up every few minutes. And she had just gone on drinking it - glass after glass. As she made her way across the restaurant to the Ladies' Room she found herself wobbling a little and giggling at the thought that possibly it wasn't the champagne, but rather the high heeled shoes Alison had persuaded her to wear. She had bought them years ago, tried them on again when she got home and found them too high, so she had never worn them again until tonight. But she had to admit they did something for her. She smiled to herself. Perhaps it **was** the shoes, but then again, she wouldn't be giggling like this if it hadn't been for the champagne - she wasn't a giggler, she had grown out of that years ago. You couldn't be a Detective Chief Inspector and giggle.

Alison came into the ladies' room while Caine was busy making faces in the mirror.

"Mummy, I think you've had too much to drink," she said. "You'd better not drive yourself home."

"Nonsense, I'm not drunk. Well, not that drunk anyway." She walked an almost straight line along the edge between the floor tiles. "Look. Well, I suppose I do wobble a bit, but I can still see where I'm going."

Her daughter giggled. "It's probably your shoes."

"It can't be. You're also drunk and you're not wearing these shoes!"

They dissolved into laughter and hugged each other.

"What do you think of Lyall, Mummy? Don't you think he's gorgeous!"

"You don't leave me much room to criticise him!" said Caine, trying hard to take the subject seriously. "If you think he's gorgeous what can I say to persuade you that I think he's just a little tingy-wingy bit less than perfect?"

"He is though, isn't he? Gorgeous, I mean!"

"For your sake I just hope so, darling. And I hope something else, too."

"What's that?"

"I hope he's not married."

Alison looked horrified and Caine was not sure whether it was because she had dared to voice her fears or because the thought had never entered her daughter's sometimes naïve head.

"I think I'd better have a few black coffees," she told the others when she got back to the table. "It's all right for you lot, you're all staying the night here, but I've got to drive home."

"I'll order you a taxi," said Lyall. The skin of his normally olive face was flushed pink from the champagne. "You shouldn't drive."

"No, that won't be necessary. I'll drop you off home," said Christopher. "If you'd like to leave the keys with me, I'll get one of my staff to drive your car back to your place in the morning."

Caine peered across at him. Her head was throbbing a little now and her vision was a little hazy. There was something she wanted to ask him, something she had meant to ask him during their earlier conversation about the Southam murders, but she couldn't think what it was. Damn that champagne!

Alison interrupted her thoughts. "But I thought you said you owned this place, Christopher! You don't mean to say you've got this huge hotel with all these bedrooms and you don't have one for you to sleep in?"

He laughed. "Actually, Alison. It's true - I haven't. Not here, anyway. But it just so happens I've just acquired another hotel and I have a rather nice set of rooms to live in there. Anton, the Chef on duty here tonight usually cooks at my other place, but I wanted the food to be especially good here tonight, so I did a swap with Ricci from the other place. Anton will drive me home and we can drop you off on the way, Jackie. Then one of my staff can run your car home to your place early tomorrow morning. It's no problem."

"And where is this other hotel?" asked Caine.

"Out at Faulkbourne - I took over the Country House Hotel there about nine months ago. It's bigger than this place - well, there's a few more bedrooms and quite a bit more land. It also has a Shooting Club there. The whole Faulkbourne complex was a bit pricey for me, I suppose, but this place has been doing so well I thought I'd stretch myself a bit. One day I hope to have a whole chain of country house hotels. Have you been to the Faulkbourne yet, Jackie?"

"No. I've hardly had time to get my feet under the desk. Should I have?"

"I thought you might have visited in the course of your inquiries into these recent murders. Come to think of it, though, somebody did mention a visit from the police, but it was an ordinary PC, I believe."

Caine looked thoughtfully across the table at him. "Yes, I see what you mean, Christopher. I'd forgotten, for the moment that Valerie Southam worked at the Faulkbourne. You knew her I suppose?"

Stone shook his head. "Hardly. I have a General Manager to look after the staff, but of course I ran into her from time to time." He toyed with his wine glass, rolling the stem between his thumb and forefinger.

"I imagine good staff are hard to hang on to in a set-up like this," said Lyall Keating.

"I leave that to my Manager," said Stone. "Of course, I take a personal interest in the kitchen staff - the cuisine is my main priority, it's the pillar on which the reputation of the hotel is built, of course. People come here and to the Faulkbourne mainly for the food - and the wine, that goes without saying. We keep very good cellars." He lifted his glass and gazed at the amber liquid before draining it. "But, yes, the staff situation is difficult from time to time, and we do have our moments. Only a few weeks ago we sacked one of the chamber maids for using one of the hotel bedrooms as a love nest. Her boyfriend used to creep in during the day."

Alison giggled. "I hope she changed the bed linen!"

Caine found herself steering the conversation back to the murders. "How did Valerie strike you?"

Stone shrugged. "She was quite attractive. Middle aged. Bit mutton dressed as lamb on occasions. Of course, I leave these minor staffing matters to my Manager, but I couldn't help feeling Valerie Southam lacked empathy - she didn't seem like a people person, if you see what I mean - hardly the correct trait for a receptionist."

"Funny. That's not quite the impression I've been getting from other people," said Caine thoughtfully.

"How so?"

"Well, according to one of her neighbours - actually a long-standing friend - Valerie was very caring towards an elderly lady they were close to when they knew her over twenty years ago. She visited her regularly, but there was no family relationship. Valerie seems to have kept the connection going entirely out of the kindness of her heart. That doesn't sound like lack of empathy."

Stone shrugged. "Really? Oh well, as I say, I leave that sort of recruitment to my Manager. There's no point having a watch dog and barking yourself is there!"

A question traced its way elusively through Caine's mind, but she lost it amongst the champagne bubbles. She yawned sleepily and looked at her watch, surprised to see that it was a quarter to twelve. "It's been a lovely evening, thank you, Christopher, but it's time I was heading home, I've got a heavy day tomorrow." She picked up her handbag and opened it. "I will leave my car keys with you, if you're sure it's okay, Christopher and I'd be obliged if one of your people could drive it back to my place in the morning. I have an early appointment, but my number two will be driving me, so if I'm not in they can drop the key through the letter box." She stood up. "But isn't it a bit early for you, Christopher, I mean you can't really shut up shop and drag the chef away, yet can you?"

Stone looked around the dining room. There were only six or seven tables still occupied. "No problem. Everyone's virtually finished eating and they won't need Anton any longer.

Besides, he has a full staff back in the kitchen and they can look after any unforeseen eventualities. I'll just go and tell him we're ready to go." He turned to Alison and Lyall. "Thank you for helping make it such a delightful evening. Have a good night and if there's anything you need in your room don't hesitate to ask. I hope you'll call in on us again soon." He strode off towards the kitchen, turning on his heel as he reached the door. "I'll get Anton to bring the car around to the front entrance and meet you there, Jackie. We'll be about five minutes."

"Nice chap," said Lyall, standing up. "Ambitious too - I wonder if he needs any advertising for this place. It deserves to be better known." Alison shot him a fierce look. "I'll just go off to the gents, if you'll excuse me." He walked quickly away.

Alison clambered to her feet, a little unsteadily and looked across at her mother. Their eyes met. "What?"

Caine tried to choose her words with precision. "I thought our friends Bleu Fogarty, or whatever they're called, were into advertising for Hi tech - not food! Why would Lyall be interested in advertising a hotel?"

Alison giggled and shook her head. "It was just his little joke - he wasn't serious!" She changed the subject quickly. "Will you be safe with Christopher in the car?"

Caine smiled. "I'm not that drunk, darling. I know what I'm doing - I'm an officer of the law - and besides I've got the most frightful headache coming on!" She was serious. She didn't know how many glasses of champagne she had consumed, but they were really taking their toll.

"No, seriously, I'm worried, Mum," said Alison. "I'm not sure he's all right - I mean, what was all that about drugs and having to run away to America to stop himself from being bumped off?"

"He was manager of an entertainment centre, darling, not a gangster. And that was twenty-five years ago. Now he's a respectable hotelier. Don't worry, I can handle Christopher Stone. And you have a good night too." They hugged. "I only hope you can handle your Mr Keating."

Her daughter laughed and she had to remind herself that Alison was over twenty- five and well beyond parental control. "You bet I can handle him, Mum!" she said. "I'm looking forward to it!"

They wandered slowly and a little unsteadily out of the restaurant, through the spacious hall and out to the entrance steps where they were to say their farewells. After a few seconds what must have been Anton the Chef, still wearing his white kitchen overalls, drove a silver Bentley around the side of the building and drew it up beside the front door. Christopher Stone climbed out of the passenger seat and, with an exaggerated bow, opened the back door of the car for Jacqueline Caine. She gave her daughter a last quick hug and made her way carefully down the steps, waving as she clambered into the car. Stone jumped in beside her and pulled the door closed behind him, nodding to Anton that they were ready to set off.

"Okay, Monsieur Stone - the lady will tell me please where is her house?" Anton spoke with a heavy French accent.

Caine, busy adjusting and fixing her seat belt, told him her address and he slipped the car into gear, guiding it carefully across the forecourt of the big house and out towards the drive, the headlights slicing through the darkness ahead. Stone sat next to her on the wide leather seat, not making contact.

"Thank you for a really lovely evening, Christopher."

"My pleasure."

"But tell me, how did you know Alison and I would be at your hotel this evening?"

"Her name - Alison Caine was on the room booking. And I'd read about your appointment as DCI at Fen Molesey. I just put two and two together and, luckily, I was right. I suppose I took a bit of a chance, but it was a chance worth taking don't you think."

They were silent as the big car reached the end of the driveway and swung out onto the road. Caine leaned back, her head resting against the leather restraint. She felt slightly sick and knew she had drunk too much. The top part of her skull was throbbing itself into a migraine. She could have left her questions until the morning, or some other time, but they were nagging at her and she thought she might as well ask them while she remembered.

"Christopher, you were working in the night club business - entertainment, casinos, that sort of thing - in the nineties." She giggled again and gave a tiny burp. "Oops! Sorry." Stone nodded, turning towards her. It was dark in the back of the car, but there was a little yellow light reflecting from the instrument panel on the dashboard and the reflection glinted ghoulishly from his eyes. She shook her head and continued. "Do you remember *The Red Dragon Club*?"

He nodded. "Oh yes - Ramilly Street, wasn't it? But that was in Soho - not my area at all. I was up here in Essex."

"No - it was Frith Street in Soho. Not Ramilly Street - where *is* Ramilly Street?"

"I don't know now you mention it. It just came to me. Anyway, I hardly knew *The Red Dragon*, only by reputation, really. It was a long time ago, you know and I was only an occasional visitor to the area. Why do you ask?"

Her migraine closed in and she shut her eyes. Stone asked her a few more questions, conversationally, but afterwards she could not remember what he had asked or, indeed, her answers, if she answered at all.

CHAPTER NINETEEN

Mark Dolby put the telephone receiver back on its rest and sighed. DCI Caine had not sounded at all pleased to hear his news that the blood-stained clothes from the Southam murder had possibly turned up in the van abandoned by the computer warehouses thieves. She sounded as if she had other things on her mind. Oh well, she was entitled not to show any interest - it was gone six o'clock on Friday evening and she had escaped for a rare night out with her grown-up daughter. It had been a hard week for both of them he reflected, yawning, but homicide was like that - there was always a sense of urgency to get the murderer locked up as soon as possible in case he - or she - tried for a repeat performance. He yawned again and looked at his watch - he ought to be on his way home now - pity he had agreed to meet Dave Milligan for a look at those famous bloody clothes! But at least he would not have to travel out to Breckon Woods to see them. Milligan had agreed he could look at them when they brought the van into the station, which should be at any time now. Dolby got up and made his way to the door.

Detective Constable Milligan stepped around the bloodstained clothes and walked towards Dolby as he entered the car park. Milligan had spread the various items of clothing on a plastic sheet ready for inspection and so they could itemise and photograph them before they were taken away for forensic examination. The vehicle in which they had been found - a white

Vauxhall van - was parked a few yards away with its back doors wide open.

Dolby stood and looked down at the crumpled clothing. "What exactly have we got here, then, Dave?"

Milligan went through the list from his notebook, double checking against each item as he ticked it off. "A pair of man's jeans - blue, well-worn and with plenty of dried blood on them. It'll be interesting if it matches Southam's. One white T shirt. Plain. No design. Also covered in blood. A pair of socks - not much blood on them, if any, but you wouldn't really expect it would you? They'd be protected by the jeans. Marks and Spencer's, so not easy to trace! Next, a pair of underpants, very soiled I'm afraid and not just with blood. Whoever this geezer was he made a good job of changing out of his old clothes, didn't he. Anyway, they're also M & S - makes it very easy for us and I don't think! Narrows it down to about thirty-five million people who might have bought them. Next, of course, is the towel - one bath sheet - almost certainly belonged to the Southams and 'borrowed', let's say, by the killer to help him dry himself after he'd taken a shower to wash away the blood."

"Could be useful for DNA testing," said Dolby, "he's bound to have left some skin cells on the fibres. Not very clever."

"Well, I dare say he was in a bit of a panic. He probably didn't come prepared for a blood bath." Milligan closed his notebook. "That's it, Mark."

"No shoes," observed Dolby. "Either he didn't get any blood on them or he couldn't find any that would fit him."

"What size did Southam wear?"

Dolby shrugged. "I hadn't thought to check, but he was a big man. Not that that actually follows for shoe sizes. Sometimes big men have surprisingly dainty feet. Anyway, perhaps we'll know a bit more when the lab has finished with all this stuff." He walked across to the van. "The stuff was in a black plastic sack wasn't it?"

"Yes. I've left that in the back of the van. Nothing unusual about it, just a standard heavy-duty sack. If I had to guess I'd say whoever dumped the clothes just took a black sack from the Southam's kitchen and used that. Always assuming that is Southam's blood."

"And this was the van used by Jason Garvey and Gary Oldham to carry out the robbery on the warehouse?"

Milligan nodded. "No doubt about that. There's the name of the previous owner printed on the side - 'Wainwright's Bakeries, Rotherham, South Yorkshire' with the address and phone number - exactly as we saw it on the security video when it was parked outside the warehouse."

"Then why do you suppose our friends Jason and Gary left the bag of bloodstained clothes in the back when they abandoned it?"

"Search me."

Dolby thought for a moment, frowning. "I can't believe that even they would be so stupid as to leave evidence like this in the back of a vehicle they've just used to carry out a robbery. Surely, if they were involved, they'd have dumped the clothes somewhere else."

"Or burnt them," suggested Dave Milligan. "That's what any even semi-intelligent killer would have done."

"Who else had access to this van? Where was it found again?"

"Breckon Woods. That's about six miles away from where the robbery took place at the Braxted Estate."

"I know where Breckon woods are, thank you, Dave!" Dolby answered irritably. "Sorry, it's Friday night - I've entered the low tolerance zone. By rights I should be on my way home now, not messing about with a pile of filthy clothes!" He rubbed his neck. It ached, probably due to stress. "So, the van must have been parked there - at the scene of the robbery - when the clothes were chucked in, that's the only reasonable explanation. There is no way the person who left them in the van went all the way out to Breckon Woods - the van was well hidden among the trees you say - just to dump these clothes."

Milligan closed his notebook and slipped it back into his pocket. "How's this for a theory? The computer warehouse where Garvey and Oldham parked the van to carry out the robbery is less than a quarter of a mile from Marazion Road where the murders took place - across the fields that is. I reckon what happened was the killer ran away across the fields - maybe he'd parked his car in the industrial estate so it wouldn't be seen in Marazion Road? - on his way he spotted the open van with a Yorkshire address on it and chucked the bloodstained clothes in the back."

Dolby nodded thoughtfully. "In the hope they wouldn't be found until the van arrived back in Yorkshire. He wasn't to know the van had been sold to some bloke in Dagenham and wasn't going back up north again - though he might have wondered what a baker's van from Rotherham was doing down here in Essex in the middles of the night."

"Probably never thought about it," agreed Milligan, "considering the state of mind he must have been in."

"Anyway, he dumped the stuff in the van and made off, hoping the person who found the clothes wouldn't report it to the police when he got back to Yorkshire - he hoped they'd assume they were just old clothes and throw them away."

"And even if they did hand them over it's unlikely the local Yorkshire plod would have connected them with a murder down here in Essex," agreed Milligan. "And that wouldn't have happened if the owner of the van wasn't in the habit of buying his second-hand vehicles up in the North of England!"

Dolby stood for a few moments, hands on hips, legs akimbo, staring thoughtfully down at the items of clothing laid out on the ground. "We are making a pretty big assumption here.

We're assuming that Jason and Gary didn't leave this stuff in the back of the van, but how do we know that?"

"But we can prove it wasn't them left the clothes, can't we?" said Milligan "Look, if they didn't put the stuff in the van and it was chucked in there by someone else while they were inside the warehouse robbing the computer store, then whoever it was did the chucking should show up on the security video."

"You mean we should be able to see that other person throwing the black sack into the van at some time while it was standing outside the warehouse?"

They found what they were looking for after running the video tape back and forth for nearly half an hour. It took them that long because the van had been parked head on towards the main video camera. When the rear doors were open, they looked like bat's wings at the end of the van and they partially hid anyone approaching it from the side, out of an alleyway at the perimeter of the warehouse. The camera had, in fact, captured pictures of a dark figure dashing the few feet from the alleyway to the van, pitching the black sack into the back and returning the way it had come. The whole sequence lasted hardly more than a second, but they were able to slow the picture and use the computer to enhance the images sufficiently to show the figure fairly clearly. The face, however, remained obscured by shadow.

Dolby stood up and walked away from the video machine, stretching his arms above his head with weariness. "Well, Dave, we've got a picture of the buggar, but there's no way we can identify him from it. Too much shadow. I suppose there's nothing else we can do, technically, to enhance the picture even more?"

Milligan shook his head. "We can ask the experts, but I'd say not. Besides, if the man had any sense he'd have obscured his face while he was exposed to the camera - actually, if you look closely it looks like that's what he did. He must have known there was a camera there, for God's sake; the whole area was floodlit - except of course in the shadow of the van."

Dolby turned suddenly on his heel and came back to the TV set, his eyes alight. "What you said a few minutes ago, Dave, about the killer parking his car on the estate…"

"What about it?"

"Run the tape back, Dave - two or three minutes before this bit, there was something on one of the other cameras…"

Milligan pressed keys on the computer linked to the video machine and held two of them down simultaneously, watching the picture scud swiftly by in reverse.

"There - hold it - now run it forward a few frames until the view changes. That's it - this view's from the other camera, pointing back the opposite way, away from the van." Dolby leaned forward and pointed at the screen. "There - that's a parked car isn't it! You can just see the back end of it."

"Yes. It's about the only one. The place is deserted at that time of night. Hang on and I'll see if we can use the zoom on it." He pressed more computer keys. "There we are, Mark, I don't know when I've seen a clearer registration plate - don't say I don't do things for you!"

"Thanks mate!" Dolby grinned widely and rubbed his hands together. "And we don't even have to check it with the DVLC computer, Dave - I know exactly whose car that is! Can you print off a copy of that picture for me?"

"I don't see why not." Milligan pressed keys on the computer. The printer in the corner of the desk buzzed and clicked itself into life, whirring faintly for a few seconds before spewing out a sheet of paper. Milligan caught it as it dropped into the tray. "Here you are."

Dolby took it from him. "Excellent. It's even got the date and time the picture was taken printed on it. Thanks. Keep that video tape safe won't you." He walked across the room and opened the door.

"You're not going to walk out without telling me whose car it is, are you, you sod!" protested Milligan. "After all I've done for you!"

"I won't tell you, just in case I'm wrong, Dave - it could be embarrassing!" said Dolby, smiling. He stopped with his hand on the door handle. "But there is something I can do for you. Remember you were wondering how Jason and his mate, Gary, managed to get into the warehouse by using a key and how they knew the code for the alarm?" Milligan nodded. "It might just be connected with a little waitress called Trudy who works at that café around the corner on the estate, The **Fat and Healthy** it's called. I've just remembered. I'm pretty sure I saw our friend Gary chatting her up in there, on the morning after the robbery. It's not a direct link, but young Trudy might just have contacts with someone in the computer warehouse; someone who eats at her restaurant on a regular basis for instance. Maybe Gary was getting the keys back to her or something the following morning. Worth checking?"

"Worth checking," agreed Milligan. "Trudy, you say, at the **Fat and Healthy**." He made a note on his pad.

Dolby walked quickly back to his office, picking up a black coffee on the way. He dropped wearily into his chair and sipped the strong hot liquid before turning his attention to his desktop. Wendy Doyle's report on her visit to Valerie's place of work lay neatly on top of the Southam Murder file. He picked it up and studied it carefully, munching the last of one of his biscuits before reaching down into the drawer for another one. Doyle's report was concise and to the point. Valerie Southam had worked at the Faulkbourne Manor for just under a year. She had got on reasonably well with the other members of staff, although Wendy had noted that the Manager had not been too keen to take her on at the beginning - apparently there had been some pressure from the Hotel proprietor that she be given a job. Her colleagues had noticed and commented amongst themselves about the batterings she had received from her husband, but they had never made an issue of it. They were shocked at her death.

Dolby placed Wendy's report in the Southam file and then turned over the pages, re-reading parts of it and making a few quick notes in the margin. He would have a lot to tell Jackie Caine in the morning.

His thoughts were interrupted by the telephone. It was the duty desk telling him there was a male visitor waiting in the reception area.

"What's his name?" He raised his eyebrows at the answer. "Is there an office free down there? Put him in there, will you, I'll come down. Then I'm off home." He hung up. Possibly this could be interesting, but one thing was for certain. He was going home when he'd finished talking to his visitor.

Barry Ford was sitting on the visitor's side of the small desk as the Detective Sergeant entered the interview room and he stood up nervously. Dolby gestured for him to sit down again and went around the other side of the desk.

"What can I do for you Mr Ford?"

"It's more what I can do for you," said Ford. He was still looking nervous, his head bobbing on his shoulders in much the same way Dolby remembered. "You know I said I couldn't remember the details of the car I saw parked on the Southam's drive that time? Well, I think I can now."

"Are you sure?"

"Oh yes - you see, I saw the car again today."

"Really? Where?"

"It was while I was out driving to the shops. I just happened to get behind this big Mercedes and I recognised it."

"How? You didn't seem to remember much about it when we last spoke, Mr Ford. And one Mercedes is very much like another I'd say." Dolby stopped apologetically. "I'm sorry, I'm not saying you're wrong, but we like to be absolutely certain of our facts."

"Oh, I understand, Detective Sergeant, but I am sure it was the same car. It was the same colour and there was a notice in the back window that I saw the first time, but I completely forgot about it until I saw it again."

"Did you get the registration number this time Mr Ford?"

"Oh yes, I wasn't going to be caught out twice. Immediately I realised it was the same car I pulled into the side of the road and wrote it down." He looked apologetic. "I didn't follow the car or anything, I thought it was more important to write down the details." He delved deep into one of the pockets of his lightweight jacket and withdrew a sheet of folded paper. "The slogan on the notice at the back of the car is also written here. I thought that would be quite helpful." He handed the paper across the desk.

Dolby leaned forward to take it, opened it and spread it on the desk in front of him. He ran his eyes across what was written there and then looked up, smiling, before opening the Southam murder file he had brought with him from his office and sliding the computer printout of the photo of the car across the desk. "This picture is not very clear, Mr Ford, but does that look like the car you saw outside the Southam's house?"

Ford took his glasses off and polished them on his handkerchief before picking up the photo and studying it closely. "Epson, 1200 dpi," he said. There was a note of appreciation in his voice.

"Pardon?" asked Dolby wondering what the man was talking about.

"Sorry. Just commenting on the printer that produced this. I think it was an Epson printing at twelve hundred dots per inch. Pretty good as it happens."

Dolby had forgotten Ford was a computer nerd. "I'm not interested in that, Mr Ford. The picture. Look at the picture - is that the car you saw?"

Ford nodded. "Oh yes. That's it all right." He peered closer. "The registration number is the same."

Dolby sighed with satisfaction. "Thank you, Mr Ford. I think this may be very useful to us in our investigations."

"Would you like me to make a statement?"

"Yes please." Dolby stood up. "If you'd like to wait here, I'll ask one of my colleagues to come in and organise that for you. It shouldn't take long." He picked the sheet of paper from the desk and, replacing it in the file, carried it out of the room with him, still smiling.

CHAPTER TWENTY

Mark Dolby lingered over his breakfast the following morning. He had tried ringing DCI Caine at just after eight thirty, but there had been no reply and he presumed she was in the shower or, perhaps, sleeping late. It was just as well their appointment with Paul Perot was not until ten. Perot had insisted they be on time as he was leaving at eleven to attend some sort of business meeting in the north of England. Dolby looked at his watch again - he must get through to the boss soon, he thought, if they were to avoid the embarrassment of turning up late at Upton Stapleford.

"Late for an appointment?" asked Lorna, smiling. She was standing at the work surface, pen in hand, going through a sheaf of papers. "One day you'll have a whole weekend off and we can get out somewhere with the kids."

He yawned. "You know how it is, darling. It's the job and I can't change it."

"It's the job and you wouldn't want to change it. Be honest, darling - you love it!"

"Well, there's never a dull moment, I can say that!" said Dolby. Lorna was right, he reflected, he really did love his job, but he had been lucky enough to marry a woman who allowed him to indulge his passion for mystery and, he supposed, what one could loosely define as justice, without balking too violently at the late nights and missed social engagements the job entailed. He had only to look around him at the numbers of his colleagues at Fen Molesey Central, who were either divorced or confirmed singles, to realise how lucky he was. "But seriously, when this Southam business is sorted out I'll take a few days off and we can spend it together."

"Make sure those few days include a weekend," admonished Lorna. "And please **please** don't forget we're having the Pavitts over for dinner tonight." She came and sat opposite him, laying her papers on the table. "Do you really think you'll wrap up this murder inquiry within a few days?"

"Yes - especially after yesterday's revelations." He smiled at the recollection of a day's work well done. "All we need is the forensic evidence to back up my theory and we're home and dry." He cut himself another slice of wholemeal bread and pulled the tub of low cholesterol margarine towards him. "What's that you're going through, darling?"

"Some notes for the Society. Simon Barnett, you know, the functions Secretary, has asked me to arrange for the next speaker - we're all expected to muck in sooner or later. Anyway, I'm trying that chap who wrote to us a few weeks ago with new evidence on Dick Turpin."

"Guilty was he then?"

"You know what I mean, the man that wrote saying he's dug up some brand-new papers on Dick Turpin's activities in the Fen Molesey area."

"I hope they're not that brand new!"

"He assures me they were in the seventeenth century. *And* he seems quite plausible." She took a slice of bread and placed it in the toaster. "Still, I'd better check him out thoroughly or the F M History Society could end up with egg on its collective face."

"You mean if he gives you a talk and then he turns out to be a complete fraud? I suppose it could be a bit embarrassing. So, you'll be out and about today looking for corroborative evidence?"

"Yes," said Lorna, "You're not the only detective in the family you know. I too shall be poking my nose into other people's dirty business and studying the habits of the criminal classes."

"Talking of the kids - what are they up to today?"

Lorna grinned and poured herself another cup of tea. "You going to have another one?" He nodded and she leaned towards him with the teapot. "You know what they're like on a Saturday morning - they'll none of them be up before eleven and then they'll be the usual scramble for the shower and they'll all be arguing as if they're in a hurry to go somewhere. Then they'll sit around and do nothing for a couple of hours before they make up their minds what particular brand of nothing they're going to do for the rest of the day."

"Oh - right - a normal Saturday then. But I thought Donna said she wanted to go shopping."

"Oh, she'll probably take the bus into town with Sara this afternoon, but she can't do much shopping can she? She hasn't got any money!" There was a pause while they drank tea. "What are *your* plans?"

"We've got a meeting with Paul Perot for ten o'clock. I'll pop into Wilsons on the way and pay the paper bill. After Perot we're going to have a word or two with the rest of his tribe."

"Sounds like Mr P will soon be helping you with your inquiries. That'll cause quite a stir with the County Nobs!"

"Could be." Dolby sipped his tea and reached across the table for another slice of bread. "Although there always was a big question mark over his head so far as the County lot are concerned. Apparently, it cost him a Parliamentary nomination some years back."

The telephone rang and Lorna went to answer it. She came back holding the portable. "It's the boss for you - she sounds distinctly like she has a hangover!"

Dolby took the telephone from her. "Morning, boss. I've been trying to get hold of you."

Caine's voice sounded distant and vague. "Sorry, Mark, I think I overslept. Didn't hear the phone at all. What time are we due at Perot's?"

"Ten. And he said not to be late because he has a meeting or something up north this afternoon and he has to leave by eleven at the latest."

"Buggar his meeting!" said Caine. "We'll be there when we get there and we'll keep him as long as we need to answer our questions. Anyway, can you pick me up from home at twenty to ten? I haven't got my car. I'll explain later."

"Right. And I've got some interesting new facts on the case for you, Jackie - I really think we're getting somewhere at last!"

"Oh good, Mark. Splendid." She sounded tired and not at all enthusiastic. He wondered what she had been drinking at the birthday dinner with her daughter the night before. Something strong, evidently. "Save it for me, there's a good man." She went on. "God! I need a shower!" There was a pause and Dolby thought for a second that she had replaced the receiver. "I suppose there's nothing further on Susie Neale?"

"No, boss. But in our game no news is usually good news."

He sensed her grimace at the other end of the telephone line. "I suppose so. I'll see you later." She hung up.

Wilsons Newsagents, the larger of the two shops boasted by the village of Notley Seward, was busy when Mark Dolby pulled up outside at just before half past nine. The shop sold a variety of different products aside from newspapers and magazines and when he went in there was an elderly man at the counter waving a box of chocolates in the air and arguing with the cashier. A queue was building up behind the dissatisfied customer and Dolby looked at his watch, decided he had plenty of time to look for a few bits and pieces and wandered off into the shop. He had his newspapers and magazines delivered and the kids looked after the supply of the comics they read regularly, so he skirted around the bank of shelves displaying these items and walked into the household section looking for men's grooming supplies. He needed some new razor blades and shaving lotion and soon found what he was looking for. Fishing into his jacket pocket for some change he made his way back towards the counter. As he turned down the side of the newspaper display he almost bumped into a tall figure leafing his way quickly through a thick, glossy colour magazine. Startled, the man stepped back, bumping into a low ice cream storage cabinet and dropping the magazine on the floor. Murmuring his apologies, Dolby bent to pick it up, noting as he did so the almost naked, well-endowed young woman featured on the cover and the name of the magazine, '**Big and Bouncy'**. He stood up and offered the magazine back to the other man, who had turned slightly away as if uncertain what to do. Dolby was startled to recognise James Parr and it took him a moment to voice his apologies.

"Mr Parr, I'm sorry. I didn't see you there." Parr had still not taken the magazine from him, seemed reluctant to take it or to acknowledge that he had recognised the police sergeant, so Dolby put it back on the top shelf with the other girlie magazines. "Sorry, thought this was yours!"

Parr flushed with embarrassment and mumbled something Dolby did not catch before turning away again and making his way hastily around the ice cream cabinet towards the door of the shop. Dolby shrugged and made his way to the cashier, who was now free, wondering why Parr had come so far to get his girlie sex magazine when there must be a stationer's shop nearer to his home in Upton Stapleford. Then he nodded to himself, remembering a comment Bernard Pitcher had made during their interview a couple of days before.

Ten minutes later Dolby stopped his car outside DCI Caine's apartment block in the centre of Fen Molesey. She was waiting at the kerbside and climbed in beside him before speaking.

"Thanks, Mark. My car's up at the Layer Marney Hotel. I left it there last night. Drank too much champagne I'm afraid. Someone's going to deliver it back to my place sometime this morning."

"Champagne? You really pushed the boat out for Alison's birthday last night then."

"Not me, really - her boyfriend was supposed to be paying, but as it happens an old acquaintance showed up and took over the honours." Dolby glanced at her, surprised. "I know it seems strange, but as it turned out he was the owner of the Hotel, so I don't suppose it actually cost him much."

Dolby was negotiating a small roundabout on the approach to the Upton Stapleford Road and it was a few moments before he asked. "Stone? Christopher Stone?"

Caine looked across at him, surprised. "You know him?"

"Not really. It's just that his name came up a few years back, when he first showed up in the neighbourhood. There was a bit of a battle between him and another local businessman over who would get to buy the hotel. Apparently, Stone offered cash - it was a lot, apparently - and his rival was spreading rumours that he, Stone, was using laundered money brought in from The States. There was a lot of bad blood between them that led to an investigation, but it didn't come to anything."

Caine nodded thoughtfully. "You mean you couldn't prove anything?"

Dolby concentrated on the road. The traffic was heavy this morning. "Yes. Well, there was an allegation made and we had to check into it, but there was probably nothing to prove as it turned out. Stone claimed to have made his fortune in the hotels and restaurants business in the US and apparently, he checked out okay on that score. They had nothing on him over there, so the whole thing died a death."

"Right." Caine mused for a moment. "Now, what is it you were dying to tell me when we spoke on the phone?"

Dolby quickly related the events of the previous day, ending by passing a folded sheet of paper across to her.

"What's this?"

"Barry Ford's note on the car he saw parked on the Southam's drive a few days before the murder." She opened it and looked across at him questioningly. "PPA 1. Is that supposed to mean something to me? And what the heck is '*bikers do it on two wheels*' - it sounds like fun, but it's not very enlightening. What's it all about?"

Dolby smiled. "PPA1 must be 'Parr Perot Associates One'. That's the registration mark of Paul Perot's car - I saw him driving it into their office car park the other day. And that thing about the bikers is one of those so-called funny posters some drivers stick on their rear windscreens. Don't ask me what it means, but Barry Ford saw it on the Mercedes parked in Valerie's drive and I also saw it on Perot's car when I was leaving the Parr Perot offices on Thursday. If nothing else, it helped with the identification."

"And what you're saying is this was the car that was parked on the Braxted Industrial Estate on the night of the murder?"

Dolby nodded. "We've got a video recording to prove it."

"You know what you're saying, Mark, don't you!"

"Yes, I know what I'm saying. But think about it. It *was* Perot, Jackie. Everything points to it." He mentally ticked off the list that had formed in his mind. "He hasn't got an alibi for the night of the murders; his car was parked within walking distance of the Southam's house on the night of the murder; and was seen parked on the Southam's driveway during the week before, in spite of the fact he told you he hadn't seen Valerie in ages; *and* he has a two million quid motive that says he killed Bruce Southam. What more do we need?"

Caine pursed her lips. "Positive proof, Mark."

"And what about the handkerchief we found at the scene of the crime? The one with a 'P' on it. If his DNA shows up on it we've got him, surely."

Caine shook her head. "But if there's no DNA it won't be easy. There must be thousands of handkerchiefs around with the letter 'P' on them!"

"Okay, but the same thing applies to the towels and the bloodstained clothing - it should be easier to prove the clothes were his."

"But until we have the forensic evidence, Mark, it's all circumstantial. We can't make a move until we have something concrete - Perot is too well connected. And what about the timing? That video in Valerie's DVD machine stopped at *11.20* so the chances are that's when she died; and so far as we know Bruce Southam was killed a few minutes afterwards. So, if Perot was in London how did he get back to Fen Molesey in time to pick up his car, drive over to Braxted Industrial Estate, park, get to the Southam's house and kill them?"

Dolby shrugged his shoulders, keeping his eyes on the road. "That depends on whether he was actually in London or not, doesn't it!"

"Look, Mark, it all sounds very plausible, but nothing you've said so far throws any light on those mysterious cash entries in Valerie Southam's bank account. I know the neighbour, Barry Ford, saw Perot's car parked on the Southam driveway, but if our theory about blackmail is correct why should Perot be her blackmail victim? Nothing points his way so far as that's concerned."

"No, but if there **was** something it gives him a motive to bump her off while he was disposing of Bruce for the insurance money. Also, we **know** it was his car outside Valerie's house a few days before. Maybe he was there to pay an instalment on his blackmail account."

"Perhaps. But we haven't got a reason - if she was blackmailing him what was it all about?"

"It could have been anything. By all accounts he didn't lead a squeaky-clean sort of life in his earlier years. Look what happened when he put himself up as local Tory candidate - he's got to have been bent in his early days even if he's kosher now. Look, by all accounts he and Bruce Southam were sailing pretty close to the wind when they were in the paras. Maybe he got into something really heavy during that time, Bruce let the cat out of the bag to Valerie and she decided to put the screws on Paul. It all fits from that point of view."

Caine shrugged. "Maybe. But wouldn't she have been too scared of Bruce to blackmail his friend Paul?" She sighed. "I don't know - it is just feasible, I suppose." She ruminated for a moment. "Going back to the question of Perot's alibi, though - or lack of one to be more precise. He hasn't said he doesn't have an alibi - what he says is he has one, but he won't tell us what it is!"

"Cobblers!" exploded Dolby, manoeuvring the car to the centre of the road and indicating a right turn into the Upton

Stapleford estate. "He told you he was at a business meeting that his own accountant says was cancelled!" He pulled across the road and into the drive, passing the Lodge house. The doors and windows were all closed and there was nobody about. He drove on into the estate. "By the way, I've had Wendy check that out and Brian Walker, the accountant, was telling the truth. Universal Insurance definitely cancelled that Tuesday evening meeting after Bruce Southam upset them while he was drunk. By all accounts they didn't want to buy into Perot's company after that little episode."

"That may well be, but the deal may not be completely off," commented Caine. She told him about the meeting between Perot and Sir Charles Ormsby at the Hotel restaurant the night before. "Look, I agree with you, Mark, it looks like Perot may be heavily implicated in the murders, but for the time being let's take it slowly. He has friends in high places."

"You mean you're going to let him get away with murder just because he's got influential friends?" Dolby couldn't disguise the disgusted tone in his voice.

"I didn't say that Mark. If he's guilty then we'll nail the bastard - but I don't want to create any waves while we're still building the case against him." She rubbed her forehead, where the vestiges of her hangover were still throbbing away. "Anyway, from what you've said about the blood-stained clothes - and the towels - we might well have a mountain of DNA evidence against him once forensics have done their stuff."

As Dolby turned the car into the bend in the road that led up to Paul Perot's house Perot's blue Mercedes swept by in the opposite direction, travelling fast. Dolby jammed his foot on the brake and looked back. "Where's he off to? It's nearly ten o'clock - he's due to see us in two minutes!"

"It's Okay, Mark," said Caine, turning in her seat to watch the rear of the other car recede into the distance. "That wasn't Perot driving. It was Philip Chantry, though what on earth he's doing driving Perot's car is anybody's guess!"

They drove on around the bend and as they turned into the drive two large dogs, red setters Caine thought they were, came bounding around the side of the big house towards them, barking wildly. The front door opened and the middle-aged woman Caine recognised as Mrs Cooper, the Perot's daily help, came down the steps, shooing the animals away.

"Mungo, Rufus, stop all this noise, you naughty people." The two dogs ran around her a couple of times and then, sensing that the visitors in the car were friendly, bolted off around the corner again, barking playfully. Mrs Cooper peered into the car and recognised DCI Caine. "Good morning - you'll be wanting to see Mr and Mrs Perot again, Inspector?"

Caine nodded a greeting and climbed out of the car. "Yes, please, Mrs Cooper. We have an appointment with Mr Perot."

She nodded and they followed her into the house.

"Why is Philip Chantry driving your car this morning?" They were in the Perot drawing room a few minutes later. Jessica Perot, looking as cool and composed as Caine remembered her, had met them in the hall and shown them into the spacious room, before excusing herself and going off to some other part of the big house. Paul Perot had appeared without delay, protesting at the way they were taking up his time. They ignored his invective, Caine asking the question as soon as they were seated.

Perot was slightly taken aback. "Philip Chantry? Why shouldn't he drive my car if I let him? I don't think that has anything to do with you."

"I have reminded you before, Mr Perot, that we are conducting a murder investigation," said Caine, a little wearily. "We would be grateful if you would co-operate and answer our questions, Does Mr Chantry often drive your car?"

Perot scowled. "Not when I can avoid it. I don't like the little poof!"

"So why this morning?"

"I suddenly realised the car's almost out of petrol and Jake Thompson isn't around. At least I can't find him. So, I asked Chantry to take the car down to the Texaco garage on the bypass and fill up the tank, to save me the time and bother later on. He may as well make himself useful."

"You obviously don't like Mr Chantry, sir," said Dolby. "Why do you continue to employ him?"

"I don't know that that's any business of yours," said Perot, "And for your information, I don't employ him. He's employed by the gardening contractors. I could have asked them to take him off the job, I suppose, but if you must know he gets on particularly well with my mother. She loves the garden and - in spite of his sexual proclivities - she likes Chantry. It would upset her if he went and she has enough problems with my father being unwell without me adding to them."

"You don't like homosexuals, sir?"

Perot scowled again. "No, Sergeant, I don't like them. If I had my way, we'd lock them all up and throw away the key." He looked across at Caine. "Isn't it time we got on, Inspector? As I told your sergeant here on the phone yesterday, I have an important meeting in the North of England, and I must not be late for it."

"A business meeting on a Saturday, Mr Perot? You are a busy man."

"When I have my business meetings is no concern of yours, Inspector!" said Perot icily. "Now, if you've got anything useful to say I'd be grateful if you'd get on and say it. I haven't got all day."

Dolby spoke now. "Where were you on the night of Tuesday 3rd June Mr Perot?"

Perot scowled. "I've been through all this with you before!" he said, shooting a glance at Caine. "If all you're going to do is repeat yourself I'm going to have to ask you to leave!"

"I shouldn't do that if I were you," said Caine. "We would only have to ask you to accompany us to the police station; answering our questions there would be a lot less congenial Mr Perot, I can assure you and it would take a lot longer. I would remind you," she went on wearily, as if to a small and recalcitrant boy, "that you refused to answer that question when I interviewed you on Thursday morning. Perhaps you would be kind enough to give us a proper answer now."

"I told you - I was at my London flat."

"No - before that - between the time you left your office and when you arrived at your flat."

"I've told you - I was at a business meeting."

"Yes, Mr Perot," said Caine, wearily, "but you've refused to say with whom."

"Quite right, too, in the circumstances. I told you it was a business sensitive matter!"

Dolby consulted his notebook and leaned forward in his seat. "Could that meeting have been with Universal Insurance, of which I believe Sir Charles Ormsby is Chairman?"

Paul Perot's mouth dropped open. His face flushed and he reached into his pocket for a handkerchief and rubbed his nose. "Where did you get that information from, Sergeant?"

"That's not important," said Dolby, continuing, with a slightly theatrical note to his voice. "I must remind you, sir, that this *is* a murder inquiry. Now, was the meeting you say you had on Tuesday evening with Universal Insurance or not? And if not - who was it with?"

Perot pursed his lips, stood up and walked across to the window. "I have told you before, that in the circumstances, I do not feel I can answer that question. At least, not at this stage."

"That's a pity, sir" said Dolby. "Because it would have helped to clear the matter up if you had confirmed that the scheduled meeting with Universal Insurance was, in fact, cancelled. By them. We understand that Mr Bruce Southam upset Sir Charles and his staff and so they called the meeting off. What do you say to that?"

Perot bit his lip and scowled. "Inspector, I don't think that in the absence of my lawyer I wish to say anything further on this matter."

Dolby glanced across at Caine. She shook her head.

"Okay, sir, we'll leave that just for the time being." He opened his notebook and smoothed down the pages with his fingers. "After your - shall we call it 'meeting' - where did you go, Mr Perot?"

"To my flat in Docklands."

"You can prove that? Did anybody see you enter the building - or did you meet anybody?"

Perot hesitated. "Only the security guard. We have twenty-four-hour security. I've been through all this before."

Dolby ignored Perot's last comment. "Did you speak to him?"

Perot nodded. "My taxi stopped just outside the building and he saw me going in. We exchanged a few pleasantries, I believe."

"And you saw nobody else?"

Perot shrugged. "No. Not that I can recall."

"What time was that?"

Perot shrugged. "About a quarter to eleven, I think."

"What did you do after that?"

"I went upstairs to my flat and fixed myself a nightcap. Then I did a bit of reading, I think. I retired to bed at midnight, or thereabouts."

Dolby paused to flick through his notebook, finally finding the page he was looking for. He read his notes quickly. "Do you know what a T E P is, sir?" he pronounced the phrase using the initial letters.

Perot shrugged. He was still standing at the window, looking out at the garden with a show of disinterest in the proceedings. "I suppose you mean a Top Earner's Policy. Yes, of course I do."

"And you do know that your company, Parr Perot Associates, has such policies on all of their top people? Bruce Southam included?"

Perot nodded.

"So why didn't you tell us about it?"

"You didn't ask, Sergeant. And what about it anyway?"

Caine answered his question with one of her own. "Do you know how much the policy on Mr Southam is for, Mr Perot?"

He shrugged again. "Not without looking it up, but I imagine it was for one or two million. Southam was a high fee earner!"

"Not a bad guess, Mr Perot." Said Caine. "It's for two million, I believe."

"So?" Perot returned slowly to his chair. His tone was aggressive, but he crossed his arms and legs defensively.

"So, when I asked you in our previous interview whether you could think of any reason why someone should want to murder Bruce Southam you said no, you couldn't." said Caine. "Which is a bit strange considering that, out of action or dead, he was worth two million to your firm."

"What are you suggesting, Inspector?" Perot stood up again, quickly, striding to the escritoire by the window and picking up the telephone receiver. "I really think I shall have to contact my solicitor!"

Caine continued as if he hadn't spoken. "Another question we have for you, Mr Perot is - why did you tell us you hadn't seen Valerie Southam for a very long time when your car was parked outside her house - on the drive, in fact - only last week?"

For the first time Perot looked really rattled. His hand was shaking as he replaced the telephone receiver. He made an effort to regain control of himself, striding back across the room to sit down again. "I can explain that, Inspector - there's a perfectly reasonable explanation." He paused. "I was delivering some papers to Bruce."

"What sort of papers?" asked Dolby.

He waved his hand vaguely. "I don't know - some policies, I suppose - Bruce wasn't in the office on that day and as I live nearby somebody must have asked me to drop some urgent papers in on him. His wife wasn't there when I called, so what does it matter?"

Caine nodded thoughtfully. "We'll accept that for the time being, but at some point, you may have to tell us who asked you to take the papers to Mr Southam and what exactly those papers were. For the time being, though you can also tell us the answer to the following conundrum - if you were in your London flat on the night of the murders, how come that for some hours that night your car was parked on the Braxted Industrial Estate not ten minutes' walk from the Southam's house?"

Perot looked flustered. "It couldn't have been. I've told you twice - I didn't have my car that night. It was at home, locked up in the garage here, in Upton Stapleford. I was in my London flat!"

"So how do you explain the fact that your car appears on a warehouse security video between the hours of eleven p.m. Tuesday and two a.m. Wednesday?" asked Dolby, "It was parked in Valkyrie Road on the Braxted Industrial Estate."

Perot shook his head. "I can't explain that!" he said. "All I know is, I wasn't anywhere near Braxted at the time - I was in London." He stopped for a moment, thinking. "Unless, of course, someone else drove the car there."

"And who might that be?"

He shrugged. "I don't know. Any number of people."

"Who has access to the keys, then, Mr Perot?" asked Caine, puzzled. "Apart from you, of course."

"My wife, I suppose." He rubbed his chin. "Jake and Bernice Thompson. Jamie Parr - not Ursula, though, she wouldn't be able to drive it. And my mother, of course, not that she would. But not my father - he's too ill to drive. Maybe that fellow Chantry as well, come to think of it."

"So, what you're saying is that practically anyone living or working on this estate can pick up your car keys at any time and drive off in your car?" Said Caine, incredulous. "It's open house on your car keys?" Perot nodded sullenly. "So where do you keep the keys?"

He hesitated. "Well, normally, they're on a hook on the garage wall." Both Caine and Dolby were astonished at the answer, coming as it did from a man who must understand the security implications of what he was saying. But at least Perot had the decency to blush with embarrassment as he told them. He rushed to his own defence. "That's not so bad as it seems, Inspector. The security system includes the garage. The alarm would go off if anyone tried to get in and take the car."

Caine nodded. "I see. But do you and your wife always set the alarm when you leave the premises?"

"I can't speak for my wife, of course, Inspector, but I always do. Without fail." He paused, said emphatically. "Inspector, I can assure you it wasn't me driving that car on Tuesday night. As I've told you three or four times already, I was in my flat in London."

"So, you did, sir, a few minutes ago - and you have a witness to back up that statement - the security guard." Said Caine. Perot stared blankly back at her; his lips set. She sighed. "Believe me, Mr Perot, we're on your side, we're only looking for the truth - but so far you've refused to identify the people who, you say, were at the meeting you attended on that evening. We can't help thinking that's a little strange - some might even say suspicious."

"I've told you the reason," said Perot tightly.

"So, you have," agreed Caine. "And we have told you that, in the circumstances, it is a totally inadequate answer!" She paused. "You must understand our dilemma - in spite of the fact that you say you were in London your car was very close to the scene of the crime. You also failed to tell us about the insurance policy in favour of your firm - which is, incidentally, going through hard times at the moment. Not to mention your rather pat answer to our questions as to why your car was parked on the Southam's drive a week or so ago. You must, as I say, sir, understand our dilemma."

Dolby broke the silence that followed Caine's monologue. "We shall also be asking you to let us have a DNA sample, sir."

"What on earth for?"

"We shall need it for forensic tests," said Dolby.

Perot glowered angrily and rose again from his chair. He stood for a moment, glaring at Detective Sergeant Dolby, before retracing his steps across the room to the telephone. "I must say, Inspector, that your tone and attitude give me the distinct impression that I am a suspect - if not your **prime suspect** - in this case. In the circumstances I refuse to say another word in the absence of my solicitor." He picked up the telephone receiver, the fingers of his other hand hovering over the keypad. "So, either this interview is at an end or I shall call him now and we can all wait until he arrives." He turned to face the two police officers again. "Needless to say, if you make me miss my appointment this afternoon I shall have no hesitation in making a very strong complaint, in the clearest terms, to your superiors."

Caine folded her hands in her lap and looked across at him, her eyes glinting. "Mr Perot, as I've reminded you a number of times, this is a murder inquiry and I shall conduct it in any way I think fit. Anyway, as it happens, I don't think we need bother you any further just for the moment. We shall almost certainly want to see you again, of course, but for the time being I would appreciate it if we could have a few words with your wife."

He replaced the telephone receiver once again. "If you require me to see you again, Inspector, I shall want my solicitor to be there, so you had better give me plenty of notice." He walked towards the door. "I'll see if my wife is available - but I warn you, try harassing her and your superiors will certainly hear about it." He opened the door and went out in search of his wife.

"I see what you mean about Perot," said Dolby.

"Yes, he's not what you would describe as co-operative, is he?"

"No, he's not, but that's not what I mean. You said he reminded you of somebody - I've got the same feeling." He shook his head as if to clear it. "I can't quite make the connection, but it is there, somewhere in the back of my mind." The Detective Sergeant's eyes alighted on the photographs on the mantel shelf. He stood up and walked across the room, picking one of them up for closer examination. "This picture here, I assume it's Perot in his younger days?"

Caine came over and stood beside him, placing her glasses on her nose and peering at the picture more closely. "Yes, it must be."

Dolby nodded. "Correct me if I'm wrong," he said thoughtfully, "but isn't there a very strong resemblance to young Adam Southam?"

Caine took the photograph from him and scrutinised it more closely. "Yes, you're right. They are very much alike - at least they were when Paul Perot was young. How do you suppose that can be?"

Jessica Perot was cheerful and breezy when she came into the room. "It's a lovely morning, Inspector, Sergeant. I was on the patio and just about to enjoy a cup of tea. Would you care to join me?"

"No thank you, Mrs Perot," said Caine. "We won't be keeping you long. There are just a few questions."

Jessica Perot sat in the chair her husband had occupied and crossed her long legs. "Fire away."

"It's concerning your husband's car, Mrs Perot," said Dolby, trying to keep his gaze from straying away from her face and down her body to her extremely shapely legs. He shifted uncomfortably. "Did you have occasion to drive it on Tuesday evening?"

She shook her head. "No, Sergeant. I have my own car. I did use that on Tuesday night - as I told you I went out for a few rubbers of bridge. But I didn't go near Paul's Merc."

"It was locked up in the garage, presumably?"

"So far as I know, yes. *His* garage, of course, we have one each. Side by side. Very cosy."

"Do you know where he keeps his car keys?"

She nodded. "Yes. Everybody on the estate knows Paul hangs them on a hook in the garage." She smiled. "For a man who is supposed to know all about insurance he isn't very security minded!"

"But we understand the garage is part of the alarm system. When you set the alarm it protects the house **and** the garages."

"Well, that's not strictly speaking true, Inspector. The garages are detached from the house and they're on a separate security circuit. You have to set it separately. I leave that to Paul. When I go out I set the alarm for the main house, but I don't bother with the garages."

"So, on Tuesday night, the garage security system may have been left switched off?" asked Dolby.

"Quite likely. Are you asking these questions because somebody used Paul's car that evening, while he was away?" Caine nodded. "Well, it could have been anyone. Even if the alarm was on **everybody** knows what the security code is."

"How do you mean 'everybody'?"

"Everybody on the estate."

"That's not very wise is it, Mrs Perot?"

"We trust our people, Inspector." She shrugged. "Anyway, it would be a bit impractical otherwise, wouldn't it? We all need to get into the various outbuildings from time to time and we don't want to keep bothering each other about security codes."

"But if everybody here knows the security codes and where your husband keeps his car keys," said Dolby "doesn't that mean anybody on the estate could drive his car away at any time?"

She nodded. "Yes, I suppose it does, Sergeant. But don't look at me - I'm not responsible for my husband's inadequacies in security or, for that matter, any of the other areas in which he falls short of perfection." She smiled, implying there were many such areas.

Caine leaned forward in her seat. "Mrs Perot, if someone was to drive your husband's car in or out of the garage late at night would you hear them?"

"No, I don't think so. My bedroom is at the other side of the house. Besides I'm a very heavy sleeper." She smiled. "But Rufus and Mungo aren't."

"Rufus and Mungo? Oh - your dogs? They greeted us as we drove up. Red Setters, aren't they?"

"Yes. They sleep in the house, in the back kitchen. They have a dog flap, of course, so they'd be out there like a shot if we had an intruder. And, of course, they'd bark to blue blazes! They didn't on Tuesday evening - not while I was here, anyway."

"But you did go out," said Caine. "The car could have been taken at any time afterwards."

"Yes, but whoever it was took it must have brought it back before I returned, which was at twenty to twelve at night, give or take a few minutes. Or I'd have heard the dogs barking, wouldn't I?" She smiled. "Is there anything else I can help you with?"

Dolby stood up and went over to pick up the photograph of Paul Perot. He brought it back to Jessica and showed it to her.

"I know it's a strange question, Mrs Perot, but would you say that your husband resembles young Adam Southam?"

She looked up at him curiously, then back down at the photograph. She took it from him and shrugged. "I suppose there is a vague resemblance. But as I was saying to the Inspector the other day," she nodded at Caine, "My husband has one of those faces that people keep thinking they recognise. It's just one of those things."

"You don't think there can be any family resemblance?"

She shook her head distastefully. "You mean that the Southam boy may be related to my husband? No, I'm sure there was no family connection between Paul and Bruce Southam - and as for his wife I would hope not! As a matter of fact, I think Charles had a genealogist do some work on their family trees some years back - well, he asked Florence to organise it, actually - and I'm sure if anything like that had shown up I'd have heard about it - we'd have *all* heard about it!" She shook her head decisively. "No, Inspector, any resemblance you can see between my husband and Adam Southam is, as they say in novels, purely coincidental." She got up from her chair and replaced the photograph on the mantle shelf above the fireplace. "Now, if there's nothing else, Inspector, I think I'd like to get back to the garden. This weather is far too good to waste sitting here in the gloom."

Jessica Perot showed the two detectives back to the front door and bade them goodbye. They stood for a moment under the porch, enjoying the shade, before making their way back to Dolby's car. The sun was high in an almost cloudless sky. Dolby took off his jacket and, opening one of the back doors of the car slipped it onto the back seat. Caine checked the bonnet of the car for cleanness and then leaned back, her bottom resting on the warm metal. She fanned her face with her hand.

"What do you think of Perot now, Mark?"

He sighed and came to stand beside her, looking out over the fields towards the dark mass of High Point Quarry. "Well, having open house on driving his car doesn't exactly help our case against him does it? He can say that practically anybody could have driven it over to Braxted and we couldn't disagree." He thought for a moment before continuing. "Of course, if the car was taken or brought back while Mrs Perot was in the house and the dogs didn't bark - as would have been the case if they knew the person taking the car - then she wouldn't have realised the car had been taken. That narrows the field a bit, don't you think?"

"You mean it must have been someone who lives on this estate? Someone the dogs knew and recognised, otherwise, they would have barked? That's true, and according to the time frame we've been working on Mrs Parr would have been in the house when the killer brought the car back in the early morning. But who would have taken the car, Mark? Who has the motive to go over to the Southam's house and slaughter them?" She rubbed her eyes, regretting the champagne of the night before and opened her handbag, taking out a pair of black framed sunglasses and slipping them on. "Of course, we don't know that it **wasn't** Paul Perot using the car. But you may be right - whoever it was brought the car back they must have been known to the dogs - what was their names - Rufus and Mungo - or they'd have barked the place down."

CHAPTER TWENTY ONE

As she spoke Paul Perot's Mercedes swept up the driveway and turned onto the parking space in front of the house. Philip Chantry switched off the engine and opened the door, springing lithely down onto the pathway, his well-worn trainers scrunching noisily on the gravel.

"Good Morning, Inspector, Sergeant." he turned away from them towards the house. Caine got up from her makeshift seat against the car and walked to intercept him. "Just a moment, Mr Chantry. Could you spare us a few minutes?"

"I do need to get these car keys to Mr Perot, Inspector."

"I'll only keep you a couple of minutes," Caine said. Chantry stopped. "You told us you were not at the Southam house on Tuesday evening, Mr Chantry." He looked down and bit his lip nervously. "You were seen, sir, by one of the neighbours, cycling along Marazion Road at about half past nine that evening. Why were you there if you weren't calling at the Southam house?"

Chantry laughed nervously. "I'm sorry, but - yes - I suppose I was - er - there, as a matter of fact, Inspector. It must have slipped my mind. When you asked me that is."

"Then you did call in at the Southam's house?"

He nodded miserably.

"Why?"

"I was picking up my tools. Yes, I know I told you that I'd taken them all with me when I left on Sunday, but…"

"But you lied!" said Dolby in a matter-of-fact way. "Tch…Tch…It never pays, Mr Chantry, you should know that."

The younger man blushed and scratched his eyebrows nervously. "Yes, I didn't tell you the truth - I was worried you might think it was me that killed them, what with the row I had with them on Sunday. I'm sorry."

"Well, the case isn't solved yet, Mr Chantry and you are still under suspicion," said Caine. "And if you persist in lying to the police you might well find yourself in a great deal of trouble. Now, tell us what happened when you called in on the Southam's that evening."

"Valerie was there by herself. I told her I'd come to pick up a few of my tools and she asked after Adam. I told her he was OK. Then I suppose things got a bit heated - well, she'd been a bit off to start with. Sort of agitated."

"What happened between you?" asked Dolby.

"Nothing - we had a few words - she called me a few names I shan't repeat and we raised our voices. I took my stuff and left."

"You didn't hit her?"

"No!" he was indignant. "Who do you think I am? Her husband?"

"And what time did you leave?"

He shrugged. "I don't know - I got there at about nine thirty, I suppose, so it must have been at about a quarter to ten. I wasn't there long!"

"Are you sure about that, Mr Chantry? Did anyone see you leave?"

"I don't know. I didn't see anyone else, so I assume nobody saw me. But then I didn't realise anyone had seen me on the way in, did I? And I can't be absolutely sure of the time - I didn't look at the clock." He looked her in the eye. "But I do know that poor Mrs Southam was still alive when I left the house."

"We'll take your word for that for the time being," said Caine. "You can take those keys in to Mr Perot now if you wish, but we may want to speak to you again, so don't travel out of the area without informing us."

Chantry nodded nervously and went into the house. Dolby watched him go with a wry smile on his face.

"He's worried, but I don't think it's him we're after, Jackie. I don't think he's got the killer instinct, do you?"

"No, I doubt he's our man." She yawned and climbed into the car. "But in our profession, it's never wise to draw your conclusions too quickly. Come on, we may as well go and see what the others have to say for themselves. We'll have a go at the Parrs first. Apparently, their house is the first one on the estate road, we passed it on the way in. It's called Beacon Cottage if my memory serves me correctly."

Beacon Cottage, the Parr house, was set off the estate road, behind a thicket of trees about two hundred yards down the tree lined road and at the top of a gently sloping hill. Dolby pulled into a lay-by beside an old wooden gate leading to the driveway and stopped the car in the shadow of a tall lime tree.

"Shall I drive up or do you fancy a walk?"

They went through the gate and walked up the hill towards the house, the thatched roof and some of the stonework of which was visible through the trees.

"It doesn't add up, Mark," said Caine.

"What doesn't?"

"Perot being the killer." She stopped and looked about her. They were halfway up the hill and they could see across the broad sweep of the estate, a vista of meadows dotted with grazing cattle and groups of trees, clear down to the Fen Molesey road. "This place is enormous and the Perots own it. You could almost say that Paul Perot is the sole owner and it must be worth a fortune. Why commit murder when you're in such a privileged position?"

Mark Dolby laughed cynically. "It might look good, Jackie, but when you look at a place like this you don't see what it costs to keep it going. It might have been manageable when they had all the money coming in from the gravel pits, but since they've dried up the Perots must be losing a fortune. That two million quid from the insurance policy'll come in real handy I can tell you

- it's probably the only thing that'll keep the wolf from the Perot door."

"But why not just sell off a bit of land?"

"And raise how much? Not enough by a long stretch. You're forgetting, this is green belt land - you can't sell it off for millions to a builder for housing development - not without changing its usage and you couldn't do that easily. There'd be public protests from here to Colchester, if not from London itself and it wouldn't go through without a full public inquiry. It would take years and there's no guarantee you'd win. If Perot needed the cash - and it's my belief he did - well, does actually - desperately - then his easiest way to it was to call in the insurance policy, especially as Bruce Southam had just loused up what was probably his only chance of being bailed out." Dolby swept the view with his eyes and turned to take a few more paces up the hill. "And I don't need convincing that Perot's capable of killing someone. He was trained to kill in the paras and it's not the sort of thing you forget."

"That's another thing," said Caine. "If he was trained to kill you would think he'd make a cleaner job of it, wouldn't you?"

"You mean that bloody mess in the Southam's kitchen? So, he lost his cool and got a bit carried away. After all, Jackie, this wasn't a killing in the line of duty, for Queen and Country. It was cold blooded murder in someone's kitchen, for God's sake!" Dolby stopped again to let her catch up. "Besides, you're forgetting that the victim was Paul's lifelong friend - they were buddies for most of their lives, call them partners in crime if you like. Even Paul Perot might have been a little hesitant when he killed Bruce - and don't forget, also, that Bruce Southam was in the Paratroopers too and knew how to look after himself. He must have fought like the blazes when he realised his buddy boy was going to stick him with a kitchen knife!"

"You may be right," agreed Caine. "But all we've got so far is circumstantial evidence. We're going to need a lot more than that to convict him."

They walked on, each of them deep in thought.

"To change the subject entirely," said Dolby as the house came almost fully into view at the brow of the hill. "You didn't tell me how you got on with Lime Tree Cottage. When was it you went to view the place?"

"Wednesday evening," said Caine. As they approached the Parr's cottage - which, she now appreciated, might better be described as a large country house - she saw there were many similarities with the cottage she had viewed in Birch Medley. "It was nice. I liked it. Actually, it was pretty well ideal for what I'm looking for - a peaceful retreat away from the world of cops and robbers. I put in an offer, but I haven't heard from the agent yet."

"Typical!" said Dolby. "I don't know what they do for their money."

"It's not entirely his fault," said Caine, finding herself in the unfamiliar position of defending an estate agent. "He did warn me that the owner is away in the States on business." She looked at her watch. "That reminds me, I was hoping Alison would have time to come and have a look at the place before she goes back to town - I think I'm running a little late though."

They crested the hill and found themselves walking across the wide parking area in front of the cottage, which was obviously old - seventeenth or eighteenth century perhaps - but well maintained. It was quaint, with many gables and square leaded light windows. Creepers grew up the old stone walls and there were roses - now in full bloom - around the doorway. The scene was one of picturesque neatness and careful husbandry, but Caine noticed that the edges of the parking space were potholed and in one small area the grass bordering its gravel surface was gouged into a deep track where a car had recently run off the pathway. The tyres had sunk deep beneath the surface leaving a crescent of ridges in the damp earth where the vehicle had run off the path, travelled across the grass and rejoined the pathway again lower down. A car was parked on the far side of the parking area and they could see a man bending over the open bonnet, his face hidden from view. It was a large vehicle, a Vauxhall Caine thought, and quite old with a few dents in the body work and the bubbles of early rust beginning to show themselves at the bottoms of the doors. As the man heard the two police officers approaching, he looked up from what he was doing and wiped his hands on a dirty piece of cloth. Caine recognised Jake Thompson.

"Wondered who it was," he said. "We're not open to the public today and anyway this bit of the estate's private." He was wearing paint-stained dungarees and his face was streaked with engine oil. He sniffed and wiped a greasy hand across his nose. "Still, I suppose you're here on murder business, Inspector."

"That's one way of putting it," said Caine. "This is Detective Sergeant Dolby. Mark, Mr Jake Thompson - I think you'd describe Mr Thompson as General Handyman for the estate."

Dolby nodded to Thompson. "Good morning. Is looking after the vehicles one of your jobs then?"

"Yep. Man of many talents I am," said Thompson. "I can turn my hand to most things." He nodded towards the open bonnet of the parked vehicle. "I've just been giving Mr Parr's car a wash and I thought I'd refill the windscreen washer bottle. It was a bit low and you need it quite a lot when you drive around the estate. There's a lot of dust in the hot weather." He scratched a small area of his chin where it was stained with oil. "Shouldn't really need it, of course, the car went in for a full service only last week. But you know what the garages are like these days! As my old dad used to say - regular servicing of a car's more trouble than it's worth. Most of the time it's only the rust and dirt that's holding it together. Take that away and the bloody thing's bound to go wrong!"

"I know what you mean," said Caine. "Our apologies for disturbing you. We had hoped to have a few words with Mr and

Mrs Parr, but perhaps you can fill in a few points for us while you're here." Thompson nodded and leaned with his bottom against the bonnet of the car. "As you know we're investigating an incident that took place on Tuesday night. Do you happen to know if Mr Parr used his car that night?"

"The night of the murders? I wouldn't know," said Thompson, "but I doubt it. He don't often go out at night on account of Mrs Parr not being able to get about easily. And she gets tired quickly so she's usually in bed early in the evening."

"But your place is a long way away from here," Dolby pointed out. "Would you hear his car from here?"

"Probably not," said Thompson "I'd only hear if he drove past the lodge house. And that would depend on where he was going."

"How do you mean?" asked Caine.

"Well, we're at the south end of the estate road, you see, in the Lodge House, so if Mr Parr - or Mr and Mrs Perot or any of 'em for that matter - are going south to Maldon or the lower end of Fen Molesey, then they'd come by ours and join the public road there. It's quicker. But if they're going North to the Chelmsford road, they'd leave the estate at the top end and they wouldn't go past the lodge. So, whether I'd hear them or not would depend which way they were going, if you follow me."

"So, you didn't hear anything on Tuesday night?"

"Only Mrs Jessica's sports car," said Thompson. "But that's got an almighty powerful roar to it, you can hear it all over the estate when she revs up."

"What about Paul Perot's car?" asked Dolby. "Did anyone take that out on Tuesday night?"

Thompson smiled, his eyes lighting up. "The Mercedes? Now that's a real car that is! Drives smooth as a baby's bum that does, if you'll excuse my French. Not like this old heap of junk!" He thumped the car he was leaning against.

"Did **anyone** drive the Mercedes on Tuesday night, Mr Thompson?" Caine asked again, patiently.

"I shouldn't think so - Mr Perot spent the night in London so far as I know." He paused, then went on slowly. "Tuesday - Come to think of it that was the day it went in for its service."

"So, it wasn't here, on the estate, on Tuesday?" asked Caine. Thompson shook his head. "But I assume it would have been back from the garage by the evening?"

"Oh yes! Leafords, the garage people pick it up in the morning and then drop it back again in the evening. Been doing that for years. It's a very good service."

"They collect it from you?"

"No - they just come in in the morning and pick it up. George, the mechanic does it. He's been doing that for a good ten years or more."

"So, George knows where the keys are kept?"

"Oh yeah. We do trust him, you know. He's been with Leaford's for over thirty years, man and boy. He comes in on his bike, collects the car and then, after he's brought it back he bicycles back to the garage. It's only just over a mile on the B road."

"And he doesn't deliver the keys into your hands when he returns the car?"

"No. he just puts it in the garage and leaves the keys on the hook, same as anybody else would."

"So, you wouldn't know what time he delivers it back? Or even if it is delivered back on the same day?"

Thompson shrugged. "No, I suppose not. But if it's going to be more than one day Leaford's would phone to tell us there was a delay and not to expect it."

"But you don't take formal delivery of it when they return." said Dolby. "Excuse me saying this, Mr Thompson, but it seems to me a very haphazard way of going about things."

Thompson shrugged again and lifted his hands in resignation. "That's us country folks, Sergeant, we don't get stressed out for no reason in these parts, not like the city folks. We trust each other."

Dolby sighed. "Then I suppose you all know where Mr Perot keeps the Mercedes keys?"

"Yep. It's no secret."

"And you know the security alarm code?"

"Yep. We have to don't we or we couldn't none of us do our jobs, could we?" Thompson's mouth fell open as if the coin of enlightenment had dropped through the top of his head and onto his tongue. "Here! What are you getting at?"

"That remains to be seen, Mr Thompson. Did *you* drive Mr Perot's car on Tuesday night?"

"No, I did not. I told you I don't even know whether Leafords brought it back that day or waited for the next morning. I certainly didn't leave the estate that night."

"So, what *did* you do?"

"Tuesday night? Me and the missus watched telly. That's what we do most nights. We're too knackered to do anything else, usually. It don't get dark until late in the summer months, so we're both at it until gone nine o'clock, most evenings!"

"And you were together all evening? You didn't go out at all?"

Thompson shook his head. "Like I said, we was watching telly. Until about half eleven I suppose. Then we went to bed. Boring ain't we?"

"No more boring than millions of other people, Mr Thompson," said Caine. "Thank you for your time. Is Mr Parr in?"

Thompson nodded towards the cottage. "He's around - he might be inside, or he might be round the back in his workshop. Works in wood he does!"

Following Thompson's directions, they walked around the side of the house into the back garden. It was neat, laid to lawn in the centre with flower beds around the borders, butting up to a picket fence that separated the garden area from the vast meadows that stretched away towards the dark shape of the quarry up on High View Point. To one side of the garden was a red brick building which, according to Thompson, had once been the garage, but which James Parr now used as a workshop. They walked towards it, passing the sliding patio doors of the lounge and skirting the wide wheelchair ramp that led up to them. The half glass side door of the garage-cum-workshop was open and as they approached, they could hear the whirr of a small machine. Caine paused in the doorway and peered inside. The room was fitted out as a carpenter's or woodworker's workshop, with a large bench in the centre, on top of which was mounted a wood lathe. There were carved wooden bowls and figures, presumably finished examples of Parr's woodworking efforts, lining the shelves on the walls, beside them tool racks populated by a number of well used tools. Parr, wearing jeans and a dusty tee shirt, his eyes protected by a pair of goggles worn over his normal spectacles, was sitting on a high wooden stool, hunched forward over the spinning wheels of the lathe, working intently at a piece of wood with a small chisel. He had a cigarette in his mouth. It hung limply from his lips, the smoke drifting up in front of his face as if it were there not to afford enjoyment, but merely to feed his habit. The ash tray beside him on the bench, which was itself laden with a heavy covering of wood dust and curled shavings, was full of half smoked cigarette ends.

"Good morning, Mr Parr," Caine called. Parr's concentration on the spinning section of wood did not waver, as if he had not heard her and she called out again. "Mr Parr, may we have a few words?"

Parr heard her this time and turned slowly to look at them, his eyes rheumy and tired, showing surprise and what might have been alarm, although the thickness of his plastic goggles made it difficult to be sure what emotions he was showing. He sighed and reached over to turn off the electric motor of the lathe, dropping the chisel heavily on to the top of the bench. He crushed the partially smoked cigarette in the ash tray and pulled the goggles up, leaving them resting on the top of his head. He pushed himself off the stool and came towards the two police officers, his hands patting nervously at the unruly shock of hair the goggles caused to stand up on his scalp. He recognised Dolby from their meeting in his office and nodded, a little sheepishly the Detective Sergeant thought.

"Good morning."

"Good morning, sir, we met a couple of days ago." Dolby made no mention of their earlier encounter in the newsagents. If Parr was inclined to indulge a penchant for girlie magazines that was his own affair, it had nothing to do with police inquiries. He introduced Caine. "As you know, sir, we're investigating the murders of Mr and Mrs Bruce Southam. We'd like to ask you a few more questions."

Caine was examining one of the wooden bowls. She lifted it up and ran her hands over the smooth, silky surface. "Is this all your own work, Mr Parr?" He nodded. "It really is very good."

He flushed. "Thank you. It keeps me out of mischief."

"Do you sell them, Mr Parr?"

"Sometimes. At charity fairs, jumble sales, that sort of thing. It's only a hobby." He reached across to the bench to take another cigarette from the packet.

Dolby was admiring a turned wood candlestick. "They really are very good. Ever thought of setting up in business?"

"Yes, as a matter of fact I have." He was still holding the unlighted cigarette between his fingers. "It's a pleasant dream to get away from working in an office, but it wouldn't be viable as a business. I work too slowly. I couldn't turn out enough pieces. Besides, they really aren't that good, you know - I've seen far better." He took a plastic lighter from his shirt pocket and flicked it open, bringing the cigarette up to his lips.

Caine looked around at the copious amounts of shavings and wood dust in the room. The place was a tinder box. "Do you think you should be smoking in here, Mr Parr?"

He ignored her and lit up, drawing the fumes of the cigarette greedily into his lungs. "You wanted to ask me some questions?"

"About Tuesday night, Mr Parr," said Dolby, "You told me on Thursday that you spent the whole evening at home."

Parr nodded, pulling himself onto the high wooden stool. "Yes. That's what I said."

"You didn't go out at all?"

Parr took off his glasses and rubbed his eyes. "No."

"You didn't drive Mr Perot's car that evening?" Parr shook his head. "But you do drive it sometimes?"

Parr drew on the cigarette again before reaching out and crushing it down onto the ash tray. His hands were shaking slightly as he reached again for the packet. "You probably know by now," He said slowly, "that I often drive my brother-in-law Paul into the office in the morning. We often use his car rather than mine. It's a better car. More expensive." He bit his lip. "Paul considers it a more fitting vehicle for the Senior Director of Parr Perot Associates."

"But you were driving your own car this Tuesday when you went into the office with Mr Perot?" asked Caine.

Parr thought for a moment. "Yes, Paul's car was in for service on Tuesday, so we couldn't have used it for the office. Yes - We went down to London in the Vauxhall. My car."

"What time do you normally leave for the office in the morning?" asked Dolby.

"Early. Usually about six thirty. It helps to avoid the traffic."

"And that Tuesday morning you drove straight in - you didn't stop anywhere?"

Dolby had asked the question. Parr turned towards Caine. "What has all this got to do with the murders, Inspector?"

"Just routine, Mr Parr. We're trying to get a general picture of what went on on the day of the murder."

Parr answered Dolby's question, somewhat reluctantly. "We were a little late in starting on Tuesday. I had to attend to Ursula for a few minutes." He giggled nervously, embarrassed. "She had an early toilet call, you understand, and she can't manage by herself and Anne Hendry's always busy with Charles at that time in the morning. Oh - and the car wouldn't start for a few minutes. But we set off eventually and we didn't stop anywhere on the journey to the office, not that I can recall." He shifted uncomfortably on the stool. "Why should we?"

"No reason, Mr Parr," said Dolby. "Just trying to establish the routine. And what time did you arrive at the office?

Parr shrugged. "I really don't know. Not much later than usual, I think. The traffic wasn't too heavy for some reason. We must have got there at just before nine."

"Going back to the subject of Paul Perot's car, Mr Parr, do you know where he keeps the keys?" Caine asked

"Of course. They're on a hook in his garage. But everybody on the estate knows that, not just me."

"How do you actually get on with Mr Perot?" asked Dolby. "Would you say you were good friends?"

Parr looked away and drew on his cigarette, his other hand running over the silken surface of one of the wooden bowls in an almost sensual caress. "No - we're not good friends. But I suppose we do manage to rub along together."

"You've known each other a long time." This from Caine.

Parr nodded. "All our lives. You might say, Inspector, that our lives have been inextricably interwoven, but at best we've only tolerated each other. We're not friends. We do not like each other."

"You were at the same school, I believe. Is it correct that Paul Perot and Bruce Southam used to bully you?"

Jamie Parr's face whitened. His fingers gripped hard at the edge of the bowl and he let it fall back the few inches on to the top of the work bench. "That's in the past, Inspector. I don't think about it now."

"I don't know about you, sir," said Dolby, "but if I was in your shoes and lived and worked with people who'd mistreated me when I was a kid I'd want to get my own back."

"If you're asking me have I tried to get back at them for the way they treated me at school then the answer is 'no'. I don't see the sense of seeking vengeance. Besides, what would I do to get revenge?" He sighed and could not hide the trace of bitterness in his voice. "I am not a vengeful man, but the truth is I am so tied to the Perot family that if I did anything against them it would rebound on me. Besides, I would not want to hurt my wife - it's her family."

"Your wife's accident, Mr Parr - how did it happen?" asked Caine.

His face darkened and he bit his lip again. He was silent for a few moments, his eyes misting over. "We were out together, Ursula and me, riding on the estate, up in Beacon woods, that's just over by the quarries." He nodded in the general direction of High View Point. "Ursula was always a better horsewoman than me - she does - did - most things better than I do, better than most people do. Anyway, I wasn't concentrating on the ride, I had my mind on other things - horses are canny you know, they know when you're not paying attention - and my horse suddenly started playing up. He refused one of the jumps - a relatively easy one, not that that makes any difference when things go wrong. Anyway, he wouldn't take it and he ran right across Ursula's path. Her horse shied and she was thrown. She received injuries to her spinal column, and she's been in a wheelchair ever since." He smiled bleakly. "I know that some members of the family blame me - and they're right you know; I should have been able to keep control of my own horse!"

"But people are thrown from their horses every day," said Dolby. "Horse Riding is a very dangerous sport. Aren't you being a bit hard on yourself?"

"I don't think so." Jamie Parr said bitterly. "It was my horse caused the accident and I should have had proper control over him. I let my concentration go - so poor Ursula ended up in a wheelchair - just because *I* couldn't get it right!" He pulled the goggles off his head, hurling them into a cardboard box that stood on the floor beneath the bench. "It totally changed our way of life! It should be me trapped in that wheelchair, Inspector, not my poor wife!"

Caine shook her head sympathetically. She did not pursue the point. "Would it be possible for us to have a few words with your wife, Mr Parr?"

"You don't have to bother her, surely, Inspector," said Parr irritably. "I don't see that she'll be able to help you with your inquiries. She's practically house bound."

"Nevertheless, I think we'd like to see her, sir," said Caine. "If you could just point us in the right direction, we can probably find our own way."

He stood up. "No, I'll show you, Inspector. She's in the utility room doing the ironing. She likes to keep herself busy and do her little bit to help, although it does tire her out, the poor thing." He stubbed out his cigarette. "She won't have me smoking in the house - can't say I blame her. I wish I could give it up. I've tried on a number of occasions - no will power, that's my problem. If you'd just like to follow me." He led the way through the door and they followed him out and across the garden, entering the house by the patio doors.

Caine and Dolby followed Parr through into the hall and walked down a ramp into the spacious kitchen which was fitted out with features that made it easier for a disabled person to use the various appliances without assistance. Beyond the kitchen was the utility room,

"There are some people to see you, darling," Parr called out as he pushed open the door. "They're from the police."

Ursula Parr was seated in her wheelchair, working at the ironing board, and as she heard her husband call out to her, she flicked the chair controls and turned towards them, smiling. She must have been a very striking woman when she was able-bodied, thought Caine. Her long blonde hair set off the fine patrician features of her face, but her skin, once smooth and delicate, was lined, her blue eyes tired, inured by years of pain. She winced slightly as she turned and held her right hand out towards them, at the same time rubbing the small of her back with her left.

"I'm sorry, I have a little back pain," she apologised.

"I'm sorry, darling, perhaps this isn't a good time..." said Parr.

"No, no - it's all right, I've just taken my pills, so I shall be OK in a few minutes." She looked at her two visitors and smiled. "What can I do for you?"

Caine introduced herself and Mark Dolby. "Sorry to intrude on you, Mrs Parr. I hope we won't keep you long. There are some routine questions we'd like to ask concerning the murders of Bruce and Valerie Southam."

Ursula Parr nodded. "Anything I can do to help, Inspector." She ran the iron along the sleeve of the shirt that lay across the ironing board, and with long, slender fingers moving with sure dexterity over the cloth, pushed a plastic hanger into the shoulders. "I hope you don't mind me going on with the ironing."

"You don't do your own washing as well do you?" asked Dolby.

Ursula Parr laughed. "Don't look so surprised, Mr Dolby - I'm not that helpless, as you can see, I still have good use of my arms - but no I don't do my own washing. We're very fortunate in having Mrs Thompson - you know, she and her husband live in the Lodge House and look after most of the chores about the estate - she does it for me - for all of us on the estate, actually. But I do insist on her letting me iron my husband's shirts and our other personal things. It's my contribution to our little community." She hung up the shirt she had been ironing and turned to pick up another from the pile at her side.

"If you'll - er - excuse me," said Parr. He had been hovering at the door while his wife was speaking, "I'm just going into town for - er - some linseed oil." He looked at Caine. "You're not going to need me any more are you?"

Caine shook her head. "We shall be wanting to take a DNA sample from you at some point, Mr Parr," she advised him, "We'll be sending a technician over."

Ursula frowned. "I hope this doesn't mean that my husband is a suspect. That would be ridiculous!"

"It's just a routine process of elimination," Caine assured her.

Parr backed towards the kitchen. "Right. Okay. I won't be gone long, darling. Goodbye Inspector, Sergeant." He turned and disappeared down the corridor, moving hastily.

"Now, what can I do for you, Inspector, Sergeant?" Ursula asked, "Oh! If you'd like to sit down, you could bring a couple of chairs in from the kitchen."

"No thank you, ma'am," said Caine. "We'll be okay standing for a few minutes. Perhaps you could start by telling us where you and your husband were on Tuesday night - the night of the murder."

"We were here at home all evening." Ursula smoothed down the collar of the shirt and ran the iron over it. She looked up. "We don't get out much, you know - well, it's difficult with me in my condition and it puts an awful strain on Jamie when he takes me out." She sighed. "I often think he doesn't get out enough by himself. I think a man needs some outside interests, don't you Inspector, and he only has his woodworking classes on Monday and Wednesday evenings. Apart from that he spends most evenings in, with me."

"He still goes to woodworking classes then. But his work seems very professional."

Ursula Parr laughed. "Oh - he's not a student, Inspector, he's the teacher." She flipped the shirt over and continued. "Anyway, on Tuesday evening I think we watched a little TV and read for a bit. Then Jamie got me ready for bed at about nine o'clock."

"That's your usual time?" Ursula nodded. "And you went straight to sleep?"

"More or less. My pills make me drowsy."

"Do you sleep soundly?" asked Dolby.

"The sleep of the drugged."

"Did you hear anything after you'd gone to bed? I mean, from outside the house?"

She shook her head. "No, I don't think so. Like what?"

"A car going by?"

"No - We're a long way from the estate road. It's very quiet here."

"What did your husband do after you went to bed?"

"I assume he was in his workshop," said Ursula. "He often does a little woodwork in the evenings. You'll really have to ask him."

"So, you heard nothing at all after you went to bed? It was totally quiet?"

"Not totally - there were some sounds - I think the rooks were a bit noisy that night, in the trees - they are most nights, until it gets dark." She paused, turning the shirt over to run the iron along one of the sleeves. "Oh - there was a phone call. Jamie took it, but he said it was a wrong number. And now I come to think of it there was a bit of noise coming from the workshop - at least, I think it was from the workshop - Jamie must have been using one of his power tools."

"What sort of noise?" asked Dolby.

She shrugged, "I don't know - a mechanical sort of noise. Sort of a whirring and grating. It wasn't very loud. It went on for a few seconds, then it stopped and started up again. It did that - I don't know - five or six times."

"Have you ever heard that sort of noise before?" asked Caine.

"Not that I can recall. But you get all sorts of noises when Jamie's working with his wood. He has a lot of machinery out there. I don't take much notice - as long as he's happy doing it."

"And what time would that have been?"

"Half past nine perhaps a little later, I don't really know Inspector. I must have been nearly asleep by then."

"Are you sure the noise was coming from the workshop?" asked Caine.

"Yes - no -" She looked confused. "I don't know - I was nearly asleep. The drugs often disorientate me." She finished with the shirt she was working on and proceeded to the last one.

"How well did you know Mr and Mrs Southam, Mrs Parr?" asked Caine.

"Hardly at all. They came up to the big house occasionally when daddy had one of his business get togethers, but we didn't mix with them much socially."

"And your parents knew Bruce Southam from an early age?"

"Yes. He was a friend of my brothers when they were young."

"And is it true that your mother introduced Bruce to Valerie?"

Ursula nodded. "I believe so."

"How did that come about?" asked Caine.

She shrugged. "I don't know. So far as I can recall Valerie just appeared on the scene. She must have met my mother somewhere, I suppose. I really don't know. Mother didn't tell me - **wouldn't** tell me." She thought for a moment, almost visibly made the decision to go on and say what was on her mind. "The funny thing was they didn't **really** seem to get along, Mother and Valerie. But yes - I do know that Mummy was responsible for getting Bruce and Valerie together."

"There was no love lost between them?"

"Between Mother and Valerie? No – I don't think they had a civil word to say to each other, but in those days - this was before my accident - I was too busy leading my own life to notice very much. To be honest, I didn't much care what went on between them. After Valerie and Bruce were married, we saw very little of them until the boy, Adam, was born. Mother seemed to take to him. I don't know why." She pursed her lips and looked down for a moment, sighed. "Maybe she had yearnings for a grandchild, and he was the closest thing to it." She looked up again and Caine could see sorrow in her eyes. "After all, she's been unlucky in her children hasn't she - we - Jamie and me - haven't produced any children. Neither has Paul."

"And your husband - you're aware that he knew Bruce Southam at school?" This was Detective Sergeant Dolby.

She nodded. "I could hardly fail to - I was around at the time. And I'm also aware that Bruce and my brother, Paul, treated Jamie very badly. But that doesn't mean my husband killed Bruce Southam. He wouldn't do that, he's much too kind. He wouldn't hurt a fly!"

"They bullied him at school, though, didn't they Mrs Parr. Why do you think they were like that to him?"

"I don't know, Inspector," she turned the shirt and pressed aggressively for a few seconds. "It's not a pleasant thought to contemplate, but you must face facts - my brother Paul is not a nice man - he never has been. I acknowledge that. Nor was Bruce Southam. They were both brutes in their younger days and, to be perfectly honest, I don't think either of them changed much in their later years, in spite of their assumption of apparent respectability."

"Perhaps they and your husband had nothing in common. Is that why they bullied him?" Suggested Dolby.

"On the contrary, Sergeant. They had a lot in common, really. We all did - when we were young, we were all of us interested in sport. Paul and Bruce were keen rugger players - they played tennis, cycled, swam like fish - they were always in the great lake. And Jamie was the same - right up until my accident - he loved tennis and riding and although he was never a muscular man, he was quick and agile and he was in the school first eleven…" Her words trailed off and she gazed out of the window across the meadows. "But after my accident he lost all interest in sport."

"And that was - how long ago?" Caine asked gently.

Ursula Parr sighed. And then she seemed to take a hold on herself and smiled brightly. "Over fifteen years. It certainly changed our lives, Inspector. I've tried to get Jamie to take up sport again - you know, he's not too old for tennis and he could certainly take up golf - but he says he's not interested. The accident seemed to knock all the spirit out of him. He used to be quite outgoing - you know, reserved but outgoing in a quiet, determined sort of way - but after my accident he lost all that - he became introverted, almost shy and very nervous. His woodwork is the only thing he enjoys doing - he seems to lose himself in it. But it's worried me recently - he's been smoking far too much, especially during the last few days, since we heard about the murders - he must be getting through at least sixty a day - and it could be really dangerous in the workshop with all those wood shavings all over the place. I keep telling him, but it makes no difference."

"We had noticed," said Caine sympathetically.

"And he spends far too much time fussing over me." Ursula said grimly. "I suppose I should be grateful to have such a devoted husband." She suddenly winced with pain and rubbed at the small of her back with her left hand. "It's fifteen years since the accident, but it really won't let me forget!" She reached across to the working surface to pick up a small bottle of pills and unscrewed the top, shaking two of them into her hand. "That's the last two - I hope Jamie finds the new bottle!"

"Can we get you anything?" Caine asked. "A glass of water, or something?"

"No, thanks, I'm fine. "She pressed the pills into her mouth and swallowed. "I've had a lot of practise!" She smiled and looked around at the pile of washing. "Oh - that's all the shirts finished." She manoeuvred the joystick control of her wheelchair and turned herself away from the ironing board. "If you'll excuse me for a moment I'll just go and hang them up in Jamie's wardrobe. Don't want them to get creased again."

"Please, let us do that for you." said Caine. "Save you the trouble. Just tell us where the wardrobe is." She wondered, when Ursula frowned, if she had said the right thing, whether she was being patronising. The woman was obviously fiercely independent and wanted to do things for herself.

But Ursula smiled gratefully. "Oh, that is kind - would you? - that would be a great help. Thank you. I do like to do these things for myself, but to be perfectly honest I am feeling just a little worse for wear - that's quite a heavy iron and I feel as if I've been at it for ages." She turned the wheelchair to face the door of the room. "And it'll save me having to use the lift - that's right at the other end of the corridor and, to be honest, it's a bit of a palaver getting in and out of it!" She indicated the ironed shirts. "They go in Jamie's room - upstairs, first on the left. The wardrobe's facing you when you open the door. I do hope he's left it tidy up there - he's been a bit sort of -" she hesitated - "**distracted** recently. Mind you, it should be tidy enough. Bernice - Mrs Thompson - was in earlier on."

Dolby moved to pick up the shirts, but Caine was there before him. "It's okay, Mark, I'll do it!" She smiled roguishly, "Woman's work!" She was still conscious of the fact they had only worked together for a few days and she did not want to give him the impression he was there to carry out the purely mundane tasks of their partnership. Besides, she had offered to assist Ursula, partly she supposed to be helpful and also, she had to admit to herself, because she had been dying to see a little more of the interior of the cottage which, in many ways, resembled Lime Tree Cottage, the Birch Medley property she had viewed. She took hold of the shirts by their hangers and carried them to the door. "I don't suppose I'll be more than a couple of minutes."

Jamie's room was reasonably tidy, and, as Caine had expected, he had made good use of wood in furnishing it, but the decor was tired, the wallpaper faded and the paint work in need of freshening up. In the centre of the left-hand wall was a double bed, covered by a heavy throw over and backed by a burr walnut headboard. Beside it was a bedside cabinet in the same wood, empty save for a brass lamp topped by a translucent glass shade. Facing the bed was a massive wardrobe, also of polished walnut and standing next to it a low chest of drawers. Two big bay windows looked out over the front garden. The curtains were open and the morning sun streamed in. Caine walked quickly across to the wardrobe, laying the pile of shirts on top of the bed while she turned the brass handle to open the doors. Inside, several suits, jackets and shirts hung from a rail and beneath them Jamie's shoes, brightly polished, were arranged neatly along the bottom shelf. The rail was almost full and Caine looked back at the shirts on the bed to try to judge if she could fit them all on the rail. There were seven or eight waiting to be hung up and she would have to make room for them by shifting the suits further along. There were three dark business suits, a couple of sports jackets - one a familiar Harris tweed, the other a grey check in what she thought was cashmere. Between them hung a navy-blue blazer decorated with silver buttons and a bright yellow monogram worked into the breast pocket. The pattern was vaguely familiar, and Caine wondered if it was a designer label, but she didn't really keep up with men's fashions and if it was she didn't recognise it. She fetched the freshly ironed shirts from the bed and hung them alongside the blazer, finally closing the wardrobe door and walking across the room to the window, pulling aside the net curtain so that she could see out. Her head was still aching a little from the effects of the previous night's over-indulgence and she welcomed the few seconds in the silence of the room gazing out over the quiet, landscaped gardens.

When Caine returned downstairs Dolby and Ursula Parr were in the lounge. Mrs Parr had manoeuvred her chair across the room to the French windows and was looking out over the garden. Mark Dolby stood beside her, his hand on the back of her wheelchair. She turned her head as the Chief Inspector came into the room.

"I was just telling the Sergeant how much I enjoy the garden," she said.

"Yes, Mrs Parr's quite a gardener," said Dolby. "She was telling me she can manage quite a bit out there."

"Oh, we do have a lot of help, of course," said Ursula. "Father contracted with Budds and Co. from Chelmsford quite a few years ago, to do the park - the area that's open to the public - and we have that young man Philip in nearly every day. He and his team do all the heavy work, although the way things are, I'm not sure how long Paul will be able to keep them on. Jamie does some of the planting for our private garden and I manage most of the pruning."

"You say your brother may not be able to keep the contractors on," said Caine. "Would that be for financial reasons?"

Ursula Par nodded. "I don't think things are very easy financially. They try to keep it from me, of course, they always have - just because I'm disabled they seem to think I'm not all there - but I know what's going on. They can't really stop me from knowing, of course, because I'm still a shareholder, but they try - they say they don't want me troubling my head over it all. Never mind that I'm interested! Anyway, I do know the family's been in financial trouble ever since the Lloyds collapse and then we had to close the gravel quarries down a few years ago and that's made a tremendous difference."

"You have shares in the family business, then?" inquired Dolby.

"Only ten percent," said Ursula, "but it's enough for me to know what's going on - and I do take an interest."

"What do you think will happen to the business then, Mrs Parr?" asked Caine.

"I think Paul has a few ideas as to what to do," Ursula looked up, musing. "He keeps saying he has some irons in the fire, but he won't give out any details."

Caine wandered across the room to the fireplace. "This is beautiful…" she said. "Is it cast iron?" She ran her fingers over the smooth cold metal. "There's a similar fireplace in a property I'd like to buy. Lime Tree Cottage in Birch Medley."

Ursula smiled. "It could be of the same period. I believe this one was put in in the early nineteenth century."

Caine nodded and ran her eyes over the framed photographs on the mantle shelf. There was one of what she thought must be Ursula and Jamie in their younger days, standing close together him with his arm around her waist, looking very much in love. Beside it the now familiar faces of Charles and Florence Perot, suitably posed by a professional photographer, gazed out on the world from the imposing entrance door of Upton Stapleford House.

"Do you have any more questions Inspector?" asked Ursula, breaking Caine's train of thought.

Caine heard the question and was about to turn to answer it when the photograph at the far end of the shelf caught her eye. It was a black and white or more accurately sepia snap, slightly faded with age. She moved closer and peered at it curiously, surprised to recognise the young woman of the photograph she had seen in the Southam's varied collection of old snaps. She was in the same nineteen thirties costume - a small hat worn at an angle, long jacket in contrasting fabric with mid-calf skirt - and, although she was not striking the same pose, this photograph had almost certainly been taken at the same period as the Southam's, for behind her towered the Arc De Triomphe.

Caine realised it had been some seconds since Mrs Parr had asked her question. She turned back towards her. "I'm sorry - I just noticed this photograph - who is the lady?"

Ursula Parr propelled her wheelchair towards her. "You mean the one at the end - the old one?" She reached out her hand and Caine passed the photograph across to her. "That's my maternal Grandmother, Emma. It was taken in Paris in the 1930s."

CHAPTER TWENTY TWO

"Was Bruce Southam related to her?"

"To my Grandmother?" Ursula was puzzled. "No. I don't think so. Why?"

"We found a very similar photograph among the Southam's effects." Caine told her. "I'm sure it was the same lady, and the background, the Arc De Triomphe, is certainly the same. I'm just wondering, have you any idea why Bruce and Valerie Southam should possess a picture of your grandmother?"

Ursula Parr looked down at the picture in her hands and shook her head. "You mean they had a photo like this in their house? I can't think why. But is it important?"

"I don't know." Caine replaced the picture on the mantle shelf and stood back. "I don't think we have any more questions for the time being Mrs Parr." She looked across at Mark Dolby for confirmation. "Thank you for your co-operation. We'll see ourselves out."

They let themselves out through the French windows and walked slowly around to the front of the house.

"She's a brave woman," said Dolby.

Caine nodded thoughtfully. "Yes, it's remarkable the way she keeps her spirits up. It can't be easy to have lost the use of your legs. It's a terrible thing to happen, but I suppose she's lucky, in a way, to have such a devoted husband."

"He does seem to look after her very well," agreed Dolby. They walked slowly across the gravelled parking area at the front of the house and down towards the drive. "This is a nice big parking area," he remarked, looking critically over at the deep furrows in the grass at the edge of the pathway. "There's plenty of turning room, especially if there's only one car."

Caine followed his gaze. "Meaning - those ruts were obviously caused by car wheels, so why should someone drive off the path and onto the grass?

"Yes," agreed Dolby. "Maybe someone's a bad driver?"

"That someone being James Parr? It wouldn't surprise me. I've seldom interviewed anyone quite so nervous. Then again, I suppose his life can't be easy. His wife's disabled - I suppose some people would describe his marriage as dysfunctional - and he's tied to a job he doesn't like, with a boss - who also happens to be his brother-in-law - that he doesn't get on with." Caine grimaced. "But, by the same token, if Parr is that bad a driver how come Perot lets him drive him into the City every day?"

"Perhaps he's not such a bad driver, perhaps he's just a thoroughly weak character," said Dolby, almost dismissively. "He's not in control of his life. It seems to me he just gets carried along by the current and allows things to happen to him."

Caine glanced at him quizzically. "Aren't you ignoring the effects of chance? Some people would call it Fate! Sometimes people can't help what happens to them no matter how hard they try."

Dolby snorted derisively. "You can always do something about your life if you really want to. Parr's just feeling sorry for himself!"

They continued their journey down the hill. Dolby had taken off his jacket again and carried it slung over his shoulder.

"But what about Paul Perot?" he asked. "Wouldn't you agree he's still our most likely suspect?"

Caine thought for a moment before answering. "I'm uneasy about him. There's a lot loaded against him and in some respects I'm sure he's lying or holding something back. But I'm still not sure he's our killer." She stopped in front of the wide wooden gate at the bottom of the hill, in the shade of the tall lime tree, watching while Dolby released the metal catch of the gate and swung it open to let them pass through. "His chief motive would be the insurance money and I just have the feeling that if he was going to bump off Bruce Southam, he would have planned it a whole lot better. The whole thing seems too messy and too unpremeditated. In the first place, why kill him at home? I would have thought making it look like a nice, quiet, random killing somewhere else - in the city, say - would have been far more effective and deflect suspicion away from him."

"You mean a hit and run car accident or maybe take out a contract? It's all a bit far-fetched." said Dolby, nodding his agreement. "I admit, that would be far more anonymous." He unlocked car doors. "But don't forget that he - or whoever the killer is - tried to make it look like Valerie had done for Bruce and then committed suicide. That showed a bit of planning and premeditation, surely!"

She climbed into the car. "Not necessarily. The point is, Mark, if Paul was going to do the job properly he would have been appropriately dressed for it - there wouldn't have been any of this nonsense about disposing of the bloodstained clothes. The kill would have been far cleaner than it was. As we've said before - the man used to be in the paratroopers and he's been trained to kill. We know that Bruce Southam was dead drunk when he came home that night - his blood alcohol level was way up! - And he'd have been no match for Perot. But there's also the problem with the timing - I don't see how Paul could have got to the scene of the crime within the time frame he's given us."

Dolby looked at his watch. "It's just gone eleven," he walked around the car and climbed in on the driver's side. "If it's okay by you, Jackie, I think I'll spend a few hours doing a spot of digging around Paul Perot's alibi."

Caine fastened her seat belt and dropped her handbag onto the floor of the car. She turned to face him. "You don't have to, you know, Mark, it is Saturday!"

"Oh! A few hours won't do any harm and I really think the man's taking the mickey so far as his alibi is concerned. He's spinning us a yarn, Jackie!" He laughed ironically. "I must admit I wouldn't mind the afternoon at home, but I've already warned Lorna I wouldn't see her until this evening, so there's no harm done. I'll do you a deal though - I do have a few days leave due, so how about you let me have a few days off when this Southam business is cleared up and we have the killer safely under lock and key? You could probably do with a few days off yourself."

Caine nodded. One of the first tasks she had set herself when she took up her new post at Fen Molesey CID had been to go through Dolby's file, which had made it quite obvious he was a keen and methodical worker who didn't hesitate to work long and arduous hours. It had also been evident that he did not take enough time with his family. "Okay, that's fine. Just let me know when you want to be away - but I'm not so sure about myself. I've hardly started the job and I can't see Hansen encouraging me to take any holidays yet!" Besides, until the purchase of her house came through she didn't have much to do away from the office.

They drove on in silence for a few minutes. "Do you think we should stop to ask Paul Perot's parents a few questions?" asked Dolby. "They might know something."

Caine shook her head. "Let's save them for Monday, shall we? To be honest I was hoping to see Alison this afternoon for a few hours if I could. She has to get back to London early for some PR promotional party! Anyway, I don't suppose the Perots

Senior will be able to tell us very much that we haven't already learnt from the rest of the family. By all accounts Charles is very much past it, but I don't know about the old lady. Maybe we would get something new out of her."

"I doubt it," said Dolby, having second thoughts. "I know they all live on the Upton Stapleford Estate, but they're not exactly in each other's pockets and the old people probably haven't got a clue what's going on." He manoeuvred the car around a particularly deep pothole in the estate road. "Personally, I'm more anxious to go down to Docklands and have a nose around Paul's apartment. He mentioned a twenty-four-hour security guard. If past experience is anything to go by the man must have something to tell us. These security guards don't often miss much. And then there's that Chinese Restaurant he's supposed to have eaten in on Tuesday evening - what was it called - *The Junk*? We may learn something from them."

They came slowly past the Lodge House and paused before joining the B road. There was no sign of the Thompsons.

"Okay if I drop you at home?" asked Dolby. She nodded. He indicated a right turn and they swung out on to the road. "I'll go on to London after that." He checked the clock on the dash-board. "Should make it easily by twelve thirty if the traffic isn't too bad." He made a quick mental calculation. "Should be able to do what I want to do and be back home by five o'clock."

*　　　*　　　*　　　*　　　*

*　　　*

The Junk Chinese Restaurant was situated on the West India Dock Road, almost in the shadow of Canary Tower and the other glass and stainless-steel skyscrapers which, since their construction in the early two thousands, had dominated this newly transformed part of the Isle of Dogs and the old London Docks. Dolby parked his car in the service area in front of the restaurant, which was part of a small row of retail units laid back from the road. A red, blue and white train of the Docklands Light railway trundled by on the elevated section of track a hundred or so yards up the road and he followed its passage between the gleaming stone of the new and recently renovated old buildings towards Canary Wharf before pushing open the car door and stepping out into the road. He had not visited the area for years and was surprised at the astonishing changes which had taken place, but the thing that struck him most was how clean everything was. Clean and new. No wonder people like Paul Perot fought each other to buy places here. The urban cycle had made a complete turn and it was one of **the** places to be in London. But it wasn't for him. The changes were superficial, ephemeral. It was too busy here. Too crowded. Too polluted. He could almost taste the pungency of the air - air that was heavy with chemical particulates that, unless something was done soon to reduce the number of vehicles passing through the area, would quickly coat the clean surfaces of the new buildings with grimy traffic film.

The illuminated sign above the entrance to **The Junk** proclaimed the restaurant to be the finest local purveyor of Peking and Cantonese food and Dolby's nostrils were met by tantalising odours as he pushed open the glass entrance door and went inside. The terrace of buildings in which **The Junk** was situated had been recently renovated and the interior of the restaurant, lit by fluorescent lighting from a suspended ceiling supplemented by the bright sunlight streaming in through the plate glass windows, was light and cheerful. The walls were covered with ivory silk wallpaper decorated with small Chinese motifs and a number of tapestries reminiscent of the Willow Pattern design adorned the walls. The small tables were glass topped and the upright struts of the chair backs were shaped and grooved to resemble bamboo shoots. Light, easy to listen to Western music drifted down from strategically placed speakers.

Apart from an elderly Chinese couple occupying a table at the far end of the surprisingly large dining area the restaurant was empty and Dolby made his way between the tables towards the bar and serving area, the heavy aroma of the food the couple were eagerly consuming reminding him he had not eaten since breakfast.

As he approached the bar a Chinese girl appeared from the kitchen area beyond. Her plain white blouse and long black skirt emphasised the frailty of her slim figure and her eyes appeared huge against her high cheek bones and the almost luminous pallor of her skin. She greeted him with a smile and asked if he would like a table or whether he required take-away.

"Thank you; I'd like a table for one, please." It was well after mid-day and the aromas had worked their persuasive will. He had to admit to himself that a few minutes ago he had not been very hungry, but in his job he rarely knew when he would be in a position to take a meal and he might as well take advantage of the fact that duty had brought him to this very pleasant restaurant. Besides, he was a great lover of Chinese food.

"You take our set meal, or you want menu?" asked the girl.

"I'll have the menu, thanks," said Dolby. "But before I sit down, I wonder if I could have a word with the Manager."

"I am Manager. I am Sue Ling." she smiled showing a set of small white teeth. Dolby found himself wondering how old she was. He introduced himself and showed her his warrant card.

She examined it carefully and nodded. "Fen Molesey - that in Essex I think." her words were stilted and she spoke them with the precision of a person speaking a foreign language, although Dolby still had the impression that she had been born and raised in England - probably here, in these same Limehouse premises, which no doubt had living accommodation upstairs.

"How I help?"

"I'm interested in one of your customers, Miss Ling. At least, he claims to be one of your regular customers."

"What his name? Perhaps you have photograph?"

"No - I don't!" he should, of course, have thought of getting one before chasing all the way down here to London's Docklands. "His name is Perot, Paul Perot. You may know it - he probably uses a credit card." She reflected on his words, her attractive eyes flicking upwards thoughtfully in their almond shaped sockets. "A tall man," he prompted, "dark hair. Probably wears a business suit."

"Ah! Of course, I know Mr Per-oe." Her pronunciation of the name was quaint, prolonging the first syllable. "He come in here often, sometimes he on his own, other times he with his lady friend."

"He has a lady friend?"

She smiled. "They very close, I see that from body language."

"What does she look like, this lady?"

"Tall. Attractive. Long blonde hair," said Sue Ling. She smiled. "Good legs. Long. She wear short skirts and all men look at them when she come in."

"Mr Perot is older than her?"

"Oh yes. Could be she his daughter, but somehow I not think so."

"And they come in here together a lot?"

She shrugged again. "I suppose. Five, maybe six times a month. I not always on duty."

"Were they in here last Tuesday evening?"

She scratched her head thoughtfully with long, well-manicured fingers. "Maybe; I not know. One day much like any other. But like you say, Mr Per-oe always pay with credit card, so I can check." She went around the back of the bar, hit some keys on the computerised cash register and peered closely at the screen. "What date Tuesday?"

"The third of June."

She hit a few more keys. "Oh Three - Oh six. Here. June three. Ah! Come look!" Dolby made his way around the to the back of the counter. A summary of the invoice was displayed on the screen; it gave no details of the meal Perot had enjoyed on the evening concerned, but his name and credit card details were clearly shown as were the time and date of the transaction - 19:53:28 on the third of June. Dolby gave mental thanks to the person or persons who had invented credit card payments. They had unwittingly given birth to a system of immeasurable assistance to the Police and to the Pursuit of Justice. It was all here, clearly recorded. Paul Perot had used his card to pay *The Junk's* bill at seven fifty-three pm on Tuesday 3rd June, which meant he had been lying when he told the Detective Sergeant and DCI Caine he had arrived at the restaurant at nine o'clock in the evening and left an hour and a half later at ten thirty. But in one respect he had been telling the truth - the size of the bill and the number of covers shown confirmed that he had - on that occasion at least - eaten alone.

"I'd like a printout of this, please."

Page 450

"No problem." She hit another key on the cash register and the printer situated on a shelf under the countertop beeped into life. After a few seconds she handed him the completed print out. "You want Chinese meal now?" She said hopefully.

Dolby smiled, pleased with the morning's work. "Thank you - yes - it smells good. I'll have a look at that menu if I may, please, Miss Ling, and I'll have a pot of Jasmine tea to drink while I'm choosing."

With a generous bowl of egg fried rice and a plate of stir-fried chicken in satay sauce lying warm and comfortable in his stomach, Detective Sergeant Mark Dolby made his way across West Ferry Road and into Limehouse Causeway. The Manageress of The **Junk** had given him directions to Antigone Wharf where Paul Perot had his Docklands apartment. It was situated in Narrow Street, overlooking the River Thames, almost opposite **The House They Left Behind** and now Dolby looked out for the appropriately named public house. Apparently, it was the only building left standing when the LDDC, in collaboration with the property developers, had razed the area to the ground in order to rebuild. It was relatively quiet here, but not far away traffic streamed into the relatively newly built Limehouse Link Tunnel, creating a constant background hum. Behind him rose Canary Tower, flanked by the Hong Kong and Shanghai Banking Corporation's London Headquarters, both of them amongst the tallest buildings in Europe and testaments to the growing importance of the area.

Dolby found Antigone Wharf a few minutes later, about one third of the way along Narrow Street, and walked quickly up the entrance steps, pushing open the glass doors into the reception area. The building was an old Victorian warehouse refurbished within the last ten years and converted into luxury apartments. The original high brick walls of the entrance area were exposed and had been preserved in much the same condition as the developer had found them, retaining the slightly mottled effect of brick seasoned by coal smoke. The floor was beech wood strip, highly polished as the fashion required and Dolby's metal capped heels clicked loudly as he crossed to the security guard's desk in the centre. The man heard him coming and looked up inquiringly from the tabloid newspaper he was reading.

Dolby showed his warrant card. "Detective Sergeant Mark Dolby, Fen Molesey CID. Could I have your name please?"

The security guard blinked nervously. "I'm John Richards. What can I do for you, Sergeant?"

"We're carrying out some inquiries, Mr Richards. There's nothing for you to be alarmed about. Now, I understand that a Mr Paul Perot occupies an apartment here."

"That's right, Sergeant, number 68." Richards was middle aged, balding, the small amount of hair he had managed to retain almost entirely grey. The tunic of the Corps of Commissionaires was a little tight on his well fleshed body and the skin of his face was tinged with pink, probably betraying high blood pressure. His eyes, scrutinising Dolby, were set a little too close together on either side of a bulbous, large nostrilled nose. "What's happened to him then?"

Dolby ignored the question. "Were you on duty on Tuesday evening?"

"What time would that be?"

"Between, say, six o'clock and midnight."

The man consulted a large day to a page diary, his thick, stubby fingers flicking ponderously back through the pages. He found what he was looking for. "Yes, I was as a matter of fact. I normally do the six till six stint, what I call the red eye, but last week-end they asked me to do the day shift now and then, to help out. That's why I'm on days today. One of the other blokes is sick or something, but I don't mind. It's all extra cash and the wife's away visiting her mother so there's nothing for me to be doing at home. I may as well be here earning. Why do you want to know?"

"You're a regular here?"

"That's what I said didn't I? I usually do the six till six and I was here on Tuesday. So, what about it?"

"Did you see Mr Perot that evening?"

"Well, I don't know about that. My memory's not what it used to be you know."

"It's important."

"Well, I'm sure it must be, or you wouldn't be asking me would you? But memory's a funny thing. Sometimes it's easy to remember what happened a month or more ago on a certain date, but at other times you can't even think what you were doing on the day before. Some people reckon they need something to trigger their memory off."

Dolby, his stomach still warm and heavy with Chinese food and feeling a little sleepy in the heat of the afternoon, was becoming more than a little exasperated at the man's apparent reluctance to answer the question. "If you're looking for a financial inducement, my friend," he said, "forget it! You are not a paid informer. You've been watching too many Hollywood films. So, did you or did you not see Mr Perot on Tuesday evening?"

Richard's voice almost squeaked his alarm. "I wasn't angling for no money, Guv'nor. I just can't remember. There's no reason why I should is there? One evening's much the same as any other in this job. They all run into each other so that you can't remember what happened when. Besides, Mr Perot isn't exactly the sort of bloke that'd cause you to remember him just because he's coming in or going out is   he? You do know him I take it?" Dolby nodded. "So, you see my point then. How am I supposed to remember if I saw him or not on a particular night? You tell me that."

Dolby sighed and changed tack. "Okay, we'll come back to that. Do you ever see him with a woman?"

The man's eyes gleamed and flickered upwards, reminiscing. "Do I ever see him with a woman? Yeah - as a matter of fact I do. Quite often. One of the other residents she is -

and she's quite a looker. Young and blonde she is and you should see those legs of hers. I'm a married man, Sergeant, but I'm telling you they don't do my blood pressure a lot of good! Not with those short skirts she wears. Sometimes they're so short you can see her pants! Phew!" He wiped his brow at the thought. "And those leathers - she wears leathers sometimes, with really tight trousers." He paused, smiling widely. "And now as you mention it I do remember, I **did** see Mr Perot on Tuesday evening - because just as he came in from the street **she** came up from the car park and they met here in the vestibule."

"Would you say they were good friends?"

"What? Good friends and the rest. I've seen them together a few times and I'm telling you it's the most he can do to keep his hands off her until they get in the lift. I'm not saying anything, but I think they're a lot more than good friends. Well, they have the opportunity don't they, living in next door flats like they do."

"And they met here in the reception area last Tuesday night? What time was that?"

The man hesitated, thinking back. "Well, I'd been on duty for a couple of hours and Eastenders was just finishing on the telly," he indicated the small set at the side of the desk. "So, it must have been 8 o'clock or thereabouts."

"And you're certain this was on Tuesday evening?" The security guard nodded. "How can you be so certain? A few minutes ago you were complaining that one evening is very much like any other evening. They all run into each other you said. So how do you know it was Tuesday that you saw Mr Perot and his lady friend meet each other and go into the lift together?"

"Ah! Because she told me she was going away the following day. She said she'd be away for a long time and to keep my eye on the flat for her until she gets back."

"I don't see how that helps."

"Ah, but it does you see," he smiled widely enjoying his moment of triumph. "Because she was on the telly the following night and I was at home watching with the wife. It was the only night I've had off this week and it was the Wednesday. That's how I know I saw them together on the Tuesday, because it was the day before I saw her on TV."

Dolby was not sure he was following Mr Richards' reasoning. "She's a TV personality then, this friend of Paul Perot's?"

"No - did I say that? She just happened to be on telly on Wednesday. I was with my wife at home and there she was on the nine o'clock news."

"But why was she on the news?" Dolby spoke the words slowly, controlling his irritation.

"She was off somewhere on an expedition."

Something clicked in Dolby's memory and he leaned forward with mounting excitement. Certain things were beginning to make sense to him. "What's this woman's name?"

"It's a funny name. Well, both her names are unusual I'd say. Can't say I've ever heard of her first name before, though. Phyllippa I think, something like that anyway."

"Phyllida - Phyllida Orsmby?"

Richards' eyes opened wide, showing his surprise. "Yes. Do you know her?"

Dolby nodded. "We have met. You say that on Tuesday evening she was coming up from the garage? Does she keep her motorcycle down there?"

"Yes, Sergeant. She has a parking bay downstairs." Richards was still impressed. "Have you seen her bike?"

"No, but I'd like to take a look at it, if I may, Mr Richards."

"I'll take you down," said Richards. He reached under the counter for a bunch of keys. "I'll just have to lock the front door while we're gone. Can't be too careful in these posh blocks, you know, once the villains are in they could get anywhere. The residents will have to use their own keys to get in while I'm away for a few minutes." He walked to the glass entrance door and swung it shut, securing the lock with a quick turn of the key. "Follow me, please Sergeant." Dolby followed him to a door at the back of the reception area, standing back as the burly Richards tapped out the security code on an electronic key pad. The lock clicked open and he reached forward and pulled the heavy door towards him. "After you, Sergeant." They went through the door and down a flight of stairs into the underground car park.

There were cars parked in rows on either side. Richards led the way between two of them and ducked through a doorway into another section of the car park. They went past a number of exterior windows covered by strong metal grilles, through the bars of which Dolby could see the street outside.

"This place is quite secure is it?" asked Dolby.

"Oh yes, very secure. You can't get in from the road without a pass card."

They passed around a circular structural pillar. On the other side, tucked neatly into a small space, was a large motorcycle, gleaming black and silver in the fluorescent light.

"It's a real powerful buggar, isn't it," commented Richards. "not at all the sort of vehicle you'd expect a young girl like Miss Orsmby to be riding about on!"

Dolby remembered the photograph he had seen in Phyllida Ormsby's cottage. "She seems to manage okay." He examined the vehicle more closely, noting the "Vincent" motif painted on the side of the fuel tank and making a note of the registration mark. "Any idea how fast this thing can go, Mr Richards?"

Richards shrugged. "She told me she'd got it up to 125 miles an hour when she was in Germany a few years back, but I wouldn't really know, I'm not a biker."

"And she hasn't asked you to look after it while she's away?"

"Well, she said would I keep an eye on it, but I don't have the keys or anything." Richards thought for a moment. "I imagine she's given them to Mr Perot. I believe he used to ride a bike like this, so I imagine he could take it out for a spin now and then to keep the engine sweet."

"Yes, I believe he did used to ride," said Dolby, breaking into a smile. "He didn't by any chance take it out on Tuesday night?"

"He may have done," said Richards. "He's got a security pass card so he can come and go out of the vehicle entrance whenever he likes. I don't keep my eyes on the security screens *all* the time and I sometimes get called away from the desk. Why?"

Dolby ignored the question. "Do you happen to know where Miss Ormsby gets the bike serviced, Mr Richards."

The guard thought for a moment. "Yeah, it's Mike Bird does it for her. I know that cos Mike delivers it back during the daytime and he leaves it with me. As a matter of fact, she had it done last Monday and he brought it back that evening, just after I clocked on. We had a bit of a natter together."

"And he has his own garage?"

"Yeah - Bird's Bikes - he's not far, just off Ming Street.

Dolby wrote the name and address in his notebook. "Thanks. We'll go back upstairs now if we may."

They made their way back to the stairs and mounted them slowly, the security guard puffing slightly from the effort, Dolby taking them easily.

"And you say, Mr Richards, that Mr Perot and Miss Ormsby are neighbours? What number is she?"

"69. They're both up on the sixth floor. Do you want to take a look? I can't take you into their flats, of course, but you could see how the land lies."

"No thanks. I'll leave that to my imagination for the present." They came back into the reception area. "One last question, if you please. Did Miss Ormsby go out later?"

"You mean on Tuesday?" Richards answered without hesitation. "Yes. She left in her little car - her "run-around" she calls it - at about ten, although it might have been as late as ten thirty. She said she was going to her place out in Essex before flying out to the Far East on the following day. It was something to do with an expedition to look for new plants. I'm not sure what she does, but I think it's something to do with flowers."

"She's a botanist," said Dolby. He put his notebook away and made for the door. "Thanks, Mr Richards, that's been very helpful."

Dolby slowly retraced his steps to his car, turning over in his mind what he had learned from John Richards. There was little doubt in his mind now as to who had murdered Bruce and Valerie Southam. He appreciated that DCI Jackie Caine had been reluctant to accept the situation so far; there had been a number of points that did not add up, but with Richards's contribution there was, Dolby thought, more than enough proof to convict Paul Perot. The forensic evidence. would be hardly more than technical confirmation that he had carried out the murders.

Dolby checked his watch. It was just a little after half past one. Time enough for him to get back to the office and write up his report of the morning's events before setting out for home and dinner with the Previtts.

CHAPTER TWENTY THREE

DS Dave Milligan was rubbing his eyes and staring at the computer screen on his desk when Dolby came into the office. "G'Morning, Dave." He sat down in the swivel chair opposite his colleague.

Milligan looked across at him and yawned, opening his mouth wide. "G'Morning, Mark." He yawned again, this time taking his time and stretching. "God! A computer screen is the last thing I need this early on a Monday morning. I feel like it's ten o'clock at night and I've been at it all day."

"How long *have* you been at it?"

"Ten minutes. But I didn't get much sleep last night on account of that shocking business up at Springfield."

"What was that then?"

"Breaking and entering at an old people's home, believe it or not." Milligan frowned. "There's an old lady dead as a result and it could have been murder."

"What happened?"

"We're not sure yet. I was called out at just after four o'clock to go up there with my Guv'nor." He was referring to DCI Hopkins. "The dead woman had a garden room at the Springfield Retirement Home - it seems someone broke in and either murdered her or scared her enough to give her a heart attack. We're waiting for the path report. The place was a right mess. Whoever it was made a good job of turning it over, but there wasn't much taken, apparently, if anything. Anyway, I feel shagged out and the last thing I want to be doing now is staring at this bloody computer screen."

The telephone rang. Milligan picked up the receiver, listened for a moment and passed it across to Dolby. "It's for you, Mark. Wendy Doyle."

Dolby took the phone from him. "Mark Dolby here Wendy. That was quick - what have you got for me?" He listened, a smile spreading across his face. "Thanks. That's great. We shall have to get the original, but that's fine for the moment. Fantastic work, Wendy - remind me to give you a big kiss when I see you! Thanks again." He replaced the receiver.

"Must be good news, you lucky beggar! I wouldn't mind having a snog with that Wendy myself."

"You're not her type, Dave. Anyway, it looks like my hunch was right on the nose!"

"The Southam case?"

"Yes, but I can't say what yet - it's just a theory and I'll have to run it by DCI Caine first." He stood up and made for the door. "By the way, thanks for your help on that CCTV recording. You done good!"

* * * * *
* *

Caine looked up from her desk as DS Dolby came into her office. She had had a restful Sunday and was feeling refreshed, but the news she had just received from PC Wendy Doyle had not been encouraging and her smile of welcome was muted.

"'Morning, Mark. Good weekend?" He nodded enthusiastically as she waved him towards a seat. "I'm afraid there's no news yet on the whereabouts of Mrs Neale. She seems to have vanished from the face of the earth."

"It is a bit baffling isn't it." He sat down and crossed his legs. "Especially in the light of what happened to the Southams."

"But there's still no proof her disappearance is connected with the Southam murders," continued Caine. "Hansen's made it clear we're to treat it simply as a case of a runaway wife and not let it take up our time or resources. Until, of course, and I quote, **'*something more concrete*'** turns up. You know what that means." She frowned again and shook her head. "I must admit it has me worried, Mark. I'm not so certain it's as simple as a runaway wife - it must be connected with the murders, it's too much like coincidence." She sat back and drummed her fingers on the desk. "I wish to hell I knew how they were connected, though. I feel so sorry for those two kids of hers, not to mention her husband."

Dolby nodded his agreement. "Any particular reason why Susie shouldn't simply have just upped and gone, though? Irrespective of what happened to the Southams?"

She stood up, making her way to the window and opening it, leaning over the bunch of mixed flowers she had bought in the marketplace on her way in. She had spent five minutes arranging them in a vase on the windowsill and now she breathed in their fragrance. "No." She smiled. "It's just a feeling, Mark. Call it intuition if you like. I just don't like the way the whole thing smells!" She turned and came back to her desk, sitting in her high-backed swivel chair and crossing her legs. "Anyway, how did your trip to Docklands go on Saturday? You've obviously got a few things to tell me - we've only known each other a week, but you can't hide that look of boyish enthusiasm!"

He blushed. "Well, yes, I have. Quite a few things as it happens." He ran over the events of the weekend.

"You're still convinced Paul Perot murdered the Southams?"

"Yes. It's got to have been him. He was obviously having an affair with Sir Charles Ormsby's daughter and he used her motor bike to get back to Fen Molesey on the night of the murder. It's fast enough - around 125 miles per hour - and we know he used to be into fast bikes, so he could've handled it. Anyway, he drove up here on the bike, did for the Southams and then hared it back to London again. Piece of cake in the time available, especially on that bike!"

Caine bit her lip. She was still reluctant to arrest Perot. Superintendent Hansen had made it very clear he did not want any more waves in that direction. Besides, there were one or two facts that didn't fit.

"I hear what you're saying, Mark, but even if Perot did use Miss Ormsby's motorbike why would he bother to collect his own car and drive that over to the industrial estate? Why not just go straight to the Southam's on the bike?"

"Maybe he was trying to divert suspicion from himself." Dolby suggested, frowning. "And add a bit of confusion to our inquiries. After all, with his open house policy so far as his car is concerned, he could implicate practically everyone living on the estate. Muddy the waters so to speak."

"Then why park the car on the industrial estate instead of outside the Southam's house?"

Dolby thought for a moment. "I don't know." He said uncertainly, "Perhaps he was hoping it wouldn't be noticed? If it wasn't then all well and good - if it was then he'd be implicating someone else. Sort of belts and braces!"

Caine frowned. "Your logic's a little convoluted, Mark. I'm not sure I'm convinced." She paused, closing her eyes in thought for a moment. "Mark, you mentioned Miss Ormsby had had the bike serviced a day or so before she left for Indonesia. Have you checked out the mileage on the odometer?"

Dolby grinned. "Yes, I put Wendy on to that first thing this morning," There was a hint of smugness. "She's just rung me with the results of her inquiries. We had the name of the service garage so she was able to make a quick phone call and luckily they were open early. They found the paperwork with the details almost immediately."

"Get to the point, Mark."

Now he was smiling broadly. "**Someone** used the bike **after** the service and they travelled a good few miles on it - enough to get up here to Fen Molesey and back again to Docklands."

"And you reckon that someone was Paul Perot?" Caine reached up and rubbed the back of her neck. It had started to ache again. "It seems plausible."

"More than just plausible, Jackie. It's obvious. Perot has the motive, the opportunity **and** the capability. He's been telling us a pack of lies from start to finish." He laughed grimly. "And it's no wonder he didn't want it known he'd been with Phyllida Ormsby on the evening of the murders - I don't suppose her daddy, Sir Charles, would be over the moon to learn that his prospective business partner was bedding his darling daughter! Particularly as said prospective partner is old enough to be her father!"

Caine nodded. "She's over eighteen, but I follow your drift and it fits into the general picture. We do know Perot was trying hard to keep Charles Ormsby on board and news like that wouldn't have helped his efforts. But still..." She leaned back in her seat and closed her eyes for a moment, steepling her fingers together. "We can't afford to get this wrong, Mark - I'll rephrase that - *I* can't afford to get this wrong - I've only just taken this job and I'm still more or less on probation." She made a decision. "Look, we still haven't had the forensic report on the clothes. If Perot's DNA shows up on those then we're home and dry and we can arrest him without Hansen going ballistic. But if not..." She let her words hang on the air.

Dolby shrugged. "I reckon we've got enough already, Chief. I don't know what more you want." He stood up, stretched and walked over to look through the window. "What's our next move then?"

Caine was about to answer him when the telephone rang. "DCI Caine." Her face betrayed her surprise as she gesticulated to Dolby, mouthing the words "It's him - Perot!" He sat down again and leaned towards her. She listened closely for a few seconds before commenting. "I'm very sorry to hear that, Mr Perot." She listened again. "Right." She reached for a pen and jotted a note on the pad in front of her. "Molesey Hills Hospital. We'll be there as soon as we can. I sincerely hope the news on your father will be better by then. Goodbye." She hung up.

"What did he want?" asked Dolby. "And what's this about a hospital?"

She answered his second question first. "Charles Perot, Paul's father, was rushed into hospital last night - he's had another stroke - this time a pretty massive one. He's in a coma. Paul wants to speak to us at the hospital. As soon as possible."

"What do you suppose he wants to say?"

She smiled. "Perhaps he's going to confess?"

"Dream on, Jackie." There was no trace of humour in Dolby's laugh. He stood up. "Come on then, the sooner we get to see him the sooner we'll find out what he has in mind."

The Molesey Hills Private Hospital was situated a few miles outside Maldon. It was a low, modern red brick building, no more than ten years old Caine judged, and it had about it an air of clean, quiet efficiency totally lacking in the majority of National Health hospitals she had visited in the course of her career. The car park was hidden from the main hospital buildings by a well-tended grassy knoll dotted with flower beds and young trees. It was crowded with vehicles and it took them some moments to find a space. They left the vehicle and made their way to the reception area along an asphalted path. The automatic glass entrance doors opened noiselessly as she and Dolby approached the reception area and closed behind them with only the barest whisper. A solitary man reading a magazine occupied one of the chairs ranged at the side of the room and a well-turned-out middle-aged lady, clad in a crisp white uniform was seated behind the polished wooden counter. A label attached to her blouse announced that she was Mrs Daphne Morris and that she was an 'Administrator'. Behind her glowed a row of closed-circuit television screens each showing a different view of the outside and entrances to the building. Mrs Morris smiled as they approached almost silently over the rubber tiled floor. She asked if she could help.

Caine showed her warrant card. "I'm Detective Chief Inspector Jacqueline Caine and this is Detective Sergeant Mark Dolby, Fen Molesey CID. You have a Mr Charles Perot in the Davenport Wing?" Mrs Morris nodded. "His son, Mr Paul Perot, is also here, I believe. Perhaps you could tell us where we can find him."

She smiled again. "Yes. I have been told to expect you, Inspector. If you'd like to come this way." She came around the counter and they followed her across the reception area to one of the doors marked 'Consulting Room'. "If you'd like to wait in here, I'll tell Mr Perot you've arrived. Help yourself to a drink if you wish."

They entered a small room. There were no windows, but it was well lit by artificial light. A circular wooden conference table, constructed of light oak, with four upholstered upright chairs ranged around it took up most of the space. A side table laden with coffee machine, teapot and two bottles of sparkling mineral water stood in the corner. A shelf beneath was well stocked with china cups and a number of cut-glass tumblers.

"Nice set up," said Dolby moving around the table towards the coffee machine. "Would you like a drink, Jackie? I know I could do with one."

"Thanks. I'll have a glass of mineral water, please. Sparkling."

He picked up one of the bottles and unscrewed the cap carefully, listening to the loud hiss as the gas escaped before opening it fully. "I don't know what it is about hospitals, but even when they're so obviously well run as this one I don't like being in them. Even as a visitor."

"I don't suppose anyone does," agreed Caine. She took the glass of water from him and sipped it slowly. "But unfortunately, they're a necessary part of life - and death." In the car on the way over they had discussed every aspect of Perot's sudden request for a meeting and there was little more to say on the subject. Now they were resorting to meaningless small talk.

After a few minutes the door opened and Paul Perot entered followed by a small, dark man they had not seen before. The stranger's well cut obviously expensive suit, meticulously laundered shirt and sober tie set him down as a professional and Caine was not in the least surprised when Perot introduced him as Joshua Goodman his family's solicitor.

"How is your father Mr Perot?" she asked when they had been through the introductions and were sitting at the table facing each other.

Perot shook his head. He looked genuinely concerned. "I'm afraid they've given us very little hope. He's in a coma at the moment and they don't expect him to come out of it." His pale face creased into a weak smile. "Still, he had a good and fruitful life and at over ninety he's had a pretty good innings, wouldn't you say so, Joshua?"

Goodman nodded. "Yes, he had a good and full life, Paul, but nowadays, even at that age one hopes for more."

The solicitor got up and went to the coffee table. "Can I get anything for anybody?" Perot asked for tea and Goodman poured him a cup from the thermos jug, adding a dash of milk.

Caine coughed apologetically. She felt as if she was intruding on Perot's private grief and she wondered how this would go down if Superintendent Hansen got to hear about it. Although she and Dolby were here at Perot's specific request Hansen would probably accuse her of 'making waves'. "Look, Mr Perot, I want you to know that DS Dolby and I are very sorry to hear of your father's condition. I know that you wanted to speak to us, but in the circumstances I would be quite happy to see you at another time. Tomorrow perhaps."

Perot smiled and for the first time Caine realised that he could be very charming when the situation warranted, as it probably did on numerous business occasions. "Thank you for your concern, Inspector. However, there are one or two things I feel I need to tell you in order to clear the air. They are matters of a rather delicate nature and that is why I've asked Mr Goodman to join us. I don't want any misunderstandings. As for whether I talk to you now or later, I think the earlier the better. My father will not come out of his coma - the doctors have told me that quite categorically and I must believe them. Therefore, I want any unpleasantness out of the way now." He stopped, then continued slowly, sipping his tea. "I would add that I called this meeting largely for my mother's sake, to save her any further distress."

Caine nodded. "I understand, Mr Perot. I should warn you though that you are under suspicion for murder and, therefore, anything you do say connected with the deaths of Mr and Mrs Southam cannot be off the record."

Perot inclined his head, acknowledging the situation. "I did think you were considering me as a serious suspect, Inspector, and naturally that did concern me. However, let me assure you that I *am* innocent of any wrongdoing and that I have no intention of confessing to anything. I am merely going to explain to you why I have withheld certain information".

"I'm glad to hear it, Mr Perot," said Caine.

Perot looked across at his lawyer. "Mr Goodman is here to witness that I am talking to you of my own free will." Goodman nodded. Perot paused to organise his thoughts. "The first thing I must tell you, Inspector, is that I was not telling the truth when I said I was at a business meeting on Tuesday evening, the night of 3rd June last. I am prepared to make a new statement."

"Where were you then, sir?" asked Dolby. His mouth was set in a thin line and his eyes showed his distrust.

"I was with a young lady up until just after ten o'clock. She left at - I would say - between ten twenty and ten thirty, or thereabouts." said Perot.

Dolby smiled grimly. "Our inquiries have already led us to that conclusion, sir. Her name, we believe, is Miss Phyllida Orsmby. You were with her in either your or her flat on that evening until just after ten o'clock, at which time she left to return to her cottage in Upton Eccles."

Perot's eyes narrowed with surprise and he bit his lip. "Well, you have been doing your homework, Sergeant. Yes, I was with Phyllida that evening. Of course, I did not want her father - who, as you know is a valued business associate - to know of our relationship. That's why I was reluctant to talk about it before." He paused. "I still hope, Inspector, that this piece of information can remain confidential, between the four of us here in this room." He paused, his gaze moving from Caine to Dolby and back. "I will, if you wish, get confirmation of my alibi from the young lady. However, that might prove a little difficult in the circumstances."

"What circumstances?" asked Caine.

Goodman answered. "Miss Ormsby, as you may know, is on a scientific expedition to Indonesia. Even with all our modern technology it might be difficult to get in touch with her."

Dolby grunted. "Very convenient for you, Mr Perot."

Perot continued, ignoring the Detective Sergeant's comment. "The other matter concerns the reason why I visited the Southam house a week or so before the murders. Again, I was not telling you the truth when I said I was delivering some papers to Bruce. It was, in fact, Valerie I went to see on that occasion." He paused again, picked up his teacup and sipped from it, once more composing his thoughts. "You see, Valerie Southam was my half-sister."

The other three occupants of the small room were silent, watching him. It was obvious to Caine that even Perot's solicitor, Joshua Goodman, was surprised. His dark eyes opened wide at his client's revelation.

"Perhaps you'd like to explain," suggested Caine, breaking the silence.

"In the early nineteen eighties my mother was, shall we say, guilty of an indiscretion." Said Perot, his eyes averted.

"You mean she had an affair?" said Dolby.

Perot ignored the interruption. "As a result of which she found herself pregnant. It happened at a time when my father was overseas for long periods and, not to put too fine a point on it, the child could not have been his. Nowadays, of course, these things are looked on in a different way, but in the eighties it was extremely difficult for her. Abortions were available, but for one reason or another my mother decided to have the baby. She had it adopted immediately." He paused.

"The baby was Valerie Southam?" Joshua Goodman prompted.

Perot nodded. "My father of course, knew nothing about it. He still knows nothing about it." He looked directly at Jacqueline Caine. "I can tell you, Detective Inspector that he was - is - an extremely conservative man who would not have taken at all kindly to the revelation that his wife had given birth to another man's child. I don't know what would have happened if he had found out, but it would certainly have been extremely unpleasant for my mother. Therefore, she went to great lengths to ensure he did not discover her secret." Perot paused again and sipped at his tea.

"So how did *you* find out?" asked Caine.

"It was Valerie who found out," said Perot slowly. "I don't know how. I gather it is possible for adopted persons to make certain inquiries nowadays. Anyway, she did. All this happened over twenty years ago. She discovered that her natural mother was my mother - Florence Perot - and came to see her. Naturally, mother was very distressed. It had been well over twenty years since she had given up her baby and she had almost forgotten the whole incident; she had put it firmly to the back of her mind. And now here was her long-lost daughter bursting in on her life after all those years. She was not happy, Inspector, I can assure you. And the last thing she wanted was for my father to suddenly discover she had given birth to another man's child, even all those years ago. There are certain wounds that time cannot heal. She denied everything and turned Valerie away."

"And Valerie blackmailed her," suggested Caine.

Perot looked across the table at her and nodded. "She made capital of her situation, oh yes! Who was it said that information is power? She had a lot of power over my mother and threatened to tell my father. The price for keeping quiet wasn't just money, though. Part of her 'blackmail' was to force my mother to help her gain social advancement. As you've no doubt found in the course of your inquiries, Inspector, she - Valerie -

had been adopted by a working-class family and she wanted a leg up on the social and financial trees. Anyway, at the time, my mother told nobody, but she managed to introduce Valerie into the local scene - I think she said she was the daughter of an old friend. Specifically, she introduced Valerie - at her own request - to Bruce Southam. He was attracted to her, although I couldn't really see why at the time and I still can't - she was a tart. I believe the attraction was purely physical, intellectually she was far beneath him. Anyway, they were married and all through the years Valerie extracted cash from my mother on a monthly basis."

"At what point did you find out about this?" asked Caine.

"About six months ago. Over the years Valerie's demands on my mother had not been too unreasonable, but recently, as you also no doubt know, the family's resources have been depleted. At the same time Valerie stepped up her demands. Mother started to find it difficult to keep up the payments and Valerie threatened to tell my father. So, mother finally came to me and told me what was going on." He spread his hands in a gesture of helplessness. "Of course, I was livid, but there was nothing I could do about it - mother wouldn't let me take any action against Valerie in case my father got to hear of it. So, after that I took it upon myself to make the payments to Valerie personally. That's why I was visiting her house on that day you referred to - to pay over the cash."

Caine nodded. "We suspected there was some family connection between Mrs Southam and the Perots," she said. "Thank you for telling us, Mr Perot."

"Yes, it's been most useful," said Dolby. "But there are a few questions I'd like to ask. Concerning Miss Ormsby."

Perot eyed him suspiciously. "Yes?"

"When she left for her field trip to Indonesia did Miss Ormsby leave you in charge of a certain vintage motorcycle?"

Perot nodded. "Yes, a Vincent 1000. But I don't see what that has to do with anything."

"Did you use it on the night Mr and Mrs Southam were murdered, sir?"

"Do you mean did I ride it, Sergeant? No, I did not."

Dolby leaned forward. "Then how do you explain the fact that there are one hundred and twenty-three more miles on the odometer now than there were when Miss Ormsby had the bike serviced the day before she left?"

Perot shrugged. "I don't know, Sergeant and frankly I don't care. I don't know what the hell you're getting at!"

Joshua Goodman spoke, quietly but with authority. "I think you owe my client an explanation, Sergeant."

"I believe, Mr Perot," said Dolby, "that after Miss Ormsby left you on the Tuesday evening you used her motorcycle to travel up to Fen Molesey and murder the Southams. You then used it to return to your flat in London."

"That is a very serious accusation," said Goodman. He turned to his client. "I would advise you not to say anything, Paul."

Perot smiled, ignoring his solicitor's advice. "On what do you base this accusation, Inspector, Sergeant?"

"You have the motive," said Dolby. "In fact, you have motives to murder both the victims - Mrs Southam because she was blackmailing your mother and Mr Southam because of the Top Earner's insurance policy - I believe we established that is worth two million pounds? And Mr Southam had been behaving erratically for some time, to the marked detriment of your business." Perot made no comment. "Your car was seen near the scene of the crime, but for a while we were unable to see how you could have travelled from Docklands to Fen Molesey in the time available. As soon as we realised you had the unfettered use of Miss Ormsby's motorcycle, that particular problem disappeared."

Perot laughed and gave a slow hand clap. "Well done, Detective Sergeant. Of course, none of it is true, but full marks for a quite convincing scenario." He stood up, still smiling. "What I didn't tell you is that I left the Vincent's keys with the day porter. I'm hardly ever there, so it was a bit impractical of Phyllida to leave *me* in charge of the thing. Yes, I left the keys with Colin, the porter and I shouldn't be at all surprised if he took the bike on one or two little jaunts. He's a bike man, you see. He probably couldn't resist the temptation!"

CHAPTER TWENTY FOUR

"He must be lying!" Declared Dolby as they strode across the hospital car park towards his car. "Perot is the strongest lead we've got and if it wasn't him…" His words trailed off and he shrugged and threw his hands into the air in a gesture of resignation.

"It's a pretty stupid lie if he is!" said Caine. "He knows we can easily check it out. And I hope you're not getting obsessional about this, Mark, Perot isn't the only one in the picture, although I admit that up till now he did seem to be the most likely."

They reached the car and Dolby unlocked the passenger door and held it open for her. "Yes, he certainly had the least number of brownie points. Anyway, if it's all right by you I'll drop you off at the station. Then I'm going back to Perot's flat in Docklands to have a few words with that porter he was talking about." He turned towards her. "I know you have your doubts, Jackie, but if this Colin person denies having the keys of the bike or taking it for a joy ride then Paul Perot is going to be in a whole lot of trouble!"

Caine smiled ruefully. "I don't share your confidence about Perot lying, Mark, but good luck, anyway." She buckled up her safety belt. "Don't forget, though - we've still got the DNA report on those clothes to look forward to. Surely there must be something on them that'll give us a firm lead! I'll have a go at the Lab when I get back to the office. Find out what's holding things up."

Dolby gave her a sour look. "Don't make any assumptions, Jackie. DNA examination isn't all it's cracked up to be by the tabloids. Quite often they can't get hold of enough of the stuff to reach a proper conclusion!" He started the car, burning rubber as he accelerated out of the car park.

Caine spent the afternoon in her office, reading through the Southam Murder File again and going over the pile of personal documents and photographs she had asked PC Doyle to bring back to the station for further examination. She did not pretend to have any liking for Paul Perot, but her instincts told her he had been telling the truth about the motorcycle's keys, which meant that if he had murdered the Southams he must have had some other means of travelling between his flat in Docklands and Fen Molesey. With Phyllida Ormsby's bike out of the picture she had no idea what that method of transport might have been.

She rang through to the Forensic Lab to inquire about the long awaited DNA report. Conceivably it might show something. She was told, somewhat curtly she thought, that these things could not be hurried and that the full report would be on her desk the following morning.

Dolby telephoned at just after two o'clock. He was ringing from the porter's desk at Antigone Wharf.

His voice was despondent. "I'm afraid it's going to take a little longer than I expected to check out Perot's story. Would you believe that it's Colin the porter's day off? I've been on to the agency that employs him and they're checking the records for his home address. Anything new at your end?"

She told him there wasn't and hung up, going back to the file and re-reading every word of the various reports slowly and carefully. Somewhere she and Mark Dolby must have missed something, just as they had missed the various clues that, with some more intensive investigation, could have told them of the family connection between Valerie Southam and the Perot family. Not that knowing Valerie had been Florence Perot's illegitimate daughter and Paul's half-sister had helped in solving the case; true, they now knew the identity of **one** of Valerie's blackmail victims, but who the other two might be remained a mystery.

Caine brought herself some coffee from the machine and sipped it slowly as she sifted through the various photographs of the Southam family. There was half a dozen or so showing Valerie and Bruce with the Perots, probably taken, she thought, at Upton Stapleford; usually they were together, she and Bruce, with various members of the Perot clan, but there were one or two of them without their partners. In one Bruce, wearing his smart navy golfing blazer with the yellow emblem on its breast pocket, and carrying a set of clubs in a large leather golf bag, stood beside Paul Perot. The next showed him, again in his blazer, in the garden beside an ageing Charles. There was one with Valerie standing beside Ursula Parr, her hand on the back of Ursula's wheelchair. It had been taken against the background of the Manor House; figures scrawled on the back dated it to about seven years ago. Another, more recent by about five years, showed Valerie with Jamie Parr; they were standing very close and the background of the photograph, an ornate fountain fronting a period Manor House behind, was unfamiliar to Caine. She wondered if Dolby, with his superior knowledge of the area, would recognise it. But even if he did, so what?

At the bottom of the box of photographs were the slides she had come across before and ignored because there was no slide reader. She switched on her desk lamp and held the first one up to the light, peering closely at it. She could make nothing of it. The image was too small; it was probably a landscape, just another holiday snap among many. She put it back in the box making a mental note that she must find a slide reader or projector.

The telephone rang. It was Alison speaking from her office in London. They exchanged pleasantries and chatted for a while before she finally brought up the reason she had telephoned.

"I've done the most stupid thing, mum. I've lost my jacket."

"Which jacket, darling?"

"The one I was wearing when you picked me up from the train station last Friday. You know, the one from my lightweight navy suit."

"Oh. When did you last see it?"

"Like I said, Friday. I remember it was a lovely hot day, so I had it over my arm when we went up to your flat. You know, to change for the evening."

"Oh yes, I remember now. That *is* a nice suit."

"It might be *was* a nice suit ," said Alison, a note of defeat in her voice. "I can't find that jacket anywhere. I thought I'd chucked it into my bag at your place, but I looked everywhere this morning and it wasn't there. I don't suppose I left it at yours?"

Caine shook her head. "No. I don't think so, darling. I would've noticed. It's not exactly a big flat."

"What about in your wardrobe? Perhaps I hung it up by mistake."

Caine laughed. If Alison had hung up the jacket it would have been a first. She had been untidy as a child and a teenager, and there was no reason to suspect anything had changed in that direction. "I doubt it, darling, it's not easy to break the habit of a lifetime. Besides, I've been to my wardrobe three or four times since then - there's not much in there, I haven't unpacked all my clothes since I moved in - there doesn't seem much point if I'm moving again in a few weeks - anyway, I certainly didn't notice it in there. Perhaps you left it in Lyall's car."

"No, it would have been in my bag if it was anywhere," said Alison with a sigh. "Looks like it's gone for good."

"Perhaps you should try the hotel," Caine suggested. "You might have left it in your room."

"I suppose it's worth a try," Alison agreed. "I'll do that later. Just in case. Haven't got time now - Anyway, I'll have to go now. I've got a meeting with some clients in a couple of minutes. Love you." She hung up.

Dolby came in at a few minutes after six.

"You're not looking happy," said Caine. "I suppose you're going to tell me you couldn't find this Colin person?"

He sat down heavily and sighed. "Worse than that. I found him - wouldn't you know he lives near Brentwood so my journey down to Docklands was totally unnecessary. Anyway, he confirmed everything Perot said."

"The porter did ride the motor bike then?"

Dolby nodded. "Yes. Perot left the keys with him and told him to turn the engine on now and then, in the garage, and run it for a bit to stop it from seizing up. Of course, when he saw the machine, he couldn't resist taking it out on the road. He was reluctant to admit it, though, bearing in mind he wasn't insured, but I managed to screw the truth out of him by telling him that if he didn't come clean, he'd have a lot more to worry about than driving without insurance." Dolby sighed and stood up. He crossed to the window and looked out on to the street. "Anyway, there's no doubt he used the bike. Apparently, he took his girlfriend for a run up the M11 - must have covered over a hundred miles he thought." Dolby's shoulders slumped. "I think that puts Perot out of the picture." He turned back to face Caine. "So, Jackie, where do you think that leaves us?"

Caine came to stand beside him before answering. "Nowhere, I'm afraid. I'm just hoping the forensic report will give us something to go on. Something concrete. I must admit I wasn't all that convinced we could make a case against Paul Perot, but we really haven't got anything substantial against anybody else either." She went back to her desk and began to pile the documents and photographs taken from the Southam house back into the heavy filing box. "I think we need a re-think of the whole case, Mark. So, my advice to you is go home and enjoy the evening. Tomorrow, we'll review everything through fresh eyes. We'll look at everything we've got and try to think of some new angles. The answer's got to be in there somewhere." She closed the lid on the box and shoved the file into the top drawer of her desk, bending slightly to lock it. "Right. I'm off home for a shower and then I shall spoil myself for once and watch some television."

An hour or so later Jacqueline Caine pushed open the door to her flat and dropped her shopping bags on the carpeted floor before kicking off her shoes and making her way wearily into her sitting room in her stockinged feet. She went straight to the small drinks trolley and poured herself a neat malt whisky, sipping it slowly as she flopped into one of the two armchairs that occupied the small room. She put her feet up on the pouffe and undid the zip and button at her waistband, sighing with contentment as the pressure on her waist eased. It was just after half past seven. She had intended to go straight home from the office, but she had realised as she climbed into her car, that there was practically no food in the flat. She was not very good at the domestic side of life, something for which her parents - whom she visited sporadically at their home in West Cliff - scolded her frequently. Mostly, she lived on convenience foods, rarely cooking a proper meal, but she had decided, as she sat in her car wondering which of the local supermarkets was to enjoy her rare custom, that she would treat herself this evening and cook herself a meal. She would empty her mind completely of any thought of the Southams and enjoy a delicious, if lonely, casserole prepared in her own kitchen and consumed, together with a bottle of crisp white wine, in the lounge in front of the television. It was to be her small act of decadence, a release from the stresses and strains of her normal daily round.

She finished her whisky and got up from the armchair, letting her loosened skirt fall to the floor and kicking it upwards so that she could grab hold of it without bending. She carried it into the bedroom, taking off her jacket and unbuttoning her blouse as she went. She opened the wardrobe and ran her hands along the rail of clothes looking for a hanger. She found one and hung her suit up carefully before completing her undressing and going across the corridor into the bathroom.

She spent almost twenty minutes in the shower washing off the heat and grime of the day, longer than usual because she enjoyed the feel of the water against her skin and she needed cheering up. But thoughts of the day's activities continued to whirl through her mind and she could not shake them off. She sighed resignedly and decided to go with the flow, shampooing her hair, massaging the creamy soap into her scalp as if trying to induce her brain to work harder, to point out the direction in which she and Dolby should be going to solve the murders. She knew it was a futile effort, that this physical stimulation would have no effect whatsoever, that she could not arouse the sleeping cells of her brain by such primitive means and yet - there **was** something in the back of her mind, some notion to which she found hard to give definite form. It lurked in the shadowy recesses, at once far from her grasp, then coming close only to vanish again as she plucked at it. Out of the shower, body and hair wrapped in towels she crossed the hall into her bedroom and flung open the wardrobe door. She didn't know what she was looking for, but still, although she had looked into this cupboard three, four maybe more times during the last few days and not seen it, she ran her eyes along the rail, searching. Until now her eyes had passed over it without the benefit of her brain, but now she found it and with a vague feeling of disbelief she reached into the wardrobe and took down her daughter's navy jacket. Every time she had opened her wardrobe over the last few days, she had looked at it without seeing it. What was it someone had once said? *The best place to hide a letter is in a letter rack*- had it been Edgar Allen Poe? She held Alison's jacket in her hands, running her fingers over the fabric and in that instant many things, insignificant in themselves, came together in her mind and she knew who had killed Bruce and Valerie Southam.

She dropped Alison's jacket on to the bed beside her and sat staring at it for some moments, letting the realisation sink in and casting her mind back to the various interviews she had conducted over the last few days. She opened her briefcase and took out the Southam Murder File, flicked though the pages of notes until she found what she was looking for and then picked up her telephone and dialled the operator. It took a few moments to reach a supervisor and explain who she was and her unusual request and then she gave her own number and hung up. She was back in the bathroom drying herself when, a few minutes later, the telephone rang. She went back into the hall and answered it, finishing the call quickly and with rising excitement. Then she telephoned Mark Dolby. He was at dinner and one of his children answered, calling out loudly for her dad who came to the telephone with a mouthful of what Caine imagined was delicious home-cooked food. Her stomach rumbled loudly, reminding her that her own meal was a long way in the future and getting further away at every moment.

"I'm sorry to interrupt your meal, Mark, but I want you to meet me up at Upton Stapleford. I think I know who our killer is."

She could hear him swallowing before he answered. "It is Paul then, after all!" His voice was excited. "I've been trying all evening to work out what we've missed - how the bastard managed it - and you've obviously been doing the same thing." He laughed; his good humour restored. "A bit more successfully than me it seems!" His voice became serious. "Mind you, whatever evidence we've got we'll have to tread carefully. His father is still on the danger list. The man's likely to turn really nasty and he has friends in high places, as you know."

"Yes - the whole of the Perot tribe must be feeling pretty sensitive at the moment. But we can't let this lie, we have to act quickly. We'll just have to make the best of it." She made no comments on his assumptions. "Can you meet me there?" She looked at her watch, it was just a few minutes after eight o'clock and she had still to blow dry her hair and get into some clothes. "At the bottom of the drive leading to Beacon Cottage. Shall we say 8.35 or thereabouts?"

"Beacon Cottage?" Dolby sounded puzzled for a moment. "Oh, I see, don't want to alert him too early do we! Right. See you there. 8.35." There was a brief pause before he continued. "I'll be in a marked car. Lorna's using ours this evening to go into town, so she'll drop me off at the station on the way through. I'll pick one up there." He hung up.

Caine left her flat at about 8.20. The traffic was easy at this time of the evening. Most people who were going out had already arrived at their destinations. The sun was low in the sky now, but the evenings were still drawing out and it would not slip over the horizon until well after nine o'clock. She was not yet familiar with the shortcuts in the area, so she drove out of the centre of town on the main road until she reached the B road, when she turned off to the left at the mini roundabout and looked for the junction which would take her to the Perot's estate at Upton Stapleford. She took very seriously indeed Mark Dolby's point about Charles Perot. She would have to tread carefully, and she ran over in her mind the various facts which, once the initial revelation had burst into her consciousness, had led her to the certain conviction that she knew the killer's identity. They had all been there, those pieces of information, firmly lodged in her brain, but they had been buried under a mass of irrelevant detail. Many of them were small and by themselves insubstantial, but the one fact that had finally broken through into her sentience was capable of being physically checked. If, of course, she was not too late. Unlike the other facts that were on the record and could not be changed the killer had had plenty of time to dispose of the particular piece of evidence she had in mind. She had no time to lose. She turned off the road and instinctively accelerated up the estate drive, bumping past the lodge house, the overhanging branches of the hedgerows brushing the car's paint work. She followed the road around the curves, passing the track that led up to High Point Quarry and looking for the Parr's house, Beacon Cottage, to appear through the tall trees. Dolby had arrived before her, parking the white Ford Scopio in the lay-by beside the entrance to the drive and he stood leaning against the boot, watching her approach. She checked the time on the dashboard clock - she was a few minutes late, it was almost twenty to nine. She pulled in behind his car and he walked around and opened the passenger door.

"We'll go the last leg in your car," he suggested. "Mine's a bit obvious with the word 'POLICE' scrawled all over it. Don't want him running away before we can nail him do we?"

She switched off the engine. "No need," she said, unfastening her seat belt and reaching into the back for her bag. "We're not going any further for the time being."

"We're going up to the Parr's house then?" She nodded and he looked puzzled. "I suppose you know what you're doing, Jackie, but I'd appreciate your telling me what's going on."

She wound up her window, opened the door and climbed out. "I'll fill you in on the way up."

He closed the passenger door and came around the car while she locked up, then he fell in beside her as she walked across to the big entrance gate. He worked the latch and held the gate open as she walked through, following her and slipping the metal bar back into place. "So, what gives?"

She smiled. "I think I know who did it " she told him. "Funnily enough I'd just told myself to have a night off without thinking about the Southams when it came to me. Strange how the mind works."

"Yes, I guess so." He looked frustrated. "Aren't you going to enlighten me then?"

She smiled. "I may be totally wrong, of course. But I suddenly remembered, this evening, that when I went to Jamie Parr's wardrobe to hang up the shirts there was something in there that should not have been there."

Dolby nodded thoughtfully as she went into greater detail about what she had seen. "Very interesting. I wonder if it's still there – you would have thought he would get rid of it at the earliest opportunity."

They were ascending the brow of the hill now, coming onto the wide parking area in front of the cottage. There was no sign of Parr's Vauxhall as they scrunched their way across the gravel towards the front door, passing into the shadows thrown by the big gabled and thatched cottage.

"The car's not here. I suppose there is someone in?" Dolby pressed the front doorbell. "Mrs Parr should be about, or maybe that nurse they mentioned."

It was the nurse who opened the door to them. Ann Hendry was a tall woman in her early thirties, full bosomed beneath her light blue uniform and with the broad shoulders of someone who spends a lot of her time lifting and manipulating other people's bodies. Her face was lightly tanned, and wisps of dark hair peeped out from under the smart blue nurse's cap. She looked tired, as though she had had too many late nights recently and was in need of a good night's sleep.

"DCI Caine and DS Dolby, Fen Molesey CID," said Caine. "You must be Miss Hendry. We'd like a few words with Mr or Mrs Parr."

"Sorry, I haven't got my lenses in," Hendy apologised for peering myopically at the warrant cards the two police officers were holding practically under her nose. She called over her shoulder into the house. "Two policemen to see you, Mrs Parr." There was an answering call from the lounge at the back of the cottage and Hendry turned back to Caine and Dolby and opened the door to its full extent to let them into the hall. "Mr Parr's not back from his classes yet, but I think Mrs Parr will see you."

They found Ursula Parr sitting in her wheelchair in the lounge in front of the open French doors reading a paperback book. She carefully placed a bookmark between the pages and put it down as they entered. She, too, looked tired and drawn. Her face was wan and for the first time Caine noticed that her forehead was lined and there were crow's feet at the corners of her eyes, which now were dull and troubled. She seemed to have aged twenty years since they last saw her. She smiled weakly as they entered the room. "Can I do something for you Inspector, Sergeant? Would you like a cup of coffee or something?" She was in her night clothes, a light blue silk dressing gown with the matching edges of her night dress peeping out above her bosom where the edges of the gown, drawn towards each other by the belt around her waist, did not quite meet.

Caine shook her head. "No thank you, Mrs Parr. We are sorry to bother you again, especially at a time when you must be very worried about your father. Is there any further news?"

Ursula shook her head. "No. I rang the hospital just a few minutes ago and spoke to Paul. Father's hanging on by a thread, but the prognosis is not good." She sighed. "They're doing all they can for him, but they are only doctors..." Her words trailed away.

"I'm sorry," Caine paused. "It was your husband we actually wanted to speak to Mrs Parr. He's not in I understand."

"No." She averted her eyes and looked out into the gathering dusk of the garden. "Jamie teaches woodcraft at evening classes on Mondays and Wednesdays. He normally gets back at just after nine." She smiled, but there was a tremor in her voice as she continued. "He offered to stay in with me tonight, in case there's any news on Daddy, but I told him he should go to his classes. I said I would be OK with Ann here and, besides, his students rely on him to be there. I thought we could easily get hold of him if we needed to." Her bottom lip trembled and she reached over to the occasional table beside her and pulled a paper handkerchief from a box. She dabbed at her eyes. "Besides, I think it does him good to get out - he's been awfully depressed recently, since the murders. He's - he's not been at all himself, Inspector."

"How do you mean, Mrs Parr?"

"As I said, he's not himself. He..." She broke off and when she continued her voice was almost inaudible. "He's been edgy and irritable - and he's been drinking and smoking much more than is good for him." She bit her lip as if wondering whether to go on. "He's been going out in the evenings, Inspector, and coming home drunk. In fact,..." She stopped and turned her gaze appealingly towards Caine.

"Go on..."

"I think that's where he is tonight, Inspector - at a pub somewhere - drinking. There was a phone call from the College earlier in the evening. Jamie was already an hour late for the start of the class, but he hadn't turned up. I've tried to talk to him, Inspector, to find out what's wrong, but he refuses to discuss it with me, says he'll work it out for himself." She dabbed at her eyes with the hanky again. "In fact, he lost his temper with me. He's been doing that a lot recently - and that's not like him! Inspector, I think he's in some sort of trouble!"

"And this has been going on since the time of the murders?" asked Dolby with a meaningful glance at Caine. "Do you think there's any connection?"

A shadow passed over Ursula Parr's eyes, but she shook her head. "It - it's disturbing," she said softly, "to have tragedy come so close, it's bound to affect you." She sighed and her shoulders drooped. "But I don't think there's any more to it than that." She breathed deeply and looked directly at Caine. "You haven't told me why you're here yet, Inspector."

"As I said, we did want to speak to your husband," said Caine "but as he's not here I wonder if you would let us take a quick look in his wardrobe?"

Ursula Parr was completely taken aback. "You want to look in his wardrobe? Whatever for?"

Caine smiled, choosing her words carefully. "When we were last here, Mrs Parr, you may remember you were ironing your husband's shirts and, to save you the trouble, I went upstairs to hang them in his wardrobe." Ursula nodded, remembering. "Well, while I was hanging them up I noticed something in his wardrobe. I would just like to look in there again to see if it's still there."

"And this is important to your inquiries?"

"Yes." Caine could see that Ursula Parr was troubled. Whatever could the Detective Chief Inspector have seen in her husband's wardrobe that was important to the murder investigation? Was it something that implicated Jamie? She was clearly worried about his recent change of character and had possibly linked it with the murders. But she refused to believe there could be any connection. The Inspector's question threw her off balance and confused her. She bit her lip, hesitating.

"I know it's not the best time to ask, Mrs Parr," Caine went on. "But I would prefer to do this informally and not to have to go through the red tape. I assure you it would be best if we could take a look now. It will only take a couple of minutes."

Ursula Parr thought for a moment longer before shrugging her shoulders. "All right. You may as well. But I don't know what you think you're going to find." Her face was pale and she was gripping the handles of her wheelchair. "You know where to find the wardrobe."

"Do you think it will still be there?" asked Dolby as they climbed the stairs and made their way across the upstairs hall into James Parr's bedroom.

"I hope so," said Caine. "Although, to be honest I find it hard to believe he put it in there in the first place instead of getting rid of it." While she was speaking, she opened the bedroom door and strode across to the wardrobe. She stopped in front of it and turned to Dolby. "I had the notion earlier on that he might have thought a wardrobe is the best place to hide a jacket. If you think about it it makes sense doesn't it? It wouldn't exactly shout at you, would it, when you saw it hanging beside a lot of other jackets and shirts? It would be sort of lost in the crowd. That's why I didn't realise its significance when I first saw it in here. It just didn't register as anything out of the ordinary."

Dolby nodded. "It does make some sort of sense. Let's hope it's still there."

"If it's not, there are one or two other things that point in the same direction. They only fell into place, though, after I remembered the blazer."

The curtains at the windows were only partially open so the room was poorly lit in the weakening evening sunlight. "Could you put the light on, please, Mark, I can hardly see anything." He moved back to the door and found the light switch. "Thanks." As the light flooded the room Caine turned the key in the lock to open the doors of the large walnut wardrobe. She ran her eyes along the rail and then she reached in and pushed a couple of shirts and a suit to one side. They slid smoothly along on their hangers. "I think it was at this end...Yes!" She reached in again and took down a navy-blue man's blazer. She turned and laid it on the bed exposing the yellow motif sewn onto its breast pocket. "Unless I'm very much mistaken, Mark, that is the logo of the local golf club. And this..." she opened the jacket up to reveal some dark marks on the lining, "unless I'm very much mistaken, is Bruce Southam's blood."

He reached out and ran his hand over the cloth. "Yes. It certainly looks that way. So, you think this puts Paul Perot out of the picture?"

"Forget Paul, Mark - think about his brother-in-law for a moment."

He pursed his lips thoughtfully. "But we don't know that this *is* Bruce's blazer. And even if it is how do we know James Parr didn't just borrow it from Bruce or Paul, or some other member of the Golf Club? We're on fairly tenuous ground here I think."

"Not if that *is* Bruce's blood. Besides, it's unlikely Jamie would have borrowed it. Why? He doesn't play golf. And look at it - it seems much too big for him. Why would he borrow a jacket that doesn't fit him?"

"How do you know it's too big for him?"

"You can see just by looking at it." She picked up the blazer again and examined the labels sewn on to the lining. "Size forty-four." She looked across at Dolby. "What size are the shirts?"

"Fifteen and a half. I think that's thirty-nine centimetres in metric."

"That confirms it - That is *not* Jamie Parr's blazer - it's almost certainly Bruce Southam's."

Dolby whistled softly through his teeth. "It was Parr then! His own clothes would have been covered in Bruce Southam's blood, so he swapped it for his blazer! Too bad he got blood on **that** as well." He examined the stains on the material again and nodded his head thoughtfully. "Not much, but enough to do for him! But there's just one thing that doesn't seem to fit - what earthly reason would Jamie Parr have to kill Bruce and Valerie Southam? Somehow he doesn't seem the type."

"Murderers often don't, Mark, but that doesn't seem to stop them." Caine picked up the blazer again and folded it over her arm. "I don't know why he would have done it; not at the moment, anyway." She frowned as a thought struck her. "Do you suppose he could have been Valerie's second blackmail victim?"

"I don't see how? He says he hardly knew her."

"That's not what the Southam telephone records tell us," said Caine.

"Come again?"

"Before I came out this evening, I remembered that Ursula Parr told us there'd been a wrong number call to here - Beacon Cottage - at around nine o'clock on the evening of the murders. I had a hunch, so I rang BT - they confirmed there was a call made to this number that evening at about that time and guess who's telephone the call was made from."

"The Southam's?"

"Yes - and that call was one of many over the last few weeks." She closed the wardrobe and moved back towards the door. "So, we know Parr knew Valerie a good deal better than he admitted. It could be she rang him to arrange some sort of tryst - especially as she thought Bruce was going to be away on business overnight. It's possible nobody told her his arrangements had been cancelled." She paused, reflecting. "And I've been thinking about all the other interesting little snippets of information we've learned about our friend Jamie Parr. For instance, he smokes Black Silk cigarettes - there was the remains of a packet of Black Silk in Valerie's bedroom - she's supposed to have given up don't forget. And then there was the handkerchief with the letter 'P' on it - we both thought it must be Paul's - but remember - Mrs Thompson does the washing for all the members of the family living up here on the Perot estate. It would be the easiest thing in the world for her to get some of the laundry mixed up. Jamie was probably using Paul's hanky and he didn't even realise it. And there were other things…still, the clincher will be the DNA on the blood-stained clothes."

They had moved now into the upstairs hall and were standing at the head of the stairs. They spoke in subdued tones to prevent their voices carrying down to the ground floor of the large house.

Dolby nodded his head in agreement. "Yes, now you come to mention it, Paul Perot told us that on the morning of the murders Jamie Parr stopped off at the Chemists to pick up his wife's painkillers; but Jamie said they'd had an uninterrupted journey to the office. Then Mrs Parr made some comment about her new bottle of pills - what was it she said? - I hope Jamie finds the new bottle. I didn't know what she meant at the time…" He nodded again. "And, of course, Valerie had drugs and alcohol pushed into her after she'd been killed by a blow to the head. But there was nothing in the house that would do the job - Parr must have gone through the contents of the bathroom cupboard and found nothing. We'd assumed it was an overdose of Ergotamine tablets that killed her, but there probably weren't enough of those in Valerie's own bottle of pills to do the trick so, he used his wife's pills to make it look as if Valerie had died of an overdose. He'd collected them from the chemist on Tuesday morning and he probably still had them in his pocket in the evening. The PM report should confirm that. But the big question is - *why*? *Why* did he kill Valerie? And why did he kill Bruce Southam?"

Caine thought for a moment. "Valerie died in her bedroom, practically naked. All she had on was a negligee and a pair of pants. There's nothing to suggest she died somewhere else and was carried into that room. So, she knew whoever killed her intimately and they must have been in the bedroom with her prior to her death." She paused. "Do you suppose Jamie Parr was her lover?"

"It fits in with what Susie Neale said and with what Bernard Pitcher, the ex-accountant at PPA, told me," agreed Dolby. "Susie said she thought Valerie was having an affair. And Pitcher said Parr was probably getting his pleasures elsewhere, outside his marriage that is and it was rumoured that he - Parr - had sexually harassed some of the women at the office. Also, as I told you, I saw him with that girlie magazine in the local newsagents." He nodded thoughtfully. "An affair with Valerie is certainly a possibility - to some she must have been an attractive woman." He paused thoughtfully. "And we mustn't forget - Jamie Parr had a lot to hate Bruce Southam for - and his brother-in-law Paul for that matter - they bullied him something rotten when they were all kids - some people don't forget that sort of experience. It probably gave Parr a peculiar sense of vengeance to be able to cuckold Bruce in his own nest, so to speak. But we still don't know *why* he killed her."

"We'll get that out of him," declared Caine confidently. "Our friend James Parr has a lot of explaining to do!" They stopped in the downstairs hall as she checked the time on her watch. "Look, I don't think we want to upset his wife too much at this stage, she's had enough to contend with today without being told her husband's on suspicion of murder. Parr's due back any minute now, always assuming he's not out on a pub crawl, of course. We'll intercept him on the estate road and take him down to the station for questioning. He can telephone her from there and tell her he's been delayed."

Dolby nodded dubiously. "I suppose that might help cushion the blow. But that little lady is in for a big upset no matter how we handle it."

They went back into the lounge. Ursula Parr was sitting in her wheelchair beside the fireplace. Her book was closed on her lap and she was staring into the grate, obviously preoccupied with her own private thoughts. Ann Hendry sat opposite her in an armchair, knitting, the needles flashing and clacking in her hands.

"Our apologies for intruding, Mrs Parr," said Caine. "We shan't bother you any further." Ursula nodded vacantly but did not answer.

Nurse Hendry put down her knitting and stood up. "I'll show you out, Inspector, Sergeant."

Neither of the women seemed to show any interest in the jacket Caine was carrying folded over her arm.

It was almost dark as they left the house and walked towards the drive, guided by the silver rays of an almost full moon. The heat sensitive security light fixed to the eaves of the corner gable of the house switched on with an audible click as they came within its ambit, flooding the parking area with brilliant white light. Caine crossed over to look again at the still visible tyre marks sunk in the grass at the edge of the gravelled drive. "Interesting. Even these marks in the grass make sense now." She turned towards her colleague as he joined her. "I don't think our friend Parr could get his car started on Tuesday evening."

Dolby stared thoughtfully at the deep tracks. "You mean he tried to push start his car and it rolled off the drive into the grass?" He scratched his head. "Makes sense! Maybe he's not such a bad driver after all."

"And when he couldn't get it started he walked over to Paul's house and picked up *his* car to use it for the journey over to Valerie's place, where, of course, he had a rendezvous with her." Caine theorised as they made their way down the drive in the bright moonlight, towards the gate at the bottom of the hill. "He probably didn't want anyone to know he'd been there, so he parked on the industrial estate and walked across the playing fields to her house."

Dolby nodded. "Sounds plausible, but of course, we haven't really very much to go on so far." He reminded her. "And we still haven't got a motive."

"We've got enough to hold him on suspicion, though" said Caine. "With any luck the results of the DNA tests should do the rest."

As she spoke they heard the sound of a vehicle approaching along the estate road. It was coming from the north, the opposite direction from which they had come   and they saw its headlights sweeping through the trees as it came towards them. A moment later, James Parr's Vauxhall swung erratically around the bend, as if the driver was having trouble controlling it. The vehicle was travelling fast, but it slowed as it approached the entrance gate to Beacon Cottage. Parr was at the wheel. He angled the car to enter the gate and then saw Caine's car and the Police vehicle parked in the lay-by. He braked violently, the tyres of the Vauxhall kicking up chips of grit and dust and sat there uncertainly for one or two seconds, looking wildly about him. Even in the closing darkness Caine was near enough to see his face. It showed surprise - and fear. His eyes swept towards the two police officers, lingering on Caine who was still holding the blazer folded over her arm, the Golf Club emblem on the pocket clearly visible in the glare of the car's headlights. He opened his mouth and muttered something inaudible under his breath.

Dolby opened the gate and walked towards him. "Good evening, Mr Parr," he called out. "We'd like a few words with you if you wouldn't mind."

Parr made no attempt to answer him. Instead, the Vauxhall engine roared as he slammed his foot down on the accelerator and swung the steering wheel. The car shot past the parked vehicles and veered away from the gate, heading straight for Dolby. The policeman threw himself to one side and Parr accelerated off down the road, rocking and bumping over the potholes. He slowed as he approached the bend, the car swaying from side to side on the uneven road surface and disappeared around the bend.

"Are you all right, Mark?" Caine pushed her way between the gate and the heavy wooden post and came out onto the road to join him. "I thought you were a goner for a moment!"

Dolby looked shaken. "I'm fine, but the man's a menace. He's obviously been out on another drinking spree. We'd better get after him before he gets out onto the public roads again and actually does kill someone." He ran towards the police car, searching in his pocket for the keys.

Shocked at Parr's sudden action it was a moment before Caine roused herself and ran after Dolby. He was turning the police car around and he stopped and waited while she opened the passenger door and clambered in.

"You'd better belt yourself in," said Dolby, fixing his own belt and ramming his foot hard down on the accelerator. "He's driving fast - and dangerously!"

The three-litre engine of the big Ford roared as they tore down the road towards the bend. Entering the straight on the other side they just glimpsed the rear of Parr's vehicle as it disappeared around the next curve. It was dark now and their headlights caught the trunks and foliage of the trees, silhouetting them against the night sky.

"I didn't expect this!" exclaimed Caine, turning to throw the blazer onto the back seat. "It seems totally out of character. And how the hell did he manage to drive home in that state?"

"He's drunk and he's panicking!" Dolby told her, wrestling with the steering wheel and trying to keep the vehicle more or less in the centre of the roadway, where the potholes seemed to be reasonably small. "Did you see his face when he saw you carrying that blazer? I reckon he realised the game was up."

They took another bend at high speed and Caine, swaying in her seat, grabbed at the restraining strap fitted into the bodywork above the door. The rear of Parr's Vauxhall was visible in the distance, the red sidelights weaving from side to side across the road as Parr, obviously the worse for drink, tried to keep it under control. Dolby accelerated and they drew closer.

"But he must know he can't get away, the stupid man! We'd better call for back-up." She reached over for the radio microphone.

"Hang on, where's he off to?" In front of them Parr had slowed at a junction where the road met a track a hundred yards or so ahead. He turned off towards the left. "He's going up to High View Point! What the heck is he doing that for?"

"Up to the top of the quarry? But there's only one road up there isn't there?" She grabbed the restraining strap again as Dolby braked and then threw the police car over to the left to follow Parr onto the track.

"You can cancel that call," said Dolby through his teeth, wrestling to keep the car on an even keel. The surface of the track was lined with fine stone aggregate that shifted under the tyres causing the vehicle to slew from side to side. "We won't need any back up - this track only goes to the top of the hill and there's no other way down. We'll be able to handle him when he stops at the top, no problem. The man's got nowhere to go - unless, of course, he's planning to go over the top into the lake!"

As Dolby spoke the lights of Parr's car winked out. The moon had disappeared behind a bank of thick cloud, plunging the road into darkness and he had accelerated suddenly, pulling a long way ahead. He rounded a bend and their headlights lost him. The bright halogen beams wavered eerily, silhouetting the uneven shapes of the hedgerows lining the edges of the track.

"As he can't get away from us," said Caine, "perhaps you'd like to slow down, Mark. There's no sense in us killing ourselves!"

Dolby slowed. "What the deuce is the man doing turning off his lights?" He fumed. "How the hell can he see where he's going?"

"He's lived here all his life. He probably knows the road like the back of his hand," said Caine. "And maybe he's thinking of giving us the slip by driving into a side turn - some sort of break in the bushes that would conceal his car? Without his lights on we wouldn't see him in there and he could double back once we'd gone by."

"Feasible, I suppose," said Dolby. "But so far as I can recall there aren't any places he could do that - there are a few passing places on the track, but that's all. Nowhere you could hide a car. My guess is the man's not thinking straight! The way he's driving he's got some sort of a death wish!"

As he spoke the beams of their headlights caught the rear of the car in front and they saw that Parr was no more than fifty yards ahead. The lack of proper lighting had obviously made him slow down, but now as they watched he accelerated again and swung the car at high speed into a sharp bend, disappearing once more from their sight.

Dolby slowed as they followed him into the curve. "There's not far to go now before we get to the top. Then we'll have him."

A few seconds later they came out of the bend and found themselves on the plateau at the summit of High View Point. Dolby slowed as they bumped over a large piece of quarry stone that had fallen onto the track. The beam of their headlights danced in the cloud of dust kicked up by the tyres of Parr's vehicle. Indistinctly through the dust motes they could pick out the dim form of the derelict workman's hut a hundred or so feet ahead, beyond it the dark silhouette of the abandoned mining machinery. Caine identified what may once have been a heavy digger, towering over it the rusting stanchions of a long-abandoned conveyor system. But there was no sign of Parr's car. Dolby brought the police vehicle to a halt. To their left, pearly grey against the darkness of the sky, a high ridge loomed fifteen or twenty feet above them, where the rock had been left in situ. To their right, some twenty feet away and sharply defined in the bright moonlight, for the bank of cloud had now scudded away towards the north, glistened the outline of the metal chain link fence bordering the edge of the man-made ravine and guarding the sheer sixty foot drop into the waters of the quarry lake.

They peered around them in the quiet, the only sound the low throb of their car's powerful engine.

"Where the hell has he gone?" asked Dolby.

As he spoke Caine saw something move, to the left, at the edge of her vision. A silhouette grew out of the background of grey rock, sliding silently forward. The sleek, curved shape of a car bonnet turned out of its hiding place behind a fold in the limestone and raced towards them, its headlights suddenly snapping on and dazzling them.

"On the left, Mark!" She gasped.

Dolby turned his head to look past her towards the approaching vehicle, his hand snaking down for the hand brake and then the gear lever. Behind the blinding light of his head lamps, through the windscreen of his Vauxhall, not fifteen feet away from them and approaching with terrifying speed, Jamie Parr stared at them, his eyes glazed, his hands gripping the steering wheel. He was going to force them through the fence and over the edge of the ravine into the quarry lake. Reacting instinctively, Mark Dolby threw the police car into first gear and slammed his foot on the accelerator. They felt the car buck and then shoot forward as his other foot came completely off the clutch. The front end of Parr's car glanced the side edge of the

Police car's rear bumper, crumpling the plastic and tearing at the metal, slewing them around to face the wall of rock, their engine still racing. With the power of over a hundred horses they careered towards the rock wall. Dolby slammed his foot on the brake.

Behind them the sound of ripping metal and splintering glass rent the air. Caine twisted around in her seat to see the rear end of Parr's Vauxhall ploughing through the hole the car had torn in the flimsy wire fence. For a fleeting moment it was silhouetted against the sky, its wheels racing as it toppled over the edge of the ravine. Then the bonnet of the police car hit the wall of rock and crumpled like so much tinsel, casting them into oblivion.

CHAPTER TWENTY FIVE

It was seven thirty the following morning before the heavy lifting tackle was finally assembled at the side of the Quarry Lake. Caine and Dolby sat in her car a short distance away and watched as police frogmen went over the side of the inflatable dinghy and disappeared beneath the murky water ten yards or more out from the edge, roughly at the spot where Parr's Vauxhall would have hit and slid beneath the surface of the water over ten hours before. There was no hope they would find him alive.

There had been nothing Caine and Dolby could do at the time Parr went over the edge into the water, for when their car hit the wall of rock, they had both been momentarily stunned and it was some minutes before they regained their senses. The impact had crumpled the car's bonnet, forcing the engine backwards and causing a domino effect that had splintered the windscreen and fascia. The shock wave had travelled the full length of the vehicle, twisting the body out of true and making it almost impossible to open the doors. Remarkably, Caine and Dolby had sustained only minor injuries. They were thankful for that, but they could still feel the soreness of the bruises where their seat belts had restrained their bodies as they jerked violently forward into the expanding air bags. Dolby had called the emergency services over the car radio and then they had struggled to open the car's doors .

When, finally, they scrambled out and made their way across the dust covered ground to peer through what was left of the fence and down into the lake they found themselves looking into a black, featureless pit. Even the beam of Dolby's torch showed nothing but a few eddies of turbulence on the surface of the water sixty feet below them. In the few minutes they had been out of action Parr's vehicle had sunk without trace. They had known then that nothing could be done to save him - it only remained to positively identify the body as that of James Parr.

Caine's stomach groaned, reminding her that she had not eaten since lunch time the previous day. Following her sudden flash of inspiration, her plans for chicken casserole the evening before had not materialised and the events of the night and early morning had moved too swiftly for her to even think about food. They had given her a cup of tea at the hospital where they had taken her and Dolby for a routine check, but she had had nothing else. Now, hunger pangs had begun to gnaw. Beside her Dolby sat silent and grim, the line of his jaw partially obscured by a small length of sticking plaster, his eyes tired, watching the scene laid out before them. She shifted her gaze back to the water. They were parked a short distance from the edge of the quarry lake, with most of the other police vehicles between them and a patch of bullrushes that grew up just beyond the water line. Within the perimeter of the taped incident barrier a number of their fellow officers were standing or sitting in their cars and vans, watching the activity taking place on the water. A group of reporters stood to one side of the barrier, talking animatedly, some to each other, others into their smartphones. The photographers fiddled with their cameras, fitting telescopic lenses or filters, their attention held by the black and yellow dinghy that bobbed on the surface of the lake, some thirty or forty feet from the bank. The anchor man, sinister in his black rubber wet suit, was peering over the edge, down into the murky water. Suddenly he leaned forward and threw a nylon line as the head of one of his colleagues bobbed up out of the water. The diver shook his head and a rain of droplets cascaded around him. He took hold of the line and swam closer to the side of the dinghy, grasping the side with one hand and with the other withdrawing his breathing tube from his mouth. He spoke briefly to the man in the boat who nodded his head and then turned in the direction of the police officers gathered on the bank. He spoke rapidly into his radio.

"What's going on?" asked Caine. "It looks like they've found something."

"It didn't take long," said Dolby. "Then it wouldn't would it? You can't hide a car in a lake this size! Not for long, anyway!"

At the lakeside Detective Sergeant Dave Milligan, assigned the night before to co-ordinate the search operation, finished his conversation with the anchor man and slipped his radio-phone back into his pocket before turning to make his way in Caine's direction, picking his way between the other vehicles.

Caine and Dolby opened the doors of the car and walked to meet him.

"What's up?" asked Caine.

Scowling, Milligan kicked at a large piece of grit stone that lay on the ground before him. "You're not going to like this, Inspector, Mark," he said grimly. "They've found the car, but they've also found a body."

"We were expecting that, Dave!" said Dolby irritably. "Parr was in the car when it went over. We were there and it was damned nearly us who ended up in the drink!"

Milligan looked contrite. "Sorry, I'm not making myself clear. Parr is there, of course. In the car. But there's another body in the water not far from the car. It's a woman."

Caine and Dolby looked at each other.

"You mean she was in the car when it hit and she fell out?" asked Caine. The lack of food was beginning to make her head ache. Or was it the certainty that she knew the identity of the dead woman?

Milligan shook his head. "No, it doesn't look that way. The car doors are all closed and the boot isn't open either. No, so far as the divers can tell at the moment she was in the water *before* Parr's car made the nosedive. She may have been weighted down and the car probably disturbed her. She's caught in the reeds on the bottom, but they reckon she'd have floated to the surface by this afternoon." He sighed. "Oh, the body's reasonably fresh by the way, probably not been in the water more than three or four days." He paused and then broke in again on their thoughts. "We obviously need to investigate further, but it looks like we've got two separate incidents here."

"You mean the woman was murdered and then dumped in the lake?" said Dolby. He rubbed his eyes and turned to look out over the water again. "It wouldn't be the first time this place has been used for that sort of thing, would it?"

Milligan shook his head and looked at Caine. "Things have certainly become active since you came out to Fen Molesey, Ma'am. No offence meant, but we don't generally have more than three or four murders a year in these parts. This is the fourth in less than a week."

Caine's head ached. She wasn't sure for a moment whether or not Milligan was being facetious. She decided he wasn't. "The fourth? You're not counting Parr's death as murder are you?"

"No," said Milligan, slightly taken aback. "I don't mean him - I mean the old lady in the Springfield Retirement Home."

Caine looked blank, but something stirred in the back of her mind. "What old lady?"

"I don't know that I mentioned it," said Dolby apologetically. "DCI Hopkins and Dave here are investigating the incident. It seems an old lady died during the course of a breaking and entering on Sunday night." He turned to Milligan. "I thought you were undecided whether it was murder or not at this stage, Dave?"

Milligan shrugged. "We're not certain how she died - we won't be until the full post mortem's in - but she must have been a plucky old girl cos it looks like she confronted the intruder **and** had a tussle with him. There's a chance there may be some fibres from his clothes on her skin or even on her own clothing that we can match up to any possible suspects." He shrugged. "Anyway, so far as I'm concerned the old lady would still be alive if the burglary hadn't taken place. In my book that makes it murder!"

Caine brushed a lock of hair back from her forehead. She had had hardly any time to change and dress before coming out. She felt a mess and she knew she must look a mess. "I'd appreciate seeing the details," she told Milligan, trying to stifle a yawn.

He nodded and turned to look back at the lake where the anchor man was once again peering down into the depths. "Anyway, it looks like the bloke in the car is definitely James Parr. The description tallies. We don't know who the woman is though. They're going to bring her up first. I don't know if you want to hang around any longer - unless, of course, you want another case on your hands."

"I think it's already there," said Caine. "We'll stay until they bring the woman's body up, if you don't mind."

Milligan nodded. "I get the drift." He smiled, said sympathetically, "But you've had a pretty bad night. You both look like you could do with some breakfast. Would you like me to send one of the men for some coffee and sandwiches?"

*   *   *   *   *   *

*

Caine pushed the Forensic Report across the desk towards Dolby. He put down the flimsy sheet of paper he had been reading and picked it up. He ran his eyes over it picking out the salient points.

"At least we know for sure now that Parr killed the Southams," he said. "The blood-stained clothes and the towels were full of his DNA."

She nodded. It was just after noon and only a few minutes before they had returned from the Neale's house after breaking the news of Susie's death to her husband, Norman. Before that they had been to the Parr's to break the news of the night's events to Ursula Parr. It had not been a pleasant interview. Paul Perot had been there and he had given them a hard time of it. Now Caine expected the telephone to ring at any moment, summoning her to a meeting with the Superintendent. It was not a meeting she was looking forward to.

"Excuse me, Ma'am," PC Wendy Doyle was at the door. On Caine's instruction she had been going through Jamie Parr's personal papers. "I think I've found something in Mr Parr's things that might throw some light on his motive for killing Mrs

Southam." Caine indicated one of the guest chairs and Doyle came in and sat down. "I found this in Mr Parr's safe, Ma'am. It seems to be part of a blackmail note somebody sent to him." She handed a torn post card across Caine's desk. It was about half of the original, torn roughly across its centre. "Whoever sent it cut print from a magazine and stuck the letters on to make up their message. There's no postmark on the card, so maybe they put it in an envelope to send it."

Caine took the piece of card from her and examined it. "It looks like it's been torn in half. Any sign of the other piece?"

Doyle shook her head. "No. And I've no idea why it's torn. Maybe he got mad when he read what was on it."

The message had been made up of small font letters cut from a magazine and stuck onto the card, rather haphazardly. *"...what you are up to..."* it read, **"secret to remain...00 in cash on first to ...ney, Springfield Ret...ously..if you do not...I will tell U know who."** Caine handed it across to Dolby. "What do you make of it, Mark?"

Dolby ran his eyes over the message. "Obviously it's not complete, but if you fill in the missing bits it does look like a blackmail demand." He read the words again. "It mentions "Springfield Ret"...that could be the Springfield Retirement Home."

"That's what I thought," said Wendy Doyle, "and the "ney" could be the last three letters of "Harney" as in "Martha Harney.""

"Perhaps this ties in with the torn-up birthday card we found in Valerie Southam's bedroom?" suggested Dolby. "That was signed "Martha" wasn't it. If you ask me this card was instructing the blackmail victim - i.e., Jamie Parr - to whom to pay the money and how much. In other words, he was to pay Martha Harney at the Springfield Retirement Home."

"So, that means that whoever sent this card - the blackmailer - must have some connection with Martha Harney," said Caine. "It **must** have been Valerie Southam. Jamie was having an affair with her and she was blackmailing him by threatening to tell his wife! "

"And that would be curtains for him so far as the Perot family were concerned!" Dolby agreed. "That could be Parr's motive for killing her."

Wendy Doyle was incredulous. "But surely Valerie Southam wouldn't have an affair with the man and then blackmail him by threatening to tell his wife. That's unbelievable - what sort of a woman would do that?"

"The Valerie Southam sort of woman," said Dolby. "She was no Angel I can assure you. We know for a fact that she was blackmailing Paul Perot's mother about her having had an illegitimate baby, i.e., **her** - so it's not stretching credibility for her to be screwing Jamie Parr - in both senses of the word."

"I still think it's incredible," said Wendy. "I wonder if she set out to do it deliberately. Talk about a honey trap! But where does Martha Harney come into it? If we're interpreting the message on this card correctly Jamie Parr was to pay the cash over to her or, at least to her retirement home."

"Anonymously," said Caine, "that's what the "ously" must mean." She paused for a moment, gathering her thoughts. "Okay. So, let's suppose that was the motive for killing Valerie. Why did the murder happen on that particular evening and how did Jamie find out Valerie was blackmailing him? Obviously, he wouldn't have known it was her."

"What if it was all down to that torn up birthday card we found in Valerie's room?" suggested Dolby. "It was signed "Martha" wasn't it. Now, we know Valerie and Martha were close - maybe she helped Valerie when she was having *her* illegitimate baby twenty odd years ago and they sent each other birthday cards and the like over the years. And what if Jamie found the card at Valerie's, and it came in an envelope with the Springfield Retirement home printed on it and he put two and two together and confronted Valerie, accused her of being the blackmailer?"

"And they had a fight over it," agreed Caine. "That blow to Valerie's head - the one that killed her…"

"…And that was hardly noticeable because of the way her husband used to beat her up… Yes - go on…"

"Suppose she got it by accident," Caine leaned forward eagerly, playing out the scene in her mind's eye. "Imagine Valerie and James Parr up there in her bedroom preparing to hop into bed together - and they get to rowing with each other over the card and the blackmailing and it gets a bit out of hand and she trips or something and hits her head. Hard. And it kills her. Right? But Jamie Parr doesn't realise she's dead, so he goes downstairs for some reason - maybe to find a jug of water to throw in her face to bring her out of what he thinks is a dead faint. I don't know, I'm just throwing ideas about. Okay, so he's downstairs when Bruce comes home - remember Jamie wasn't expecting him. Anyway, he discovers Jamie Parr in the house and they have a fight. Bear in mind they didn't like each other, Bruce and Jamie - by all accounts they probably hated each other. Bruce wouldn't be too pleased to find Parr in his house - maybe he's already guessed Valerie has been carrying on with him. Anyway, they get into a fight - Parr is no match for Southam - he realises he's going to be beaten to a pulp unless he does something drastic, so he grabs a knife out of the block and stabs Bruce to death."

Dolby nodded. "It makes sense, Jackie. And when Parr realises what he's done and that Valerie *is* actually dead, he decides to set up the scene so it looks like she did for Bruce - stabbed him to death - during one of their regular fights. You couldn't blame her for defending herself, could you? So, he dusts down all the fingerprints, stuffs Valerie full of drugs to make it look like she's committed suicide after murdering her husband and then he washes all traces of blood off himself in the shower..."

"And throws away his old clothes, substituting some of Bruce's so that he can make a clean getaway."

"But where does Susie Neale fit into all this?"

"Perhaps she doesn't," suggested Caine. She was about to continue when the door crashed open and Superintendent Hansen banged into the office. He was breathing heavily as if he had come up the stairs rather than used the lift and the muscles of his red face were working with anger.

"Hell of a mess you're making of this case, Caine!" he said, without any preliminaries, holding on to the door handle for support. "I've just had a visit from Paul Perot - his father has just died and to cap it all he tells me you've been going around saying his brother-in-law murdered that couple up in Little Cornwall! Not to mention the fact that you and Dolby here chased the brother-in-law all the way up to High View Point and - apparently - forced him off the edge of a precipice into the lake. As a result of which he drowned. The press beggars are all over the Perot place! And what about this woman's body in the lake?" He finally let go of the door handle and closed the door with a crash, swooping across the office to drop down into one of the visitor chairs. "Would you be so kind as to tell me what the hell's been going on, Detective Chief Inspector?" He emphasised the last three words.

Caine allowed a few seconds to pass before she replied. "James Parr **was** responsible for the deaths of Bruce and Valerie Southam, Sir." She looked the Superintendent straight in the eye, showing no trace of the emotions she felt inside. "We had suspected it - that's why we went over to Upton Stapleford yesterday evening to interview him. The DNA report came in this morning - traces of his skin cells were on the discarded clothes and the towels he used to clean himself up. There's no doubt, Sir. He *did* kill them - his body hairs were also found on the towels and the clothes have been positively identified as his. As for our pursuing him to his death, Sir, it simply isn't true. We followed him up to High View Point, yes, but only after he tried to run down DS Dolby in the lane outside his house. And then, up on the Point, he tried to ram our car and force us off the top into the lake. DS Dolby took evasive action, but unfortunately, in the process of trying to kill us, Parr drove his car off the edge. I will be filing a full report, sir."

Hansen nodded his large head, "Then I suppose we have to be grateful that Dolby here only wrote off a thirty-thousand-pound car - we could have been facing two very heavy life insurance claims!" He seemed partially mollified at the thought. "Well, Perot's been talking about putting in an official complaint, so that report of yours had better be bloody good!" He shifted in his seat. "And what about this woman's body - the one the frogmen found in the lake near the car? Where does *she* fit in to this mess?"

"As I was just remarking to DS Dolby," said Caine. "I don't think she does. Not directly, anyway."

"You mean Parr didn't kill her as well then?"

"I don't think so, sir."

"Any leads as to who might have done it?"

"Not at the moment, but we're waiting for a lab report from the Pathology people. Apparently, they found some skin under her fingernails. If we can match that up with a suspect we'll be getting somewhere." *If*, she thought, we have any suspects.

Hansen stood up, still eyeing the two detectives suspiciously, as though they had done something heinous. Finally, he grunted. "Well, at least that's something. I shall want your report by tomorrow morning, Caine, without fail." He made his way back to the door and opened it. "And get this other murder cleared up as soon as possible too - we've had a damned sight too many suspicious deaths around here since you showed your nose in my manor!" He went through the doorway and into the corridor without glancing back.

Dolby closed the door quietly behind him. "I don't think we're flavour of the month at the moment, Jackie!"

Caine smiled. "He was just a little bit ungrateful, wasn't he!" She leaned over the desk to pick up the sheet of paper Dolby had previously been reading. She cast her eyes over it again before replacing it on her desk. "There's not much to go on here, Mark, but what do you think? Is there a connection between the death of this old lady, Martha Harney and the murder of Susie Neale?"

He thought for a moment, fingering the thin strip of Elastoplast on his jaw. "There might be - Mrs Neale knew the old lady from way back. Valerie Southam also knew her - they were quite attached apparently, and Valerie kept up the acquaintance.

Susie told me she - Valerie - used to go and visit Martha regularly. Susie went with her on a couple of occasions. So, there *is* a connection - there must be - it's too much of a coincidence they should all die - or be killed - within a few days of each other."

"And remember also, Mark, that all of the victims had their houses broken into just a few weeks before they died. The killer was looking for something."

He nodded. "But what makes you so sure Jamie Parr didn't kill Martha and Susie as well as Valerie?"

"I'm just thinking of the practicalities," said Caine. "Look, so far as the old lady was concerned Jamie Parr couldn't have been out at Springfield at the time the break-in to her flat occurred. That happened in the early hours of Sunday night - about the time when the whole of the Perot family - including Jamie - were together, fretting over Charlie Perot's stroke. Their nurse, Anne Hendry, was with them and I shouldn't be surprised if the Thompsons were also up and about offering to help - we can check to make doubly sure Jamie was with them, but I've no doubt he was."

Dolby nodded slowly. "Right, so if that's the case he couldn't have been out at Springfield at the same time, burglarising the old lady's apartment. But what about Susie Neale? Who's to say he didn't kill *her*?"

"Susie disappeared last Wednesday evening. She was in the water for a few days, we know that much without the formal post mortem, so it's sensible to assume that she was killed very shortly after she disappeared. And Jamie Parr took a woodworking class at Chelmer College on Monday and Wednesday evenings. They usually run from about 6.30 to 8.30 - so at the time Susie met whoever she met in the Car Park of The Bald Griffin Pub in Birch Medley Jamie was probably up in front of a dozen or so woodworking alibis."

"Well, we don't know that Jackie, until we check it out, but I follow your drift. So, what you're saying is there's somebody else involved. Yes. That also ties in with our notion that Valerie Southam was blackmailing *three* different people; we know who two of them were, but there's a third." Dolby drummed his fingers on the desk and looked across at her. "But who are they and where the hell do we start looking for them?" A strange look came into his eyes. "You don't suppose it was Paul Perot, do you?"

Caine smiled. "No. So far as we know he had no connection with Susie Neale *or* Martha Harney. And don't forget, Mark, he would also have been at the family gathering around Charlie's hospital bed on Sunday night. So, I think we can forget him for the time being at least so far as Martha Harney is concerned."

Dolby nodded reluctantly. "Well, what *do* we know about the killer, if anything?"

Caine sat back and stretched her legs. "Well, firstly, he was probably being blackmailed by Valerie Southam - he'll be number three blackmail victim. What a busy person she was!

When he burgled her house, he was looking for whatever she was using to extort the money out of him. When he didn't find what he was looking for at the Southam's he presumably took it into his head that she and Susie Neale must be working together and she'd given it - whatever *it* was - to Susie, maybe for safekeeping. But it wasn't there either when he broke into the Neale's house."

She paused and Dolby took up the train of thought. "So, he let it go for the time being. A few weeks passed. Then Valerie went and got herself murdered and things got hotter for him. He thought that whatever *it* was it might be found by us - the police."

Caine nodded. "Yes - We'd have a lot more time to carry out a proper search of the house than he had - not that we have actually found anything, but that's the theory! So, he turns the heat on Susie and presumably gets nowhere. He decides she knows too much and does away with her. But before he kills her she gives him the notion - it may even have been true - that because of her connection with Valerie, Martha Harney might have what he's looking for. So, he breaks into Martha's place. He may or may not have found it when he broke in there, but things go wrong and she ends up dead. It's possible. The thing is we don't know **what** he was looking for."

Dolby nodded thoughtfully. "But whatever it was it's something that links the three women - and him - together. Sounds plausible, Jackie. And if you think about it he must have known Susie Neale quite well - so far as we know she met him in the car park of The Bald Griffin in Birch Medley. She met him and she left behind her handbag and her car keys, a most unusual thing for a woman to do. She would only do that if she left the car in a hurry - if, for instance, she was meeting someone she really liked."

"Rushing into his arms do you mean? In other words, she may have been having an affair."

Dolby thought for a moment, running through in his mind the interview he had had with Susie Neale. "It's possible. An affair presupposes there was something wrong with her relationship with her husband - at least it would in normal circumstances - and come to think of it, although she had some nice things to say about Norman, her husband, there was always a certain reservation, as if their marriage was good, but not *that* good!"

"So, she may well have been having a fling."

Dolby shrugged. "It's the best explanation so far as to why she should meet up with another man."

Caine nodded. "I guess so. But it looks like it's Mr Plod work for us again - checking the women's backgrounds, looking for common denominators. We'll have to go back and re-question the landlord of The Griffin and his wife, of course, and talk to all the locals to see if anyone saw anything suspicious on the evening that Susie Neale disappeared. I know we've questioned a few of them, but now we're investigating an actual murder, not just a possible disappearance."

"I suppose we should also start turning over a few stones up at the Neale's place and at this Retirement Home out at Springfield," suggested Dolby, "See what we can dig up that might throw some light on the subject." He stood up, yawned and stretched. "We'd better not poke our noses into the Harney case without clearing it with DCI Hopkins first though, he might think we're muscling in on his territory."

Caine looked blank. "DCI Hopkins? I don't think I've met him, but I suppose you're right. I'll check it out with him," She reached for the telephone. "If you'd like to cover the Neale place, I'll do the old people's home. What's Hopkins' phone number?" Dolby shrugged his ignorance. Caine opened her desk drawer and consulted her directory. She dialled and listened to DCI Hopkins' telephone ringing for about twenty seconds before replacing the receiver. "He's probably gone for lunch. I'll try him again later, but in the meantime we'll take in a quick snack in the canteen. We may even see him there."

*　　　*　　　*　　　*　　　*　　　*

*

The Springfield Retirement Home, just outside Chelmsford, was a combination of an old converted Victorian house set on top of a hill overlooking meadows and farmland and a series of purpose-built blocks recently erected around it in the extensive grounds. A wide gateway led on to a sweeping drive bordered by horse chestnut trees and well-tended flower beds riotous with summer blooms. Caine drove slowly, noting the well-kept lawns and returning with a smile the curious looks of the residents who were out taking the afternoon air. They walked singly or in groups or were pushed in wheelchairs by smartly dressed staff, along the pedestrian paths that criss-crossed the lawns. Others sat on benches beside the small lake enjoying the early June sunshine and watching the ducks cavort on the water. She turned finally off the drive onto a wide paved area in front of the house and followed the signs to the parking lot. Leaving her car there she made her way back to the steps leading up to the front doors, which were also approachable via a wheelchair ramp. The doors were all glass and slid open automatically. The inside of the house was light and airy, lit by big windows on either side of the spacious hallway which led on to a quiet reception area. A young woman was working at a computer keyboard behind a high counter and she looked up as Caine approached.

"Mrs Saunders is expecting you, Detective Chief Inspector," she said glancing at Caine's warrant card. "If you'd like to come this way."

Caine followed the receptionist along a corridor and into a spacious sun-lit office where a heavily built woman advanced on her from behind a large desk, thrusting out her hand in greeting. "Do come in, Inspector Caine. I'm Isabel Saunders." After a hearty handshake she ushered Caine towards a wing backed armchair in what was obviously the conference area part of the room. She eased her body down into a similar chair on the opposite side of a glass topped coffee table, laden with hand painted china crockery and a voluminous matching tea pot. "You will take a cup of tea won't you!" She started pouring before Caine had a chance to answer and she kept up the monologue as she handed a brimming cup with accompanying saucer across the table to her. "I can't tell you what a terrible shock it was yesterday, Inspector!"

"What exactly happened, Mrs Saunders?" asked Caine, taking a sip of the tea. She shook her head at the biscuits offered. "And it would be helpful if you could tell me what your position is with the Retirement Home."

"I'm the Chief Superintendent of The Home, Inspector," Mrs Saunders told her squaring her shoulders proudly. She adjusted the hem of her tweed skirt as she put down her teacup. "I've been here now for over two years and I must say that nothing quite so dreadful as this has happened in all that time. Everybody here is most upset at the passing of Mrs Harney. Mind you, we're not exactly sure what did happen, your people are still investigating - but it seems quite clear that some dreadful person broke into poor Mrs Harney's room in the early hours of Monday morning and turned the place upside down. Poor Martha must have had a terrible shock. It almost certainly killed her."

"My colleagues in the CID are looking into it, of course, Mrs Saunders, but do you know if any of Mrs Harney's belongings are missing?"

"Nothing valuable, of course," Mrs Saunders broke off a piece of short cake biscuit and chewed on it reflectively before sipping at her tea. "We advise all our guests - we don't call them patients here at The Springfield, by the way Inspector - they're not in need of medical attention, you see, any more than any other healthy elderly people - they are literally 'guests', almost like hotel guests, I like to think. And thinking of them as 'guests' rather than patients instils a feeling of respect into our staff. Anyway, we advise all our guests not to keep valuable items in their rooms. We do have a safe in the office, but most of our people keep their really valuable jewellery in the bank." She brushed a few biscuit crumbs from her white silk blouse. "But what exactly is your involvement, Inspector Caine? I understood the other officers were dealing with the case."

"We think there may be a connection with one of my cases," said Caine. "It's something which may involve Mrs Harney's background. But, before we get on to that can you confirm that a part of her rent was paid by an anonymous donor, in cash?"

"You mean Accommodation', or 'boarding' fees, Inspector." said Mrs Saunders snootily - "we don't call it *'rent'* here at The Springfield. But yes, I can confirm that Bursar and I were aware of this - er - special arrangement. It was I admit highly unusual. "

"And you have no idea who was making the payment?"

"None. It's a complete mystery. It was always in cash - monthly - and it didn't come through the post, it was deposited by whoever it was directly into our letter box."

"And how long has this been going on?"

Mrs Saunders thought for a moment. "From the very beginning. From when Martha came to us just over five years ago. Of course, she had her own bank account, and she paid the other half of her fees from that."

"And did *she* know who her benefactor was?"

"No. In fact, to be honest, she thought she was paying the full amount; she didn't realise there was another payment being made."

"How come? Who set the whole thing up?"

Mrs Saunders shrugged. "I don't really know. It started before my time here, but I have discussed with Burser and he said he'd originally had a phone call from a lady - who would not identify herself - saying the cash would be coming and it was to be credited against Mrs Harney's account every month."

"And you obviously went through with that arrangement?"

"Why not? Burser and I couldn't see any harm in it. After all, if a well-meaning person wants to help an old lady afford to live in better circumstances than her own resources will allow then that's *a good thing* isn't it? We thought it was a very charitable gesture from someone who wished to remain anonymous."

Caine thought for a moment. "And it never occurred to you, Mrs Saunders, or to your burser, that the money might be coming from - how shall I put it? - an irregular source?"

Mrs Saunders looked genuinely shocked. "Certainly not, Inspector! So long as our guests pay for their accommodation on time, we do not concern ourselves as to how they come by their money!"

"So - Mrs Harney had been with you here at Springfield for about five years."

"Yes" Mrs Saunders finished her tea and daintily replaced her cup and saucer on the tabletop. "How far into her background would you like to go?"

"Quite a bit further than the five years, actually," said Caine. "Twenty years or more maybe, but I don't suppose you have anything going back that far!" The other woman shook her head. "We're also interested in any friends she may have had, who visited her while she was here, anyone who might have written to her, or that she wrote to, that sort of thing. And, of course, we'd like to take a look at whatever these monthly cash donations came in - envelopes I assume?"

"Yes - envelopes with "For Martha Harney" written on them. That was all - but I doubt we would have kept them. I will ask Burser of course."

"What about other information on her background?"

"There won't be much - not in our official records anyway - it's too personal. Some of the other guests may be able to tell you something, not that she was particularly close to any of them. But let's have a look at our records first, shall we." She stood up and went to her desk. A computer console stood on a side table, a colourful screen-saver passing slowly across the screen. It vanished when she moved the mouse, to be replaced by the background of the Microsoft Windows 'desktop'. The speed with which her fingers flew unerringly over the keys suggested that she had risen to her present heights from the more humble level of 'Personal Secretary' or 'copy typist' and, as Caine crossed the room to sit in one of the guest chairs on the other side of the desk, she said brightly, "Here's Mrs Harney's record - I've been looking at it rather a lot recently and, to be frank, there's not that much on it. Just her name, date of birth, her National Insurance Number and the date she came into the home." She clicked the mouse to scroll up the screen. "Then there are a few notes on her bank details, next of kin - there's nobody listed under that heading - to be frank, although she calls herself 'Mrs' we have no proof she was ever married. So long as they are able to meet their fees we don't inquire into our guests' personal lives. And there's some comments on her medical condition. Not much there, a lot of high blood pressure problems and extensive arthritis. That more or less covers it."

"Nothing else? No previous addresses?" asked Caine, feeling the trail - such as it was - beginning to run cold.

Mrs Saunders shook her head. "No. Although I suppose the DSS could tell you something from her national insurance number. This system isn't that clever if you ask me - not the one I would have put in myself, you know, but my predecessor knew nothing about computers! Wait a minute, though..." She thought for a moment, picking up the fountain pen that lay on her desk and tapping it on the blotter reflectively. "You know, I'd forgotten, but we may have something else for you, Inspector. There was an old system in operation when Mrs Harney came to join our little community. It was on microfilm and I think we've still got those old records." She leaned over and pressed a button on her telephone console. "I'll just see if Margery, our receptionist, knows where we can lay hands on them. She looks after all those sorts of things."

It was likely to be quite a while before the old records could be located Mrs Saunders advised Caine after a short telephone conversation with Margery, the receptionist. Caine took the opportunity of requesting a look at Martha Harney's room while she was waiting and Mrs Saunders summoned a young girl dressed in a mob cap and overalls decorated with fruit and vegetables, (Caine discovered this designated her as one of the kitchen staff) to escort her out of the main house and across to one of the blocks of annexe buildings.

Mrs Harney had enjoyed a garden room on the west side of the block. It was spacious and airy, recently decorated and boasting double glazed patio doors that looked out over the extensive grounds. There was a view of the lake and, in the far distance, the outskirts of Chelmsford. On DCI Hopkins' instructions the room had been left just as it had been found after the old lady's death and Caine stepped carefully around the various items scattered across the floor by the intruder. He had ransacked Martha's cupboards and left the contents where they fell. There were items of clothing, underwear, a few sweaters and cardigans, dresses and skirts that had been pulled from the wardrobe and drawers, strewn all over the room, along with shoes emptied out of the cupboards. There were a few more personal belongings, broken ornaments, a large print book she had been reading before she died and, in the corner, open and on its back an empty leather writing case. The writing paper embossed with the Springfield Retirement Home logo was scattered over the floor as if the case had been opened and searched and then discarded in disgust. There were no letters in the case and nothing of a really personal nature, no photographs of family and friends displayed about the room and none scattered on the floor; presumably the old lady had had no family she wished to remember. Caine left Martha's room having found nothing of significance; almost certainly Hopkins and Milligan would have taken away anything they thought important to their investigations, but they had mentioned nothing to her when she had inquired.

She was on her way back to the main house, thinking about what she had seen and had just reached the stage of concluding that her visit to the Retirement Home had been a complete waste of time, when Mrs Saunders came out to meet her and told her that Margery, the receptionist, had found something she might find interesting.

"All the old records are down here," Margery told her as they descended a dark stairway into the cellars beneath the house. "The old Superintendent, Mrs Offal - 'Grumbleguts' we called her - was a real hoarder. She wouldn't throw anything away if she could help it, so when we had the new computer system installed, she insisted we put the old files and records down here. *Just in case* she said, and they've been down here ever since."

They reached the bottom of the stairs and entered a narrow corridor lit by a single low watt bulb hanging from the ceiling on a piece of worn cable. They approached a closed and locked door and Margery selected a key from the motley collection she carried on a large ring and opened it. She reached inside the doorway for the light switch. "According to the notes old Grumble - er - Mrs Offal - left us, the microfilm for the patients' - I mean guest's - records should still be in here."

The dim light showed rack upon rack of paper files in the large, square room. To one side, at right angles to the wall, was what appeared to be a counter, possibly a working surface on which the records could be opened and searched. Side by side on the neighbouring shelf were two microfiche readers, their screens dark with dust.

"There must be hundreds of files down here," observed Caine.

"Oh yes, Inspector," agreed Margery. "Thousands I'd say - well, they probably go back to the 1950s - long before my time, of course," she laughed, "I've only been here for twelve years. The place was a lunatic asylum in those days you know - I suppose nowadays we would call it a mental home, that's nicer isn't it? Anyway, these are most likely the files relating to those patients." She waved her hand to break through a cobweb. "Sorry the place is such a mess, but we hardly ever come down here." She walked over to the fiche readers. "There should be some boxes here somewhere with all the microfilm things in them. Ah! Here we are." She wiped a layer of dust off the top of a box and peered at the label stuck to the top. "Yes, these are the most recent." She picked up the box and took it over to the working surface, wiping away more of the dust with a small cloth as she went. "This covers the last five years before we went completely over to the computer system about eighteen months ago. The records for poor old Mrs Harney should be in here."

"Thanks." Caine lifted the top off the box. Inside was a stack of transparent plastic sheaths, each containing a microfiche record. She reached in and lifted out the one at the front, holding it up to the dim light and peering at it. The name of the 'guest' - 'W. Ames' - was handwritten in black marker pen in the top right hand corner, together with a date, but the light was too weak for her to make out anything at all on the surface of the actual fiche. Tiny print in the corner of the semi opaque plastic border proclaimed that the film had been manufactured by Kodak; in the opposite corner was printed the name of the company that had carried out the filming operation - **'Microcell Ltd, Chelmsford'**, followed by a telephone number. Caine rubbed her eyes and peered at the name of the company again. Where had she seen that name before? Recently - she had seen it written down, recently. But where? She thought for a moment and it came to her and she shook her head to try to clarify the curious notion that was developing in her mind. She felt a sudden flood of confidence.

She smiled and nodded towards the microfiche readers. "Can I use one of these? I suppose they are working?"

"So far as I know, they are," said her companion. "But you can't use them down here. There are no power points working any more. We'll have to carry one of them upstairs I'm afraid. Sorry."

Caine hefted one corner of the machine. It wasn't very heavy. "I'd like to take it back to the station with me. I'm going to need one to have a look at some of these records and if you can lend me the reader it'll be easier than trying to locate one. I shouldn't imagine the local police force have still got this type of viewer, if they ever had any."

"I shouldn't think so - they are a bit antediluvian nowadays aren't they." Margery laughed apologetically, "The microfilm readers I mean, not the police!" She reached over and picked up the box of fiches. "Can you manage that? I could get Albert, the odd job man, to come down and help us if you like."

"It's not heavy," said Caine, arranging the strap of her handbag over her shoulder and picking up the reader. "It's just awkward." She carried it towards the door.

*   *   *   *   *   *

*

"I've sent the children to stay with friends," said Norman Neale with a long sigh as he showed Dolby and PC Doyle into the lounge of number 23 Marazion Road. "Susie hasn't - *didn't* - have any family worth speaking of. Her parents passed away some years ago and she was an only child. The girls'll be better off away from all this for the next few days. It's not going to be easy arranging things." His big, lined face was crumpled with misery and Dolby noticed there was a bottle of whisky and a half full glass on the table where he had left it when he went to open the front door. "You will get the bastard, won't you?" He said suddenly, vehemently, his eyes narrowing with anger. "The one that killed her!"

"We're doing all we can," said Dolby. "And we'd appreciate any help you can give us." They sat on the fawn leather settee and watched him retrieve the half full glass of whisky and gulp its contents down as though it was water. "I know we asked you this before, Mr Neale, but do you have any idea at all who your wife went to meet last Wednesday evening?"

Neale refilled his glass. "No. I told you. No. She didn't have any friends that I didn't know about!"

"If you're sure..." Dolby chose his words carefully. The man was distraught and he did not want to add to his burden by asking insensitive questions, but they had to know. "How were relations between yourself and your wife, Mr Neale?"

Neale looked at PC Doyle and blushed. "What sort of a bloody question is that Sergeant?" He drank quickly from his glass, swallowing hurriedly and coughing. He wiped his mouth with the back of his hand and struggled to recover his composure. "My wife was a good woman! I know what she was before I married her, but she was a dancer not a bloody prostitute! We were okay. We were fine!" The two police officers said nothing. Neale looked down and his face coloured again. "Okay, you may as well know it from me," he went on in a small voice, that was barely audible, "you'll find out from my GP I dare say if I don't tell you myself. Yes, we did have some difficulties in the - er - in the **bed** department. Nothing unusual - I'm quite a few years older than Susie is - **was** - and she was a passionate woman!" He paused to fill his glass again. "But she understood **and there were no other men in her life, Sergeant.** She wouldn't do that to me!" He swallowed back the tears that were moistening his eyes and stood up, swaying slightly. "You said you wanted to see my wife's papers and personal things - I don't know why - they were of no consequence to anyone but herself, but you seem to think looking at them may be useful." He sighed. "I suppose you know best, so I've put them on the table," he gestured across the room. "She kept them in those shoe boxes.

There isn't much, and I don't know what's in them, but you're welcome to look."

"Thank you," said Dolby, "but as I told you on the telephone earlier, Mr Neale, I'm afraid we may have to search the rest of the house as well. We can't just make the assumption that what we're looking for will be in these boxes."

Neale scowled. "What exactly **are** you looking for, Sergeant?"

"I don't know, sir," said Dolby apologetically, "but I'm sure we'll know when we find it!"

Neale shook his head ruefully. "I suppose you know what you're doing," he said. "Just get the bastard that did it, that's all! He should be hung!" He sighed yet again, wiped the back of his hand across his forehead. "Now, if you'll excuse me, I'll leave you to it..." He picked up the whisky bottle and carried it to the hall door, his glass in his other hand. "I'll be upstairs if you want me..."

Dolby and Wendy Doyle were silent for a few moments after he had left and then Dolby stood up and walked over to the table. Four shoe boxes were arranged side by side on the polished wooden surface.

"Come on, Wendy; the sooner we get started on this lot the better."

"Do you think she **was** carrying on?" she asked as she stood up, smoothing her dark blue skirt. "I mean, having an affair?"

"To be honest, yes, I do," Dolby told her. "It's one of the few reasons she would have gone out last Wednesday evening to meet a so called 'friend'. And between you and me, I think Mr Neale thinks that too."

"Poor beggar!" She came over to the table and sat down, lifting the lid from one of the shoe boxes. "Don't you ever get sick of this, Sarge? Meddling in other people's lives, going through their intimate belongings?"

"Of course, I do. But it has to be done. It's all part of the job, and if it helps to catch a killer well, that speaks for itself!"

She riffled through a wad of bank statements and receipts. "I suppose *he's* under suspicion as well?"

"Mr Neale? No reason why he shouldn't be at this stage, Wendy."

"But he couldn't have done it - he's so upset!"

"I admit he **seems** upset, but we hardly know anything about him. For all we know he may be a brilliant actor, a star of the amateur stage giving the best performance of his life."

"He's not though, is he? I've never seen him at any of the local theatres!"

"Neither have I, but he may have been an actor in his younger days. We know nothing about him," He opened another shoe box and shook the contents on to the tabletop. "But in a couple of days or so we'll know everything about him there is to know." He picked up a small wad of papers. "In the meantime, let's get through this stuff."

"Can't you go through these bank papers?" Wendy asked. "I can't make head or tail of figures!"

"There's nothing to it," said Dolby, "You just look on the statements for any abnormally high payments - either in or out - or any entries for the same or similar amounts paid on a regular basis. Say each week or month. You're looking for patterns." She gazed back at him unhappily. "All right, Wendy, you win, pass them over - you can go through these photos and the odd papers."

She smiled and handed the bank statements and cheque book stubs over to him. "Thanks! I owe you one."

"I'll bear that in mind," said Dolby with a crooked smile, "but don't let on to the wife!"

He worked quickly through the statements noting nothing of interest and becoming bored by the endless strings of figures that passed before his eyes. He could sympathise with Wendy's preference for photographs and the multitudes of other documentation we all habitually store in files or boxes over the years and, usually, never look at again.

It was after about fifteen minutes that Wendy found the folded piece of newsprint tucked into an old and creased A5 manila envelope. Somebody had scrawled the word "Susie" on the outside. She pulled out the thin sheet of printed paper and smoothed out the creases. "Here, Sarge, look at this newspaper cutting," she said. "It's a picture of somebody getting married, with a write up underneath. The date on it is..." She peered at the top corner more closely, "12ᵗʰ May two thousand and one. I wonder why Mrs Neale kept it for all these years."

"Let's have a look," said Dolby. He leaned over the table and they looked at the cutting together. "Read the caption underneath the picture, Wendy, I'm a dab hand at reading upside down, but it's a bit faded."

"*Daughter of local businessman marries*," Wendy read, "That's the headline. It goes on to say '*Marilyn, daughter of local businessman Robert Roberts, was married at All Saints Church last Saturday at 2.30pm to Mr Arthur Patterson, son of well-known local contractor Derek Patterson. Seen with the new Mrs Patterson are bridesmaids Annabelle Poole and Deborah Sweet, the bride's nieces, Maid of Honour Susie Lake and other guests. A reception was held at The New Brunswick Banqueting Rooms, Frimley Street after the ceremony.*'" Wendy looked up. "Susie Lake - would that be our Susie Neale?"

Dolby nodded. "Yes. Lake was her maiden name. Let's have a closer look at the face just to be sure. I've got a magnifying glass here somewhere." He dug down into a canvas bag he had leaned against the leg of his chair and produced a large circular glass. "Here we are - yeah, that's her all right. What's the date of this 'do' again?" He moved the magnifying glass, peering closely. "May '01. She was looking quite a bit older when I interviewed her last week, but you couldn't mistake her - it's definitely our Susie!"

Wendy peered through the glass at the figure standing next to the bride and nodded. "Yes, that's Mrs Neale. Why do you suppose she kept the picture?"

"Sentimental reasons," he suggested. "The Roberts' girl must have been a good friend at the time, I suppose." He stopped as a sudden thought struck him. "Hey! You don't suppose this so-called businessman is Bobby Roberts the gangland mobster, do you?"

"How should I know, this picture was taken in two thousand and one, Sarge," said Wendy Doyle indignantly. "I was about three years old at the time." As she spoke, she was moving the magnifying glass slowly over the photograph. She stopped it suddenly and peered closer. "Isn't that Valerie Southam? Here, among the other guests."

Dolby leaned closer. "Yes - it certainly looks like her; a younger version, of course!"

Wendy was scrutinising the photograph very closely now. "That man beside her - the one she's linked arms with - do you know him?"

She moved her head aside for Dolby to look more closely. "No - I can't say I do."

"I'm sure I've seen him somewhere," said Wendy thoughtfully. "Recently. I've seen him recently - he would look much older now of course, than in the photo, but I'm sure it was the same man." She peered down through the glass again, screwing up her eyes to see better. "And come to think of it there was a photograph of these two together - Valerie and this guy - amongst Valerie Southam's photos. I'm sure there was. I didn't think anything of it at the time, of course!"

"Could it have been the same photo?"

"No. No, but it was probably taken at about the same time. Let me think - yes, it was them at the beach somewhere - the two of them together on a beach!"

"And you say you've seen this man recently, Wendy - where?"

She frowned. "I think it was about two weeks ago. It was my birthday and my boyfriend, Daniel, treated me to an evening out up at that posh hotel on the hill. You know, the one that looks down over the Blackwater estuary. We had the works, you know, champagne and all."

"And this man was there?"

She nodded. "Yes. I'm sure it was him."

CHAPTER TWENTY SIX

As Jacqueline Caine drew her car to a halt in the police station car park Detective Sergeant Dave Milligan stepped out of the car in the space beside her. "Afternoon, Ma'am; how did you get on up at Springfield?"

She smiled. "Very well, thank you, Sergeant. I think I have a lead at last."

"That's great. Me and the Guv'nor have been going round in circles so far." He nodded towards the microfilm reader on the back seat. "Something to do with microfilming then is it? All the clues written on a micro dot are they?" He laughed. "I thought old Mrs Harney looked like a KGB spy!"

"I don't think she was a spy," said Caine as she opened her door to climb out. "But microfilm may be involved. You obviously know about these things. You wouldn't like to come up and see if you can get that machine working for me, would you?"

"Yeah - why not? I haven't had a better offer all day," Milligan said, grinning. "I'll carry it in for you." He opened the rear door of the car and reached in to pick up the reader. "I used to work one of these things way back before we had computers. I've always been interested in gadgets and microfilm was quite an innovation - very handy for storing records in as little space as possible. Where did you get this one?" She told him, opening the boot to retrieve the box of microfiches.

She led the way across the car park and into the building, nodding to the desk sergeant who looked curiously at the machine Milligan was carrying. They entered the lift together and she pressed the button for the third floor.

"Second for me, please, Ma'am," said Milligan. "I've just got to nip into my office for a word with DCI Hopkins. I'll tell him I'm debriefing you on the Harney case, then I'll be along with your machine. We'll get it working for you, no problem!"

He got out on the second floor and hurried off along the corridor, carrying the microfiche reader. She stepped out on the third and walked quickly to her office, putting her bag and the box of film on her desk before going to her filing cabinet and opening it, eager with anticipation. She had just retrieved the box of photographs taken from the Southam house and put it on her desk when the telephone rang. She answered it impatiently.

It was Daniel Carmichael, the estate agent. "Your offer's been accepted, Detective Inspector Caine," he told her, sounding pleased with himself; "perhaps you'd like to give me your solicitor's details."

"Pardon?" She replied absently. Her mind was running on a completely different track and she resented the interruption.

"Lime Tree Cottage," said Carmichael, as though uncertain he was speaking to the right person. "The vendor has accepted your offer. You know, you made an offer, Inspector Caine."

"Oh! Right!" Her brain was now back in gear and she was delighted at the news. "Good - I'll get back to you shall I? - With those details - I've something rather important on at this very moment!" She put the phone down with a quick apology and turned back to the Southam photographs. She lifted the lid off the box, turning most of them out until she found the small plastic container of slides. She took one of them out and examined it closely, turning on the desk lamp and holding it under the glare of light. She smiled to herself when she read, across the top of the cardboard border, in the very tiniest print, **Microcell Ltd, Chelmsford.** She looked at it for a long time, thinking.

Milligan came in carrying the microfiche reader. He set it down on her desk.

"Is it okay here, Ma'am? I'm afraid I can't stop more than a couple of minutes!" He looked distinctly disappointed. "DCI Hopkins wants me to run an errand for him! But I'll get this thing up and running for you before I go." He snickered and looked around the room. "I just love gadgets! Now - Where's the nearest power point?" She told him and he plugged it in and then came back to the machine, running his hands around its base. "There should be an on-off switch someplace around here." He found it and clicked the reader on. The screen glowed with bright white light. "Bingo!"

"Good. You can try it out with this," Caine handed him the microfiche that Margery, the receptionist at the Old People's

Home, had identified as Martha Harney's record. "It'll be interesting to see what's on it, anyway."

Milligan took the fiche and slipped it into the spring-loaded glass guide in the front of the machine, pushing it under the magnifying lenses in the reader's case." It's a long time since I had one of these to play with!" His brow puckered as a blurred image appeared on the screen and he twiddled the small adjuster wheel to bring it slowly into focus. "Oh, this is from the Springfield Retirement Home." He read from the screen and looked up at Caine with a grin. "It's the murder victim's file. Nothing much to get our teeth into here, though, is there?"

Caine stood behind him and read the details off the screen. They were much the same as Mrs Saunders had given her from her computer record. There was nothing new. "At least the reader's working okay, Sergeant. Thanks for setting it up for me."

He stood up, letting her slide into the chair. "What's all this about? Do you reckon there's a connection between the Southam murders and this latest two?"

"Maybe," said Caine, "This reader should help me eliminate - or confirm - a little idea I've had, that's all. Mark and I will keep you and DCI Hopkins in the loop - if that's the right expression."

"Right" He seemed satisfied. "I'll have to go now and leave you to it. The reader's quite simple to use. You just push the film in and out using that slider guide," he pointed, "it's spring loaded to hold the film in firmly. And you turn the little furled wheel under the front of the screen to bring it into focus - the one on the left - and the little wheel beside it on the right is to adjust the screen brightness. Dead simple." He walked to the door. "Let me know how you get on."

"Thanks, Sergeant!" As he went out and closed the door Caine pulled the guide towards her and extracted the fiche, placing it back with the others. Then she took one of the photographic slides from the box of Valerie Southam items and held it up against the brightly lit screen. As she had expected there was no picture on it that she could see, just the very faintest trace of a few dark lines. On the off chance that she would be able to read it like a piece of microfilm, she placed it in the microfiche guide. It was much smaller than a microfiche and even in the grip of the spring loading it was difficult to keep straight as she pushed it into the machine. Eight groups of dark, jumbled images leapt out at her from the screen and she adjusted the focusing wheel, resolving them into an incomprehensible series of strokes and whorls that meant absolutely nothing to her. She sagged with disappointment. Her hunch could not have been more wrong. *The slides were just slides*. They were *not* micro dots containing incriminating evidence Valerie Southam had been anxious to hide and that she had consequently made to look like ordinary photographic slides when she worked for Microcell Ltd; and obviously, therefore, she had *not* used the information contained in them to blackmail the person who had murdered her accomplices, Susie Neale and Martha Harney. They **were** just slides - perhaps just holiday snaps - but whoever had made them from the original photographic negatives had done an extremely bad job and ruined them.

Caine sank down into her chair, staring at the motionless, almost mocking images on the screen and steepling her hands in thought. There was something wrong here. If they were useless, badly produced slides of holiday photographs, **why had Valerie Southam kept them for over twenty years**? She **must** have considered them important, but the one now projected onto the screen was nothing but a jumble of meaningless marks and streaks. Caine ejected the slide from the machine and with a shrug pushed another one into the glass guide. Again, the images were blurred, but this time, as she turned the focusing wheel, a recognisable pattern of dark shapes swam slowly into view. There, on the screen, were eight groups of two columns of figures, the first of which were obviously dates, the second cash amounts; the series of letters beside them may have been initials. All were written in a fine copperplate hand.

Caine gave a little laugh of triumph and shook her head at her foolishness - of course, she had probably put the first slide into the machine upside down and back to front. She leaned towards the screen to read the figures and characters, but apart from the column that may have been dates they meant nothing to her, so she ejected the slide and put another into the guide. This one was the same, columns of meaningless numbers and figures and so were the three that followed. She began to doubt the soundness of her theory. Surely, if Valerie had used this information as a lever to blackmail it had to be comprehensible. The fifth and sixth slides were the same, but the seventh was proper script, written with what looked like a ball point pen and in a quite different hand - a hand that she recognised from examples she had seen in some of Valerie's other papers.

The next slide contained two photographs. Caine's pulse quickened in anticipation. They were of poor quality, but this could be what she was looking for. Taken in bad light she had to lean close to the screen before she could make anything of them. The first was of two men standing close together, their faces side on to a concealed camera. One of them was handing the other a package. She rubbed her tired eyes trying to make out the faces. The microfilm reader was not a suitable way of viewing ordinary photographs, the images were too small and indistinct. She opened her drawer and rummaged around for a magnifying glass. She held it close to the image, twirling the small wheels beneath the screen to bring up the brightness and adjust the focus. Slowly the picture became sharper. She leaned forward and then started with shock, her heart beating faster. She knew now who the two men in the picture were. She turned her attention to the second image and gasped again, this time in horror. The man on the left of the image had drawn a gun. It was clear from his pose and the reactions of the second man that he was firing it at point blank range.

For a long moment Caine sat staring at the screen in disbelief, fighting back the tears that were welling up in her eyes.

A cup of hot sweet tea from the machine at the end of the corridor revived her, bringing her mind back to the present and she continued to scroll through the slides. There were other similar photographs among the dozens in the boxes. The eight sections into which each of the other slides was divided, she realised suddenly, were eight separate pages and she read rapidly through a number of them, a troubled smile growing on her face. The ones with Valerie's writing on them were an explanation of the others containing the figures, dates and initials. They also tied in with the photographs and represented a key to the information contained in the slides. They were Caine's Rosetta stone enabling her to read and understand the incriminating evidence preserved for so long by Valerie Southam and used by her as a tool to blackmail. Caine was certain now that she had only to assemble the slides in their correct order - they had become hopelessly jumbled over the years - and the whole story would come together. She already knew the identity of Susie and Martha's killer.

She finished her tea and went at the task with renewed energy. The pages contained within the slides, she realised, were numbered, although only with a ballpoint pen, which the microfilming camera had not captured clearly, as a result of which it proved difficult and time consuming to assemble them into their correct order. Finally, however, she had the task completed. Slide by slide she read through the complete set of pages, piecing together the story Valerie was telling her from the grave. The first time she read the name of the person Valerie had blackmailed - the person who must have killed Susie Neale and broken into Martha Harney's room - Caine smiled grimly, but with satisfaction. Now there was no doubt in her mind. Certain events, things said and noticed during the last few days, took on new significance.

Her heart still beating with excitement she read through the slides a second and third time and then she reached across the desk for her telephone and dialled Dolby's mobile number. It was engaged. She sat for a few minutes gazing at the information on the screen and just as she reached again for the telephone the Detective Sergeant pushed open the door and came in, followed by PC Doyle.

Dolby looked pleased with himself. "We've found something we think is important," he said. "Well, actually, it was Wendy who found it. We've just been checking out a few details." He looked curiously at the microfilm reader on Caine's desk. "Looks like you've also been busy. What's up?"

Caine waved them to the chairs. "You show me yours and I'll show you mine," she offered.

"Go ahead, Wendy," said Doyle.

The young PC went to Caine's desk and handed her the envelope containing the press cutting. "We found this among Mrs Neale's personal papers," she explained. "It looks as though it was taken from the local paper. If you look closely you'll see Mrs

Neale in the photograph," she pointed to the woman standing beside the bride. "And over here amongst the guests," she moved her finger, "is Valerie Southam - with the man we think may have been her boyfriend at the time."

Caine moved the magnifying glass across the press photograph, the constituent dots that made up the print standing out clearly. She nodded carefully and then caught her breath. "I know him!" She said. The link was forged beyond any shadow of a doubt. "Well done, children - I think we're home and dry!" She beckoned, "Come around to this side of the desk, the two of you and I'll show *you* what *I've* found!"

Chapter Twenty Seven

They took a marked police car, PC Doyle driving. The Faulkbourne Country House Hotel was about twenty minutes from the centre of Fen Molesey and it was past seven o'clock before they turned through the tall ironwork gates and into the long drive.

Leaving the police car in front of the hotel they climbed up the stone steps and, passing the bronze plate that proclaimed its kitchen one of the finest in England, entered the panelled reception area. Their heels clacking on the Italian tile floor they strode three abreast past an elderly couple seated side by side on a long leather couch and enjoying a pre-dinner drink. Followed by their curious stares the three police officers - the policewoman in uniform - passed through into the carpeted reception area and made for the desk. There was nobody about so Dolby pressed the bell and then walked impatiently around the counter to meet the young lady who came slowly out of the ante-room behind.

He held up his warrant card for her inspection. "Fen Molesey CID. Where can we find Mr Christopher Stone?"

"He's not here. He left in his car about two hours ago."

"When will he be back?" asked Caine.

"I don't know - he didn't say," the young woman told her nervously. "He didn't say where he was going either – he was sort of *vague* - but I gathered he would be away for two or three days. He had a suitcase with him you see."

Dolby looked at Caine. "What do we do now? Do we wait for him to come back or go into his flat and see what we can find?"

"Not that - not without a warrant," cautioned Caine. She sighed heavily. "We can get one, but I doubt we can do that before tomorrow. For now, the best we can do is go home and re-assess the situation in the morning."

"He won't be back by then, though" said Doyle. "Not if he's gone off with a suitcase."

"You're right - but there's not much else we can do. He could be anywhere. We don't even know *if* he's coming back."

"Maybe he's not - maybe he's realised we're onto him and done a runner," Dolby suggested.

"Yes. It could be," Caine agreed, her face grim. "Get onto the Station and have them put out an APB. Wherever he is I want him found."

Dolby took out his mobile phone and dialled. "We should get into his place and have a look," he suggested.

"Not without a warrant," insisted Caine. "We'll get one and go in tomorrow morning. Stone's a slippery customer, the bastard, and we're not going to give him any way of getting off on a legal technicality. In any case," she went on, "if he has done a runner I'll bet he's had it planned for some time, so it's hardly likely we'll find anything incriminating." She turned back towards the hotel exit. "We can't do anything here - let's get back to the Station."

It was nearly half past ten before Caine pushed open the door to her flat and stumbled inside, kicking off her shoes in the hall and dropping her jacket onto a chair in the lounge. She yawned and made her way across the room to the drinks cabinet and poured herself a whisky. She drank it quickly, throwing her head back, feeling the amber liquid rush down her throat. It brought a warm and contented feeling and she poured another generous measure into the glass and took it with her into the bathroom, placing it carefully on the shelf at the side of the bath. She emptied the remains of the bottle of bath oil into the tub and turned on the hot tap, watching the water gush down onto the oil, agitating it into lather, before sitting on the toilet seat and stripping off her stockings.

She was almost undressed when the telephone rang. She ignored it and leaned over the bath to test the water, turning on the cold tap when she realised it was too hot. The answer phone cut in and she heard her own voice floating down the hall towards her, telling the caller she was out and to leave a message. It was Alison. With a sigh she went out into the hall and picked up the receiver, interrupting her daughter's message.

"Sorry darling, I was just about to have a bath. It's been a long day!"

Alison sounded fed up. "Oh, I'm sorry Mum. I just felt like a chat."

"Anything wrong?"

"Not really. I was just feeling a bit down – well, a lot down." She sighed, "But more important - did you get the cottage?"

"Yes - the agent rang this afternoon. They've accepted my offer." Was it just a few hours ago? It seemed so much longer; it had been a busy two days. She remembered the running taps and the bath she was longing to immerse herself in, but her daughter's voice told her she needed a shoulder to cry on. "Hang on - I'd better go and turn the bath taps off - a flood is the last thing I need at the moment." She traced her way back into the bathroom. "It's Lyall isn't it, darling - he's married isn't he!"

"How did you know?" Alison was almost always surprised when her mother guessed things correctly.

"I'm a detective, aren't I? Darling it was *obvious* - what would a good-looking man of his age be doing without a wife?"

Alison giggled despite herself. "Yeah - I suppose. Anyway, his wife is welcome to him, the little shit!"

"That's the idea - you can well do without him, darling!"

"Yeah! But it's not just that Lyall's married, the lying sod! Do you know what he did to me, the double crossing little...?" She searched for a word that would adequately express her opinion of her ex-boyfriend without offending the modesty she attributed to her mother. "...little shit!"

"Let me guess - he pinched your ideas and used them to outbid you on the Ashby Foods Proposal," suggested Caine. "The one he was supposed to be helping you with!" Alison was silent for a few seconds. "Hello, darling, are you still there?"

"Yeah - you're right of course. How do you always know everything, Mum?" She sounded cross, but Caine knew it was with herself.

"I told you, I'm a detective! Don't worry about it, darling, chalk it up to experience. You've just got to learn that some men are not what they seem! Did your boss say anything?"

"No - he was gutted we didn't get the account, but I don't think he realised what was going on with me and Lyall. He's a bit of a dork really!" She changed the subject quickly. "It's good news about the cottage then."

"Yes - I've got to get things moving on that or I'll lose it!" Caine had a sudden thought. "Could you make it up here for the weekend, darling? We could go and look over the cottage and start planning the decor and curtains and things. And we'll have Chinese in the evening - there's a very good restaurant here in the town centre. You'd enjoy that wouldn't you? You can spend the night here on Saturday and Sunday and travel back to town on Monday morning."

"Yes please, that'll be fine." Alison paused for a moment and then said, "But won't you be tied up with all these dreadful murders? I've seen it all in the papers. There seems to be no end of dead bodies in Fen Molesey recently!"

"I know - my Superintendent says it's all happened since I arrived." Caine sighed. She felt a sudden wave of fatigue, the late night and busy day were catching up on her. "But we've more or less got it wrapped it up."

"OK. See you on Friday evening then Mum. We'll have a real girls-in weekend!" She sounded like a little girl who'd suddenly got her mummy back.

"Looking forward to it, darling. Take care." Caine hung up. Suddenly she felt insanely hungry and realised she hadn't eaten since lunch time. Even then it had been just a snack. She went into the kitchen and interrogated the fridge. It was adequately stocked, but there was nothing in there she really fancied. She groaned and looked in the larder cupboard above the kitchen surface. She didn't fancy tinned tuna fish, in a sandwich or otherwise. She noticed a lone banana on the fruit dish and quickly buttered two slices of bread, crushing the banana between them. She carried her hastily constructed sandwich into the bathroom, shedding the rest of her clothes as she went and plunged into the frothy water, luxuriating, with her head back and her legs stretched out as far as they would go. Then she took a huge bite of her banana sandwich, washed it down with a large mouthful of whisky and closed her eyes, contemplating a thousand and one ways she would like to punish Christopher Stone.

*　　　*　　　*　　　*　　　*　　　*

*

Mark Dolby put the small tray of coffees on the edge of Caine's desk and handed a brimming cup to each of the two women, taking the last one for himself.

"It looks like he's got away. There's been no sign of him anywhere!"

PC Wendy Doyle sipped at her coffee and made a face "You've forgotten the sugar, Sarge, but at least it's hot and strong." She turned towards Jacqueline Caine. "So, you actually knew this character Stone, Ma'am, in the olden days?"

"Twenty or thirty years ago were *not* the olden days!" Caine declared. "And I didn't know him all that well. He was an acquaintance of my husband, Jonathan - not even a friend. They just happened to grow up in the same neighbourhood."

"Do you reckon he's got clean away then?"

"It seems likely."

"He's obviously gone to ground somewhere," offered Dolby. "We've had no result from the APB."

"If you want my opinion, I think he's already out of the country," said Caine. "Let's face it he managed it all those years ago and now it looks like he's done a repeat performance."

"Well, if he's gone back to The States, we can get him extradited," Dolby suggested.

Caine nodded. "*If* he's gone back to America - which I doubt. *And* if we can find him. No - he's cleverer than that. He'd have had another escape route lined up. We'll just have to wait and see if he surfaces anywhere."

"But what's his connection with Susie Neale and the old lady, Martha Harney?" Wendy wanted to know.

"It's complicated," explained Caine. "In fact, the full story goes back nearly thirty years when Stone was mixed up with a bunch of crooks under the stewardship of Bobby Roberts who was running a big-time crime syndicate.

"Your husband, Jonathan, knew Stone back then?"

"Yes," volunteered Dolby, who had spent some time earlier in the day discussing the situation with DI Caine. "Stone was running a night club of some sort out here in Essex and we think he got into a bit of trouble with Roberts."

Caine took up the story. "Bobby Roberts was keen to expand his evil empire out into the provinces. He set up a chain of Casinos and used them as a front for his various rackets, which included drugs, prostitution, porno books and magazines etc., etc. It was quite a business! The Police didn't realise it at the time, but he took a large slice of the racketeering that was going on in this part of the world as well as a big chunk of the London scene. What we now think happened is that he latched on to Christopher Stone who, up till then, had been fairly clean. Our take is that Stone probably lost a lot of money in Roberts's Casinos; at which he, Roberts, probably stepped in and put him under his 'protection' if you can call it that. Maybe he offered him a 'loan' which Stone, very foolishly, accepted. The interest rate would have been way up in the stratosphere, of course, so it was impossible for Stone to pay it back out of his legitimate earnings. That made him easy meat to be lured into the drugs business."

"We think Stone, was soon up to his neck in pushing drugs supplied by Roberts," continued Dolby. "The club he ran here in FM was a useful extra outlet for pushing the stuff and it enabled Roberts to get a foothold in the Essex market. But Stone still wasn't making enough money to pay off his loan and feather his own nest, so, he started dealing on his own account and he dipped his sticky little fingers into Bobbie Roberts's treasure trove."

"Which wouldn't have made Uncle Bobbie very happy!" suggested Wendy.

"Not ecstatic, no," agreed Caine. She sighed and leaned back in her chair. "At the time, unfortunately, my late husband, Jonathan, was a Detective Sergeant with The Met. He was with the drugs squad and he went into Robert's organisation in Soho as an undercover agent, not knowing that out here, in the wilds of Essex, Christopher Stone was under Roberts's control…"

Dolby took up the story again. "Here again we're working on assumptions, but we think that somehow Stone got to know that Jonathan had joined Roberts's mob - Jonathan was using an assumed name, of course, but Stone recognised him and he spilled the beans to Roberts who, of course, wasn't well pleased to find a police 'mole' embedded in his organisation. In the meantime, he'd also tumbled to the fact that lovely little Christopher was dipping his fingers into the till. We're not sure, Wendy, but we think Stone was having an affair with Valerie – in which case he's probably the father of, Valerie's daughter, Karen. Anyway, the upshot of it all was that Valerie somehow got her hands-on evidence that Stone was dealing in a big way.

"And all this was recorded in Valerie Southam's micro fiches?"

"More or less. What we do know from them," said Caine "is that Stone was stupid enough to keep a record of his dirty dealings with Roberts - apparently, he had some idea that he might be able use the information against Roberts if the going ever got tough - which was a bit cloud cuckoo land if you ask me - he was really playing with fire! Anyway, when he suddenly had to make a dash for it he didn't have time to go back to Valerie's place to collect any of his things. Valerie probably found his papers, realised their implications and decided to keep them for a rainy day. She was pretty angry, don't forget. Stone left her on her own, pregnant with his child. She wanted her revenge, but she couldn't make any use of what she knew until he returned to the UK."

"But what about that photo – the one showing Stone shooting your husband?" Wendy Doyle asked Caine tentatively. "It was so incriminating – why would Stone keep hold of that?"

"We're not sure how Valerie got hold of that. It may have been taken by another undercover police officer, or more likely by one of Robert's hoods; but somehow Valerie got her hands on it. Of course, she couldn't use it or any of the other incriminating evidence until Stone appeared back on the scene.".

"Which he didn't do until Roberts snuffed it more than twenty years later." Doby added. "He certainly had it all worked out!"

"Yes, he had it all worked out all right!" said Caine unable to hide her bitterness. "Just as he did last Friday when I met up with him again. I thought he was being nice, but he did it all with the sole intention of getting Martha Harney's address from our file - which just happened to be in my car. What an idiot I was! No wonder he offered to drive me home after the dinner - I handed it to him on a plate!"

"Putting all that information onto micro fiches was a pretty brilliant idea!" Wendy commented. "She could keep it forever and nobody would even guess it was there!"

"Yes, that must have occurred to her when she worked at Microcell," said Dolby, "With all that microfilming equipment around she could preserve all the incriminating evidence she had against Stone, on Micro fiches. Then she disguised them as ordinary photo slides so they wouldn't look out of place amongst all the other family snaps."

"I suppose everything went into hibernation then," said Wendy. "Stone was off in America and Valerie struck off on her own and got married etcetera."

"That's right," agreed Caine. "For twenty odd years nothing happened. Then lo and behold Bobbie Roberts kicked the bucket and Stone decided it was time to return to Blighty - that's England in case you're wondering, Wendy. He came back and set up in the hotel business here in Fen Molesey where he bumped into his old girlfriend, Valerie - now known as Valerie Southam, and already a past master at blackmail. She'd been taking Florence Perot, her long lost mother, to the cleaners for years!"

"A respectable lot we're dealing with here," commented Dolby. "The way we reckon it is that as soon as Valerie spotted Christopher Stone, she turned the screws on him. She told him she had evidence that would send him to jail for a goodly stretch. Then she started milking him for a few hundred quid a month and, I dare say part of the deal was that he should give her a job at his new hotel; though I can't see why she bothered, she didn't do it for the money! He didn't like that arrangement one little bit, but there wasn't much he could do about it."

"He must have thought he'd struck lucky when he ran into Valerie's old friend, Susie," Caine continued. "He played on her marital difficulties - her husband was quite a bit older than she was, as you know - and Stone purposely got into a relationship with her. He wanted to use her as a weapon against Valerie, of course, because he thought - mistakenly as it turns out - that Susie was aware of what Valerie was up to. He was confident Susie wouldn't tell Valerie about her affair with him because she, Susie, was afraid Valerie would let it slip to her husband. Susie wanted her goings on with Stone kept as hush hush as possible!" Caine paused. "It gets complicated doesn't it – they were all a bit dodgy! Then Valerie started to get greedy and that few hundred a month she was squeezing out of Stone grew into over a thousand - we know that from her bank statements. Stone didn't like that very much, so he broke into Valerie's and Susie's houses trying to lay his hands on the evidence against him."

Caine finished her coffee and placed her cup on the table. "Then fate took a hand. Valerie was having an affair with Jamie Parr and somehow - we think almost by accident - she and her husband Bruce, as well as her lover, Jamie, all ended up dead. Christopher Stone realised that his blackmailer was no longer in the picture, but he still hadn't got the evidence. He was worried that we - the police - would find it while we were investigating the murders, so he tried to get Susie, his lover, to tell him where it was. She probably didn't know, but now that he had shown his hand, she knew too much about him and she had to go. So, he killed her and dumped her body in the quarry lake, weighting it down and hoping it would lie there undiscovered for years." "Even if she was found," Dolby commented, "he reckoned her death would be put down to the Southam's killer. And, of course, he must have learned about Martha from Susie and thought she might know where Valerie was keeping the evidence - so he went along to try to persuade her to tell him. He literally frightened her to death."

Caine took up the narrative again. "By then, of course, Stone realised we must already have the evidence – they were amongst Valerie's belongings - and sooner or later we'd find them. So, he decided to make a run for it,"

"So, in actual fact, the deaths of Valerie and Bruce Southam had nothing to do with Christopher Stone," Wendy concluded.

"Nothing," agreed Caine. She stood up and walked to the window. Storm clouds were gathering in the western sky and the first fat drops of rain had started to fall in the streets outside. She turned back to face her two companions. "But the irony of it is that we may not have been able to get a conviction based on the evidence Valerie had against Stone; not after all these years. In which case he'd have killed Susie Neale and Martha Harney for nothing!" She sighed and sat down at her desk again. "You wouldn't like to write the report to the Super would you, Mark?"

"No thanks, Jackie, if it's all the same to you," said Dolby with a grin. "I think I'll take those few days off - you know, the ones we talked about last week."

Alone, Caine booted up her computer. Outside the rain gathered momentum, rattling on the tiles of the roof a few feet above her head. She pursed her lips and began to write.

Printed in Great Britain
by Amazon

60523216R00325